TALES OF
DOMINION
WAR

STAR TREK®

TALES OF THE
DOMINION
WAR

EDITED BY

KEITH R.A. DeCANDIDO

Based upon *Star Trek*® and
Star Trek: The Next Generation®
created by Gene Roddenberry
and *Star Trek: Deep Space Nine*®
created by Rick Berman & Michael Piller

POCKET BOOKS
New York London Toronto Sydney

 POCKET BOOKS, a division of Simon & Schuster, Inc.
1230 Avenue of the Americas, New York, NY 10020

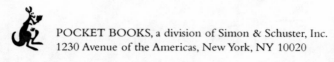 STAR TREK is a Registered Trademark of Paramount Pictures.

This book is published by Pocket Books, a division of Simon & Schuster, Inc., under exclusive license from Paramount Pictures.

ISBN: 978-0-7434-9171-6   ISBN: 0-7434-9171-8

First Pocket Books trade paperback edition August 2004

10 9 8 7 6 5 4 3 2 1

POCKET and colophon are registered trademarks of Simon & Schuster, Inc.

Manufactured in the United States of America

For information regarding special discounts for bulk purchases, please contact Simon & Schuster Special Sales at 1-800-456-6798 or business@simonandschuster.com.

To all those who gave their lives in war that others may go on with their lives in peace—may your service never be forgotten.

Contents

TALES OF THE
DOMINION
WAR

Introduction

This book owes its existence to *Star Trek: Deep Space Nine* for two reasons.

The obvious reason is that the Dominion War was chronicled on the last two seasons of *DS9*. That show introduced the Dominion, the Jem'Hadar, the Vorta, and the Founders, and many of the stories you are about to read relate to episodes of *DS9*, either by expanding on references in them or chronicling events that happened simultaneously with them.

But the second reason is far more fundamental than that: when *DS9* debuted in 1993, it changed the face of *Star Trek* forever.

Until *DS9* came along, *Star Trek* was pretty much defined by the words spoken at the beginning of one of the most famous show-opening voiceovers in television history: "These are the voyages of the Starship *Enterprise.*" It could be Kirk's *Enterprise* or Picard's *Enterprise* (or, if you wanted to get radical, possibly Pike's *Enterprise,* April's *Enterprise,* or Garrett's *Enterprise),* but for twenty-seven years, it was the *Enterprise* that was always at the forefront of most any *Star Trek* adventure.

Then in January 1993, *DS9* debuted, taking place on a space station, featuring a cast that was only about half Starfleet—and the floodgates opened. Now, the whole *Star Trek* universe was fair game. *Star Trek* was no longer limited to one ship. The storytelling possibilities, already pretty wide with a ship of exploration at its center, got even wider.

This extended not only to television, but also to the *Star Trek* novels, which have been, in one form or other, an integral part of the franchise since *Mission to Horatius* was published back in 1968. In 1997, *Star Trek: New Frontier* debuted, with Peter David chronicling the adventures of an all-new ship and crew created just for the novels—something that wouldn't have been imaginable before *DS9*. The success of *New Frontier* in turn led to more prose-only projects: *Star Trek: Stargazer* by Michael Jan Friedman, showcasing a young Jean-Luc Picard in his first command three decades prior to *Star Trek: The Next Generation; Star Trek: S.C.E.*, a monthly series of eBooks by a variety of authors featuring the Starfleet Corps of Engineers; and my own *Star Trek: I.K.S. Gorkon,* focusing on a vessel in the Klingon Defense Force.

"This," you may say, "is all well and good, but what does it have to do with this anthology?" A fair question.

The Dominion War was a massive endeavor, one that involved the Federation, the Klingons, the Romulans, the Cardassians, the Dominion, and so much more. But *DS9* was really only able to show a small portion of it. Just as *M*A*S*H* showed the Korean War through the lens of one particular group of characters and one general location, *DS9* likewise gave us a view of the Dominion War. But it's not the complete picture of the whole conflict.

That's where *Tales of the Dominion War* comes in. I love the opening up of the *Star Trek* universe because I love to explore all the nooks and crannies, the roads not traveled as often, expanding on the bits that are talked about but not shown. With the war, I found myself asking many questions. Some previous novels and eBooks had dealt with the conflict to some degree or other (see the timeline at the back of this volume), but I was still left wondering: What was Picard's *Enterprise* doing? What about the original series characters Spock, McCoy, and Scotty, all of whom are still alive and kicking in the late twenty-fourth century? What about the *Excalibur* crew from *New Frontier* or the *da Vinci* crew from *S.C.E.* or Klag from the *Gorkon?* What about the surviving crew of the *Stargazer?* How was it that Shinzon served the Romulan Empire with distinction during the war, as established in *Star Trek Nemesis?* And what about the events that were mentioned on *DS9* but not dramatized, such as the fall of Betazed from "In the Pale Moonlight" or the Breen attack on Earth in "The Changing Face of Evil"?

And so I gathered some of the best *Trek* prose stylists out there, and set them to the task of sewing some new threads in the tapestry that *DS9* provided. Some pairings of author and subject were obvious, e.g., Peter David providing a *New Frontier* tale, Josepha Sherman and Susan Shwartz—authors of several excellent novels focusing on Ambassador Spock—offering an insight into Spock's doings on Romulus during the war years, etc. Some will surprise you; I, for example, chose, for reasons of my own, to tell the story of the fall of Betazed, leaving the able Robert Greenberger to dramatize Klag's adventures. Other authors I just let run loose and tell whatever story they wanted.

The result is the book you hold in your hands, one that endeavors to show the *entirety* of the *Star Trek* universe. All five television shows are at least touched upon, as are all the above-mentioned prose series. You will see the war from the point of view, not only of Starfleet, but of the Klingons and the Romulans, the Cardassians and the Jem'Hadar, and even that old *Star Trek* standby, a being of pure energy. Within these pages are battles, disasters, fables, medical thrillers, espionage tales, murder mysteries, and so much more.

I must give thanks to the many people who aided me in ushering this book into existence: Jessica McGivney and Elisa Kassin, the in-house editors, who kept the mills grinding. Scott Shannon, the publisher who oversaw those mills. Marco Palmieri, John J. Ordover, and Ed Schlesinger, who kibbitzed marvelously at various points. All the authors, who were true joys to work with, and who were all very patient with their deadbeat editor. Paula M. Block, the wonderful person at Paramount who approves all this stuff, and does so with a keen eye, a fine sensibility, and a marvelous ability to catch things the rest of us are too dumb to notice. And most of all, to the love of my life Terri Osborne, about whom I can't say enough good things, so I won't even try to say them all here.

And now, to the front lines . . .

—KEITH R.A. DECANDIDO
somewhere in New York City

What Dreams May Come

Michael Jan Friedman

War correspondence: In the first season of *Star Trek: The Next Generation,* it was established that, before taking command of the *U.S.S. Enterprise*-D, Jean-Luc Picard served a distinguished twenty-two-year tour as captain of the *U.S.S. Stargazer.* The novel *Reunion* established several members of the *Stargazer* crew, such as his first officer Gilaad Ben Zoma, his Gnalish chief engineer Phigus Simenon, and the twins Gerda and Idun Asmund. Subsequent novels *The Valiant, The First Virtue,* and the ongoing *Star Trek: Stargazer* series have chronicled the early adventures of the *Stargazer* under Picard's command. However, Picard isn't the only former *Stargazer* crew member to survive into the 2370s.

"What Dreams May Come" takes place in the early days of the war, in the three-month gap between the final episode of *Star Trek: Deep Space Nine*'s fifth season, "Call to Arms" and the sixth-season premiere "A Time to Stand."

Michael Jan Friedman

Michael Jan Friedman has written nearly forty books about the *Star Trek* universe, including *Reunion* (the first *Star Trek: The Next Generation* hardcover), *Crossover,* the novelization of the episode *All Good Things. . . ,* *Shadows on the Sun, Kahless,* the *My Brother's Keeper* trilogy, *The Valiant, Starfleet: Year One,* and the ongoing *Stargazer* series (featuring Jean-Luc Picard's first crew). He also wrote the *Star Trek: The Next Generation* series published by DC Comics, co-wrote the *Voyager* television episode "Resistance," and is currently at work on yet another *Star Trek* novel—this one concerning the fate of his favorite romantic couple in the wake of the movie *Star Trek Nemesis.* As Mike has noted on other occasions, no matter how many Friedmans you may know, he's probably not related to any of them.

Sejeel sat up in his luxuriously overstuffed bed, stretched out his arms in his soft, silky bedclothes, and reflected—not for the first time, by any means—that it was good to be a Vorta on a backward but strategically located world on the edge of Federation territory.

Most of his fellow Vorta had drawn significantly more demanding assignments—the sort that involved the grim prospect of injury and even death. After all, the tune of armed conflict was being played now in earnest in the Alpha Quadrant, and injury and death were its natural accompaniments.

But not on Illarh, the world of gentle humanoids to which Sejeel and his ship full of Jem'Hadar had been dispatched. There was no struggle here, no fight to repel the invader.

And no possibility of Starfleet interference, either.

For reasons that escaped Sejeel, the Federation had made it a rule not to get involved with pre-spaceflight civilizations—even those like the Illarhi, that were situated in or near Federation space. So when Sejeel's ship slipped into orbit around Illarh, it did so with complete and utter impunity.

Feeling pleased with himself, the Vorta pulled aside his covers, got out of bed, and dressed himself in a set of clothes he had brought with him from the Gamma Quadrant. They had seemed perfectly comfortable before he arrived on Illarh, but now they seemed altogether too stiff and scratchy.

Of course, *anything* would have seemed stiff and scratchy in comparison to Illarh's native fineries. The people here might not have been particularly aggressive or advanced with regard to technology, but they certainly knew how to make an alien feel comfortable.

Removing his personal communications device from the pocket of his tunic, Sejeel contacted Baraj'aran, the First of his Jem'Hadar task force.

"Anything to report?" the Vorta asked.

"Nothing unusual," Baraj'aran told him.

"Splendid," said Sejeel. "Let me know if anything changes." With that, he terminated the conversation and replaced the device in his pocket.

It hadn't been much of a report. But then, in truth, there was little for either the Vorta or the Jem'Hadar to do at the moment. They had come to Illarh to establish a communications and supply depot, a critical element in an imminent wave of military advances from which the Federation wasn't expected to recover.

However, without any opposition from the Illarhi, Baraj'aran and his soldiers had been able to set up the depot in just a few days. In another few days, they had constructed a powerful, ground-based shield generator capable of thwarting any weapon Starfleet could bring to bear.

And because the Illarhi were so primitive and naïve, they had believed Sejeel when he told them that he and the Jem'Hadar weren't staying long. All they wanted, the Vorta had said, was to use Illarh as a temporary stopover in their migration from a dying world to a new home in a distant star system.

During Sejeel's talks with the Illarhi, the Jem'Hadar had been a little brusque, true, but otherwise they'd been quite inoffensive. When one got to know them, the Vorta had said, they were actually a fine and noble species.

Not invaders, oh no. Merely pilgrims on a journey that would soon compel them to leave Illarh, at which point the lives of its original owners would return to normal.

None of it was true, of course. Even the Illarhi would figure that out eventually. But for the time being, the situation was a stable and serene one, and Sejeel meant to keep it that way as long as he could.

He didn't like wholesale slaughter any more than the next sentient being. And when the Illarhi launched their inevitable revolt, that was exactly what the Jem'Hadar would inflict on them.

No one dealt death and destruction quite like the Jem'Hadar. It was what they had been designed for.

In the meantime, the Vorta meant to enjoy the creature comforts of Illarhi—not the least of which was the cadre of servants he had assembled to attend to his needs. Before Sejeel's arrival, these Illarhi had worked in the employ of prominent citizens.

Now, they worked for *him*. As always, their day began by preparing Sejeel's morning meal.

It was a wonderful concept, and one the Illarhi had more or less perfected. Savoring what was in store for him, Sejeel exited his bedchamber—which had also belonged to a prominent citizen before the Jem'Hadar evicted him—and emerged into his residence's forward living space. As usual, his servants had laid out an assortment of native delicacies for him, illuminated by cylinders full of luminescent insects.

Sejeel stopped in front of the display and admired it component by component. Dark, fried *ogliila* eggs. Fresh melon-meats, ranging in color from pale gold to dark red. The succulent, blue roots of the *aderrja* bush, and a frothy, white juice whose name he could never seem to remember.

The Vorta picked up one of the melon slices and bit into it. It was a shame that he couldn't truly appreciate the differences in tastes and smells. Still, the Founders had had their reasons for giving the Vorta such a limited sensory range.

As he thought that, one of the Illarhi entered the room. Like all his people, the fellow had copper-colored skin, a spattering of mossy, white hair, shiny black eyes, and a series of bubbles on his cheeks that facilitated auditory perception.

"Draz," said Sejeel. "So good to see you."

The Illarhi inclined his head, displaying the patchwork pattern of his hair. "Good morning, Master Sejeel. Did you sleep well?"

"I did," Sejeel assured him. He smiled wistfully. "A deep, dreamless sleep, Draz. As always."

After all, he was a clone, and clones weren't given to dreaming. Those who had created him had considered nocturnal visions a waste of time for someone with such large responsibilities.

He had believed the same thing until he came to Illarh. He had imagined that dreams were but a series of unintelligible images, irritating at best.

Then one day—Sejeel's third on Illarh, as he recalled—Draz had mentioned one of his dreams in passing. It was a simple dream, about Draz's childhood and his brothers and sisters.

To the Vorta's surprise, Draz's dream wasn't at all irritating. It was by turns storylike and realistic, logical and bizarre, and the combination was something that seemed to strike a chord in Sejeel's psyche.

When he woke the next day, he couldn't wait to find out if Draz had had any other dreams. To his delight, the Illarhi said he had, and went on to tell Sejeel of it.

Every morning thereafter, he had asked Draz to describe his dream of the night before—and on no occasion had the Illarhi disappointed him. In fact, of all the delicacies the Illarhi set before the Vorta each morning, Draz's dreams were the ones Sejeel found most appealing.

"So," he said to the Illarhi, "what sort of dream did you have last night?"

Draz's brow creased. "A disturbing one."

He was about to elaborate when Sejeel's communications device began to beep. Holding a finger up to keep the Illarhi from continuing, the Vorta retrieved the device and said, "Yes?"

"We have lost contact with our vessel," said Baraj'aran. *"We are attempting to isolate the cause."*

Sejeel frowned. Communications lapsed occasionally—it was a fact of life in unfamiliar systems, with unfamiliar magnetic fields.

But there was nothing *he* could do about it. That was the province of the Jem'Hadar.

And he found himself intrigued by the look on Draz's face. *Disturbing,* the Illarhi had said. It was the first time he had ever used that word to describe one of his dreams.

"Isolate it soon," Sejeel told Baraj'aran, "or I will put someone in charge who can."

Then he put away his communications device and turned to Draz again. "Disturbing in what way?" he asked.

Draz shrugged. "It's . . . difficult to explain."

"Try," said the Vorta, plopping himself into an overstuffed chair in the corner of the room. He made a "hurry up" gesture with a flip of his hand. "Please, proceed."

Draz nodded. "Very well, then."

But he didn't speak of his dream right away. Instead, he moved to the room's only window, pushed a bit of its covering away, and looked outside.

It wasn't like the Illarhi to hesitate so, Sejeel mused. Clearly, the fellow's dream had affected him even more deeply than he had indicated.

Finally, Draz said, "This will sound strange, I know, but—last night, I dreamed I wasn't the servant you see before you. I dreamed I was a man of power, a man of authority." He looked back over his shoulder at Sejeel. "Your equal, in fact."

How perfectly ridiculous, the Vorta thought, reveling in the absurdity of the idea. He couldn't help laughing.

Draz winced.

"Forgive me," said Sejeel, attempting to control himself. "It's just that you caught me off guard. I mean . . . you, Draz? A figure of authority? My *equal?*"

His servant looked embarrassed. "Clearly not, Master. But in my dream, you see, I wasn't Illarhi. I was from another planet, just like you and the Jem'Hadar."

Sejeel smiled. This was getting good. "Then where was your ship, Draz? Hidden somewhere, perhaps? And what did you look like? An Illarhi . . . or something else?"

The servant's brow puckered deeply as he tried to remember. "I don't think my ship was here anymore, Master. It was called away on urgent business."

Sejeel nodded. A pleasing answer. "And your appearance?"

"No different from what it is now," said Draz. "In my dream, I looked the same."

The Vorta sighed. He had hoped for more. "And how is that possible, I ask you, if you came here from another world? Neither I nor the Jem'Hadar look like the Illarhi. How would *you*?"

Draz thought for a moment. Then his eyes black eyes seemed to brighten. "I didn't look like the Illarhi originally. I was *altered* to look like them."

Sejeel had a feeling that this wasn't part of his servant's dream at all. It seemed to him that Draz was making the story up as he went along—no doubt, in an attempt to entertain his master.

Nonetheless, the Vorta played along with it.

"It's true that people on other worlds can arrange to surgically alter their appearances," he allowed. "But why, I wonder, would someone from a world where that was possible wish to become a denizen of *this* world?"

Again, Draz paused, as if trying to come up with a plausible answer. "I . . . was a scientist," he said finally. "A scientist who wished to study the Illarhi without their noticing. That's why I was altered to look like them—so I could mingle with them and examine them at close quarters."

"How intriguing," said the Vorta. Indeed, it was a clever answer, especially for a member of such a simple species. "And what happened to you in your dream? Did you carry out your scientific study?"

"I did," Draz seemed to decide. "That is, until you and the Jem'Hadar appeared on Illarh. Then my study was interrupted."

"Of course," said Sejeel. "And was that the end of your dream? The arrival of your master and his Jem'Hadar?"

He hoped it wasn't so, but he sensed that his servant's ingenuity might be reaching its limits. Indeed, he was both surprised and pleased that it had gone this far.

"Not quite," said Draz.

Sejeel leaned forward. "Really? There's more."

"Yes, Master. You see, in my dream, I had retained the technology I needed to send a message to my people—my true people, not the Illarhi."

"Yes, yes, I understand which people you mean," said Sejeel a little impatiently. "And did you send them a message with this technology you had?"

"I did. I contacted them and I told them what the Jem'Hadar were doing to Illarh."

The Vorta felt his smile fading a little. This truly *was* a strange dream. "And what was it the Jem'Hadar were doing, if I may ask?"

"In my dream," said the Illarhi, "the Jem'Hadar were setting up a depot here to serve a war effort. A rather *large* war effort, you understand."

Sejeel grunted softly. How strange that his servant should say such a thing. Was it possible that Draz was more perceptive than the Vorta had given him credit for?

"Seeing this," Draz continued, "I obtained operational data on the shield generator the Jem'Hadar set up. Then I sent it to my people. Not the Illarhi—"

"Your *real* people," Sejeel said, more eager than ever for his servant to finish—if for a different reason now. "As I indicated before, I understand the distinction."

"Yes, my *real* people," Draz echoed, as if he needed to do so in order to get himself back on track. "It was my hope that with such information, my people could pierce the Jem'Hadar's shield. Then I studied the Jem'Hadar's duty schedules, and recommended the best times for my people to attack."

The Vorta felt a chill climbing the rungs of his spine. "How absurd," he said, "how positively absurd."

Suddenly, he had an urge to get in touch with Baraj'aran. Taking out his communications device, he opened a link.

But there was no response from the Jem'Hadar First. Only a series of loud, guttural sounds that sounded eerily like barked commands.

Sejeel's mouth was remarkably dry. He eyed Draz, wondering what in the name of the Founders was going on.

"Excuse me," he told his servant, and got up out of his chair. Then he advanced to the window where Draz was standing, meaning to fling aside the window covering and see what was going on outside for himself.

But Draz blocked his way. "Your pardon," he said to Sejeel, "but it would please me immensely if you would allow me to finish."

"Finish . . ." the Vorta echoed numbly.

"Finish my dream," the Illarhi explained.

Sejeel's fists clenched. "What is happening, Draz? What is this about?"

His voice sounded shrill in his ears. It was the voice of someone who was suddenly very afraid.

"Finally," said Draz, "my people *did* attack. And the first thing they did was disable the vessel the Jem'Hadar had left in orbit."

Sejeel's mouth felt dry. As dry as dust.

"That was why the Jem'Hadar on the surface lost contact with the vessel. It was because it had been attacked. In my dream, however, the Vorta in charge of the depot didn't respond to that news. He was too eager to hear—"

"What is going on?" Sejeel shrieked, surprising himself with the violence of his outburst.

"The Jem'Hadar are obliged to follow the instructions of their Vorta," said Draz. "But he was too busy to give them any. So when my people—not the Illarhi, but my *real* people—went after the depot, and the shield generator was of no help . . ."

"Who *are* you?" the Vorta demanded.

Draz looked hurt. "I am who I've always been, Master. Your humble servant."

Sejeel tilted his head and looked up at the Illarhi. "Then . . . it was just a dream? *Truly* a dream?"

He desperately wanted to believe that. *Still*, despite everything.

Draz shrugged. "Sometimes," he said archly, "it's difficult to say where reality ends, and dreams begin."

Then he removed something from his own pocket—a Starfleet insignia, of all things. Tapping it, he said, "Ben Zoma to Picard. What's our situation, Jean-Luc?"

"A successful one," said a voice on the other end of the comlink—a human voice, unless Sejeel was mistaken. *"We've disabled the shield generator and all but secured the depot. But if I were you, Gilaad, I would remain indoors for the moment—until we are quite certain all the Jem'Hadar have been accounted for."*

The Vorta hung his head, the magnitude of his blunder only now filling him like the breakfast foods he'd been consuming. How could he have so thoroughly betrayed the trust the Founders had placed in him? *How?*

"Don't go out there and try to be a hero," the comm voice said.

Draz—or, rather, Gilaad Ben Zoma—smiled at Sejeel. "Don't worry, Jean-Luc, I wouldn't *dream* of it."

Night of the Vulture

Greg Cox

War correspondence: In the *Star Trek* episode "Day of the Dove," the so-called Beta XII-A entity menaced a Starfleet and Klingon crew before they joined forces to drive it off. The *Star Trek: The Next Generation* trilogy *The Q Continuum* established that the entity was an old and powerful being. In the *Star Trek: Deep Space Nine* episode "Call to Arms," the area surrounding the entrance to the wormhole was mined by the DS9 crew shortly before they abandoned the station to the Dominion, thus preventing the latter from summoning reinforcements.

"Night of the Vulture" takes place about the same time as the *DS9* episode "Favor the Bold."

Greg Cox

Greg Cox is the *New York Times* bestselling author of *The Eugenics Wars* Volumes 1-2, *The Q Continuum* trilogy, *Assignment: Eternity, The Black Shore,* and other *Star Trek* novels, including the upcoming *To Reign in Hell: The Lost Years of Khan Noonien Singh.* Recent short fiction can be found in *Star Trek: The Amazing Stories, Star Trek: Enterprise Logs,* and *Tales of the Slayer* Volume 2. He lives in Oxford, Pennsylvania, and is shocked to realize that this is the first time he has ever written a Cardassian, Vorta, or Jem'Hadar . . .

The Starfleet database referred to it as the Beta XII-A entity, named for the planet where the Federation, in the person of James T. Kirk and his crew, first encountered it. The database further described it as "extremely dangerous." The entity called itself (*), and most of the time it was simply hungry.

But not now.

The galaxy was at war, flooding the cosmos with waves of unleashed hate and anger. (*) had not supped so well in ages.

It spun through the vacuum of space, a shimmering sphere of incandescent crimson energy. *Yes,* it thought with satisfaction, savoring the violent emotions radiating outward from the vast interplanetary conflict. *This is as it should be.*

For nearly a century, ever since the day two warring species had joined forces to laugh (*) out into the void, the entity had been careful to avoid both Klingon and Federation space. (*) feared exposure above all else, for it preyed most easily on the unsuspecting, and those two loathsome nations, along with their allies, had learned far too much about (*)'s essential nature to risk trying to exploit them once more. Instead it had been compelled to skulk like a craven assassin through the most desolate backwaters of the quadrant, taking only such ships as were unlikely to be missed. Smugglers' vessels, mostly, and the occasional exploratory vehicles from less developed worlds.

Such lean pickings had left (*) merely a flicker of its former self—until the war had begun. Now, with the ambient aggression of the entire quadrant raised to unprecedented new heights, (★) felt its powers and perceptions expanding at a geometric rate. Not since Cheron, fifty millennia ago, had its hunger been so abundantly rewarded.

Now there was a banquet, (★) recalled with pleasure. Racial bigotry had provided the foundation for a truly delicious repast, one that had endured until scarcely a single survivor remained. This new war promised to be even more invigorating. *I have waited generations for a feast such as this. . . .*

The more (★) fed, the more powerful it became. Tendrils of intangible thought reached out from its glowing red core, searching out the freshest springs of unbridled wrath and hatred amidst the overall carnage of the war. Then, to its dismay, (★) became aware of a situation, less than a parsec away, that threatened to bring the exquisite strife to a swift and premature end.

Unless (★) acted at once. . . .

"Ready to beam up passenger."

The name on the freighter captain's papers was Jeremy Paul Gleason, but that was a fiction. Zonek Karle, Cardassian sleeper agent, sat at the helm of his ship, awaiting word from the planet below. On the viewscreen ahead of him, Earth rotated like an enormous taspar egg. It looked deceptively placid for all the grief and inconvenience its people had inflicted on the Cardassian Union over the decades.

"Copy that, Solanco," a voice announced from the planet's surface. *"You're good to go."*

Karle nodded at the comm. "Thanks," he said with a flawless Federation accent. Security had tightened on (and above) Earth ever since the Cardassian Union, along with its new Dominion allies, had reclaimed Terok Nor several months ago, but Karle had not anticipated any problems at this stage of his mission. As far as

Starfleet was concerned, the *Solanco* was simply picking up an ordinary civilian passenger.

He activated the transporter controls. A familiar hum filled the bridge of the freighter, and Karle spun his seat around to watch as a humanoid materialized at the rear of the bridge.

Like Karle himself, the new arrival appeared revoltingly human. She was the very image of a middle-aged Terran female, not particularly attractive, wearing a nondescript olive-colored suit. A compact travel bag about the size of a standard medikit materialized along with her. Her fleshy pink features bore a notably severe expression.

"Welcome aboard."

The woman did not deign to reply to Karle's greeting. Her pale gray eyes dubiously inspected the smallish interior of the bridge as if expecting to find it beneath her standards. Her gaze swept over the sturdy duranium walls and mass-produced Federation control consoles. Although auxiliary workstations ran along both the port and starboard sides of the bridge, Karle could control all of the ship's major functions, from navigation to sensors, from the crescent-shaped helm station facing the viewscreen. Between the glow of the screen and the overhead lighting cove, the woman had more than enough illumination with which to scrutinize her new surroundings.

"Adequate," she pronounced finally. Karle repressed a stab of irritation at the woman's attitude. "Are we quite unobserved?" she asked.

Karle nodded. "The bulkheads are shielded against even the most invasive scans."

His answer appeared to satisfy the woman, who underwent a striking metamorphosis. Her exposed face and hands glistened wetly as human flesh was supplanted by a gelatinous golden slush that flowed and melted into a new configuration before solidifying once more. The woman's face now bore the smooth and masklike features her kind routinely presented to humanoid lifeforms. Karle felt a pang of jealousy. His own surgical transformation had not been nearly so painlessly accomplished.

"You may depart now, Captain," the Changeling instructed him. "I am anxious to be under way."

Karle waited until they were safely clear of Earth's solar system before admitting the rest of his passengers to the bridge. Confident that the *Solanco*'s departure had not roused Starfleet's suspicions, he went to warp and then pressed a concealed button on the helm's control panel.

A door slid open at the rear of the bridge, revealing a hidden passenger compartment between the bridge and the cargo bay. A Vorta emerged from the compartment, accompanied by a combat unit of scowling Jem'Hadar warriors.

Typically, the Vorta, whose name was Methras, ignored Karle and immediately began fawning on the Changeling. "Founder," he gushed, "I cannot tell you how honored I am to be in your sublime presence. It is my unworthy privilege to assist you in this, your momentous journey back to Dominion space."

The Changeling accepted Methras's devotion as her due. Still clad in the same olive suit, she occupied a seat at the bridge's starboard workstation like a monarch astride a throne. The glowering Jem'Hadar soldiers took up defensive positions about the bridge, standing guard over the Changeling with their rifles poised and ready.

The Founder's entourage left the *Solanco*'s bridge feeling considerably more cramped than usual. Karle had, in fact, objected to ferrying such a large party to Earth just to escort the Founder home, but had been overruled by his superiors. Heaven forbid that the Changeling spy should travel back to Dominion space without her bodyguards and Vorta minion.

"How soon, Captain, until we reach Terok Nor?" the Changeling demanded. She rested a protective hand on the bag in her lap. "It is vital that I deliver these codes to our military forces as soon as possible."

Her peremptory tone irked Karle, but he held his tongue. Their joint mission was far too important to waste time objecting to the Founder's lack of manners.

Via her shape-changing abilities, the Changeling had obtained a piece of vital Starfleet information: the command codes to the deep-space mines currently preventing the Dominion from sending reinforcements from the Gamma Quadrant through the Bajoran wormhole. With these codes, the Dominion would be able to deactivate the mines and send a flood of fresh ships and soldiers through the wormhole, bringing the war to a quick and brutal end.

Unfortunately, as Karle was all too aware, they couldn't risk transmitting this information through Federation space for fear that Starfleet might discover that the codes have been stolen. Thus, they had to deliver the codes in person, which was why the *Solanco* was currently warping toward Terok Nor.

The mission is all that matters, Karle reminded himself. *That and winning the war.* "Approximately five days," he informed the Changeling.

"Is that the best you can do?" she replied, clearly displeased by his answer. She cast a disparaging glance aft, as though examining the freighter's all-too-inadequate engines. "Was this the only vessel available to you?"

Karle had captained the *Solanco* for over ten years, and he bristled at the Changeling's impertinent queries. "It is, if you want to make it out of the Federation unnoticed." He could not resist adding a touch of sarcasm. "Perhaps you would have preferred a *Galor*-class attack cruiser?"

The Changeling frowned, alarming Methras. Ever the diplomat, the Vorta inserted himself between the captain and the Founder. "I am certain that the captain means no disrespect," he burbled. His ribbed ears flushed in embarrassment, in contrast to the sickly pallor of his face. "We are all agreed, surely, that stealth is of the utmost importance?"

"Very well," the Changeling conceded. "Five days will suffice, if that is what we absolutely must make do with."

"The Founder is most wise," Methras said, genuflecting in the Changeling's direction. "Your patience is gratefully appreciated."

Karle found the Vorta's obsequious prattle distasteful. *Allies or not,* he thought, *I'll be damned if I'll kowtow to a heap of animated protoplasm.*

Tension suffused the atmosphere of the bridge. Karle glanced back over his shoulder at one of the looming Jem'Hadar soldiers. With his scaly gray reptilian skin, the fierce bodyguard looked more Cardassian than Karle, but there the similarities ended. Karle couldn't imagine worshipping the Founders the way the Jem'Hadar did. *They're no better than those superstitious Bajorans.*

The bodyguard met Karle's gaze with a baleful glare, reminding Karle of just how uneasy Cardassia's newly forged alliance with the Dominion was. *Politics makes strange bedfellows,* he reflected, *and war even stranger ones still.* But it would be worth putting up with the Changelings and their slavish underlings if it meant crushing the Federation and the Klingons once and for all. *When Cardassia rules the Alpha Quadrant, all my sacrifices will be rewarded.*

He keyed the proper coordinates into the helm controls. The route he had chosen would take them to Terok Nor via one of the less trafficked spaceways in the quadrant. A dangerous space-time rift located along the route encouraged most travelers to give the entire region a wide berth. Karle judged the course enough off the beaten path to keep them clear of the major Starfleet checkpoints without seeming suspiciously evasive. Fortune willing, they would reach their destination without incident.

To his annoyance, the Changeling left her seat and approached the helm. She halted only a few paces behind him, looking intently over his shoulder as Karle manipulated the controls. If Changelings could breathe, of which Karle was uncertain, she would have been practically breathing down his neck. "Can I help you?" he asked impatiently.

"I am merely ensuring that our mission is completed successfully," she said, continuing to peer over his shoulder like a disapproving headmistress. "Would it not be more efficient to cut across the Ohop system directly?"

Acid churned at the pit of Karle's stomach. *How dare this imperious blob of goo keep second-guessing me, and on my own ship, no less!*

"That would send up red flags throughout the entire sector," Karle said. "We'd be lucky not to end up with half of Starfleet on our tail." He turned away from the viewscreen in order to look the Changeling squarely in the eye. "You may rest assured, madam, that I have already considered every aspect of our voyage."

"Perhaps," the Changeling said coldly, "but you will forgive me if I do not trust the outcome of the war to the unproven judgment of a minor Cardassian operative."

She made *Cardassian* sound like a slur.

Karle could not let the Founder's disdainful words go unchallenged. "Might I remind you," he pointed out, "that you would not have acquired the command codes were it not for contacts made years ago by the Obsidian Order."

The Changeling sneered, unimpressed by his reference to the once-dreaded intelligence service. "The Obsidian Order is extinct," she retorted, "a victim of its own colossal arrogance and stupidity. We crushed the life out of it in the Omarion Nebula two years ago."

Karle leapt angrily to his feet. He had not forgotten the way the Dominion had once lured the Order into a trap deep in the heart of the Gamma Quadrant. Many valiant Cardassians had died that day, long before the present alliance.

The Jem'Hadar reacted immediately to his hostile motion. In a heartbeat, five fully charged rifles were aimed at Karle's skull, impressing upon him the need for a cool head. Raising his hands in a nonthreatening manner, he took a deep breath and stepped backwards, away from the Changeling.

"Well, Captain?" she asked coolly. "Have you anything else to add?"

He shook his head, not trusting himself to keep the rancor from his voice. *It's just as well,* he thought, *that I'm not carrying any sort of weapon.* He had no doubt that the Jem'Hadar would have shot first and asked questions later if he had so much as reached for a pistol or blade. *Plus, I probably couldn't have resisted the temptation to blast the smirk from this Changeling's waxy face!*

Turning his back on the Founder and her servitors, he resumed his place at the helm. He did his best to swallow his pride, for the sake of the war, but he could be pushed only so far. . . .

Hours passed, during which Methras kept up a constant stream of small talk in a futile attempt to alleviate the strained atmosphere aboard the bridge. Karle had to admire the Vorta's persistence, if nothing else.

"Once the Alpha Quadrant comes under the benevolent sway of the Dominion, I look forward to touring some of the more scenic regions of the Federation," Methras declared. "I'm told that the Azure Peaks of Betazed are truly magnificent to behold, not to mention Earth's legendary Victoria Falls. . . ."

In fact, Karle knew, Vortas had weak eyesight and an even feebler sense of aesthetics. Methras was lying shamelessly, as was second nature to his kind. The Vorta's blatant mendacity chafed at Karle's nerves. *At least a Klingon tells you what he really thinks before he cuts your throat.*

A warning Klaxon interrupted Methras's incessant chatter. "What is it?" the Changeling demanded.

"The proximity sensors have picked up something," Karle reported. "A vessel approaching at warp speed." He hastily adjusted the sensors until a distinctive silhouette appeared on the viewscreen. His heart sank at the sight of the saucer-shaped contours, which bore a marked resemblance to a fossilized trilobite. "It's Starfleet. A *Saber*-class starship."

The Changeling hissed angrily. "You said we would not be detected," she accused Karle.

"I made no promises!" the captain snapped. How was he supposed to know there would a Starfleet ship on patrol this close to the rift? "There's a war on, haven't you heard?"

A blinking annunciator light signaled that the *Solanco* was being hailed. Karle activated the comm system, audio only. A commanding male voice abruptly echoed across the bridge.

"Attention, unidentified vessel. This is the U.S.S. Bellingham, conducting a routine security check. Please drop out of warp immediately."

Karle glanced back at the grim-faced Changeling and shrugged helplessly. What else could he do? As requested, he powered down to impulse.

The Changeling released an exasperated sigh and reassumed her human disguise. Looking away from the viewscreen, she cast a meaningful look at Methras, but the cowardly Vorta was already slinking back toward the entrance to the hidden compartment. The Jem'Hadar didn't budge, however. They were not about to leave a Founder undefended in the face of the enemy. Their dark eyes gleamed in anticipation of a battle to the death.

Not if I can help it, Karle thought. Perhaps this really was just a random security check after all. "Greetings, *Bellingham,*" he addressed the oncoming starship. Although small by Starfleet standards, the *Saber*-class vessel possessed more than enough firepower to obliterate the *Solanco* in a heartbeat. "This is Captain Jeremy Gleason of the commercial freighter, *Solanco.* What can I do for you?"

The Starfleet vessel pulled up alongside them. *"Something wrong with your transceivers, Solanco?"* the nameless voice inquired. *"All we're getting is audio."*

Karle glanced anxiously behind him. The door to the hidden compartment slid shut, concealing Methras, but the Jem'Hadar remained in plain view. "Hang on." He stalled, while mouthing an urgent warning to the heavily armed bodyguards. Predictably, the Jem'Hadar ignored him entirely; it was not until the Founder nodded her assent that the stubborn warriors shrouded themselves, employing their innate ability to vanish from sight. Karle expelled a sigh of relief, then opened a visual channel to the *Bellingham*.

A stocky Andorian wearing a captain's uniform appeared on the viewscreen. *"That's better,"* the blue-skinned humanoid said gruffly. His antennae perked in approval. *"You're a commercial freighter, you say?"*

"Yes, sir," Karle answered. "I'm transmitting my manifest and course coordinates to you." He licked his lips, which suddenly felt as dry as Vulcan's Forge. "I'm think you'll find all my data is in order."

The Andorian's eyes dropped to scan Karle's doctored credentials, then rose back to the screen. He stared across the void into the *Solanco*'s bridge. *"Who's that with you?"*

"A passenger," Karle said hastily, "chartering a ride to the Enkidu system." A trickle of sweat ran down his back. The bridge felt uncomfortably warm, even for a Cardassian. "Her passport should be with my documentation."

"My name is Evelyn McDougal," the Changeling volunteered. Karle knew that the real McDougal had been discreetly terminated months ago, the better to facilitate the Changeling's impersonation. "I have family on Enkidu Prime."

"Vraath ch'Evram, captain of the Bellingham," the Andorian said. His stony expression and twitching antennae offered little clue to his suspicions or lack thereof. Geological epochs seemed to pass as Vraath carefully reviewed their paperwork. *"You're flying awfully close to the Hunyadi Rift,"* he commented finally.

Karle shrugged. "It's the quickest way to Enkidu." He tried to present the semblance of a cash-strapped skipper willing to cut a few corners. "Don't worry, I intend to keep a safe distance from the edge of the rift."

Is he buying this? Karle fretted silently. He suddenly saw himself spending the rest of the war in a Federation detention camp, perhaps with the resentful Changeling as his cellmate. An irrational urge to flee came over him, but he knew that escape was impossible. The *Bellingham* would overtake his humble freighter almost before he reached warp speed.

There was no choice but to brazen it out and hope that Vraath did not see through their deceptions. *What if he insists on searching my ship?*

"How safe?" Vraath asked, but, before Karle could begin to answer, a Deltan first officer appeared on the viewscreen beside the Andorian. She bent over and whispered something in her captain's ear, and Vraath immediately appeared to lose interest in the *Solanco.* *"That will be all,* Solanco," he informed Karle, now sounding somewhat distracted. *"Thank you for your cooperation—and watch out for that rift."*

The transmission broke off curtly, replaced by an image of the *Bellingham* pulling away from the *Solanco.* Karle watched, holding onto his breath, as the Starfleet vessel warped out of sight.

A tremendous wave of relief washed over Karle. He had no idea what pressing business had called the *Bellingham* away, but he felt as though he and his entire extended family had just been granted a stay of execution. *That was a near thing,* he acknowledged. *I thought we were skewered for certain.*

Unlike Karle, however, the Changeling behind him was in no mood to appreciate their good fortune. "It seems our mission will continue, no thanks to you." She sounded far more aggrieved than grateful. Her features melted back into those of a Founder. "So much for your expert piloting!"

"There was *always* a chance that we'd run into a Starfleet patrol." Karle was tired of being treated like an incompetent lackey. "But our cover stories held up, just as they were supposed to."

At the moment, it was easy to think that he and the arrogant Founder were alone on the bridge. Then the Jem'Hadar unshrouded themselves and Karle was outnumbered once more.

"Spare me your pitiful excuses," the Changeling said. "I see that, as I feared, I must take a firmer hand in this operation." She gestured brusquely at the viewscreen. "Call up your navigational charts. I wish to plot an alternative course."

Karle was offended by the very suggestion. He was the captain of this ship, not the Changeling. "There is no need for that," he insisted. "The odds that we will encounter yet another Starfleet vessel are infinitesimal."

"Your judgment is no longer credible," the Changeling stated scornfully. "Call up the charts."

Behind her, Methras emerged from his hiding place. Karle knew he could count on no support from the sycophantic Vorta. Bile rose at the back of Karle's throat as he grudgingly complied with the Changeling's request. A star chart materialized on the viewscreen, representing the space between them and the Bajoran system. An illuminated green line marked their present (and entirely satisfactory) course, while, less than a dozen light-years away, the amorphous borders of the Hunyadi Rift were carefully marked in red.

The more Karle stared at the charts, just as he had done extensively prior to this mission, the more he resented the Changeling's presumptuousness. "As you see," he observed, "our current heading brings us to Terok Nor in less than five days, while bypassing the major inhabited systems."

"Unacceptable," the Changeling said bluntly. "We have narrowly avoided disaster once already. I demand the highest degree of stealth. The gravity of our mission requires nothing less."

Methras hurriedly seconded the Founder's assessment. "Of course, Founder." He looked beseechingly at Karle. "No doubt the good captain recognizes the paramount importance of delivering the codes to Terok Nor."

"Frankly," the Changeling said, "I have my doubts in that regard."

Karle had heard enough. *Very well,* he thought savagely.

On the chart in front of him, the Hunyadi Rift lurked like a pool of deadly quicksand. Beyond its invisible boundaries, neither matter nor energy could ever hope to escape. A thin, humorless smile lifted the corners of his lips as he swiftly adjusted the ship's heading.

At Karle's command, the *Solanco* warped toward the rift. The sudden acceleration momentarily overcame the bridge's inertial dampers, throwing the Changeling and her minions off balance. The startled Founder had to grab onto the back of Karle's chair for support while Methras, stumbling, slammed into the angular corner of a workstation. The Jem'Hadar growled and cursed, but somehow managed to stay on their feet.

"Wait!" the Changeling cried out. "What are you doing?"

"Giving you what you asked for!" he shot back, his eyes glued to the navigational controls. "We're going to skirt the very fringe of the rift—where no one else in their right mind is going to venture, not even Starfleet!"

"No!" the Changeling shouted. Karle relished the fear in her voice. "It's too dangerous!"

"I know exactly what I'm doing!" the captain proclaimed. He'd show this insufferable pile of ooze what a Cardassian was really capable of. His eyes narrowed as the *Solanco* came within forty-five minutes of the outer regions of the rift. This was going to be tricky. . . .

To his surprise, the Founder's dismay gave way to contemptuous outrage. "Fool! I should have known better than to entrust our fate to one of your despicable breed!" Her right arm devolved into a viscous golden tentacle that wrapped itself tightly around Karle's throat, choking him. "You Cardassians do not deserve the blessings of the Dominion. Do not think we have forgotten your treacherous attack on us in the Omarion Nebula—for we most certainly have not! Your time will come, after you have served your purpose. The sooner your wretched species is exterminated, the better!"

I knew it! Karle thought furiously, even as he tugged uselessly at the slimy tentacle around his neck. The choking appendage resisted all his strength. *I knew we couldn't trust you! Lying blobs of pus!*

Methras and the Jem'Hadar looked on impassively as the Changeling throttled the ship's captain, who expected nothing less of the idolatrous creatures. Of course they would not lift a hand to interfere with the Founder's will! Karle realized he didn't stand a chance—

—until, without warning, a disruptor pistol suddenly appeared in his hand.

Karle was in no position to question this miraculous occurrence. Gasping, he raised the weapon and fired it point-blank at the Changeling's head. A blast of incandescent amber energy lit up the bridge, and Karle felt the tentacle about his throat go limp. He sprang from his seat and fired relentlessly at the headless body of the Changeling. The protoplasmic form bubbled and blackened before collapsing into a heap of ashes upon the floor.

Never cross a Cardassian! Karle thought triumphantly, all thought of his original mission forgotten. *We'll see who's exterminating who!*

He had only an instant to savor the Changeling's destruction. Caught off-guard by the freakish arrival of the disruptor, the Jem'Hadar were too late to save their divine Founder, but quick to avenge the Changeling's death.

A lethal cross fire reduced Zonek Karle to atoms.

Amidst the flare of the rifles and the chaos of the moment, no one noticed a shimmering red sphere hovering only centimeters beneath the bridge's ceiling. Indeed, anyone looking up might easily have mistaken the radiant crimson nimbus for a red-alert beacon activated by all the furious weapons fire.

(*) surveyed the scene with immense satisfaction. It had almost been too easy; the bitter divisions underlying this so-called alliance had already been simmering just beneath the surface. It had required only the slightest of effort on (*)'s part to telepathically stoke the entrenched animosities to a fever pitch—with the desired results. By the time (*) tipped its hand by arming the Cardassian, the unleashed hatred and bloodlust had already escalated beyond these puny creatures' control.

Delicious, (*) purred to itself. *Truly delectable.*

And the games had only just begun. . . .

★   ★   ★

"What do you mean there is no white?" First Virak'iklan barked at Methras.

The frightened Vorta swallowed hard, panic mounting at the back of his brain. He felt his control over this entire nightmarish situation rapidly slipping away. "I don't know. I can't explain it. It's impossible, but . . . it's gone."

In his shaking hands, Methras gripped the engraved metal chest that, in theory, should have contained a more than adequate supply of ketracel-white. Methras had thought that dispensing white to the Jem'Hadar, along with the accompanying ritual, would calm the agitated warriors in the wake of the Founder's shocking demise, but exactly the opposite reaction had resulted when he'd opened the chest to discover that his entire stock of white was missing.

How can this be? he wondered in fear and confusion. *I carefully checked my supply right before we left for Earth—and the chest is genetically encoded so that only I may open it!*

"Gone?" the First repeated ominously. He bent down until his horned face was only centimeters away from the Vorta's. The other Jem'Hadar closed in around Methras, trapping him at the center of a knot of discontented warriors. "All of it?"

"Every drop," Methras whispered, flinching in anticipation of the soldiers' reaction. He had no illusions regarding the Jem'-Hadar's distaste for Vortas in general; only his control of the white, and the authority of the now-carbonized Founder, had guaranteed the warriors' obedience. Without the white, Methras was like a tribble tossed into a cage of ravening saurovores. "It's not my fault!" he pleaded shrilly. "It isn't possible. . . ."

But the Jem'Hadar weren't even listening anymore. The butt of Virak'iklan's rifle slammed into Methras's face, shattering his jaw and dislodging several teeth. The rest of the soldiers joined in, knocking him to the floor. Heavy blows rained down on Methras like a meteor storm, while a blood-red glow filled the Vorta's fading vision. He groped frantically beneath his fractured jaw, struggling to activate his termination implant and spare himself a far more painful death. Yet, to his horror, the subdermal mechanism refused to work. He could not even kill himself.

It isn't fair! his mind protested to the universe. *How is this happening?*

Again and again, the merciless rifles pounded him. In his final moments, he wondered if the Founders would even bother to clone a new Methras, given the complete and utter failure of his mission. . . .

Perfect, (★) gloated. With the Vorta dead, and the *Solanco* accelerating heedlessly toward the cosmic rift, there was no chance of the crucial command codes ever making it to their destination. And by denying the Dominion an easy victory, (★) had successfully prolonged this sumptuous and savory war. *Exactly as I desired.*

But though it had already accomplished its primary objective, (★) could not resisting lingering aboard the doomed vessel while there were still living creatures to torture and violent emotions to foment. . . .

The ring of steel against steel echoed through the cramped confines of the freighter. Brownish-yellow bloodstains streaked the uncaring walls and consoles as the Jem'Hadar warriors clashed violently upon the bridge. The venerable commander of the unit perished by the edge of his former Second's *kar'takin,* then rose up once more, his fatal wound miraculously healed, to avenge his own demise. Spittle sprayed from his mouth of First Virak'iklan as he hacked mercilessly at the other warrior, aiming for the life-giving tube that flowed into his jugular vein. He struck a glancing blow at his target, nicking the reinforced plastic tubing, and drops of precious white leaked from the perforated conduit. The scent of the white, lost and wasted, inflamed his righteous anger further, spurring him to still more frenzied attacks, while all around him a half dozen Jem'Hadar soldiers slashed and stabbed at their brothers-in-arms.

Caught up in the heat of battle, the dueling warriors remained oblivious to the flickering sphere of crimson energy spinning fiercely above their heads, and to the fact that their rifles had inexplicably disappeared, leaving them only to fight each other endlessly with their *kar'takins*.

(★) devoured the unleashed fury of the Jem'Hadar. Turning the unit against itself had been child's play; it had merely implanted the idea in each soldier's mind that the others were hoarding a hidden supply of white and withholding it from him. Their genetically programmed addiction made them peculiarly susceptible to manipulation, much to (★)'s delight.

Alas, (★) knew it would soon have to depart the doomed freighter, before the vessel disappeared forever into the approaching rift. The voracious space-time rupture waited to consume energy and matter alike, and not even (★) was immune to the danger it posed. (★) briefly considered resurrecting the Cardassian captain in time to save the ship, but, no, it was better that the *Solanco*, along with the stolen command codes, vanished from the cosmos altogether. *I must abandon this vessel shortly,* (★) resolved.

But not quite yet.

The ongoing carnage was just too succulent.

This was the very peak of its feeding cycle. The more the organic specimens hated, the stronger (★) grew, and the stronger it became, the better it could fan the flames of the conflict, toying with the minds and matter below it to yield ever greater levels of homicidal mania for it to dine upon. Hovering beneath the gore-splattered ceiling, it flexed its power to make another minor adjustment to the scenario it had created.

Virak'iklan had his traitorous Second right where he wanted him, backed into a corner and down on one knee. More white dripped from the Second's punctured supply tube; like all the soldiers aboard the vessel, the Second had just enough white to stay alive, but not enough to curb the madness of withdrawal. (★) had seen to that, discreetly adding and subtracting to each soldier's rations as needed. The First raised his *kar'takin* to deliver the killing blow, but on its downward swing the sharpened blade inexplicably transformed into a blunt truncheon. The metal club slammed into the Second's skull, knocking him to the blood-stained floor but not yet killing him. Virak'iklan had to strike the officer again and again before he finally collapsed lifelessly onto the floor. The First clubbed him one more time to be sure, then took advantage of his momentary victory to glance around the bridge.

For a second or two, Virak'iklan was puzzled to see that, as with himself, every soldier's *kar'takin* had been replaced instantaneously with an identical truncheon. *How?* he pondered, dimly remembering that he had wondered much the same when the Cardassian had mysteriously received his weapon, and when his own rifle had mysteriously disappeared.

Something is terribly wrong, he realized for a moment, but then the grappling bodies of two of his soldiers, locked together in a furious struggle, smashed into his side, dashing such concerns from his mind and tossing him back into the savage fray. It was all these two's fault, he realized instantly, not pausing to question where this sudden certainty had come from. It was they who, along with the dead and vanquished Second, had stolen the last of the white, sparking this riot. But he'd teach them to let their greedy craving get the best of them. He'd beat some discipline back into his troops, even if he had to kill them all to do it. He swung his club and felt it connect satisfyingly against flesh and bone.

Ignored and discarded on the floor behind him, the body of the murdered Second began to twitch spasmodically as shattered bones reknit themselves and mortal injuries healed with impossible speed. A fresh layer of overlapping, chitinous, gray scales spread over a skull that no longer looked nearly as pulped as it had a few heartbeats before. Limp fingers jerked to life, then tightened around the shaft of his abandoned club as he lurched onto his feet, pursuing his First into the chaotic free-for-all that had erupted on the bridge. Already he had forgotten his own short-lived death, forgotten everything except his own unquenchable need for revenge.

Yes . . . (★) basked in the intoxicating enmity suffusing the scene. Blunt weapons instead of edged ones prolonged the struggle and increased the brutality. This was more than mere sustenance now; it was an exquisite delicacy.

A graphic on the viewscreen charted the *Solanco*'s steady progress toward the fateful event horizon of the rift. (★) registered that the freighter was now less than a single light-year away from oblivion. *Soon,* (★) reminded himself. *I must escape soon.*

But not this very minute. (★) had never encountered a species like these Jem'Hadar. Their single-minded focus on combat made them the perfect prey. The intensity of the warring Jem'Hadar, genetically engineered for maximum ferocity, was almost more than (★) could resist. *Just a little bit longer,* it promised itself. . . .

On the bridge, First Virak'iklan died once more as both his Second and his Third battered him so hard the blows left dents in their shining metal clubs. No sooner had they finished killing him than the two soldiers turned on each other, trampling over their victim's body in their frenzy. *This is wrong,* Virak'iklan thought as his brain came back to life seconds later. *This is not the Founders' will.*

(★) spun silently above the crazed Jem'Hadar, lapping up the hate that spilled like blood from the maddened soldiers, caught up in a rapture such as it had never known.

Too late (★) realized that it had lingered too long at the feast. The *Solanco* crossed the event horizon into the Hunyadi Rift, and immense cosmic forces seized hold of the fragile freighter. Lighted display panels blinked out, and the viewscreen went blank, as the rift sucked every last volt of electrical energy from the ship's sys-

tems. The battle-scarred bridge was cast into near-darkness, lit only
by the incarnadine glow of (★) itself. The floor beneath the
Jem'Hadar lurched violently as the ship was buffeted by the
chaotic turbulence of the rift. Life-support and artificial gravity
shorted out, and the helpless bodies of the Jem'Hadar were tossed
about the bridge like chaff in the wind. They gasped hoarsely, feeling the lifeforce drain from their bodies as surely the rift consumed
the hate-spawned vitality (★) had leeched from its unwary victims.
The flickering red sphere tried to escape, to leave the collapsing
starship behind, but the pull of the vortex was too great. For the
first time in uncounted millennia, (★) found itself in the presence
of a hunger even more demanding than its own.

But that was not the only irony. As the walls of the freighter
buckled inward, and (★) descended inexorably into the abyss, a singularly bitter truth struck at the core of its being:

Without intending to, (★) might have just saved both the Klingon Empire and the United Federation of Planets.

And it had nothing to blame but its own insatiable appetite.

Wait! (★) wailed in despair. *Give me another chance! This cannot be
the end . . . !*

The banquet was over forever. An eternity of hunger began.

The Ceremony of Innocence Is Drowned

Keith R.A. DeCandido

War correspondence: This story chronicles events referred to in the *Star Trek: Deep Space Nine* episode "In the Pale Moonlight."

Keith R.A. DeCandido

Keith R.A. DeCandido's contributions to the *Star Trek* universe since 1999 have been numerous, including the novels *Diplomatic Implausibility, Demons of Air and Darkness,* and *The Art of the Impossible;* the two-book series *The Brave and the Bold;* the comic book miniseries *Perchance to Dream;* over half a dozen eBooks in the *Star Trek: S.C.E.* series, which he codeveloped; and short fiction in *What Lay Beyond, Prophecy and Change,* and *No Limits.* He is also the author of the *Star Trek: I.K.S. Gorkon* series, novels starring the franchise's most popular aliens, the Klingons. Forthcoming works include the novels *A Time for War, a Time for Peace* and *Articles of the Federation,* the Ferenginar portion of the *Worlds of Star Trek: Deep Space Nine* miniseries, further *I.K.S. Gorkon* adventures, and a great deal more. Keith, whose original novel *Dragon Precinct* was published in 2004, has also written in the universes of *Buffy the Vampire Slayer, Doctor Who, Farscape, Gene Roddenberry's Andromeda,* Marvel Comics, *Resident Evil, Xena,* and more. His other anthologies include *Imaginings: An Anthology of Long Short Fiction, The Ultimate Dragon, The Ultimate Alien, OtherWere: Stories of Transformation, Urban Nightmares,* and an upcoming *Star Trek* anthology called *Tales from the Captain's Table.* He has long since abandoned such outmoded notions as "sleep." Learn more exaggerations about Keith at DeCandido.net.

Lwaxana sent Mr. Homn to the door to let Nathan Gold and Elaine Welsh in nine seconds before they arrived at the door.

Her eyes did not see Mr. Homn open the door for the two humans as they walked up the three stairs that led to it, but thanks to her telepathy, she perceived the actions just the same. Nathan was thinking about the questions he'd be asking Lwaxana; Elaine was studying the old house's architecture and coming up with some questions of her own; Mr. Homn, bless him, was going over the inventory of the pantry, and hoping that the two new arrivals wouldn't ask for anything that he didn't have in stock. They had a replicator, of course, but Lwaxana hated the damn thing, and much preferred original foodstuffs. Sometimes, however, the needs of guests went beyond what was stocked in the larder, and so Lwaxana had to swallow her irritation—which always went down badly—and let Mr. Homn use the wretched device. Such were the burdens of a Daughter of the Fifth House, Holder of the Sacred Chalice of Rixx, and Heir to the Holy Rings of Betazed.

As soon as Mr. Homn led the couple into the cavernous living room, Lwaxana stood up from the genuine *amra*-skin couch to stand on the *Eridat* rug that had been in her family for generations, and extended her arms. "Elaine, Nathan—welcome to my humble abode! It's so good to see you both again!"

Nathan grinned. *"This* you call humble? I'd hate to see lavish."

"Thank you, Lwaxana," Elaine said, putting her hands together. "It's a singular privilege to be allowed into your home."

"Of course it is, dear. Oh, and to answer your question, yes, this house was built as a combination of the early Dantric style and later Torinese." She frowned. "I'm not sure why, really, but I always liked it. We've—well, *I've* lived here for—" she blinked "—goodness, almost forty years now. Time passes so quickly, doesn't it?"

"That explains why I keep losing my hair," Nathan said.

This prompted Lwaxana to actually look at her guests for the first time. So often she neglected to pay attention to people's physical appearances, aside from her own, of course. But she knew that nontelepaths placed such a huge emphasis on it that it behooved her to acknowledge them—which was part of *why* she paid such close attention to her own appearance.

Nathan was a short, balding man, though he hadn't reached the elegant baldness of, say, Jean-Luc Picard or Timicin. No, he was still achieving baldness, a work in progress. The hair he had was black, flecked with gray, his nose was a bit oversized, his cheeks a bit too puffy, and he had awful posture. Worse, he insisted on wearing a beige cardigan sweater, even though it was a fairly warm day, that washed out his already pale skin. Despite the fact that, in many ways, he looked like he'd been put together by three different people going for three different appearances, it all seemed to fit together.

Much like the house's architecture, in fact.

Elaine's next words matched Lwaxana's thoughts: "I've never seen those designs combined before—and I've been living here for three years now."

"As far as I know, this house is unique. That's what led me to it, to be honest."

"I can see the appeal." Elaine smiled, revealing a wide mouth of white teeth. The smile seemed a bit big for the rest of her face, truth be told. She wore her sand-colored hair tied back in a large ponytail, but even with that, her hair seemed to dwarf her small, round face. However, as with the seeming imperfections in her husband's form, on her it worked.

This was the third time she had met with Nathan and Elaine, and once again Lwaxana found herself mildly envious of them. They were so wonderfully *comfortable* with their appearances. And with each other.

Lwaxana indicated the *amra*-skin couch; she herself took the plush conformer chair. "Both of you please, sit down. Can Mr. Homn get either of you something to eat or drink?"

"Just an *allira* punch for me," Nathan said, as he took a seat on the couch, sitting with his legs straight ahead of him, his arms resting on his lap, his posture still awful.

"Nonsense," Lwaxana said, "you also want a Reuben."

Nathan chuckled. "Well, yeah, I *want* one. Been wanting a Reuben for three years, but I've seen what you people call corned beef on this world. The cheese is great. Love the cheese. Could die a happy man eating cheese here, but the corned beef? Forget about it. I wouldn't give my dog the corned beef here."

Lwaxana laughed. "You don't even like dogs, Nathan."

"My point."

"Well, as it happens, you are lucky enough to be in a house that was once home to a human who adored Reubens."

Nathan blinked. "Really?"

"No, not really, but he did love to have corned beef on rye bread. The upshot, my dear Nathan, is that our replicator is programmed to provide Earth corned beef, so you *can* have a Reuben."

He threw up his hands. "Fine, you sold me. One Reuben."

Elaine had taken up a more relaxed posture on the couch, tucking her long legs under her and leaning on the back of the couch with her right arm. She fixed Lwaxana with a look. "As I recall, last time, at the restaurant, you said that your Mr. Homn made a much better blue-leaf salad than the atrocity the restaurant fed us."

Lwaxana turned to her valet. "Mr. Homn, in addition to the

Reuben and *allira* punch for Mr. Gold and some oscoids and a Samarian sunset for me, please prepare a blue-leaf salad and a glass of sparkling water with a jakarine twist for Ms. Welsh."

"Wish I could do that," Nathan said with a smile. "Just pull things out of people's heads. It'd certainly simplify the interview process."

Elaine added in a mock-conspiratorial tone, "And it'd be nice if he knew what I wanted without my having to repeat it eight times."

"That's ridiculous," Nathan said archly. "You usually only have to repeat it five or six times."

"Actually," Lwaxana said, "it averages out to nine times, but who's counting?"

Nathan shot his wife a look. "Everyone, apparently."

Lwaxana knew that Nathan's irritation with his wife was feigned. That made Lwaxana both happy and sad, but she managed to rein in her emotional state. Ever since little Barin was born, she had made an effort to keep her emotions from affecting those around her. It was tough at her age—she was a sufficiently powerful telepath that, as she grew older, it became harder to keep her own emotional state from bleeding out to others, as it were—but Lwaxana was up to the challenge. She was up to any challenge.

"So, Nathan, you may as well go ahead and ask me about my first husband and my first daughter, since that's what you've wanted to ask ever since I told you when we moved to this house."

Chuckling, Nathan reached into the pocket of his sweater and pulled out some kind of gadget or other, which Lwaxana knew would record their conversation.

When Nathan and Elaine first moved to Betazed three years ago, it was for Elaine's work: she was an architect and, in Lwaxana's admittedly amateur if still very well-informed opinion, a rather good one. She was heading up the design team for a small village being built along Lake Cataria, meant to accommodate the greater number of people coming to live on Betazed over these past few decades. Lwaxana had always taken pride in the planet's growing reputation as one of the garden spots of the Federation, crediting her own tireless goodwill efforts over the years to help promote that reputation.

Elaine had feared that the outbreak of the Dominion War nine months earlier would mean the work would come to a halt, but it was close enough to finished that the planetary government permitted it to continue. Lwaxana knew that this relieved Elaine, but the fear that the project would end prematurely lingered.

In the meantime, her husband, a writer, was working on a book about prominent Federation figures. The one change that the war had brought on was that travel was more hazardous than Nathan was entirely comfortable with. While Nathan's father was a Starfleet captain, commanding the *U.S.S. da Vinci,* Nathan himself preferred to avoid even the possibility of encountering the conflict. He instead decided to work specifically on the chapters relating to the subject of his that was on the same planet as he was: Lwaxana.

"All right, we're recording." Nathan leaned back on the couch, his arms again resting on his lap. "And yeah, you're right, soon as you said almost forty years ago, I immediately thought of your first husband and first daughter. Did you move here after Kestra died?"

It was rare that Lwaxana ever felt the need to compose herself before she spoke, but she did right now. It was still *so* difficult to speak of Kestra . . .

Finally, she began. "There was a time, not very long ago, when the answer to that question would've been 'Kestra who? My only daughter is my darling Deanna.' Kestra died in a terrible accident when she was six. I was so distraught, I—I pretended she didn't exist. I erased all memory of her, I eliminated all my diary entries from the day I learned I was pregnant with her to the day she died, I—" She hesitated, remembering the look on Deanna's face on the *Enterprise* when she found out only four years ago. "I kept her existence from her sister. It was foolish of me, I know that now, of course, but at the time, it seemed the only thing to do. Kestra was so full of joy."

"Kids're great that way."

"I'm sure you both take great pride in Danielle and Simone," Lwaxana said, referring to Nathan and Elaine's two grown daughters, both of whom leapt to the forefront of the humans' thoughts the instant Lwaxana started speaking of Kestra. "But it's so much more with us. When you're a telepath, you don't just *see* the children's happiness, you *feel* it." She took a breath. "And you feel it even more when they die. So much so that it becomes much easier to deny reality than it is to actually deal with the death."

Elaine leaned forward, untucking her legs, and putting a hand on Lwaxana's arm. "I'm sorry. My husband's an idiot; we can change the subject."

"Hey!"

Mr. Homn virtually glided into the room, holding a tray in one giant hand, and offering Lwaxana a handkerchief with the other.

Lwaxana gratefully accepted the handkerchief, and dabbed her eyes to absorb the tears that were welling up. "Thank you, Mr. Homn. And it's fine, Elaine; your husband isn't an idiot." She forced herself to smile. "No more than most men, anyhow."

"Hey!"

Mr. Homn placed the tray on the glass coffee table that sat on the *Eridat* rug between the sofa and the conformer chair. Lwaxana immediately grabbed an oscoid shell and sucked down the luscious fish.

While she ate the oscoid, Mr. Homn tapped the side of the glass containing her sunet, turning the clear liquid to a many-hued drink that matched the sunsets on Samaria. Then the valet continued laying out the food.

Lwaxana continued. "It's good to talk about it. To remind myself of what a fool I was. What I denied poor Deanna. And especially Ian. I never really gave him the chance to grieve for Kestra. Then *he* was taken from me . . ."

His distribution completed, Mr. Homn stood and looked inquisitively at Lwaxana. She sensed his thoughts: *Will you need any-thing else?*

"That'll be all for now." As the tall valet drifted out of the room, Lwaxana said to Nathan, "Wonderful servant, Mr. Homn."

Elaine swallowed a leaf. "You were certainly right about his salad. How long has he been with you?"

"Since I was forced to fire his predecessor, Mr. Xelo. The man was thinking such foul, lascivious thoughts about me that I simply could *not* take it anymore, and—" She cut herself off, closed her eyes. "No. No, that's not fair. What was it I said about denying reality instead of dealing with death?" She took a long breath. "The fact is, I found out that Mr. Xelo had hidden away some keepsakes of Kestra's. It was something he and Ian had done after she died, in the hopes that I would—come around. I found it one day when I was looking for something, and I—I blew up at him." She snorted. "I almost fried his brain, the poor man. I got rid of everything he had kept and fired him on the spot. Then I made up that whole sexual thoughts nonsense. Well," she added with a smile, "I didn't make it up *completely*, he *did* have occasional thoughts in that direction, but it's nothing I'm not accustomed to. Anyhow, he got rid of almost everything, and left. The only thing he saved was one picture of Ian, Deanna, and Kestra that I took right after Deanna was born. He gave it to Mr. Homn, and Mr. Homn gave it to me after I finally—finally admitted to Kestra's existence." Lwaxana dabbed her eye with the handkerchief once again.

Nathan carried a genuine regret for this entire line of questioning, and it was with that regret in his thoughts that he asked: "How did you meet Ian?" Or, rather, he asked, "Hm dud yuh mitt in?" since his mouth was full of corned beef, melted *espra* cheese, and bread when he did so.

All three people in the room felt a wave of relief at the change of subject. Lwaxana hadn't intended this interview to be so—so *heavy*. "He was the head of the Starfleet team that installed our or-bital defense grid. This was—" she thought a moment "—forty-

seven years ago. Such a darling man. Reittan Grax introduced us—
he was the liaison between Strafleet and the parliament. And, if I
do say so myself, my darling Ian did an excellent job. Our orbital
defenses were the envy of the sector."

"Bet they still are."

"Well, probably not to the same extent." Lwaxana immediately
recalled the recent arguments in the parliament building, arguments in which she'd played a prominent role. So, for that matter,
had Grax. "They've been talking about upgrading the system since
the war started, which strikes me as a waste of time."

"Why do you say that?"

A nontelepath might have taken umbrage at Nathan's question,
but Lwaxana knew that his query was without malice, simply an
honest request for information. "What would be the point?
They've even constructed shelters under the Loneel Mountains, as
if we were already under siege. It's just completely ridiculous, and I
see no reason for us to get excessively paranoid. Why, even if the
Dominion *wanted* to attack us—and I honestly can't think of a
good reason why they'd go after Betazed over some other Federation world—we're protected by the Tenth Fleet. I've known Admiral Masc for *years*—he's the head of the Tenth Fleet. He served
with my daughter fifteen years ago. Good man, if a little too scared
of commitment. Anyhow, he'll protect us."

"Scared of commitment—that certainly isn't something that'd
apply to you. You've been married, what, three times?"

"Strictly speaking, yes. I came close on a couple of other occasions—they're both dead now. Campio died last year of natural
causes, but he and I weren't really—compatible. As for Timicin . . ."
Lwaxana's mind drifted, remembering the most beautiful mind
she'd ever encountered. She'd known Timicin such a short time,
and yet she felt his loss as keenly as she did that of Ian and Kestra.
"Timicin was a great man, a scientist, a man of subdued passion."

"Okay, you lost me there."

Lwaxana chuckled. "I suppose that doesn't really follow, does it?

It's hard to explain to a nontelepath, but he had a quiet intensity about him." She took a refreshing sip of her sunset. All this talking was making her parched. "It's funny, but if you asked me to describe what he looked like, I'm not sure I could, but I remember his mind *so* clearly."

"Doesn't that disturb you a little? That you can't remember his face?"

Shrugging, Lwaxana said, "Well, it's not that important. His face. You're thinking like a mundane, dear. Looks aren't everything—unless you're me, of course. Somebody once told me, after we'd been married about five years, that Ian had a kind face. And once it was pointed out to me, I realized that it was true, but I'd never noticed that about him until then."

"Interesting." And, unlike when most humans used that word in such context, Nathan really did find it interesting. Lwaxana tensed as she prepared herself for his next question. "What about your other two husbands? A Tavnian named Jeyel and the changeling Odo. Which, by the way, makes you five for five—three husbands, two almosts-but-not-quites, and not a single Betazoid in the bunch."

"Oh, there are a lot more than two almosts-but-not-quites," she said with a laugh, thinking of Jean-Luc and so many others. "But, to answer the question you *didn't* ask, I suppose I tend to gravitate toward non-Betazoids because they're more of a challenge. There's very little privacy on Betazed—"

"We *know*." Nathan spoke with great emphasis, and Lwaxana saw in his thoughts how aghast he was when Elaine explained how few doors there were in Betazoid architecture.

"You have to understand, dear, we can see into each other's thoughts. Physicality is hardly taboo when the mind is an open book. But that also means that with a Betazoid man, I pretty much always know what I'm going to get."

"I know that you ended your marriage to Jeyel because of custody issues—why did you annul your subsequent marriage to

Odo? Was it because of the war? After all, Odo may be on our side, but he *is* of the same species as the Dominion's Founders."

"Nathan, dear, I may be a politican, but I don't do anything for political reasons. Life's too short. No, Odo is a dear dear friend, and I wish him the—"

"I am dead."

"Lwaxana?"

"Hm?"

"You cut yourself off. What do you wish him?" Nathan asked.

"I go into battle to reclaim my life."

"I'm sorry, I thought I heard—something."

"This I do gladly, for I am Jem'Hadar."

"Anyhow, I know Odo and his friends on that space station of theirs are fighting the good fight in this war, and I'm sure they'll lead us to—"

"Victory is life."

"VICTORY IS LIFE!"

"Lwaxana? Lwaxana!"

Dimly, Lwaxana registered that she was now lying on the *Eridat* rug, having been suddenly overwhelmed by the thoughts of thousands of Jem'Hadar soldiers uttering their prebattle mantra simultaneously. Nathan and Elaine were standing over her.

The only way she could have sensed that many Jem'Hadar that clearly was if they were right on top of Betazed.

"They're coming," she whispered.

"What?"

"Who's coming?"

Lwaxana ignored them, and focused all the energy she could on a telepathic cry to Kan Mryax, the woman in charge of maintaining the orbital defenses. *They're coming!*

We're already on it. We'll take care of them.

Mryax's thoughts were terse, and carried none of the confidence Lwaxana was hoping for.

"Lwaxana, what's wrong?"

She finally focused on her two guests, who knew only that their host suddenly collapsed onto the rug in mid-sentence and started whispering gibberish. "I'm sorry, Nathan, Elaine, please—could you help me up?"

Before they could do anything, she felt the soothing presence of Mr. Homn entering the room, taking her gently by the shoulders, and guiding her to her feet.

"Thank you Mr. Homn. Please, go check on Barin."

He nodded and took his leave.

"I'm afraid that the Dominion is attacking. They—"

Mryax grits her teeth as she activates the defense systems and sends out a general distress call. The phasers cannot penetrate the Jem'Hadar shields, and are doing only minimal damage to the Cardassian ones. The ships keep moving closer.

"*Where the hell is the Tenth Fleet?*"

Admiral Masc is in the midst of supervising a training exercise when the distress call comes in.

"*Why the hell didn't Intelligence warn us of this?*"

A Vorta named Luaran basks in the ineffectiveness of Betazed's orbital defenses. It is as the intelligence reports stated: Betazed is populated by pacifists and fools who, like so many other members of this weak Federation, believe themselves to live in a peaceful galaxy.

"*How much longer before we can land troops?*"

Gul Lemec's smile grows as wide as his face. Ever since the embarrassing defeat at Minos Corva, he's been waiting for an opportunity to conquer the Federation, and here he is at the vanguard of this invasion. This is the farthest the Dominion has penetrated into Federation space since the war started. He is going to enjoy subjugating these telepathic cowards . . .

"*Bring us about for another pass!*"

"Lwaxana, what's *happening?*"

Shaking her head, Lwaxana tried to focus on Elaine and Nathan, but she couldn't. Instead, she was assaulted by the eagerness of the Cardassian soldiers to stomp on the planet (such joy they took in being the conquerors), the zealous single-mindedness

of the Jem'Hadar prepared to do their duty to their gods (truly the
perfect soldiers, how could *anyone* stand against *that?),* the calm as-
surance of the Vorta directing the battle (so smug, so sure of themselves), the anger, embarrassment, and panic on the part of the
Starfleet officers caught with their proverbial pants down (as well
they should be, the dolts!) . . .

But most of all, she felt the rising panic of her fellow Betazoids.

"We're being invaded."

The look of horror on Elaine's face matched her thoughts,
which had turned decidedly dark—and frightened. "My God. We
have to get to the shelters."

"So much for excessive paranoia," Nathan muttered.

Lwaxana barely registered Nathan's snide comment as she felt
Mryax scream in her mind. Orbital Defense Control fell to pieces
all around her, consoles exploding, shrapnel tearing into her flesh,
Dominion weaponry ripping into the defenses and reducing them
to nothingness.

*We're being invaded! The Dominion (Hurry up!) is coming! Where is
Starfleet? What's (That's impossible,) that noise? (the orbital defenses) The
orbital defenses are down! (will stop them.) Did you hear something? We
have to (What's happening?) get to the shelters.*

*I can hear the Jem'Hadar (Starfleet's on its way) the Cardassians (I can
feel Admiral Masc.) oh no, they're coming! Get to (Hurry! What was
that?) the shelters. Do you (Don't worry, I'm sure the orbital defenses and
Starfleet) sense something? (can stop them easily. It's what) We've got to get
(they do, protect us from threats.) out of here before they—*

"I have Barin. We must go."

The soft, whisper-like voice of Mr. Homn cut through the telepathic chatter and got Lwaxana's attention. The valet carried the
child with his left arm. The boy was sound asleep, resting against
Mr. Homn's massive shoulder. In the other hand, Mr. Homn held a
suitcase.

Elaine looked up in shock at Mr. Homn. "He talks?"

Lwaxana forced down the voices in her head, even as they rose to an appalling crescendo. "Of course he talks, dear."

Nathan muttered, "Probably just can't get a word in. We need to get to those shelters."

"Agreed," Lwaxana said. "I just hope you packed enough, Mr. Homn. Though it shouldn't be too long. I can sense Admiral Masc getting closer. I'm sure he'll take care of everything in very short order. Those Dominion reptiles won't be able to stand against—"

"Fire on the capital city now."

"Oh no . . ."

The ground shook, knocking Lwaxana to the floor. She reached out mentally to see how her son was, but Barin was still asleep. She had joked just the other day that the sweet child could sleep through anything. Now it seemed that would be put to the test.

Lwaxana focused all her concentration, all her thoughts, all her energy on keeping her telepathic shields up. Normally, she didn't concern herself with the background noise of all the minds around her, but now it was everything she could do to keep them out. Because if she didn't . . .

. . . she could feel the white-hot agony of one woman as shrapnel from an explosion ripped through her torso . . .

. . . the fear of one man as he lost track of his son in the suddenly panicking crowds in the midst of the capital city who found the sky filled with Jem'Hadar strike ships . . .

. . . the dying minds of the hundreds of people in the nearby Art Institute as it was hit with weapons fire, obliterating entire floors of the ancient structure that had stood for centuries . . .

. . . the screams of the dying . . .

. . . the fear of the living . . .

. . . the pain of the injured and maimed . . .

. . . the sound of the weapons fire mixing with the rending of matter under its onslaught . . .

. . . the screams of everyone around her . . .

. . . Barin, waking up and wondering why the world was coming apart . . .

. . . Nathan, the ceiling collapsing right on his head, caving in his skull, his final thoughts of his children, whom he'd never see again . . .

. . . Elaine, the wall falling against her back, knocking her to the floor, shattering her spine, her last, lingering thoughts of how Nathan will get along without her . . .

. . . Mr. Homn, calmly interposing his body between the destruction of the house and little Barin, to the end his only thoughts those of protecting the child in his care . . .

. . . and then, unable to hold it in anymore, Lwaxana screamed and screamed and screamed . . .

. . . then nothing.

"There are survivors down here!"

Lwaxana felt the presence of the medic before seeing her. An Andorian, a medical student on Betazed to spend time with her mother, a teacher at the Art Institute, now volunteering to help in the rescue endeavors.

She opened her eyes to find herself surrounded by pieces of her home. Tatters of the *Eridat* rug—the rug that Lwaxana's great-great-grandmother had commissioned specially as a wedding present for her son, Lwaxana's great-grandfather—mixed in with shreds of *amra* skin and other pieces of building material that had been constructed hundreds of years ago, combining the finest elements of Dantric and Torinese in a unique way that was now lost forever. She did not have to look to know that the vase Deanna had given her for her birthday right before she left for the university, the patterned mantelpiece that Ian had designed and had built specially for her when they moved in, the magnificent kitchen that she had had redone for Mr. Homn five years ago, not to mention the Sacred Chalice of Rixx and the Holy Rings of Betazed, were all lost.

But those were *things*. Of greater import were the people. Her first action was to reach out to Barin's mind, to make sure that her son was still alive.

It was easy to do. Along with the Andorian woman, who called herself Thriss, and a few other rescue volunteers, it was the only mind she found.

Thriss managed to shift a piece of rubble off of Lwaxana's leg. Until then, she hadn't even registered that the rubble was there. Behind her, another volunteer, a Betazoid named Jeea, was holding Barin, going over him with one of those tricorder things that Starfleet was always playing with. The child was crying, poor dear. Lwaxana was amazed that she herself wasn't doing likewise.

Thriss had a tricorder of her own. "I'm reading more DNA traces. There may be more survivors."

"The—" Lwaxana cut herself off and started coughing. Her throat was raw, and her tongue felt like it was coated in dirt. Thriss handed her a bottle of water, which Lwaxana hungrily gulped down the bulk of.

"There aren't any." Even with the water, her voice sounded whispery and hollow.

"I'm sorry, ma'am, but I have to be sure—"

Lwaxana grabbed the Andorian child's arm. "There *aren't* any others. Don't you understand, you stupid girl, I *felt them die*!"

"Ma'am, I—"

"They were guests in my *house!* I was feeding them *lunch* and we were just *talking* and then they came and the house was destroyed and they *died!* Have you ever felt someone die inside your mind? *Have* you?"

Quietly, Thriss said, "No, I haven't. I'm sorry."

"You're lucky, then."

"Right now, ma'am, none of us is lucky. We have to get you to one of the shelters. The Jem'Hadar ground troops are focusing on the city right now—"

"—but they'll be getting to the outskirts soon enough," Lwaxana finished. She could feel the single-minded clarity of the Jem'Hadar soldiers, matched only by the bloodthirstiness of the Cardassians. She found, bizarrely, that she preferred the Jem'Hadar. "We have to go."

Lwaxana, you're alive!

Enaren? Lwaxana was grateful to hear the thoughts of Cort Enaren. If her cousin survived, perhaps other members of Betazed's parliament did as well.

Yes, I'm still alive, though many are not. Sark, Damira, little Cort, and I are heading to the Loneel shelters. Enaren was referring to his son, daughter-in-law, and infant grandson. *We should be able to hide from the Jem'Hadar indefinitely there.*

Don't be silly, we won't need to hide indefinitely, just until Starfleet takes care of these Dominion creatures.

I hope you're right, Lwaxana. I'll see you soon.

Jeea handed Barin over to Lwaxana. "He'll be fine. I was able to clear his lungs of the dust."

"Thank you."

The group proceeded up the hill that was just down the road from Lwaxana's house toward a group of ground vehicles parked atop that selfsame hill. Lwaxana was holding the coughing Barin in her arms. She took one glance back at the wreckage of the house she had lived in for so long, the house she raised Deanna in.

When this is over, I'll give all three of you a proper burial, I promise.

The vehicle looked like it was about a hundred years old. Even though she saw the answer in Thriss's thoughts, she had to ask the question. "We're taking one of *those?*"

"We're not—*you* are," the Andorian said. "We still have several more places to check out. Don't worry—"

"I understand, dear. Go, do what you have to do." Lwaxana read the details in Thriss's mind. The vehicles were preprogrammed to take any passengers to the shelters, and ground vehicles were necessary because they were less likely to draw the attention of the Jem'Hadar strike ships. The vehicle had massive treaded wheels that Lwaxana assumed allowed them to drive through the forests surrounding the Loneel Mountains.

"Good luck to you, ma'am," Thriss said, then moved on with Jeea and the rest of her team, determined to save more lives.

Lwaxana couldn't help but admire her dedication. *We'll need people like this in the days ahead, once Starfleet drives these monsters out of here.*

"Don't worry about me, dear," she called after them, mustering up her confidence. "I'm a Daughter of the Fifth House. I survived the Sindareen raids, I survived three childbirths, I'll survive this. This is a terrible day, it's true, but Betazed will survive. I'm sure of that."

"I hope you're right," Thriss said, mirroring Enaren's thoughts, as she and her team continued with their rescue efforts.

"Of course I am."

Lwaxana assumed that the dust in the air would dissipate as she moved farther from the house, but it didn't. If anything, it grew worse as she walked up the incline. Her eyes welled with tears, and her throat still felt like several layers of sandpaper.

When she reached the groundcar at the top of the hill, she got a good look at the capital city.

Or, rather, what was left of it.

With her eyes, she saw smoking ruins in places where buildings that were built before Betazed joined the Federation once stood. The Parliament House where she had just last week argued against the planetary defense upgrades was on fire and half-destroyed. Byram Hall, the gorgeous neo-Valdane-style structure where she and Ian had their wedding was nothing but a cloud of dust. And small ships of Dominion design flew through the air, firing on more buildings.

With her mind, she felt the pain of the injured and the cries of the dying and the brutality of their attackers as they roamed the streets.

Eventually, she was able to turn her eyes away.

Turning her mind away proved more difficult. But she managed it.

The door to the groundcar opened at her approach. She climbed in, placing Barin, still coughing, on the far seat, then taking the near one for herself. Straps came out of the sides of the chair to hold her and her son in place.

"Number of passengers?" the computer asked.

"Two."

"We will arrive in seventeen minutes," the computer said as the door closed.

Within five of those seventeen minutes, they were traversing the forest, and Lwaxana could no longer see the wreckage of the capital city. Twelve minutes after that, the groundcar arrived at the fistrium-laden crevasse that hid the entrance to the shelters from view.

Silently, she brought Barin in through the entrance, down a corridor that had been carved out from the cooled volcanic rock into the tunnels beneath the mountains. The fistrium would keep them invisible to Dominion sensors until the way was clear.

Halfway down, she stumbled, overwhelmed by the thoughts that pounded past her shields.

Where is Olfran? (The screams,) My arm! (I can't drown out the screams,) I can't feel my legs, (why can't they stop screaming?) what happened to my legs? (Cardassian bastards,) I saw her die (I remember fighting them in the war,) right in front of me. (it just figures they'd get in bed) Where's Starfleet? (with those Jem'Hadar monsters.) What happened (It's gone, all gone.) to the planetary defenses? I spent all my life living there, (Has anyone seen Marit?) I built that house, (Why do they want us?) and now it's been destroyed.

"Lwaxana!"

Shaking her head, Lwaxana turned and saw the haggard face of her cousin. "Enaren. Are you all right?" Behind him was another person Lwaxana didn't recognize, but read her name as Mara.

"Not especially. Damira's hurt, and we're running out of space down here. Sark's gone off to explore some more tunnels."

"Let me take little Barin," Mara said. Lwaxana saw in her thoughts that they had set up a section for the children. Risking casting her mind outward, she felt the thoughts of the youths. Interestingly enough, they were less panicked than the adults—though many of them, especially the younger ones, didn't really understand what was happening. Some even thought this was a simple adventure.

"I wouldn't worry too much," Lwaxana said as Mara took Barin off. "I'm sure Starfleet will—"

And then she felt it. Through the panic of the Betazoids in the shelter. Through the pain of the Betazoids still trapped on the surface, not to mention the non-Betazoid visitors who, like Nathan, like Elaine, like Thriss and her mother, came to Betazed thinking it one of the garden spots of the Federation, a place that was safe from the strife of the war. Through the bloody single-mindedness of the Jem'Hadar and Cardassian soldiers and their Vorta leaders.

Through all that, Lwaxana felt the thoughts of Admiral Masc, ordering the Tenth Fleet into retreat.

"Send a message to Starfleet," the admiral was telling one of his other officers. *"Betazed has fallen to the Dominion."*

Betazed has fallen.

In less than an hour, Lwaxana lost her home, her valet, her possessions, her world—everything, except her son. She had gone from having almost everything she could ask for to almost nothing. And what little she had was now in the hands of the Federation's enemy.

For the first time, she began to understand what it was that Deanna, Will, Jean-Luc, and the rest of Starfleet had been facing for the last year. *Oh, little one, I had no idea . . .*

We should have been safe, she thought stubbornly. *Our defenses should have been enough.* But she was unable to cling to that thought, as the memory of Mryax's horrible death as the Dominion forces tore through their half-a-century-old orbital defenses like tissue paper forced its way into her thoughts.

She realized that she had been just as delusional as those children who thought they were on an adventure.

Betazed had fallen.

Mr. Homn was dead. So were Nathan and Elaine and so many more.

Starfleet was not coming their rescue, at least not right away, but that didn't mean they were helpless. *I am the Daugther of the Fifth House, Holder of the Sacred Chalice of Rixx, Heir to the Holy Rings of Betazed, and I* will *not be defeated.*

She turned to Enaren. "Gather up as many people as you can, Cort. We need to start organizing."

"Organizing?"

"You're damn right. We're about to form the Betazoid resistance. We'll show the Dominion that taking a world and holding it are two completely different things."

Blood Sacrifice

Josepha Sherman & Susan Shwartz

War correspondence: In the *Star Trek: The Next Generation* episode "Unification," Ambassador Spock took a personal long-term mission on Romulus to attempt to reunify the Romulans with their sundered cousins, the Vulcans. In the *Star Trek: Deep Space Nine* episode "Call to Arms," the Romulan Star Empire signed a nonaggression pact with the Dominion.

"Blood Sacrifice" takes place concurrently with the *DS9* episode "In the Pale Moonlight."

Josepha Sherman & Susan Shwartz

Josepha Sherman is a fantasy novelist, folklorist, and editor, whose latest titles include *Son of Darkness; The Captive Soul;* the folklore title *Merlin's Kin;* two *Star Trek* novels, *Vulcan's Forge* and *Vulcan's Heart,* together with Susan Shwartz; two *Buffy* novels, *Deep Water* and *Visitors,* together with Laura Anne Gilman; and *Mythology for Storytellers.* She is working on the *Vulcan's Soul* trilogy with Susan Shwartz, the novels *The Black Thorn Gambit* and *Gene Roddenberry's Andromeda: Through the Looking Glass,* and compiling *The Encyclopedia of Storytelling,* as well as various other projects. For her editorial projects, you can check out www.ShermanEditorialServices.com. Sherman is also a fan of the New York Mets, horses, aviation, and space science. Visit her at www.JosephaSherman.com.

Susan Shwartz's most recent books are *Second Chances,* a retelling of *Lord Jim;* a collection of short fiction called *Suppose They Gave a Peace and Other Stories; Shards of Empire* and *Cross and Crescent,* set in Byzantium; along with the *Star Trek* novels (written with Josepha Sherman) *Vulcan's Forge* and *Vulcan's Heart.* Others of her works include *The Grail of Hearts,* a revisionist retelling of Wagner's *Parsifal,* and more than seventy pieces of short fiction. She has been nominated for the Hugo twice, the Nebula five times, the Edgar and World Fantasy Award once, and has won the HOMer, an award for science fiction given by Compuserve. Her next novel will be *Hostile Takeovers,* which draws on more than twenty years of writing science fiction and twenty years of working in various Wall Street firms: it combines enemy aliens, mergers and acquisitions, insider trading, and the asteroid belt. Some time back, you may have seen her on TV selling Borg dolls for IBM, a gig for which she actually got paid. She lives in Forest Hills, New York.

"I say yes! Let us make a full alliance with the Dominion!" Senator Terak, young, thin, and furious, whirled as he spoke, trying to face as many of the other senators as he could. "Let us take the Federation and the Klingon Empire as they claim we have longed to since we had the misfortune to meet them—"

"Impossible!" shouted a senator who had to be at least two hundred years old.

"How much did you sell yourself for?" another hissed.

"More than he is worth," Senator Oratil, lithe as the warrior she still was, sprang to her feet. Her eyes blazed with scorn. "We know the Dominion has been coaxing us while trying to entice the accursed Breen. If we join the Dominion, and they ally with the Breen . . . the very thought is more disgusting than allying with Klingon savages."

"No! That—"

"Yes! Better the Federation, better humans, better even *Vulcans* than Cardassians and Changelings!"

"Silence!" Praetor Neral's voice cut through the noise like a blade. "I said, silence! Listen to yourselves. Are you senators, or children squabbling over a toy?"

They do sound like children, Spock thought. *Children who might pull Honor Blades at any moment.* But then, on Romulus, politics had always been war by other means.

Disguised in a citizen's plain gray hooded cloak, Ambassador

Spock sat in the gallery of the Hall of State in the Imperial Romulan capital city, Ki Baratan, and wondered yet again how his genetic cousins could flash from ice to fury in an instant. "There, but for the grace of Surak . . ." Jim Kirk had once teased him. Surak, Spock had replied, had nothing to do with grace, and everything to do with logic.

Irrationally fierce as the senators sounded now, so far during the Dominion War, the Romulan Star Empire had chosen neutrality. Shortly before hostilities erupted nine months ago, they had signed a nonaggression pact with the Dominion.

Possibly because at least four different factions were arguing four different possible actions.

Logically, they were stalemated. As Jim would have said, it was a standoff.

The fact that the verbal battles on the senate's floor also increased Spock's personal jeopardy was irrelevant. He already faced a death sentence for espionage, working with the Underground on Romulus toward unification of the Two Worlds and Vulcan. If Spock were caught, he would also face charges of sedition and conspiracy.

The valiant never taste of death but once. Spock remembered Shakespeare's line from the time he had touched the mind of another captain of the *Enterprise*. Spock had already proved an exception to that rule. Still, what were capital charges against him compared with even the remote possibility he could persuade the Empire to abandon its neutrality and enter the war on the Federation's side?

Spock could almost hear Leonard McCoy's wry, *So much for being a Vulcan, bred to peace.*

A moving shadow fell across him, and he lowered his head, turning just enough that the guard patrolling the upper gallery beneath the hall's immense dome could not see his face. Spock was, he admitted to himself with Vulcan honesty, as close to worry as it was logical for a Vulcan to be. Saavik, his wife, had been transferred to home duty, healing from a wound received in ship-to-ship action (quick flash of memory: her bemused comment when Captain Howe, her former first officer, had sent her a "get well cactus" that, on Vulcan, was a superfluous xerophyte). Just two days ago, she had sent Spock both her estimate of an 86.987% chance that the Dominion would lay siege to Vulcan in the next six months and the news that she had accepted command of Vulcan's defenses.

Her new position, as much as the intelligence she had sent, troubled him. He was gravely concerned for Romulus too: he knew how precarious its economic recovery was.

Beside him on the long, hard bench, Kerit, a slight young woman, stirred uneasily. One of the most faithful members of the Underground, she didn't just play the role of dutiful kinswoman attending a slightly eccentric elder in dangerous times; she also guarded him with her knowledge of systems and her "street smarts." Already this morning, Kerit had identified spy-eyes embedded in the carvings of the gallery's rails, set like gems into the elaborately patterned mosaics gleaming on the ceiling, and even glinting from the segment of a captured Federation starship's hull bolted to one wall.

In a more urbane tone, Neral continued. "We are all revolted by the possibility that we might find ourselves aligned with a power that would even think of alliance with the Breen. I consider even the suspicion of a Breen treaty sufficient grounds for breaching our neutrality agreement."

The Praetor raised a hand before a second uproar could begin. "Yes, that would indeed mean a temporary alliance with the Klingons—*temporary, I say*—and yes, that too is a distasteful proposition. But I believe our duty requires us to make that sacrifice for the Empire."

"Ah yes." The voice of Senator Avelik hissed like an Honor Blade drawn from its sheath. "My fellow senators, consider for one mad instant what would happen if we did allow our honored Praetor to ally with the Federation and those Klingon savages . . .

why, we might all actually benefit! After all, the people who suffer most from Praetor Neral's alleged principles are his friends and relatives . . . assuming he has any left by now."

The hall fell silent as senators tried not to glance behind them to see if their guards remained in place. Neral's family had been killed by Klingons, and every senator knew it.

"I would make any sacrifice for the Empire," Praetor Neral told Avelik, his voice dangerously quiet in the stillness. "If that includes a temporary, a *very* temporary alliance with the Klingons, so be it. Savages they may be, but they can fight. Unlike some fools here, who fight only with words. So I repeat: yes, the Federation's plan of using Klingons as shock troops to weaken the Dominion shows an almost Romulan cunning. And that cunning tells me that supporting it makes good political sense. After all, should the Federation and Klingons fall, what senator with any wit doubts that the Dominion would attack us next?"

Avelik flushed olive with fury. "The Dominion offers trade, not treachery, should we enter the war! The Federation offers only peril!"

"If Senator Avelik believes every secret the Changelings whisper in his ears, he is a bigger fool than I thought."

The woman who had just spoken was Senator Cretak, controlled and sleekly groomed. She got to her feet. "Consider how much honor we would lose if we allied fully with the Dominion and if the Changelings then joined with the Breen on equal terms. We would never recover from the disgrace. The Breen don't even have a word for honor!

"As for the Federation and the Klingons: If our old enemies are foolish enough to take this war upon themselves, why should we waste our own soldiers or our ships? Let them weaken the Dominion for us! In my opinion, Praetor Neral would do better to continue his efforts to help the hearthworlds recover from the economic excesses of the past two administrations."

A formidable speaker, this Cretak, Spock thought. Perhaps not as elegantly fierce as a lady he had once seen here, but, potentially, a powerful ally. What logic could he use to convince her to back Praetor Neral's proposal to ally with the Federation and the Klingons against the Dominion?

"Now I must speak." A deep, smooth voice interrupted Cretak's next words.

The figure that rose was a tall, strongly built Romulan. His high coloring was muted by the black robes he wore, bound with what looked like Old High Vulcan sigils embroidered in metallic bloodgreen.

Archpriest N'Gathan.

The archpriest was head of a cult of state that centered nearfanatic devotion on the Emperor and on the Empire's honored ancestors.

"I come to serve," declared N'Gathan, the phrase bringing Spock's eyebrow up. "I have left my duties in the Hallows beside the Firefalls of Gal Gath'thong, honoring the final resting place of the Imperial family and the Noble Born of the Romulan Star Empire so I may counsel their descendants. My sons and daughters, why is it that we trouble ourselves with these Klingons, these Changelings, these Cardassians, this rabble of a Federation, or even the Breen? All are alien, all unworthy of our notice."

Ah yes, Spock mused. N'Gathan dominated a faction that traced their family histories back to the first Exiles from Vulcan. Isolationists, they might call themselves—xenophobes even among Romulans.

"Remember why we left the Motherworld," the archpriest intoned. "Because Vulcan had turned its back on pride, on loyalty, on family. We, in turn, abandoned Vulcan so that we might preserve the purity of our heritage, the glory of our race, and, of course, the honor of our rulers. Indeed—"

The great metal doors crashed open. A frantic underpriest, his robes disheveled, rushed into the hall, closely followed by the two young uhlans who had been guarding the doors.

"N'Lellan," said the archpriest sternly, "is this a priest's decorum?"

"The Emperor!" N'Lellan cried breathlessly. "Emperor Shiarkiek is dead! Assassinated!"

There was stunned silence in the hall, broken only by someone's plaintive, "No! Impossible!" Shiarkiek had ruled so long that probably no one in the room could remember a time when he had not been Emperor. Even Spock felt a pang of . . . yes, grief. Shiarkiek had been a reluctant Emperor. A wise, shrewd scholar, he should have lived out his immensely long life in some peaceful university.

Rising heavily, Neral turned and bowed profoundly to the throne that was now, finally, empty.

"No one grieves more than I for my Emperor's death. Not even when my own family was slaughtered by Klingons." He clenched his jaw, interrupting the flow of painful memory. "But my charge is the safety of the Emperor's people. His Majesty's death, make no mistake, will be investigated and mourned to the utmost. But war rages on our borders, and duty requires us to complete our deliberations." Neral drew a deep breath. "What is next on our order of business?"

There was a concerted roar of outrage and grief.

"No!"

"The Emperor!"

"We can't just—"

"You don't even mourn," N'Gathan said. He strode forward toward Neral's seat, stopping just out of blade-reach. "Our Emperor. That sacred, good old man. May I remind the Praetor: we are *Romulans*. We cannot just mourn the Emperor when it seems expedient: We must mourn Shiarkiek, on whom shine eternal honor, with all our hearts and all our might."

Spock suspected that if N'Gathan had anything to say about it, the funeral rites would be so long, elaborate, and time-consuming that Romulus would have no time or resources to prepare for war. And they would leave the Empire even more reluctant to deal kindly with aliens, any of whom might have had a hand—or some other appendage—in the beloved old Emperor's death.

"But who would kill so good an old man?" Avelik cut in sharply. "Does anyone else agree with me that the Emperor's death is just too convenient?"

Neral turned sharply. "What is that you say, Avelik?"

"With the Emperor dead, who decides policy? The Praetor. The Emperor was too wise to ally with Federation and Klingons." He turned to the others. "But Neral is not. What if he is already in the pay of the Federation?"

Koval, head of the Tal Shiar, stirred in his seat among the observers. Spock watched as Neral shook his head almost imperceptibly, restraining the man.

Another senator shouted, "What better way to provoke a war than kill our Emperor?"

"We have to get out of here," Kerit whispered, pulling at Spock's sleeve. Tears of unfeigned grief flowed down her face. "The place will be swarming with spies."

She raised her voice. "Please, Uncle. You know your heart is not strong. Let me get you home. Officers, in the name of a sick old man, I beg you, let us pass!"

"Better leave now, Citizen. In an hour, the streets won't be safe for an old man who can't push through," said a guard. Kindly, he unlocked the door and held it for them.

There is goodness in this people. I must persevere.

Nevertheless, Spock had to yield to the logic of Kerit's position. He drew his hood down to shroud his face, allowed himself to lean heavily on her arm, and let her guide him from the gallery toward their safe house.

He had investigations to make.

An old building, serviceable but with nothing about it to draw envy or attention, the Underground's new refuge had been provided by a kinsman of the defector M'ret. It was safer—and, Spock thought, warmer—than the caves beneath the city that had been the Underground's principal retreat for decades.

Just now, they needed a refuge. The guard had been right. Less than 0.63 hours after Emperor Shiarkiek's death devastated the senate, Ki Baratan's streets teemed with shouting, chanting, weeping mourners. Mourning quickly turned to violence as rumors spread through the streets and each new group claimed its rumors were the truth. Spock saw Neral's logic in sending out security teams to quash the riots before they turned Ki Baratan into chaos. But that only united the crowd against the guards, creating a 93.24% probability that war would replace funeral games as part of the rites honoring the late Emperor.

Spock retired to meditate in the bare, windowless chamber, with its single mat and firepot, that he had claimed for himself. He could see no logic at all in the day's events. On the surface, a case could be made that Neral had hastened the Emperor's death. How easy it would be for Neral to blame the Emperor's death on Changelings! After all, they could take the form of anyone—the Emperor's physician, an academic, even his personal chaplain, or some politically convenient scapegoat of Neral's choosing. But something about that hypothesis felt contrived, simplified for popular consumption.

Spock stared into the firepot. Shiarkiek's death had genuinely shocked him. He had met the old Emperor once and seen him on several occasions: The man had been learned and, for a Romulan, relatively gentle.

"I grieve for thee," he murmured.

Spock remembered Neral as a cold-eyed, amoral young uhlan who had grown powerful enough to take down his predecessor Narviat, who had been one of the shrewdest political manipulators in an Empire famed for them. In fact, had Spock been Romulan, Narviat's fall would have been cause sufficient for blood feud. But Neral would never be so foolish nor so self-destructive as to commit a crime for which he could so easily be blamed.

I cannot trust Neral. But if there is any chance of persuading the Romulans to aid the Federation, I must learn the truth about the Emperor's murder—yes, and Neral's innocence, ironic though that may seem—before it brings down yet another Praetor and plunges the Empire into civil war.

Some of the younger men and women who followed Spock were in the next room over, indulging in what had become their obsessive focus on the news. Over and over, viewscreens tracked Neral. Now, he appeared on the Praetor's balcony dressed in the dull blackish-green (the precise shade of dried blood, Spock thought) of Romulan mourning. Now, he made his well-guarded way to the Palace. Now, he viewed the Emperor's body. Broadcast after broadcast displayed all the preparations for an oppressively magnificent funeral.

Shiarkiek, Spock thought, would make his final journey to the Halls of Erebus accompanied by the souls of all the Romulans who died in the riots after his death. Hardly a guard the old scholar would have wanted.

Ignoring the broadcasts, Spock continued to analyze the position of each major power in the Dominion War.

"Kerit," he murmured. Leaving his meditations, he accessed the powerful computer that the two of them had built and began to work out the movements of the leader of each faction in the senate and their most loyal aides. Alibis, he knew, were as easily dismissed as created. But until Spock had more information—and until he knew it was safe to return to the streets of Ki Baratan—it was illogical to endanger himself or any of his supporters.

Neral will be hunting—or at least seeming to hunt—for the assassin as well, for the sake of his administration. But he will not dare divert too much power away from keeping the peace.

Toward the end of the tenth day of their seclusion, when composure, sleep, patience, and accurate information had all become equally scarce, Kerit glanced at one of her scanners and came alert.

"Oh . . . oh, yes! Yes! Amarik's back! He made it!"

Then Kerit flushed, looked shamefacedly at Spock, then away.

If concern for your mate requires apology, Spock thought, *I should be abject.* He signaled to her to go to her husband, and she rushed to Amarik's side. Once, Spock thought, she had been a scrawny, almost feral adolescent with a genius for invading hardened computer systems, and Amarik had been a lanky, fearless boy with shaggy, unkempt hair. She and Amarik had held jobs in Narviat's government and lost them when Neral came to power. Now, they picked up work when they could, but remained close to Spock.

But closer, of course, to each other.

Still thin, dark, and in need of remedial grooming, Amarik was smudged and bruised from forcing his way through the city streets. But that didn't stop him from catching his wife in a quick embrace.

Then Kerit, glancing over his shoulder, pulled back from Amarik's embrace with a yelp of most un-Romulan glee.

"Look who's here," Amarik called to Spock. "I ran into him at the door. He had the right passwords, so . . . are you back for good now?" He clapped a grimy hand on his taller companion's shoulder. "Kerit, do you remember Subcommander Ruanek?"

"I believe Ruanek left the Homeworld with the rank of full commander," Spock heard himself correct Amarik as though it were merely an academic point. "A battlefield promotion."

At least Spock had control enough not to shout at Ruanek in purely Romulan anger, *Are you out of your mind?*

Ruanek, born and bred a Romulan, had exiled himself thirty years ago to save Spock's life; his return didn't just put him under pain of death, it subjected Spock's entire Underground to further danger. And for this . . . this absurd flirtation with death, Ruanek had abandoned his work on the Vulcan Spock longed to see! Could the world that had adopted Ruanek mean so little to him?

He built a life with us. Were we wrong to take him in?

Not surprisingly, though, the rest of the Underground greeted him as a returning hero. Clustering around him, they clasped his wrist or his shoulder in greeting. At least, Spock thought, though they barraged him with questions, they had the sense to keep their voices subdued.

Ruanek thumped Amarik on the back as if he were a brother officer, then flung his other arm around Kerit's narrow shoulders.

"I still have the disruptor clip earring you gave me," she told him.

"But now you wear Amarik's bracelet instead," Ruanek said. But his attempt to tease her sounded forced. This was no time for jests.

"What about you?" Kerit asked. "Spock told us you found someone on Vulcan."

Ruanek pushed up his sleeve to display the marriage bracelet given him by T'Selis, who had decided that some adherence to Romulan tradition was logical for a Vulcan who took a Romulan as bondmate.

"She's a healer," he told Kerit, "just about your height, very pretty, and with such a temper." But Ruanek's grin quickly faded.

He detached himself from the younger Romulans, threw back the hood of his cloak, and moved to Spock's side. The reprimand Spock had planned to deliver went unsaid. On Vulcan, Ruanek had allowed his hair to grow out of its severe Romulan military cut. Now, he had shorn it, and his eyes were haunted.

How not? He has not seen his birth world for three decades.

Under Ruanek's drab cloak, his tunic was the blackened green of mourning. Although his smooth brow and regular features had always made him look more Vulcan than Romulan, there was no mistaking him now for anything but a son of the Empire, and a heartsick one at that.

"Explain," Spock ordered in Vulcan.

"I used my guest friend M'ret's old Underground contacts to get me back into Romulan space," Ruanek replied in the same language.

"Elaborate." Let the Romulan explode in anger if he chose.

Spock could only express his . . . his extreme disapprobation of Ruanek's actions by speaking so curtly.

"For the Emperor, of course!" Ruanek snapped. "Do you think I *wanted* to leave everything I've built? Am I the hero Azeraik to tear open my wounds and laugh as I did it? It's logical for you to calculate how that good old man's death affects the war and what you need from the Empire. I don't fault you. But the Empire needs . . . it needs . . . *we* need to find out who killed the Emperor and avenge him. And if no one else will do it, I will!"

Spock shut his eyes on Ruanek's emotional outburst. Even after thirty years of life on Vulcan, of family responsibilities, a joint appointment as lecturer in the Vulcan Science Academy and legate in Vulcan's diplomatic service, when stressed, Ruanek still reacted like a warrior.

"What if you had been conscripted?"

"As far as I know, the Empire remains neutral," Ruanek said. The irony in his tone could have drawn blood. "I considered the possibility that the Empire might be recalling veterans. So I traveled in stasis." He shuddered. "I swear, I had bad dreams the entire trip."

"No doubt, your subconscious remembered the responsibilities you abandoned on Vulcan."

A muscle twitched along Ruanek's jaw. "Vulcan! After all these years, Vulcan remembers I was born in an Empire that signed a nonaggression pact with the Dominion. So, I did not enjoy a great deal of credibility on Vulcan when I left. In fact, my presence there was a liability to all concerned. Incidentally, Captain Saavik agreed. I wasn't offended. And she's doing so well, Spock," Ruanek added in a rush. "T'Selis has already certified her fit to return to full duty."

"And what was *your* consort's reaction to this . . . preposterous excursion?" Spock demanded.

Ruanek looked down and away. "Extreme displeasure," he admitted. "But I served the Emperor long before I met T'Selis." He glanced up again in anguish. "How can I honor my wife, or Vulcan, or you, for that matter, if I don't do what honor demands to repay a master who was kind to me? 'False in one, false in all,' " he quoted a Romulan adage. The people around him nodded.

Ruanek had sacrificed a bright future on Romulus for Spock's sake because his honor, as well as his friendship with Spock, required it. Now, Ruanek's honor demanded he sacrifice the life he'd built in exile. As the late Praetor Narviat had once remarked, honor like Ruanek's could be a confounded nuisance.

He is, as he has ever been, true to himself. Illogical not to expect him to act in accordance with his nature. "You want vengeance. I want an ally I can trust."

"I anticipated you would find it logical for us to join forces," Ruanek said.

"Provided that you control yourself." Spock raised an eyebrow. "I will not tolerate your going out and assassinating every senator whose actions you distrust."

Over the years, Ruanek had picked up the habit of that Vulcan quirk of an eyebrow. "I don't think I could kill that many senators before their guards got me," he said dryly. "You have my full cooperation. As long as your investigation does not interfere with my duty to the Emperor."

With that, Spock had to be content.

Ruanek got to his feet, stretching, then poured himself a fresh mug of hot *khavas*. "I don't suppose you want—no, I don't blame you. People never understand that *khavas* needs to be strong enough for an Honor Blade to stand in."

Spock, expressionless, beckoned him back to work.

Ruanek sighed. "The Emperor was so well loved—and yet he still did have enemies."

"Be content that he was never affected by 'All power corrupts—' "

" 'And absolute power corrupts absolutely.' The humans' Lord Acton would have made a good senator."

"At least, we have managed to shorten the list," Spock said. "We have eliminated all those who might have harbored resentment but lacked opportunity or true motive. What do you make of this?" Spock gestured at the viewscreen. Ruanek's emotional kinship with the people they analyzed would be of great value even if his information were decades out of date.

"Motive is as shaky a basis for a case as alibis," Ruanek said, cynically. "Let's assume—though I know you don't—you think Avelik and his friends are smart enough to engineer a murder like this. What do they stand to gain? Just one rumor, one hint that someone was seen changing shape outside the room where the Emperor died, and they are, as I've heard humans say, dead meat. Very messy dead meat.

"Cretak's record is not of one who uses violence to gain her ends. In fact, she is one who works to preserve life rather than take it.

"Neral? I don't like him any more than you do, and don't tell me that you don't have personal reactions, Spock, because I know better. To summarize: I see neither logic nor opportunity to make a case against Neral."

"Clarify," Spock said.

"Look what Neral is facing," Ruanek said, clicking onto another screen. "The death toll from the riots has climbed to—" he winced "—three hundred and fifty. Those deaths are a political liability he doesn't need, moral repercussions aside. Besides," Ruanek added with his usual irony, "Neral lacked opportunity to commit the crime. The Emperor's household is governed by the Hearth Guard. Neral may control the military, but the Guard reports day and night to the . . ." He hesitated, staring at Spock. "To the arch-priest."

"Precisely," said Spock.

"Spock, you're supposed to be the logical one. That's preposterous."

" 'Once you eliminate the impossible, whatever remains, no matter how improbable, must be the truth,' " Spock quoted.

"Arthur Conan Doyle, old Earth author." At Spock's raised

brow, Ruanek explained, "The books were in the Vulcan Embassy. Shelved under 'alien logic puzzles.' But this isn't fiction. Yes, N'Gathan seems a logical enough suspect. But I'd still like some physical proof. Starting with a look at his current Holiness."

"It is hardly safe for any of us out on the streets. Especially you—"

"You've survived this long," said Ruanek. "If they question me, I'll make something up. I certainly remember how to lie."

"I do not doubt it," Spock said, absolutely without expression.

Amarik hunched over the viewscreen, making the smallest of adjustments.

"Praetor's on," he said as the images resolved themselves more sharply.

Neral appeared on the screen, groomed to look the very image of Romulan invulnerability. *"To forestall civil war,"* he announced, *"I had been forced to declare the senate in recess for the past ten days. Yes, I have heard some mutter that this was but the preamble to a new dictatorship. Now, however, the senate will reconvene at the Hallows at Gal Gath'thong."*

Clearly, the Praetor hoped that the ancient surroundings might overawe, or at least shame the senate into peaceful behavior. And the recess meant that the Emperor could lie in the Hall of State, which could be opened to the citizens of Ki Baratan.

"Security for the viewing of the Emperor's body will be extremely tight," Spock murmured to Ruanek. "The odds against your escaping detection are so high that calculating them might demoralize our associates."

"If my mission is in jeopardy," Ruanek murmured back, "so is yours, my friend. And our missions are similar in so many ways."

"Indeed?"

"Why, you too are relying on faith rather than any calculation of the odds."

"I see no reason to insult me."

"This is no insult. Clarification: what you are doing is more important to you—more important to what you serve—than cold logic. You cannot logically take that privilege for yourself, while denying it to me."

Now, Spock allowed himself the almost-smile he reserved for the very few friends who had gotten past his guard over the years. "I assumed that would be your reaction. I suggest we go to the Hall of State to pay our respects to the Emperor."

For 2.3 hours, Spock and Ruanek, heavily cloaked, waited to enter the Hall of State, its doors open to allow free passage of the Emperor's spirit to the Last Review. Drums pattered at the speed of a Romulan heart, punctuated by the ear-piercing jangle of *systra*, those silver bell-banners made to a pattern that had been old even when the Great Ships left Vulcan, and the mournful bray of horns.

Incense fumes drifted through in the air, growing heavier as they worked their way into the Hall of State. The altar held many offering cups, many bowls of spices, and knives attached to the gleaming stone by chains too strong to break.

The Praetor's seat had been replaced by a massive catafalque of viridian stone, draped with latinum-pressed cloth. On it, surrounded by torches burning in lofty, ancient bronze holders, lay the Emperor. His body, preserved by a stasis field, was robed with the splendor Shiarkiek had tried to avoid while he lived. Honors hung overhead, academic and military.

"I wonder they didn't roll in a fish tank," Ruanek muttered. The late Emperor's scholarly bent had been ichthyology, mostly carnivores.

Spock bowed and tossed fragrant spices into the brazier, then turned to pay his respects. Kneeling beside the catafalque, eyes downcast, he studied Shiarkiek's body. Death had eased the lines that centuries of stress and disillusionment had etched into Shiarkiek's face. He looked . . . resigned, and so pale that Spock was startled.

Did Romulans embalm their imperial dead? This was hardly the time or place to research the question. Spock seemed to recall the procedure began with draining blood from the corpse.

Spock bent closer. If anyone noticed, they might think he was simply one of the dead Emperor's ancient academic colleagues. He gazed at the Emperor's hands where they lay on his breast, clasped around his Honor Blade.

His *gloved* hands.

Fascinating.

What would Spock see if he could peel back those gloves? Wrists, slashed longitudinally to let the blood drain freely and fast, he suspected. Shiarkiek had been so old that even minimal blood loss could have brought on a fatal level of shock, just as it was intended to.

Ruanek had gone almost as pale as the late Emperor, although his face was Vulcan-calm. He bowed deeply. Taking the offering cup, he scooped up incense and cast it into the brazier. The flames blazed, an indication to the superstitious that his gift was accepted.

Spock turned to summon Ruanek, and froze.

Archpriest N'Gathan had emerged from a side door. To a chorus of awed murmurs of welcome, he approached the altar, holding out a goblet filled with the sacramental wine pressed from the grapes grown on the slopes below Gal Gath'thong.

Seeing Ruanek make his offering, the archpriest beckoned him forward, offering him the chalice. Ruanek dipped his head in respect, but held up a hand: a moment more, the gesture requested.

Then, each of his actions precise, as befitted a warrior in the presence of his Emperor, he knelt, unsheathed his Honor Blade, raised it in salute and kissed the blade. Drawing it across his palm, he let the blood flow. Only then did he tilt back his head to receive wine from the archpriest. It might have been poison, but Ruanek drank anyway.

It was difficult to tell which man looked the more exalted, the priest or the warrior.

Ruanek rose, bowed, and left the Hall of State.

Spock followed, meeting up with him at a distance that might not be safe but was not, at least, instantly suicidal.

" 'No matter how improbable,' " Ruanek repeated.

"I agree our hypothesis is improbable," said Spock. "This is why I am also going to extract a confession from him and have Amarik record it."

Spock had never been to the Hallows nor, in all the time he had spent on Romulus, had he ever been too warm. Now, he thought, the word *warm* was definitely an understatement.

The Hearthworld was more blessed with lakes and seas than Vulcan had ever been; even here, near the firefalls, emerald pools of water, heavy with minerals, bubbled, fire in their depths.

The slopes of the Gal Gath'thong range were richly fertile, but as one neared the actual firefalls, the land grew barren and strange and the air hot and dry. The ground trembled underfoot. Fumaroles roiled in mud pools, and steam rose from cracks in the bleak terrain.

Here, the sky was overcast, granting only glimpses of frozen Remus and the star the Two Worlds shared. Dust and ash weighted what few trees survived into eerie, hunched shapes. Wise pilgrims hastened by lakes of acid, masks clasped to their faces. Glittering filaments and dust wafted through the air.

Spock was dressed as an academician, giving him sufficient status to move freely in the Hallows. On his chest glinted the medallion given to him so long ago by the late Narviat's wife (*Liviana,* his mind whispered, unbidden). As he, together with Amarik and several others from the Underground, reached one of the ablution pools outside the tombs, Spock looked up—and had to stop short, staring.

Magnificent. Truly magnificent.

No surprise at all that the first Romulan to see the firefalls had thought them sacred. From the lip of Gal Gath'thong, the one flawed peak in a vast range of snow-capped mountains, poured a constant torrent of flame and lava. The firefalls hissed, roared, and crackled as they fell. From time to time, lightning lashed out high above. Sparks and ash flew, burdening the gaunt petrified trees. From time to time, pyroclasts exploded, their fragments shattering still further on immense sulfur crystals.

Here, in a narrow strip of barren land between rock and flame clustered the basalt domes and temples that guarded the Empire's most revered dead. Here was the Romulan heart; here was the Romulan soul.

"Dr. McCoy would have said, 'Doesn't this just look like hell,' " Ruanek murmured, in a fair imitation of the doctor's Georgia drawl. " 'Hotter n' hell, too,' he'd probably have added."

Battle nerves, Spock thought. If all went as they planned, Ruanek stood a 78.213% chance of confronting his enemy today and avenging his Emperor. This was his adversary's ground. Ruanek knew he had to win the battle over his awe lest it, and not the archpriest, defeat him.

Spock glanced toward the immense domed temple whose foundations were reinforced by buttresses faced with jade. A stream of people in the robes of senators, accompanied by uniformed guards, brushed past pilgrims on their climb up winding steps to the temple.

Off to one side, closer to the firefalls than any other building in the Hallows, was a miniature copy of the temple. This was the dwelling reserved for the archpriest.

No doubt N'Gathan was waiting for just the right moment to make an impressive entrance.

He will find his entrance delayed even more, Spock thought. He gestured to Amarik and Ruanek to take cover, Amarik to record whatever conversation Spock had with the archpriest, Ruanek to witness.

Not 3.5 minutes later, the archpriest strode out of the portico of his house.

"Go on ahead," he ordered the underpriests and acolytes who served as his aides. "N'Lellan, once everyone is seated, flash the light in the dome, and I will enter."

Bowing his head, the underpriest hastened up the shallow ash-strewn stairs. Others followed, carrying records, disks, pads, and even an ancient scroll or two that afflicted Spock with a most logical yearning to preserve them from the polluted air and study them himself.

Archpriest N'Gathan stood staring up at the firefalls, as if communing with them. Flame glinted in his eyes.

"Your Holiness, may I trouble you for a word?" Spock called in an imitation of an academician's over-precise diction. "I wish to inquire about some details of ritual." He maneuvered to stand between the archpriest and the temple so that N'Gathan could not push past him and escape.

A practiced benevolence masked the impatience in the arch-priest's face so swiftly Spock could almost doubt he had seen it. Nodding respect at an older man bearing the medallion of academic accomplishment, N'Gathan steepled his hands and asked, "How may I counsel you?"

"I wish to ask about the rite of blood sacrifice," Spock continued. "Not just for my family—we have a tomb here, very humble, but at least we are an old enough clan that our ancestors are honored in the Hallows—but in general. When His Imperial Majesty, may he sleep in honor, lay in state in Ki Baratan, I witnessed several warriors shedding blood. They actually drew blades in the Hall of State. How is that consistent with security?"

"We should give thanks that the Praetor's security is very good," said N'Gathan smoothly. "If that is all?"

"I know the Praetor's security is very good, but how is that consistent with the practice of not permitting arms within the Hallows? How do you reconcile the two?"

"*I* do not," said the archpriest. "Records of prior Emperors' funerals, stored in the Hallows' archives, establish the precedent that security to protect the living coexists appropriately with honor to their ancestors. Now, if you will pardon—"

"I should be glad to study those records," Spock said, moving parallel with the archpriest, not letting him get away. His own rudeness almost astonished him. Judging from the high olive flush on the archpriest's face, it astonished N'Gathan, too.

"You must apply at the temple in Ki Baratan," the archpriest said shortly. "Or anyone at the shrines here would, I am sure, be glad to assist you."

Up in the temple, the drums and *systra* had begun to play, insistent, commanding.

"I thank you, Holiness," Spock persisted. "Do you think I shall find evidence to reconcile the concepts of blood sacrifice and Final Honor? Consider the hero Azeraik, who ripped open his wounds and died, rather than accept life from his enemies. Because he drew no weapon, can we truly conclude that he accepted Final Honor?"

"If you will *excuse* me . . ." N'Gathan looked past him. Horns brayed over the shrill ringing of the *systra,* compelling all within range to come forward.

As Spock had foreseen, N'Gathan tried to walk away. Spock clung like a Terran limpet, finding the deliberate discourtesy almost as taxing as physical combat.

"But what if Azeraik had been unable to tear off his bandages? If he had asked for help and been assisted? Would intention alone be interpreted as taking Final Honor?"

"I really do not see what this has to do with ritual." N'Gathan's eyes flashed.

"Do you not?" asked Spock, his voice as sharp as an Honor Blade. "It is a slippery slope, is it not, this matter of blood sacrifice. A slope made, we may say, slippery *by* blood. For example, what if a man long past his prime was unable to accept Final Honor, but someone believed that he wanted it and assisted him? Would that be accounted to his merit?"

"If the man had led a good and honorable life, yes."

"So, the blood falls upon the land, and the land is healed," Spock said. "Even land as barren as this?"

"I think," said the archpriest, "that you might do better to inquire at the temple. They have healers there, and clearly you are in need of more assistance than I can give you—"

"One more word is all I ask," said Spock. "The truth. An old man, a sick man, but an honorable one. Is it right to hasten him to Final Honor that the land may live? That is, live in all places but here, where there is no life but only honor?"

"That is right. It is for the old, the feeble, the useless to take themselves out of the way. Or be taken thus, lest the Empire be weakened." N'Gathan spoke with absolute conviction.

He scorns the lie, Spock thought. *Good. I shall not have to trick him.* "Like the late Emperor?"

"Will you stop dancing back and forth and let me pass?" demanded Archpriest N'Gathan. He put out a hand to push Spock out of the way, but Spock sidestepped it adroitly. "Yes, we respect our elders. Yes, we respect those who have lived lives of honor. But when they are old and dishonor themselves by their continued existence, if nothing else may be done, they should be set on the path of honor. Of Final Honor."

"And is that, then, true of an emperor?"

"The Emperor—" N'Gathan broke off when he realized his slip from "an" to "the."

"In other words," said Spock, "you are saying that it was Emperor Shiarkiek's obligation to take Final Honor, and since he didn't—"

"I showed him his duty."

"Showed him? Or performed it for him?"

To his own surprise, Spock found himself angry. The Emperor had been had been very fragile since his recovery from the drugs that Narviat's predecessor Dralath had used to control him. A sick, ancient man, unable to fight—and it was becoming more and more evident that the archpriest had murdered him.

"What would you have me do?" N'Gathan demanded. Then, as if realizing he'd just said too much, he rushed on fiercely, "His days were trickling from his life like wine from a cracked glass. The Empire faces unprecedented challenges. It needs someone strong, virile to take command . . ."

"Like you?"

"I live but to serve. A ruler will emerge."

"So you would kill an Emperor who harmed no one and plunge his Empire into civil war *out of respect*?" Logical the concept might be, Spock thought, but like all theologies run amok, it was anything but reasonable.

The archpriest snarled. "War is the forge that hardens us! How else to choose the best ruler? By the time that ruler emerged, the Emperor's sacrifice would have brought us back onto our true course, free of all these *aliens!*" He spat out the word.

Spock saw how N'Gathan's glance shot about the Hallows, looking for guards or acolytes. He would have to move swiftly lest he himself become the archpriest's next sacrifice.

"Did you record all that, Amarik?" Spock called.

"Got it, Ambassador!" Amarik yelped, an echo of the youthful enthusiasm Spock remembered. "Compressed, encrypted, and on its way to the Praetor, the fleet admiral, and all the other right people!"

Again, the bells rang out. They sounded triumphant, Spock thought.

"Ambassador!" cried the archpriest. "You're no academician at all, and no loyal Romulan!"

"I never claimed that I was," Spock said. "I am, as you surmise, Spock of Vulcan."

He had miscalculated somewhat. N'Gathan was younger and heavier than Spock, and advanced like a warrior.

"Archpriest!"

Ruanek sprang from hiding, shielding Spock with his body and holding up his hand so N'Gathan could see his palm, healing from his blood sacrifice in the Hall of State. "I do not wish to fight to replace you as archpriest. I act only in the name of Emperor Shiarkiek and the life of which you robbed him. And so, hear me, heed me: *I thee challenge!*"

He spoke the last three words in Old High Vulcan and whipped out his Honor Blade. Its ancient, polished metal reflected the fire-falls onto his face.

N'Gathan stared. "The warrior I saw in the Hall of State! Who *are* you?"

"I am Ruanek, son of Stavenek of House Minor Strevon, former commander in His Imperial Majesty's Fleet, now Legate in Vulcan's Diplomatic Corps. Worry not. My bloodline suffices to let me spill your blood on the ground."

"Weapons drawn in the Hallows, my son?" N'Gathan's voice was all priestly concern and authority again.

Ruanek laughed sharply and hurled down the knife, point-first. It stuck in the ground, hilt quivering in the air. "A false priest has no sons. At least, none who are legitimate. Here is one blade. For the swiftest!"

He sprang at N'Gathan. The archpriest grasped at the air, then flung what he held—a drift of the gleaming filaments tossed free of the firefalls—in Ruanek's face and shoved him brutally aside.

As Ruanek fell, he grappled with the archpriest and hurled him to the ground. The priest swung at him and, to Spock's surprise, connected. Ruanek's head jolted and he rolled with the blow. Another blow. The priest lunged toward the Honor Blade. Ruanek hurled himself at his enemy and brought him down. Again, though, he was not quite fast enough.

I thought Ruanek had kept himself in training since his exile, Spock thought.

The archpriest was first to reach Ruanek's Honor Blade. "You dare not shed my blood here in the Hallows, do you?"

Ruanek pushed back up onto his feet and sank into a fighting crouch. He focused his eyes not on his ancient blade but on the center of his enemy's chest, from which his next move would be signaled.

"Ah, you prepare to flee. Then, you are a weakling as well as a traitor. Such a disappointment. When I saw you in the Hall of State, here, I thought, was one wedded to the old ways: one worthy to succeed me, or the Emperor himself. But contaminated as you are . . ."

The archpriest lunged. Ruanek leapt aside, then backward again until his back was to a gap in the barrier between the Hallows and the firefalls.

"Stop dancing, coward!" said the archpriest.

"Stand here and wait to be killed?" Ruanek laughed. "That is illogical. You found His Majesty easier prey, didn't you? An old, sick man who'd earned the right to live out his last few days in quiet. Damn you to the eternal ice of Remus!"

The archpriest launched himself at Ruanek, who leapt aside once more. As N'Gathan rushed him once again, Ruanek flashed a sharp grin at Spock.

He twisted round, caught the archpriest, and shoved. Taken off-guard, unable to either recover his footing or stop, N'Gathan hurtled off the cliffside and into the firefalls.

Flawless logic, Spock thought. *Not to mention superb timing.*

Ruanek had known his old reverence for N'Gathan's office and the Hallows themselves might keep him from slitting the archpriest's throat. So he had had turned N'Gathan's weaknesses—and momentum—against him.

But it had cost him his Honor Blade.

Ruanek sank to his knees, gasping in the hot, smoky air. "My Emperor is avenged," he said. He put his head down and drew deep breaths, struggling not to cough.

After a moment, he raised his head and looked down at his empty hand. "I guess my Honor Blade's gone home. It really wasn't much use on Vulcan. Still, I had wanted it for my eldest." He sighed and met Spock's eyes. "Now, I'll have to do what you do: wear my honor from within. At least it's whole again."

It always was, Spock thought.

Rising to his feet, Ruanek reached for the crystals he kept within his tunic and tossed the entire pouch into the firefalls after the archpriest. Then he followed Spock back into the Hallows.

Amarik had started to look for them. "Ambassador?" he asked. "I'm getting a message. Someone wants to talk to you. A senator . . . It's Senator Cretak! Damn, she's got good people on her staff if they could track me this fast."

Spock tapped the Federation-style combadge he had built into his medallion. "Patch me through, please. Senator? What may I do for you?"

"This is truly Spock of Vulcan?"

"Indeed."

"Then you have done enough already. I received your transmission and will—no doubt as you intended all along—put the confession of the archpriest—"

"The late archpriest," Spock cut in smoothly.

"Excellent! I shall put it to its proper use. I believe the senate will be very interested. Some minds may be changed as mine has been. Or opened."

"Ambassador!" Amarik cried. "Got a message coming through. Heavy encryption . . . hmmm, that's one complex algorithm. It's about Senator Vreenak. His ship blew up! They think it's the Dominion!"

"Did I hear that correctly?"

"My assistant has received intelligence that Senator Vreenak died in an explosion. I should caution you, Senator, that it is not substantiated."

"Thank you for the warning. If Vreenak's assassination can be confirmed independently," Cretak's voice went thoughtful, *"neutrality is a luxury we can no longer afford, and so I will say in the senate. Vulcan you may be, Ambassador, but you have done the Empire good service today."*

"I come to serve," Spock said.

"So I will do you a service in return. I suspect where you are, but I do not want to know for certain. Moreover, it would be a poor reward for your service if I allowed anyone else to find you. Take my advice and quickly remove yourself."

Spock ended the transmission. "I suggest we follow Senator Cretak's sound advice." Around him, his companions prepared to leave.

Ruanek shook his head. "I have to stay," he said. "I'm supposed to meet Senator Varyet. She's a cousin of M'ret's. The relationship's distant, but blood's still thicker than water."

Spock felt his face change. Ruanek moved closer to him and spoke quickly, urgently. "Don't worry, Spock. We've already got her vote, and she can exert leverage on three other senators. Here's the plan: I follow Varyet home, pretending she's my patron, and she gets me onto one of her House's ships. I'll have to work my passage but—" he drew a deep breath "—it's better than stasis."

"If the Empire revokes its nonagression pact, no ship will be safe," Spock cautioned. "You may yet get your chance to fight Jem'Hadar."

Ruanek raised an eyebrow. "I estimate a 28.99% chance of making it to Vulcan. See, I actually learned something in thirty years on Vulcan!"

The odds were low. Still, Ruanek had always been a gambler. He started to head upslope toward the temple, then turned back.

"You know," he said to Spock, "low as the odds are, I suspect they could be stretched to accommodate us both. Why not come back home with me?" he asked. "Vulcan needs you. Saavik needs you."

Spock shut his eyes. "I will not leave here until the war is over and my work is done."

"Shall I tell that to your . . . to the captain?"

"Saavik has always known my mind," Spock said. Which made matters no better . . . and no easier.

Ruanek drew himself up. "In that case, live long and prosper, Spock."

Spock bowed. Since he had a Vulcan's emotional control, this moment had to be easier for him than for Ruanek, he told himself.

When he looked up, Ruanek had vanished into the temple on the first step of his long voyage back to Vulcan. He would spend his strength, and possibly his life, safeguarding the world he had adopted.

Meanwhile Spock would remain on Romulus, working toward the day when Romulus and Vulcan, the worlds so long kept sundered, could be unified once more.

"Peace and long life," Spock whispered. It was illogical to think that the firefalls thundered as if they heard that blessing for the first time. He trusted it was not illogical to hope they would hear it again.

Mirror Eyes

Heather Jarman & Jeffrey Lang

War correspondence: This story takes place in the three-month gap between "Tears of the Prophets," the final episode of *Star Trek: Deep Space Nine*'s sixth season, and "Image in the Sand," the first episode of *DS9*'s seventh season.

Heather Jarman & Jeffrey Lang

Jeffrey Lang seems to enjoy having the word "and" next to his name. In addition to "anding" with Heather Jarman on this tale, he has enjoyed anding with J. G. Hertzler on the *Star Trek: Deep Space Nine: The Left Hand of Destiny* duology and David Weddle on *DS9* novel *Section 31: Abyss*. He does occasionally write stuff all by himself (including *Star Trek: The Next Generation: Immortal Coil* and stories in the *DS9* anthologies *The Lives of Dax* and *Prophecy and Change*), but it always makes him a little jittery and he has to lie down afterwards with a cool washcloth on his forehead.

On the flip side, Heather usually works alone, as she did on the *DS9* novel *This Gray Spirit*, the *Star Trek: S.C.E.* eBook *Balance of Nature*, her short story contribution to *Prophecy and Change*, and *Worlds of Star Trek: Deep Space Nine: Andor*. After years slogging through the wilds solo, she realized she was tired of having no one to play with so she signed up to work with Jeff on this project. A great partnership—in the spirit of Spock & Kirk, Frodo & Sam, and Bonnie & Clyde—was born.

Jeff and Heather are hard at work on a new project 'cause they had so much fun with this one. Jeff swears up and down that he's going to whip that original novel into shape someday soon, too. For her part, Heather has actually finished her outline for her original novel and plans to have it completed by Winter 2004. We'll see—Heather's quite the optimist. Jeff lives in Haverford, Pennsylvania; Heather in Portland, Oregon.

Entry #1037

I've decided I'm going to steal a runabout. The term I spent mastering the basic fundamentals of larceny—all part of my comprehensive training—might actually prove valuable for once. No one—not even Odo—will suspect my plan but even if they did, I'd still have to chance it. If I stay here any longer, I will be driven utterly and completely mad.

So current circumstances have driven me to consider petty thievery, an appropriately ignominious climax to my lackluster career. Not a patriot's death. Not a death dealt by my Dominion foe during combat. No, I'm sneaking out of here, hoping that in all the confusion of refueling and repairing ships, the launch of one insignificant spacecraft won't be noticed. There's nothing like a war when you need a diversion.

Pragmatically speaking, running away is my only option if I want to make it out of here in something other than a coffin. They don't tell you that part when you sign up—that if you don't like your job the only way out is death. No, they feed you a steady diet of propaganda and lies. "Serving the mother planet is the highest of all purposes in life." And my personal favorite, "Of the thousands of volunteers who have offered to fill this post, we have selected you to receive this honor."

I didn't *volunteer* for this position. They might have made me think I volunteered, but there's no chance I would have taken this job if I'd been in my right mind. Which raises another question: have I been in my right mind anytime since I started the training? The drugs *can* have unusual side effects and I've been faithful with my medication regimen. It's only logical (did I just use the word "logical"? my roommate must be wearing off on me) that a drug used to stabilize the secondary identity can prompt odd neuro-reactions. One man I knew lost his sense of taste for the first six months he took his dose—swore up and down that everything tasted like rancid warp lubricant. That could be my problem with this assignment too—the drugs, that is. They could be the real problem and I'm somehow missing the big picture.

Or maybe not. Maybe this place is as awful as I think it is.

Deep Space 9 was supposed to be a plum assignment, the job everyone wanted, the most important outpost in the quadrant. And I might have been able to offer worthwhile information to my superiors—these people have absolutely *no* conception of se-curity—but as soon as I established myself as a dependable, bor-ing, quiet little wallflower that can flit about unobtrusively, the Empire forms an alliance with the Federation and the thrice-bedamned Klingons! Who needs deep-cover operatives when the major power players have become chummy? And worst of all, everyone in the damned quadrant *knows* about anything that ever happens around here. Jem'Hadar raids! Lost Orbs found! Time travel! Dimensional rifts! Mirror universes! It's a paradox: despite all the insane things that happen here, *nothing* that only a self-respecting operative could discover happens here. I'm at my wit's end! What do I do on a normal day in the infirmary? *I'm a nurse!* Would anyone in command actually *care* how many inebriated customers from Quark's bar suffered from severe gastric distress and consequently expelled digestive contents all over the Prome-nade floor? That's a fact worth building a battle strategy around. Meanwhile, if one of our generals needs to know when a supply convoy is going to pass through a specific region of space, *they simply ask.* The lowest-ranking ensign on DS9 can answer their question. What do they need me for?

And then there's the annoying aspects of day-to-day living. For example: I hate the way this place smells. Maybe I should be used to it by now, but I'm not and I don't think I ever will be. The whole station stinks of atomized silicon or whatever it was the Cardassians used to keep the mining machinery lubricated. After all this time, you'd think the smell would be gone or that someone else would complain, but they don't or maybe it's just that my senses are more acute than the Terrans' or the Bajorans'. Still, you would think the "other" Vulcans would have commented on it, even to each other. Or maybe they're too polite. I don't mention it because I'm afraid someone might see my sensitivity as odd and start asking the kind of probing questions that would earn me a one-way ticket to headquarters—especially from the overeager Bashir. The most inane factoid sets the man off on a rabid quest. I can only imagine how he'd respond to my "smell" issues:

Me (innocently): "Has anyone else ever said anything about the strange smell that permeates every corner of Deep Space 9? You know the *stench?*"

Dr. Bashir (concerned): "Hm. That's a potentially troubling symptom. We absolutely should run a complete neurological and genetic scan on you, Seret. Who *knows* what could be wrong with you? Maybe you've contracted a horrible, debilitating disease and we have a limited time to save you."

Me: "Oh, no. That's fine. Don't worry. Really."

Dr. Bashir: "No, I *must* do this." (Applies neuro-sensors to my scalp, runs scan.) "Say, this is interesting: You're a Romulan."

That would be bad.

Or maybe not. Under those circumstances, Bashir might have me deported. Could be less complicated than trying to steal a runabout.

Entry #1038

A double shift prevented me from studying the station's docking logs. Damn. Must do tomorrow.

As I've mentioned in at least six hundred of my over one thousand entries, if the Tal Shiar ever found out I was keeping this journal, I would probably meet a very mysterious and undoubtedly terminal fate. Well, *fine.* If it meant I could get away from here, death would come as a profound relief. If I have to eat one more of Quark's "vegetarian" casseroles, I may be forced to bake him into one of his own "flaky crusts." Tonight, when Stok is at the gym, I'm going to order a steak from the replicator in my room. A *rare* steak. A *raw* steak and I'm going to eat it with my fingers.

Entry #1039

I'm feeling much better today. The protein infusion obviously helped. Or it helped psychologically.

I might *look* like I'm living on stringy, wilted green things, but I've programmed the computer to include animal proteins in my replicated nutrition shakes. Just two days ago, Stok asked for a taste of my personal favorite—Rigellian Fungus w/brown algae—and I was happy to oblige. I took great pleasure in watching her suck down half a *wreet* cat liver. At least I was deceiving *someone,* even if it was as elementary as handing too-trusting Stok, the Vulcan vegetarian, a whipped liver shake masquerading as tree fungus. I need to keep my skills sharp somehow. Not like my work gives me many opportunities to be duplicitous. How does running a computer analysis of Bolian waste products make me a better intelligence operative? Fudging *those* test results would be the perfect way to undercut our enemy. Hah! I graduated top in my class! I should be a model of stealth and subtlety! Instead, I'm reduced to hiding in the dark and eating raw meat with my bare hands to assure that my blood chemistry stays stable.

So, I don't think I'll be killing Quark today, though here I am still writing in this journal.

A thought occurs: Maybe the Tal Shiar already knows about my writings. Maybe they tell us not to do this, but know all the time that we will anyway. Maybe they even manipulate our minds to make sure we *will* start a journal.

Maybe nothing I do is my own idea.

Last night, in bed, after I had cleaned up the bloodstains on the counter from the raw steak and Stok was asleep in her room, I laid there in my own, tiny, narrow bed, flat on my back, arms at my sides, eyes squeezed shut, and tried to say my name out loud. Not "Seret," but *my* name, my *real* name.

I couldn't say it.

They warned us, back in the school. They told us not to try, and back then I thought, "Why would I want to? I'm not *her* anymore. Now I'm Seret. That's who I am."

Except I know I'm not. Maybe my implanted identity is faulty because I still want to hear someone *say my name.*

I might be able to write it down, but I'm not going to try. If I try and I can't, it would be more than I can take. Perhaps I should increase my drug dosage. If I escape the station, would I still be Seret? Or would the person that I was, I mean—the person that I am—come back eventually? They never answered the question in training. I imagine it's because we wouldn't like the answers.

Entry #1040

I have been a fool. The Tal Shiar might know what they're doing after all. I am too exhausted to say more. Have another shift. Must be on my way . . .

Entry #1041

Where to begin to sort out the events of the last two days? Should I begin with how I was awakened in the middle of the night, or dwell on the hours I kept watch beside biobeds, or should I attempt to tally up how many thousands of tissue samples I ran through the computer for analysis? My skin is pulled tight over my skull, tender to the touch like one massive bruise. Each muscle aches with a low, dull throb, screaming out for rest, but deep inside me I can feel my heart thrumming with anticipatory dread, knowing that at any minute I'll be back on duty. All the humans milling around the replicators waiting for their turn to order *raktajino* or coffee have puddles of droopy blue-gray skin around their eyes. I'm used to seeing them look shiny and healthy. Even during the worst hours of the war to date, none of them has looked this bad. A colleague from the visiting ship, *Enterprise,* Ensign Mayer, lost a boot in his rush to help a coding patient; he didn't notice until he stubbed (and broke) his stocking foot when he walked into a console. Nurse D'Rosta knocked over an instrument tray when she fell asleep—standing up.

I should be composing and encoding my official report instead of rambling on to my journal, but I'm afraid I might miss critical details if I wrote the report now, details that might lead to the kind of assignment discharge that even *I* want to avoid. My superiors would surreptitiously snatch me from my DS9 quarters for debriefing. They'd say, "How could you forget such a thing? You weakling! You would be more useful planted in a pot and fertilized!" (An old lover used to say, "Do what you're told or you're Vulcan food." I never understood that saying until today when, try as I might, I can't seem to remember how to undress, let alone recount the mind-numbing details of five consecutive shifts.)

This image lingers in my imagination: Very slowly and theatrically, a neuro-analyst would reveal a mind-probe needle, hoping my horror might dislodge any lingering reticence I might have.

They would then proceed to root through my mind to take by force each particulate my report should have had in the first place. By pouring it out here, I'm hoping to make sense of what I've seen and experienced for myself, and then I can consider them in a more clinical light.

Too many details, too many images, too many sensations to process systematically. I close my eyes and see flashes of light and color, I hear beeping consoles and the shouts of the infirmary staff. I hear the squeaking gurney wheels as the corpses are wheeled out of the way into ancillary hallways until the time comes that the insanity subsides and the dead can be tended to.

Stop. Too much. Discipline, idiot. Here is what happened.

Dr. Bashir woke Stok and me mid sleep-cycle and instructed us to join him in the infirmary as soon as possible. We were instructed to take a less traveled route to avoid being seen and to offer no explanations to any crewmates or civilians we might encounter. Of course we made haste, finding upon approach to the infirmary that a quarantine zone had been established. Within, chaos reigned. Impromptu patient stations had sprung up in every available square meter, creating a maze to navigate. I scanned the crowd, looking for someone to report to. Gloved and suited-up doctors and medical technicians, most of whom I didn't know, scurried about; I lost count after twenty, each of them seemingly attempting three tasks simultaneously.

Stok and I made our way to the center of the chaos, where I found Bashir and a tall redheaded woman directing traffic and having a nearly indecipherable conversation that seemed comprised of two-thirds diagnostic terms and one-quarter drug names, interspersed with the occasional verb. Patients in antiseptic sleeves, life support leads dangling around the edges of the plastic covers like polymer vines, were being wheeled into the isolation ward, and though I could not make out individual faces, it quickly became obvious that every man and woman being pushed by me was a Vulcan.

"Seret," Bashir called out, interrupting his colleague. "Excellent. Suit up." Pointing at the airtight suits isolation ward nurses are required to wear, he continued, "I need you in there now. You too, Stok. Full tissue panel, fluids, radiation scans. ADBs and composites. Everything. Bring me the results when you have them."

My medical training took hold. "What are we looking for?"

The red-haired doctor—there was no question in my mind that she was a doctor—replied, "We don't know. Initial readings indicate a neurotoxin, but that's only conjecture. We're probably dealing with symptoms right now. Determining the actual causative factor behind those symptoms will happen when we have more data."

"Delivery method?"

"Unknown." Thus, the isolation sleeves.

"Where did they come from?" I asked, reaching for the garment, the monofilament crinkling unpleasantly in my fingers.

"You don't need to know—" Bashir began.

"Julian," the other said in modulated tones. "I grant that this has been need-to-know up till now, but keeping information classified at this point might slow down our diagnostic process. Trust has to start somewhere. And they're her people, after all."

Bashir paused for a long moment.

"I'll answer to Captain Picard and Colonel Kira on this," she said, reassuring him.

"You're right, Beverly. Of course. I'm simply trying to figure out what information is most useful to them." Turning to me, Bashir said, "Our patients were rescued from a survey ship, *Damask Plain*. The *Enterprise* senior staff has just begun to review the logs, but we believe the crew might have recently landed on a planet that had been held by the Dominion. The doctor, Virek—did you know her? no?—left behind chart notes hypothesizing that the Dominion may have engineered a biological or chemical agent, something particularly lethal to Vulcans, that the crew was exposed to during their expedition."

"A specious conclusion in light of the available data," I observed. "What factors lead her to consider such a—?"

"She wasn't able to say," the one called Beverly—Crusher, I now know, the chief medical officer of the *Enterprise* and former head of Starfleet Medical—said. In lowered tones, she added, "And we're not going to have an opportunity to ask her now."

"I see." Stepping into the suit and touching the seal tab, I said, "We will obtain the profiles you have requested." I glanced at Stok, who was also suited up. "How many?" I asked, deliberately oblique.

"How many what?" Bashir asked.

"Have died?"

"Five so far."

"And how many are infected?"

"Twenty-three," Crusher said. "All of them. The entire crew."

I followed another trolley into iso, Stok at my heels. "We will be back in forty minutes."

And we came back in forty minutes only to receive another list of tasks to accomplish. We quickly discovered that as quickly as we completed one round of diagnostics, the results became obsolete requiring yet another round. Patient status fluctuated wildly from moment to moment. Eventually, Bashir and Crusher assigned pairs of us to sets of patients and it became our job to address all the monitoring, testing, and treatment for our patients. Tissue analysis, enzyme recalibration, and neuro-pattern stabilization were only the commonly performed tasks. One of my patients developed a web-like purple rash on his extremities. Another's optical nerve hemorrhaged, requiring Dr. Crusher to step in to perform surgery. It was not her first procedure nor was it her last. All the doctors moved from biobed to biobed until they were reduced to stumbling over their own feet. Until last night—or was it the day before, I can't honestly say I recall—I've never seen Dr. Bashir appear tired. The man is indefatigable. Without proper knowledge, one would suspect cybernetic implants, not mere genetic enhancements.

What we're facing I can't yet say. Maybe that's part of my reluctance to file my report. I have my own guesses. Being a trained medical practitioner and an intelligence officer, I know the tactical value of using microorganisms to accomplish insidious, deadly chores. Like the deep-cover spy, a nearly invisible biological assassin can live, unsuspectingly, in the company of its victims, waiting for the precise moment when the target is most vulnerable . . .

Because answers haven't been forthcoming—and because of the highly sensitive nature of the *Damask Plain*'s mission—Crusher and Bashir have relocated the isolation ward to a more secure, contained sector of the station. I overheard Crusher commenting on Captain Picard's concern that the infirmary is too easily accessible to the station public, making their work there subject to questions—or visible to enemy informants who might be on the prowl for intelligence.

Like me! I thought as I eavesdropped on Crusher, allowing myself a tiny hint of a smile. Vulcans don't smile, so I know I must be cautious when indulging myself in such a fashion.

They've also transferred the *Enterprise*'s EMH into this makeshift ward to provide round-the-clock attention to the ailing Vulcans. Why Starfleet gave their medical hologram such a persnickety, irksome personality escapes me. Many of the Starfleet medical officers I've dealt with have much less grating personalities—like Dr. Bashir for instance. The EMH has few, if any, of the physical traits that humans tend to deem attractive. His eyes— what is the word Lieutenant Newar used?—are "beady" and he suffers from advanced alopecia. Perhaps that is the point: If the EMH were desirable to look upon, the medical staff would be distracted from their duties. That reasoning, however, doesn't explain his irritating bedside manner. Patients are not soothed by his presence.

I did observe Stok composing a communiqué intended for headquarters—she used the highest-level encryption algorithms to send it so it will take me some time to decipher it once I find it in the logs. Apparently there is an admiral there—a famous and well-known doctor—who has expertise in treating Vulcans. When I learn the identity of this specialist, I will include it in my report.

And I find, without trying, yet another reason why I should wait to send information to my superiors. They would undoubtedly want to know who this mysterious specialist is.

So what do I know? Over the course of my shifts, I learned that the *Enterprise* towed in the *Damask Plain* after finding her adrift in interstellar space near the Trivas system. In retrospect, I recall having seen this ship's name on more than one occasion in docking logs. Though, now that I know something more about its mission, I realize in retrospect that I have never treated any of its crew nor have I encountered them in any of the station's public areas. *Damask Plain* was not Starfleet or Bajoran registered, but DS9 was unofficially listed as its homeport, a fact I found buried deep in a security database. (All those months weeding through programming modules finally prove useful!) Putting these facts together with snippets overheard in the infirmary, it becomes clear to me that the *Damask Plain* is a covert intelligence-gathering vessel. The Dominion has their Vorta. The Federation has their Vulcans.

Ironic, that I have been tasked with an assignment to save the lives of my fellow spies, the very individuals who, under other circumstances, I would be interrogating and casting aside after they'd outlived their usefulness.

I am certain I am forgetting much, but my prolonged hours in the infirmary threaten my clarity and I'm bound to err due to fatigue-induced dullness. Another steak might rectify my depleted endurance, but I fear I lack the sense to adequately cover my clandestine dietary behaviors. Stok would not understand and she would ask questions. Undesirable questions.

Though it's conceivable that she might, upon seeing me hunched over the table masticating the bloody flesh, walk right on past without noticing, the desensitizing events of the last four of five shifts rendering her as numb as I am.

Entry #1042

"You have not been well."

These words, which I heard when I awoke, explained why every joint in my body felt thick with gritty sand paste—why I felt like I'd been swimming in the tissue-searing radiation of an anti-matter containment tank. Later, when I had time to reflect, I realized I had been hearing for quite a long time before I became completely aware, but sounds, images, sensations, all were swirled together in my memory to form a discordant mélange.

I opened my eyes. Familiar sounds and smells settled into my senses and I realized I was lying on a biobed in the infirmary. I probed for my last memory, unable to recall how and when I'd arrived here. Stok and I had come off our shifts. I was sure of it. I tried to speak, but my dry tongue clove to the roof of my mouth. An orderly slid a straw between my lips and I sucked on it automatically, inhaled a sweet, thick medicinal-smelling liquid. Despite the unpleasant texture, my body craved fluids and I drank greedily.

"That's enough for now," Bashir said. "Can you sit up?"

I knew from long experience that the question was not meant to elicit information, but was a suggestion. With help, I pushed myself up into a lounging position and looked around. Yes—as I suspected—the infirmary. The quarantine section set aside for the Vulcans, except most of the beds around me were empty. A few orderlies milled about; those that moved went slowly, without urgency.

I wet my lips and croaked, "How long?"

"Less than two days," Bashir said. He consulted the chrono on his padd. "Forty-two hours, to be precise. When you and Stok didn't report for your shifts, we sent an orderly to your quarters and found you both unconscious."

I tried to focus on the faces of the one or two Vulcans in the beds nearby. Bashir anticipated my question. "Stok is in stasis. The disease moved quickly in her, faster even than the others. We might be able to help her if we can figure out how to control this organism, but I'm really not sure . . ." He passed a hand over his eyes and I saw the light of reason briefly flicker. Bashir had passed the borders of exhaustion and was deep into that other country beyond.

I found myself saying, "I am a Vulcan, Doctor. You do not have to—" what was the expression? I looked at the cup with the straw in his hand and thought longingly of the sweet syrup it had held "—sugarcoat the truth."

"Our Vulcan patients are hovering at critical or on the cusp of death," Dr. Crusher said. "And we've exhausted every path of inquiry we can think of. We only have a rudimentary idea of what we're dealing with." She had been standing behind Bashir, a padd in either hand, carefully scanning two charts. "But that might change with you, Seret: you're the only Vulcan patient who has come anything close to recovering."

Noting Crusher's use of the qualifier "Vulcan" in reference to the word "patient," I seized on it to direct the conversation away from a potential discussion of the differences between me and "my people." "Others have fallen ill? Non-Vulcans?"

"Whoever designed this organism is a genius." Crusher held one of the padds up for me to see. I recognized the diagram as a simplified representation of a Vulcan ribosome. The diagram became animated and I watched as the tiny chemical factory functioned in normal mode. Then, after a few seconds, tiny foreign bodies attached themselves and the action of the ribosome began accelerating. Studying the structure descriptions in the margin, I concluded, "Proteins inimical to iron-based life-forms."

Bashir nodded. "Give the girl a cookie."

It was an indication of how badly my blood sugar was depleted that I very badly wanted the cookie Bashir felt I deserved.

"How bad is it?" I asked.

"Bad enough," Crusher said. "But not deadly. Not yet. I don't think it was meant to be. These proteins weren't meant to kill humans or Bajorans or Centaurians . . . well, you know. The rest of us. They were only meant to make us very, very sick."

"And it is unbelievably contagious," Bashir added. "Airborne. Travels like flu. Symptoms develop in less than twenty-six hours and then you're down."

"We anticipate secondary—

"—and tertiary—"

"—infections could start within the day as those immune systems fighting the Vulcan protein become run down, and thus vulnerable to opportunistic viruses and bacteria. We're prepared for everything from the garden-variety pneumonias that can be cured with a hypo to cases of cellular failure that aren't so easily diagnosed."

Bashir and Crusher exchanged weary, worried looks.

"How have you two managed to avoid being infected?"

When Bashir grinned, I could see his gums were a sickly shade of gray. "Who says we have? We have the organism in our systems, but it doesn't seem to like my genetically altered system quite as much." He glanced at his colleague who was, I saw, sagged against the biobed beside my own, the one I imagine Stok must have occupied. "She's just pumped full of antivirals, antibacterials, and—what was that other stuff?"

"Turkish coffee," Crusher said. "Nothing else can coexist with it in my bloodstream."

Bashir snorted, and it was sign of how tired he was that the little laugh turned into a fit of giggles. Crusher tried to glare him into submission, but she was just as exhausted as Bashir and gave in, though guiltily, to laughter. I, of course, maintained my reserve.

Crusher regained her composure sooner than Bashir and, trying to ignore the sniggering doctor, turned her attention back to me. "How do you feel?" she asked.

I conducted a swift personal inventory. "Achy. My joints are sore and my eyes feel dry. I believe I have an elevated temperature." Crusher nodded, all of this consistent with what she knew already.

"I'm hungry, but I also feel queasy. Is that consistent with your findings?"

Bashir, calm again, nodded. "It's part of the continuum of symptoms we're seeing. You're lucky you haven't succumbed to the hallucinations some of the others have had."

"We found one of the *Damask Plain*'s officers attempting to claw his way out of a stasis chamber. His fingers were broken and bleeding before we sedated him," Crusher said.

"Obviously, you have some kind of resistance to the organism, though not complete immunity. We need to find out why. Here," he said, handing me a set of sterile-wrapped specimen containers.

I attempted to maintain a neutral expression. "What would you like me to do with these?"

"Take specimens. Run tests."

I willed my slamming heart to slow as the ramifications of my present situation settled in. Because of my illness, Starfleet might have in their possession irrefutable proof that they had a Romulan operative working in their midst. I pushed back the veils of bleary sickness and grasped hold of my training. "You have not already run the . . . ?" my voice trailed off. I steeled myself for the answer.

Bashir sighed. "Beyond the crew of the *Damask Plain,* we've spent the last two days running tests on the more than five hundred individuals of twenty different species who've become symptomatic. There are another three hundred aboard the *Enterprise* in quarantine. We haven't had the time or the staff to do anything beyond identifying the presence of the organism in your bloodstream. When we discovered that you'd fallen ill, we followed the protocol we'd developed for the other Vulcans."

"Sorry," Crusher offered. "I know your work would go more quickly if you had a body of data to work with. If you think it will help, you'll have access to what we've discovered in working on the *Damask*'s crew. We have all their sub-cellular profiles in the infirmary records."

Bashir checked his wrist chrono. "We'll meet in a few hours, Seret, and go over your findings then. "

"You can use the workstation in the remote isolation unit," Crusher said. "Since all the Vulcans are in stasis at this point, it's relatively quiet down there. And the EMH will be available to answer any questions you might have."

I studied her face and saw guilelessness. How could I help but stare at them with incredulity! Questions? *Questions?* Like how I can deceive the computer into believing that a Romulan is a Vulcan?

Now I laugh bitterly as I recall the absurdity of the doctors' proposal. Thankfully, they would have attributed any oddities in my behavior to my illness. I know they found nothing out of the ordinary in how I comported myself or I wouldn't be sitting here now, making yet another journal entry. Still . . . how did I manage to survive without exposing myself?

In that moment, chaotic bits of information tumbled about in my head; I struggled to find a discernable pattern. What was Tal Shiar training, what was medical training, what was Seret, what was that other person, the person who lived beneath the surface of Seret, who was attempting to peer out from behind these mirror eyes? I attempted to grasp for a recognizable piece of the puzzle only to have it fade, recede from memory. Struggling to discern what information was useless and what was critical to preserving my mission, I considered the known issues before me.

1. Bashir and Crusher wanted me to run comprehensive cellular diagnostics on myself in the hopes that I would discover the secret to my resistance to the infection. I know what the tests would tell them: I'm resistant to the organism because Romulan ribosomes are different from Vulcan ribosomes. Nothing spectacular there if you don't count treachery, which, somehow, I think they might.

2. The doctors are allowing me to run these diagnostics be-

cause they have an unmanageable patient load and a scarcity of resources.

3. They trust me to do my job.
4. If I want to avoid captivity—by either side—I only needed to exit this infirmary. I could then devise an escape plan.

"Seret?" Bashir asked.

I started, suddenly aware that I had been lost in my thoughts.

"Do you need more time? Are your symptoms getting worse?"

"You're releasing me," I stated, making sure I understood their intentions. I didn't dare hope that circumstances could have unfolded so perfectly.

Crusher glanced at Bashir, who stared blankly back at her. Finally, she said, "You're not that sick. Compared to most of the staff, you're looking pretty good. Compared to all the other Vulcans, you're a picture of rosy-cheeked good health."

Her combadge chirped. A voice I did not recognize said, "Enterprise to Crusher."

"Go ahead, Data."

"Doctor, we have patched in that call from Earth. Do you wish to return to the Enterprise to take it?"

Crusher glanced at Bashir. "Your office?"

Standing up quickly, Dr. Bashir straightened his tunic and said, "Certainly."

"Push it through to the infirmary's main office, Data. We'll take it there."

"Certainly, Doctor."

"Come with us, Seret," Bashir said.

Close, I thought. So close . . .

The two of them helped me stand and I was surprised to find that I was not nearly as wobbly as I had anticipated being. In fact, except for the noticeable emptiness in the pit of my stomach (raw steak, here I come) and a slight lightheadedness, I felt almost well, better even than when I had fallen asleep two days earlier. Realizing that this might not be the best image to present, I leaned rather more heavily than necessary on Bashir's arm, which turned out to be an error. We would have fallen together in a heap on the ground if Dr. Crusher had not counter-balanced us on my other side. Turkish coffee—whatever that was—seemed to be an effective fortifying agent. I shall remember to mention it to the Tal Shiar.

The infirmary's main hall remained as congested as it had been during my last shift. Several of my busy colleagues paused mid-workload to offer a smile or otherwise greet me and I found myself surprisingly touched by their concern. I noticed their rumpled uniforms, the intermittent sniffing, how they rubbed at their bloodshot eyes with their fists and supported their body weight by leaning against their workstations. Most of them looked weary or ill or a combination of the two, but none so much as Bashir or Crusher. Now that I had the opportunity to compare, the doctors' hunched postures and pallid complexions had more in common with several morgue residents I'd examined than their obviously sick and drooping staff. The head doctors had obviously been pushing themselves harder than anyone.

And I have to confess surprise at this realization. I am not accustomed to those in seniority taking on tasks requiring menial drudgery. Such duties are consigned to those of lesser rank—those whose health and energy are expendable. Highly skilled personnel are kept in reserve for occasions more befitting their status. I do not find this way—Starfleet Medical's way—of conducting their operations as repugnant as I should. In fact, I consider the behavior of Drs. Crusher and Bashir . . . meritorious. Why is that? There was nothing remotely glorious about the scene that I witnessed.

Patients from dozens of worlds squeezed into every available nook—on exam tables, seated in the waiting room, stretched out on the floor—everywhere. None of them looked to be at death's door, but all evinced the same pale complexion, their eyes rheumy, noses running, coughing, or shivering. As Crusher had said, the disease created by the Vulcan ribosome did not kill, but the misery it caused was enough that those afflicted would wish they were dead.

Surprisingly, I saw that the disease's discomforts had obliterated the usual cultural prejudices and annoyances that kept species from mingling. Garak, the tailor, sat on the floor next to Quark, the two of them grudgingly sharing a blanket. I watched as one (Quark) would tug at the blanket, trying to secure more covering for himself; a moment later, the other (Garak) would tug back. Nearby, I saw my friend Morn—the only person on the station whom I've felt an intellectual kinship with—stretched out on a half-collapsed cot, a fleck of drool running down his face as he slept.

"Dr. Bashir," Quark rasped as we toddled past him. "When is someone going to see me?"

"Did you take a number when you walked in, Quark?"

Quark glanced at a tiny slip of paper in his hand. "Well, yes, but I didn't know what it was, so I traded mine to someone else. I assumed you were running some kind of raffle."

"Traded?" Bashir asked.

"All right. Sold."

"Have you been through triage?"

"If you mean did someone wave one of your magic wands over me and pronounce me 'Not all that sick,' then yes."

"You'll be seen when the medics have time, Quark. We have a lot of sick people here on the station and the disease doesn't seem as fond of Ferengi as it does some of the others." He nodded in Morn's direction.

"It seems inordinately fond of my mucus membranes, Doctor," Quark whined. "I think I've blown about a gallon of snot out of my nose in the last half hour."

Bashir lost his patience. "Then you should *bottle* it, Quark, then sell it at the bar as a rare unguent." This was clearly the last thing he wished to say on the subject and continued to shuffle on his way. I took a quick look over my shoulder and saw an expression on Quark's face that made me think to that I should look very carefully at whatever sauce he put on the vegetarian lasagna the next time I ate at his restaurant.

In Bashir's office, he turned the monitor on his desk to face the pair of chairs he kept for guests, then rolled his own rather larger chair around so he could sit with us. When he was seated (with a palpable sigh of relief, I noticed), Dr. Crusher tapped her combadge and said, "Data, we're in the office. Put the call through."

"Affirmative, Doctor."

Moments later, the monitor came to life, and I found myself staring at the most elderly human I believe I have ever seen or, for that matter, may have ever lived. Tangled wisps of white hair trailed down around his ears and over his high forehead giving him an unkempt, ragged appearance. Below, his face was a mass of sagging flesh, the skin around his eyes so loose and wrinkled that I wondered how he could see out from the folds. Then, catching sight of us, he cocked his head to the side and his left eyebrow climbed halfway up his forehead. Light fell on his eyes and they flashed a deep, sparkling blue that made me think simultaneously of deep water and, oddly, my mother's father, a man whose name has been taken from me, but whose visage I still remember from the days of my youth.

"There you are," the old man said, though it sounded more to my untrained ears like he was saying "Tha-ya you awre." His words came out so thickly, like he had paste in his mouth, that I thought he must suffer from some sort of neurological damage, though later I learned that this was not the case. Leonard McCoy—for that was who he was—comes from a region on Earth where everyone talks in this manner. *"I was beginning to think y'all had forgotten about me."*

"No, Leonard," Dr. Crusher said. "Our apologies. It's difficult to get from one place to the next with so many patients about."

McCoy moved his head very slowly in a motion I took to be a nod, then said, *"Understood, Bev. It's getting pretty bad?"* He phrased this as a question, but I felt certain that there was no uncertainty in his mind.

"Bad, yes. I'm running out of ideas. If we don't do something soon, Jean-Luc will be forced to quarantine the station and probably have to put half a dozen ships through an extensive sterilization procedure. With the war on . . ."

"Yeah, I believe I've heard something about that. Be a shame to take all those ships out of the fight."

"Your theory about the ribosome was correct, Admiral," Bashir interjected.

" 'Course it was," McCoy grumbled. *"Only thing that made any sense. Bastards who thought of that little trick . . ."*

"That's why we're fighting them, Leonard," Crusher said. Two observations prodded me. The first was that McCoy, despite his advanced years, was both technically brilliant and also insightful. The second was that he was obviously a person that required careful management. Crusher knew the trick of it, while Bashir did not. "Have you had time to review my notes about the agent manufactured by the RNA clusters?"

"Yeah, I read it. Good work, Bev, but I think you're headed down the wrong road there. We can't stop this thing from doing its job. There's already too many of them and they're everywhere in the station, probably into other ships, too. Biofilters wouldn't have stopped it. Slippery little sneaks, they are."

"Then vaccination," Bashir said tersely.

"Only way," McCoy said as if there was nothing else to say. *"I assume this is your Vulcan who recovered."*

"Yes, this is Seret."

McCoy glared at me through his bushy eyebrows. *"You a full Vulcan, m'dear?"*

The question took me aback. At worst, I anticipated being asked if I were a Romulan. At best, I was expecting to spend the afternoon attempting to fabricate test results while at the same time planning an escape route. I wasn't anticipating being asked if I was a partial Vulcan.

"Of course she is, Leonard," Crusher said. "Vulcans don't interbreed with other species."

McCoy's eyebrow crept up his forehead again like an irate caterpillar.

Crusher rolled her eyes. "Except in rare instances."

"Better," McCoy said, somewhat smugly. *"We going to do some tests on her?"*

"She's going to do some tests on her," Crusher said. "We're fortunate in that she's one of the best technicians in the service, or so says Julian."

Studying Bashir, McCoy asked, *"You the genetically altered boy?"*

Bashir attempted to look as dignified as he could, but knew there was no way to dodge such a straightforward question. "I am," he said.

"Don't know what all the fuss was about," McCoy said, his tone softening. *"You don't look like you're about to grow a third arm."*

"No, Admiral," Bashir said, a smile creeping onto his face.

"Though I used to know a fella that had a third arm. Seemed to do just fine with it."

"I . . . see. Well, well . . ."

"You should get some sleep, son. You look tired."

Now Bashir grinned and rubbed his eyes. "You have me there, sir. I'll see what I can do when this is all over."

"Don't call me 'sir,' boy. Or Admiral. I'm just an old country doctor. Bev tells me you're pretty good."

When he lowered his hand, I could see that Bashir basked in the man's praise. I've only known the doctor for a couple of years and I would not say that we have been socially intimate, but I knew him well enough to know he had a high opinion—justifiably, I might add—of himself. It was a rare thing to see him, as he was that moment, sincerely enjoying a compliment. "Thank you, sir," he stammered. "I mean . . . Doctor. That's . . . You're very kind."

"Fine," the old man said. *"Now we've got that out of the way, get to work on that vaccine."*

"We will."

McCoy mused for a moment and I wondered if he had lost

focus on the conversation as the elderly sometimes do. Then he remarked, *"Seems to me I remember reading something about a situation similar to this one from before my time, which means, naturally, that it's ancient history to you. What kinda database depth you got there, Bev?"*

"The *Enterprise* has the full Starfleet medical database, of course," Crusher replied.

"Anything pre-Federation?"

Crusher considered. "Perhaps. I'll need to check with Data."

"Do that," McCoy said. *"Medicine didn't start in the twenty-third century, despite what some folks think."*

"Yes, Leonard."

"And Bev?"

"Yes, Leonard?"

"Tell our Mr. Data that if he doesn't send me his next chess move I'm going to forget all about the game."

Crusher smiled. "I'll mention it to him. He's been rather busy . . ."

"He's an android, *Bev. He can multitask."*

"Right. I'll remind him."

Then, the kindly old man disappeared again and the gruff old professional took his place again. *"All right. That's enough foolin' around now. You people are back on the clock. Get to work."*

Bashir and Crusher stared at the blank screen for several seconds. Finally, Bashir turned to her and asked, "So you worked with him for how many years at Starfleet Medical?"

"Not enough, Julian," Crusher said. "Never enough."

"I should go visit him someday."

Crusher said, "You'd have to give up being the smartest person in the room all the time."

Bashir rose from his seat and brushed his hair away from his forehead. "It would be worth it," he said and went back to work.

Dr. Crusher then ordered an inner-station transporter to send me back to my quarters—she couldn't spare an orderly to see me safely home. As soon as I materialized, I sat down at the console and began this recording, finding that my craving for a steak had become secondary in importance to sorting through the day's events. Would that I had any precognitive ability! Instead, I must depend on reason. Logic.

Ironic, considering.

Possibilities . . . possibilities . . .

Deceiving Bashir and Crusher. My first choice and certainly the preferable one.

Being captured by Starfleet Intelligence. While I'm certain the Federation's food is better and their penal colonies have fewer and less vicious pests than anything on Romulus, a prisoner's life is a prisoner's life.

Being designated as ineffective by the Tal Shiar and subsequently being "decommissioned"—not a pleasant option either.

So what do I want? If I could choose my fate.

I want to live.

Remaining alive shouldn't be too much to hope for, and yet, if the Tal Shiar don't get me, the Dominion's bioweapon still might.

I have five hours to plan my next move. Five hours to have my fate measured by mere minutes in comparison to my years of training and months of deep cover seems rushed, but that is what circumstance has handed me.

The room—the quarters that I shared with Stok—is very quiet without her here. I had never realized that despite the fact that she was a Vulcan, she was a rather loud person. When she would read or meditate or even when she was merely sitting, she would breathe with her mouth open, a hollow *whoosh-whoosh* that used to drive me mad.

I miss listening to Stok breathe.

Entry #1043

I've run out of time.

The pile of decimated sample collection trays I've hurled

against the wall is a testament to this fact. I have spent four hours devising every variant on fabricating test results that I can conceive of and I've yet to come up with anything that will withstand the scrutiny of Bashir and Crusher—not to mention that wizened old human physician from headquarters. Even if I could fool Bashir and Crusher in the interim, I have a feeling that Admiral McCoy would find me transparent.

And why do I care about crafting an elaborate deception? If I had any sense at all I'd signal the Bajoran sector handler that I've been made and that I need an emergency extraction. The problem with that plan is that requesting an emergency extraction is generally looked on, by my superiors, as admitting failure. Never as "the enemy is far more clever than we made them out to be," more like, "clearly you've done something wrong or you wouldn't have been exposed." Agents who fail to avoid detection often find a disruptor wedged in their neck vertebrae and are aware of it only long enough to know that their subatomic particles will shortly be scattered about the quadrant.

And then there's this irrational sense of wanting to please the doctors. Where did *that* come from? They said they trusted me. Called me a fine technician. Told me that my own ribosomal structure might hold the solution to helping the Vulcans. My non-Vulcan self nearly blushed with pleasure from the doctor's encouragement. Romulan physicians don't exhibit nearly that level of kindness. If you aren't afraid of them, they aren't doing their job. Perhaps I'm falling prey to a carefully calculated propaganda campaign and the doctors are luring me carefully, slowly into their trap.

Or maybe this infection is softening me up. Crusher mentioned something about hallucinations being a side effect.

Speaking of side effects . . . I began composing this latest entry after an odd occurrence. A short time ago, while sitting at my workstation in my quarters, I drifted off—probably due in part to illness and fatigue—but when I startled back into awareness of my surroundings, I had the oddest sensation. It began when I saw the hands resting on the computer terminal and decided they weren't mine. The knobs of joints and curve of the fingernail beds belonged to someone else. I touched my face and the skin felt alien, cold, as if I was a consciousness inside this alien shell of flesh. Rushing into my dressing area, I looked into a reflective surface and I *honestly didn't know who I was looking at.* I had separated into layers. My identity, this carefully constructed edifice of deception, is collapsing. Dr. Crusher called down to my quarters to check on me. *"Seret, how are you feeling?"* she'd asked. I touched my combadge by instinct, but wasn't sure how to answer, so I thanked her for her concern and told her "I" was doing well.

"I," who? "I," Seret-the-Vulcan? "I," nameless Romulan? "I," who?

The chrono tells me I have less than two hours before I am expected to produce my test results.

At this point, I have nothing but a pile of shattered vials and trays to show for my efforts.

I'm talking through this in the hopes that a new solution might occur to me—I've certainly tried all the conventional ones. From the beginning, I was implanted with multiple cellular transceivers that can "trick" a sensor into believing I'm a Vulcan. It's a small precaution taken to prevent a routine sensor sweep or scanner from exposing me. If Mr. Data up on the *Enterprise* swept the station's infirmary looking for Dr. Crusher, he shouldn't find a Romulan. At least, before the alliance, he shouldn't, and even now it would be a fact worth commenting on. Simple enough.

Problems show up when I'm subjected to specific diagnostics or invasive procedures. Deceiving a trained medical professional isn't as easy as pulling a sleight of hand with a computer.

To wit, I've stolen DNA samples from Starfleet Vulcans and "blended" them with my own (quite clever if I do say so), but discrepancies in the samples start appearing in the analysis almost right away—the fakes simply don't hold up. I broke into the main database and swapped my Starfleet ID's medical datalinks with those of a Vulcan presently stationed on a ship patrolling the Denoris Belt, and, again, such a measure will pass surface scrutiny. But an in-depth probe or—stars forbid—a full-on DNA expression profile? They would reveal an individual with an entirely different physiology than mine. If I'm subjected to follow-up testing, the data readings and samples taken from my person wouldn't match what's in the computer.

Still, due to the current crisis, all medical information pertaining to Vulcans has been tagged and classified, including subcellular profiles. Any swapping I might do would be revealed if any compatibility studies or comparison analysis is done.

In short, I'm done for.

I need weeks, not hours, to devise the type of deception these circumstances require.

So, sitting here before me, I have a schedule of all the outgoing station traffic. I have committed it to memory. After all the events of the past few days—when my assignment finally becomes interesting and I feel like I have something of value to contribute—I'm forced to resort to my original plan: stealing a runabout.

Stowing away works too.

I will take my crude efforts to fabricate test results and load them into the isolation ward's database. That way, the doctors can check up on my progress without me having to make an appearance in the infirmary. From the iso ward, I can slip into the docking ring and find outbound transportation. I have the name of a species reconstruction specialist on New Sydney, a physician whose skills have been widely used by the Orion Syndicate. I've heard rumors he can make a Cardassian look like a Bajoran, if needs be. Perhaps he can make a Romulan look . . . like someone that no one would notice. Someone who could move through crowds anonymously until someday, she could start over as a nurse on a far-away backwater world.

What does it matter anyway? I hardly know what part of me is real and what is fiction. Starting again with a new face should be simple enough for an individual who isn't sure of the identity of the person living inside her own skin.

Entry #1044

"What makes you believe you have the right to be using this workstation? Hm? If you hadn't noticed, this is a quarantined area, accessed restricted to medical personnel with level-four clearance only. We're not one of the seven wonders of the quadrant or selling 'I Survived The Epidemic' buttons, so move along."

The abrupt comments startled me, even momentary disoriented me. With each passing hour, my identities were edging away from each other, blurring around the edges; I feared that I was becoming further removed from my field-conditioning regimen. What would have been intuitive not even seventy hours ago had become laborious. Split-second hesitation can cost you your life in my business. So I paused, swallowed hard and forced reason to discipline my careening emotions.

From where I crouched beside the workstation, I looked up to see the EMH, his face pinched with disapproval, arms crossed. Any second, I expected his foot would begin rhythmic tapping.

During my time in Starfleet, I have observed specific behavioral patterns in humans (such as the EMH who was based on a human) with strong compulsions to control the behavior of others. Those not wanting to offend would describe the EMH as "bossy." More clinically oriented colleagues—medical professionals such as Bashir—drawing on their knowledge of humanoid psychology, would use the designation, "passive-aggressive." Others, more plain-spoken than tactful, would call him a complete pain in the ass. Whatever terminology others might use to describe Starfleet's Emergency Medical Hologram program, my own inclination, were he not made of photons and forcefields, would be to quash his verbosity via excruciating pain in his sensitive male parts. Such techniques are legitimate methods to weaken hostile operatives. (Note for future consideration: The EMH is not a technological innovation I'd recommend purloining for the Empire—unless, of course, the Tal Shiar decides that annoying their prisoners to death is a viable torture technique. Perhaps I've stumbled on a way I can be of use to my planet after all.)

"Well?" the EMH said and began to tap his foot. Predictable.

I forced the Vulcan façade to the forefront of my consciousness. "Drs. Bashir and Crusher informed me that this workstation would be available to me so that I could run diagnostics they'd requested I work on."

"Ah! You must be the nurse who recovered from the Vulcan Scourge."

I looked at him quizzically.

"That's what we're calling this infection—I thought of it. Quite clever, don't you think? I do." He clasped his hands together and leaned toward me conspiratorially. "Would it be too much to ask to let me oversee your work? I'm dying to know what kind of sneaky mutation you've got going in your cells that makes you invulnerable to all this phlegm."

Think fast. Think fast. Think fast. "I've already completed the collection of the samples and run the preliminary tests. Due to my compromised physiology, I did the bulk of the work in my quarters. I've just now loaded the data into the system. I expect the results will be available in about—" how long will it take me to escape the station? "—ninety minutes."

He looked disappointed. "I suppose I'll have to content myself with dissecting the conclusions and looking for flaws in the methodology. Once again, I'm reduced to being a database—a sophisticated, handsome one—" he sighed "—but still a database. Carry on."

I nodded in reply, and watched him stroll off, muttering to himself as he walked between the rows of biobeds and stasis chambers where the Vulcans rested, before I finished programming the computer to send my fabricated test results to the infirmary.

I wondered if Stok had been transported down here. Had she been conscious, I would have liked to say good-bye.

But I decided, in lieu of farewell, that I would finish this last entry and give the entire record to Stok. That she ultimately understand my whole situation is irrationally important to me right now, further evidence of my deteriorating state. I should be wending my way to the docking ring! Instead, I am rigging a subvocalizing processor beneath the civilian clothes I will change into and I will continue this narrative until I'm safely away. At that juncture, I will transmit these entries to Stok. She can do with them what she will. Turn them over to Starfleet Intelligence. Dismiss them as the ramblings of a mentally unstable Romulan operative. Listen with the ear of a former roommate and—dare I say and hope—friend.

Entry—I forget the next number. Isn't that pathetic?

Vulcans move serenely. They float high above confusion and chaos. Before I took this assignment, I spent hours, if not days, studying newsfeeds from Vulcan, watching how deliberately they stilled their physical energies, utilizing intensive focus and self-discipline until such calm became instinctual.

Damned if I'm not trying to keep my hands from shaking. If anyone was actually *looking* at me, I'd be doomed, exposed. I've slung a duffel bag containing a few meager belongings over my shoulder and I'm moving swiftly through the crowds. Countless ships are loading and unloading at this hour. Such is the nature of wartime, which, in reality, is little more than organized chaos.

Today, the schedule is particularly busy since many nonmilitary personnel are concerned that Captain Picard might issue a quarantine order that will prevent any starships from departing. Right now, only Starfleet personnel and DS9 residents are restricted from leaving. Visitors who've undergone a medical screening have an endorsement on their files that allow them to depart from the station. When I fabricated the identity papers required for boarding a transport, I "borrowed" an official endorsement from the infirmary—the very last task performed by Vulcan Nurse Seret, may she live long in the memories of her colleagues.

An officer I've had lunch with exits the turbolift. Must. Keep. Walking.

Breathe.

Breathe.

I resist the reflexive instinct to stiffen with fear or run. I raise my hood, drop my head and pick up my pace. A hundred more meters. A hundred more meters and I'll be at the airlock.

A woman hefting an infant bumps into me. I brush aside her apology, continue walking.

Eighty meters.

A beep-beep-whine sounds behind me, indicating an oncoming inner station transport vehicle. Crowds part before a hovercart loaded with shipping cartons and oh no, oh no, oh no—Odo sitting beside the driver, scanning the sea of swarming persons. I shield my face with my hand, spinning away from the crowd so I face the wall.

And then I see them.

The red hair. Impossible to camouflage. Someone ought to tell Dr. Crusher that if she wants to avoid being noticed she ought to do something about her hair. And of course, Dr. Bashir, his skin tone a little grayer than when last I saw him, but still remarkably alert and focused—

On me.

I stop, feet rooted to the floor. For a long moment, I look at them.

Dr. Crusher smiles.

Insanely, I smile back.

And reason reasserts itself. I take a few hesitant steps back, ruing the day I disposed of my suicide caplet. I scan the corridor, seeking an escape route . . .

Hands grasp my arms. Two security officers stand on either side of me, but discreetly. No one in the crowd even notices. These men could teach even the Tal Shiar a thing or two about silently and efficiently removing a "suspect." I consider screaming for help, a foolish impulse. Who would help me? Why would anyone believe Crusher and Bashir, the kindest of individuals, would have a reason to harm me? The security men carry me toward them, my feet barely scraping the deck. "How did you—?" I manage to sputter.

Dr. Bashir waves his hand for me to lower my voice. Strangely, he neither smiles triumphantly nor grimaces with disgust. More than anything, he appears to be embarrassed. What a bizarre species they are! "The EMH is enough of an egomaniac that he believes that anything you could do, he could do better," Dr. Bashir said, speaking just loudly enough to be heard over the crowd. "Five minutes after you left, he had already re-run half your tests."

"I would have done a better job, Doctor," I said. "But I haven't been well lately. And I've had a lot on my mind, too."

"The spy business will do that," Bashir replied, mock knowingly. "The stories I could tell you . . ."

Crusher rolled her eyes. Obviously, she understood the reference, even if I did not. "Julian, there isn't time for this now. We have to get back to the infirmary . . ."

"Not the brig?" I asked.

"Only if the EMH isn't there," Bashir said, ignoring my question. "He'll start acting up again, pointing his finger at random people and demanding they submit to a subcellular probe. Thinks he's quite the spymaster now."

"I sent him to the library section and asked him to check on Leonard's question. It will keep him out of our, uh, hair . . ." She tousled her red tresses. "For a while, anyway."

Finally, Bashir looked at me and asked, "Any theories on which element in your Romulan blood gives you immunity?"

I stared at him gap-mouthed, the tension draining out of my muscles only to be replaced by a deep weariness. "I . . . I . . ." I stammered, then tried to focus my thoughts. "In the course of my research, I formed a few theories."

"Did you make notes?"

"I kept . . . Well, yes. I kept a journal of sorts."

"You'd better make copies then and give one to each of us. We don't have much time. I had to put three more patients in stasis this afternoon. Come on." Bashir gestured at the security guards who released their grip on my arms.

"That's it?" I asked incredulously. "You're not arresting me?"

"Not just yet," Crusher said turning toward the infirmary. "We have work to do."

And so we did.

Entry #1

My new journal.

I had to give the old one to Drs. Bashir and Crusher, and they haven't given it back, so I assume it's lost for now, possibly for good. Whatever the case, I will begin again at number one. Cheap symbolism? Perhaps, but there are worse things.

One of them, I assume, is being arrested as a spy. Another, I know, is *waiting* to be arrested as a spy. I am reasonably certain neither of these things will be happening in the immediate future.

This from the immediate past: The Vulcans are cured. Having reviewed notes with one of Dr. Crusher's colleagues, I am of the opinion that she was already exploring close genetic analogs to Vulcans—Romulans, that is—in hope that a cure would present itself, but my "contribution" certainly sped up the process. She has already sent her findings to Starfleet Medical and the template for the vaccine is being distributed throughout the fleet. In the end, the Dominion may have been successful in their immediate goal. The station was disrupted for over seventy-eight hours, and the Vulcan intelligence group working here in secret will have to be disbanded. If I were judging this outcome from a Romulan intelligence officer's perspective, I would have to consider it a success. As a member of Deep Space 9's medical staff, my judgment would be that the impact was negligible.

Dr. McCoy's suggestion that the pre-Federation databases be searched bore results. The EMH found a case file written by a Denobulan doctor named Phlox, something of an expert in Terran-Vulcan comparative physiology, that led to a cure for the—gods help us—"Vulcan Scourge." Fortunately, we will not be hearing that name again anytime in the near future. As soon as the treatment was developed, Dr. Crusher put us all out of our misery and turned off the EMH. Never have I enjoyed silence so thoroughly.

And what of me? Ah, well, now there's the question: What to do with the spy when the spy can no longer do her job? Dr. Bashir suggested a simple solution: Give her a new one. "As it turns out," he said, "you're a wonderful medical technician."

But will my handlers accept this? Captain Picard and Colonel Kira assure me they will. The word "leverage" was used. I am not precisely certain what that means in these circumstances, but someone somewhere must have done something that they should not have done and someone else knows about it. I must assume my safety is secured, at least until the end of this war, this alliance. After that? Who can say for sure? One of my Terran associates in the infirmary tells me that there is a phrase from old Earth: "Que sera sera." She seemed to think this explained everything.

Terrans still baffle me, all conflict and self-contradiction, but I am beginning to find their ways strangely comforting. They mirror something within myself.

Stok is recovered completely now and has returned to our rooms. She regards me with curiosity, though not, I am relieved to see, with any noticeable animosity. Do Vulcans permit themselves to feel suspicion? If not, then perhaps betrayal? I do not know. I might ask her later. Though there have been no pointed questions about my former profession since settling back in, last night, just before going to sleep, she asked me, "Is Seret your real name?"

"It is one of them," I said. "You may continue to use it if you wish."

"But not the name you were born with."

"No."

"And that was?"

And so, without thinking, I told her.

Twilight's Wrath

David Mack

War correspondence: The movie *Star Trek Nemesis* introduced a
Romulan-produced clone of Captain Jean-Luc Picard. After the
project for which he was created was abandoned, the clone,
named Shinzon, was exiled to live in the mines on Remus
amongst the Reman slaves. However, as stated by Commander
William Riker during a briefing seen in the film, Shinzon did
serve the Romulan Empire with distinction during the Dominion War. "Twilight's Wrath" tells one story of Shinzon's service
to the Empire . . .

David Mack

David Mack is a writer whose work spans multiple media. With writing partner John J. Ordover, he cowrote the *Star Trek: Deep Space Nine* episode "Starship Down" and the story treatment for the *DS9* episode "It's Only a Paper Moon." Mack and Ordover also penned the four-issue *Star Trek: Deep Space Nine/Star Trek: The Next Generation* crossover comic-book miniseries *Divided We Fall* for WildStorm Comics. With Keith R.A. De-Candido, Mack cowrote the *Star Trek: S.C.E.* eBook novella *Invincible,* currently available in paperback as part of the collection titled *Star Trek: S.C.E.* Book 2: *Miracle Workers.* Mack's solo writing for *Star Trek* includes the *Star Trek: New Frontier Minipedia;* the trade paperback *The Starfleet Survival Guide;* the best-selling and critically acclaimed two-part *S.C.E.* eBook novel *Wildfire* (to be printed in paperback form in early 2005); "Waiting for G'doh, or, How I Learned to Stop Moving and Hate People," a short story for the *Star Trek: New Frontier* anthology *No Limits,* edited by Peter David; and the *S.C.E.* eBook *Failsafe.* Mack's upcoming works include the *S.C.E.* eBook *Small World* and two *Star Trek: The Next Generation* novels, *A Time to Kill* and *A Time to Heal.* Mack currently resides in New York City with his wife, Kara.

Shinzon strode through the veils of oily smoke that rose from the burning Jem'Hadar corpses littering the battlefield. His footfalls pressed crisp bootprints into the soft, blood-soaked earth with muffled, grotesque squishing sounds. The sickly sweet odor of decaying flesh perfumed the sultry, predawn air as the youthful, slender human paused to look up at the stars.

The sky above the crater's edge grayed with the approach of the Goloroth dawn. *I've never seen a sunrise,* Shinzon thought as he palmed a sheen of sweat off his smooth-shaven head. He had read elegant literary passages that described the sight of a solar mass emerging from beyond a planetary horizon, but living among the darkness-bound Remans had deprived him of certain experiences that he knew other humans took for granted.

Across the galaxy, trillions of humans lived their lives in the warm embrace of sunlight, as if it were their birthright and not a privilege. He envied and hated them for it.

He stepped carefully over the lifeless body of E'Mek, one of his Reman soldiers. Pale and fierce, the Remans were the only kin Shinzon had ever known. Creatures of eternal night, born of Romulan need and disdain, they were the Empire's laborers and cannon fodder—both terms that, Shinzon noted grimly, were merely synonyms for what the Remans truly were:

Slaves.

Several dozen meters ahead of him, beyond a dense wall of

smoke belching from the scattered wreckage of one of their *Scorpion*-class fighters, his few dozen surviving brothers in arms awaited him in the transport ships. Sixteen hours ago there had been hundreds more of these brave warriors, all since sacrificed in the name of victory—and Reman freedom.

Pain knifed through his gut. His vision blurred. He clenched at his abdomen and wished he could push his fingers through his armor, wished he could reach inside himself and tear out his soft, vulnerable parts. His knees buckled under him and his breath caught in his throat. *Vkruk warned me this would happen,* Shinzon thought. *But it's too soon . . . it's not fair.* His knees dug into the muddy ground. A shift in the wind enveloped him in the hot, choking smoke from the wrecked fighter. He felt himself pitch forward. Still clutching at his middle, he planted his free hand on the ground for support. Slime oozed up and swallowed his blood-caked fingers.

I cannot die here, not like this. Not yet. He fought back against the agony that dominated him. In the past sixteen hours he had risked everything for his people . . . for freedom . . . for *revenge.* He would not let it slip away now.

Sixteen hours earlier . . .

"They're beaming over now," Vkruk said, his baritone voice echoing in the mostly empty, windowless conference chamber. Shinzon nodded once to his monstrous-looking, gray-skinned Reman second-in-command and stood up from his chair.

Minutes ago, he'd been informed by T'Reth, the commander of the battle-scarred Imperial Warbird *Draco*—which Shinzon and his regiment of Reman shock troops had called home for the past five months—that they had been ordered to hold position and await VIP visitors from the Warbird *Lykara*. No other information had been offered, and Shinzon knew better than to inquire.

He pulled down his frayed tunic and straightened it as best he could. After five months and more than a dozen brutal engage-ments against the Dominion, his already rough-textured wardrobe had been left tattered and reeking of everything from blood to ketracel-white to sewage, depending on the mission.

A low-frequency hum built into an almost musical ringing. Swirling atoms materialized into three Vulcanoid shapes. They were surrounded by the shimmering, violet aura of the transporter beam, which cast long, muted shadows behind Shinzon and Vkruk. The duo shielded their eyes from the glare. As the pale glow subsided, Shinzon recognized two of the three Romulan dignitaries standing in front of him.

The first was Senator Tal'Aura, a high-ranking member of the senate. She was just as slim and regal as she had appeared in trans-missions from Romulus.

The second was Imperial High Commander N'Vol, the supreme commander of the Romulan armed forces. Thin, graying hair framed his chiseled features, which were rapidly becoming creased by the pressures of prosecuting a much-dreaded war against the Dominion.

The third was an intense-looking Romulan man who Shinzon surmised was nearing middle-age, perhaps 140 or 150 years old. Despite his age, his hair was still jet-black, and his eyes gleamed with a keen intellect and a passionate, violent will.

To Shinzon, they all smelled immaculate—as if they had just washed and donned crisp, clean new uniforms. He doubted that these back-room schemers had ever seen the horrors of war with their own eyes, from the unique vantage point of a foot soldier on a battlefield.

He bowed his head, closed his right hand into a fist and pressed it to the left side of his chest, the ancient form of the Romulan salute. Out of the corner of his eye, he noted that Vkruk gritted his fangs and grudgingly did likewise, but kept his icy glare focused on the Romulans.

"Senator Tal'Aura," Shinzon said, cautious to keep his tone

diplomatic and untainted by the bitter contempt swelling in his heart. "High Commander N'Vol. We are honored to receive you."

"Centurion Shinzon," Tal'Aura said with a polite nod. N'Vol nodded curtly to Shinzon without speaking.

The one whom Shinzon didn't recognize stepped forward. Shinzon noted with interest that Tal'Aura and N'Vol both stepped aside and slightly back, almost unconsciously subordinating themselves to the third Romulan. "I am General Valnor," the intense Romulan said. "I'm here on behalf of the Tal Shiar. Time is short. Let us sit."

Shinzon gestured with a sweep of his arm toward the conference table. He and Vkruk seated themselves to one side. Tal'Aura and N'Vol sat opposite them. Valnor sat down at the head of the table and inserted a data rod into a slot on the table surface. A holographic map of star systems along the Romulan-Federation Neutral Zone was projected above the table. The projection quickly zeroed in on one star system, then onto the fourth planet in that system.

"In the Neutral Zone lies the planet Goloroth," Valnor said. He spoke quickly but with perfect diction as a blinking red dot marked a location on the planet surface. "On Goloroth is a top-secret Tal Shiar laboratory that is not supposed to exist." The red dot expanded into a detailed schematic of the camouflaged underground facility. Shinzon eyed the schematic intently as the general continued. "It was created without official imperial sanction, and its presence in the Neutral Zone is a violation of our treaty with the Federation."

Valnor pressed another touch pad, and a blue blinking dot appeared on a different part of the planet. "Forty-six hours ago, an advance team of Jem'Hadar landed on the planet and erected a Dominion communications relay."

The hologram shifted to a detailed scan of the Jem'Hadar forces on the planet surface. "Thirty-seven hours ago we lost contact with our lab. Long-range scans have confirmed that it has not self-destructed. Because all attempts to remote-trigger the lab's self-destruct system have failed, we must assume the Jem'Hadar have captured the lab."

High Commander N'Vol reset the hologram to its original star-map configuration. It now showed numerous Federation and Klingon emblems accompanied by ship-registry data.

"Less than twenty-one hours from now, a combined force of Klingon Defense Force and Starfleet personnel will launch a counterattack against the Jem'Hadar forces on Goloroth," N'Vol said. "Their objective is to capture the Dominion relay for analysis. Once they arrive, they will almost certainly discover the now-exposed Tal Shiar lab."

Senator Tal'Aura deactivated the hologram and fixed Shinzon with a deadly look. "Such a discovery would be an extremely embarrassing incident for the Empire—"

"And a fatal one for many high-ranking members of the Tal Shiar," Valnor interjected.

Shinzon studied the three Romulans' faces. He saw contempt masked by transparently polite smiles. "How may I serve the Empire in this matter?" he said, mirroring their insincerity.

"We want you and your regiment to land on Goloroth ahead of the Klingon-Federation strike force," Valnor said. "Destroy every trace of the lab's existence."

"No one must *ever* know of this meeting," N'Vol said. "The senator, the general, and I were never here. Is that understood?"

"Perfectly," Shinzon said. "And in return for our loyal silence . . . ?"

The senator leaned forward and regarded Shinzon with a conspiratorial gleam. "If you succeed . . . command of your own warbird, with officers and crew of your choosing."

Shinzon returned her unblinking gaze. "I accept."

Beside him Vkruk drew a breath, a prelude to a protest. Shinzon silenced the hulking Reman with a gesture so subtle that it went completely unnoticed by the three Romulans. As recently as a few months ago, Shinzon would not have dared assert such authority over Vkruk. The elder Reman had adopted Shinzon when the human was abandoned by the Romulans in the mines of Remus. Shinzon had once regarded Vkruk as a surrogate father. But with the outbreak of war against the Dominion and the blossoming of Shinzon's natural talents as a tactician and strategist, their bond had become more fraternal. And now that Shinzon was in command, he remembered the first lesson Vkruk had taught him as a child: Never show weakness.

Valnor stood and removed the data rod from the conference table. Tal'Aura and N'Vol rose from their seats half a second later. Shinzon and Vkruk followed suit.

"Success and glory," Valnor said as he handed the data rod to Shinzon, who accepted it from the general with a courteous nod. Valnor touched a signal pad on his wrist. Moments later, the Romulans vanished into the unearthly nimbus of a transporter beam. The echo of the transporter's high-pitched, melodic hum lingered after their departure.

Shinzon felt the rapid pulse of the *Draco*'s warp engines throb up through the deck. He looked at the data rod in his hand, then at Vkruk, who scowled at him.

"This is a fool's errand," Vkruk said. "The Tal Shiar cannot be trusted."

Shinzon chuckled bitterly. "I never said I trusted them." He put the data rod back in the slot on the conference table and called up the scan of the Jem'Hadar deployments.

Vkruk shook his head. "Accepting the assignment was a rash decision, Shinzon."

"We had no choice. They weren't *asking.*"

Vkruk turned his attention to the hologram. "The Jem'Hadar garrison is strong, well-equipped, and deeply entrenched," he said in a voice that sounded like bootsteps on gravel. "Even if our warbird reaches orbit before they penetrate its cloaking device, there is no way to reach the surface without being detected." The ashen-hued Goliath turned toward Shinzon and glowered disapprovingly. "This is a suicide mission."

"Of course it is," Shinzon said with a half-smirk. "That's why they're sending *us.*"

Shinzon deactivated the hologram, ejected the data rod and clutched it in his fist. This was the opportunity he had been waiting for since the day he and his Reman brethren had been conscripted as imperial shock troops. "Assemble the regiment," he said. "I'll brief them within the hour."

Valnor stood in Senator Tal'Aura's stateroom aboard the *Lykara.* He stared through his dim, semitransparent reflection on the panoramic window and gazed into the endless reservoir of darkness between the stars. Moments ago he had watched the *Draco* streak away at warp speed; now that it was too late to turn back, he was plagued by second thoughts.

He turned away from the window and faced Tal'Aura, who watched him with a well-rehearsed look of loving concern. "He accepted the mission far too eagerly," Valnor said. "Either he has an agenda, or he has the wits of a bloodworm."

Tal'Aura said, "He has neither. Shinzon is a good soldier who follows orders, nothing more."

"He's a *human,*" Valnor said with disgust as he walked away from the window, toward the table in the middle of the room.

Grinning beneath a wanly lifted eyebrow, Tal'Aura said, *"He* would say he's a Reman."

Valnor shook his head and frowned. He felt her eyes on him as he reached the table. "That's hardly confidence-inspiring." Picking up the bottle of violet-hued Saurian brandy from the table, he half filled a smoked-crystal tumbler. "I used to think the Remans were just savages, but they're worse than that." He lifted the squat, slightly opaque glass and sipped the sour beverage, swallowing hard to conceal his slightly puckered grimace. "They're parasites, all of them."

Tal'Aura strolled slowly along the room's perimeter, drawing gradually closer to him. "Those 'parasites,' " she said slowly, "built some of the most powerful weapons on this ship. They aren't without their talents." She let her fingertips glide over a computer panel. Half a second later, the adagio swells of bittersweet Deltan chamber music descended gently from speakers concealed in the ceiling.

Valnor had never found Tal'Aura the least bit attractive; he had never even tried to deceive her into believing that he did. However, that hadn't stopped her from making it clear that if he wanted her help in a matter that could put her at odds with the senate, she expected from him certain discreet favors in return. Some of those favors were political in nature; others, apparently, were to be of a more personal variety.

It sickened him to stoop to such crude bargains, but it was necessary. The Tal Shiar had become politically vulnerable after its plan to cripple the Dominion backfired; a massive preemptive strike on the Founders' homeworld had been thwarted by a devastating Jem'Hadar ambush that wiped out a Romulan-Cardassian fleet in the Omarion Nebula. He knew that one day soon the Tal Shiar would reassert itself, reclaim its rightful place as the shadow power of Romulan politics. But today was not that day.

Tal'Aura slunk away from the edge of the room and moved to Valnor's side in front of the table. "As for Shinzon," she said, "he couldn't be better suited to this mission." She poured a glass of brandy for herself. "He's a gifted field commander, and the savagery you despise in the Remans makes them ideal for assaulting a Jem'Hadar stronghold."

Valnor took another lip-tightening sip of his drink. "I don't doubt their combat skills," he said, trying to avoid eye contact. "What concerns me is their loyalty. If they see a chance to betray us, they're certain to exploit it."

The edge in her voice became naked and sharp. "Your need to keep your precious secrets—especially from the senate—is what made Shinzon's regiment your only option." She frowned, closed her eyes and took a deep breath. When she opened her eyes, her face reverted to its usual mask of sinister calm. She leaned intimately close to him.

"As for their loyalty," she said in a hot whisper scented with the tart perfume of brandy, "I've taken more than adequate precautions to contain the situation." As her lips teased his own with the faintest tremor of contact, Valnor struggled to override his mouth's reflexive desire to pucker.

"This is our real reason for landing on Goloroth," Shinzon said to the more than six hundred pointed-eared silhouettes watching him from the shadows of the *Draco*'s lower hangar. Besides being the only space on the ship large enough to hold the entire regiment at once, it was also the only one that Shinzon and Vkruk had personally swept clean of the Romulans' clandestine listening devices. The lithe human paced slowly before the rows of Reman warriors, who watched him with unblinking eyes.

Behind him was a blue-tinted hologram schematic, a dozen meters tall, of the Tal Shiar's underground laboratory. One detail of the blueprint was highlighted in red.

"Connected to the lab's auxiliary power system is what appears to be a reserve fusion generator," Shinzon continued. "But the systems connected to this device betray its true nature. Only one kind of technology would require these intricate safeguards: a thalaron core."

His pronouncement was met by grim silence. As he had feared, he would have to explain every detail; these were front-line soldiers, not scientists or engineers. He continued, taking care to keep his statements simple. "The core is the real reason the Romulans want this lab destroyed. They aren't concerned about violating the Neutral Zone. Their fear is that the Federation and the Klingons will discover that the Tal Shiar has taken the lead in the biogenic-weapons arms race."

A few Reman silhouettes turned to confer in distant whispers. Shinzon realized they still did not grasp the true scope of what he had shown them.

"Until now, a thalaron generator was no more than theory," he said. "Now a working core is within our grasp. We will transform it into the heart of a weapon of unspeakable power—one that will enable us to crush all who oppose us: the Federation . . . the Klingons . . . even the Romulans themselves will bow before us." Shinzon's eyes shone with fiery passion. He raised his voice as he pointed at the hologram. "What you are looking at . . . is the first step in the liberation of Remus!"

The hangar buzzed with the susurrus of excited voices and enthusiastic growls. Shinzon raised his hands and gestured for silence. The hangar quickly fell quiet.

"Our orders are to destroy the lab," Shinzon said. "And we will accomplish our mission—*after* we have taken the thalaron core and the lab's central computer for ourselves."

Vkruk stepped forward from the shadows, his gruesome visage lined with long shadows by a dim, overhead utility light. "Most ambitious, Shinzon," Vkruk said. "But what of the Jem'Hadar garrison in the lab? Or the rest of their battalion, less than two thousand kilometers away?"

Shinzon could feel the Remans' attention press forward, as if their thoughts had physical mass. He met the cold, level gaze of Vkruk and responded with a malicious, gleaming smirk.

"We're going to kill them all," he said in a frightening near-whisper, "and be gone before Starfleet and its Klingon dogs arrive."

Commander T'Reth leaned slightly forward in her chair and steepled her pale, delicate fingers in front of her. On the *Draco's* main viewer the planet Goloroth was distinguishable as a large, bright point of amber-tinted light amid the random stipple of the starfield, and it was growing larger and more distinctly spherical even as she watched.

She swiveled her chair slowly to one side, then the other. Around her, the bridge of the *Draco* was quiet, the very model of efficiency. More than a dozen officers staffed their stations in silence as the warbird pulsed with the steady, muted throb of its warp engines. She surveyed the scene with cool satisfaction and turned her attention back toward the main viewscreen.

"Time to orbit," she said.

Subcommander J'Nek, her second-in-command, moved swiftly but with an unhurried, almost feline grace to the helm officer's station. He checked the helm display and turned smartly on his heel to face her. "Nine minutes, twenty-seven seconds."

T'Reth nodded her acknowledgment and keyed her internal comm channel. "Bridge to Centurion Shinzon. We make orbit in nine minutes. Prepare to deploy your troops. The *Draco* will cover your descent and provide supporting fire from orbit."

It had been an easy lie to tell because it was a lie of omission camouflaged with an obvious truth. T'Reth *would* defend Shinzon's attack force as it made the perilous dive from the *Draco* to the planet surface. She would do everything within her power to keep the main Jem'Hadar battalion on a defensive footing while Shinzon led the assault on the real target, the specific details of which she had not been told and knew better than to ask for. Her lie was in not saying what she had been ordered to do when the battle was over.

If Shinzon and his unit failed to secure their target, she was to unleash a firestorm of torpedoes and vaporize every last trace of their existence from the surface of Goloroth. If they succeeded in their mission, her orders were exactly the same.

Another officer might have questioned why victorious soldiers of the Empire would be treated so callously. But these were not Romulan soldiers; these were Remans, little better than animals.

More important, the orders officially had come from High Commander N'Vol—but they had been whispered to him by Senator Tal'Aura while a third, unnamed guest from the *Lykara* had watched the senator and remained silent.

T'Reth hadn't risen to the command of a warbird by ignoring small details. She heard the voice of the Tal Shiar in these orders, just as she had heard the icy whisper of death lingering on the wind during her last visit to the graves of her ancestors in the Rikolet on Romulus.

The Tal Shiar, the High Command, and the senate all wanted Shinzon and his troops dead. T'Reth didn't need to know why. The orders had been confirmed; that was all she needed to know.

The innocuous swish of the aft turbolift door opening was all that preceded the shrieking disruptor blast that tore through the back of T'Reth's chair and exploded out the front of her chest. The force of the blast and the sudden searing pain shocked her to her feet. Her legs betrayed her. She pitched forward, slamming face-first to the cold, gray-green metal deck. The angry whine of disruptor fire filled the bridge. With tremendous effort she twisted her head to the right.

Subcommander J'Nek and the other bridge officers struggled to fight back, but the ambush happened too quickly. Within moments it was over. The bridge, now shrouded in acrid smoke and the pungent odor of burned flesh, fell silent.

T'Reth clung bitterly to consciousness and to life. She couldn't conceive of how the Jem'Hadar had penetrated their cloak and infiltrated the ship at high warp. Then she heard Shinzon's voice calmly giving orders. A Reman soldier stepped over her. His spiked boot scraped her soft, angular cheek.

"Vkruk, this is Shinzon. Report."

"All decks secured," Vkruk said over the comm. *"The Romulan crew has been neutralized. The* Draco *is yours."*

"Excellent," Shinzon said. "Report to the hangar and get the dropships ready. I'll be with you shortly."

"Acknowledged."

T'Reth fumed silently. The thought of her crew being slaughtered by Reman scum made her quake with fury. Her bridge being seized by an arrogant, upstart human drew hot, stinging tears of rage from her cobalt-blue eyes.

Shinzon stepped into T'Reth's field of vision. He guided four Remans to take over at conn, operations, tactical, and engineering. "Remain just outside their weapons range, and keep the cloak up," he said to them. "Then wait for my signal. Understood?" The Remans nodded. Shinzon placed his fist against his chest in the classic form of the Romulan salute. "Victory, and freedom!" he said as he extended his arm toward his men.

"Victory and freedom!" the Remans shouted back in unison.

T'Reth coughed out a mouthful of bitter, emerald-green blood. "Traitor," she rasped. Shinzon turned and looked down at her. He walked over to her and used his foot to roll her onto her back. He gleamed at her, his smirk both smug and brutal.

"Last words, Commander?" he asked. T'Reth struggled to push the words up and out of her throat. Her final breaths foamed the blood pooling in her mouth. She spat at him. He stood above her and received her hate gladly.

"The Empire . . . will have your head for this," she said.

His eyes narrowed. He cocked an eyebrow and leveled his disruptor at T'Reth's face.

"Success forgives all sins," he said, and T'Reth's world vanished in a blinding burst of sound and fury.

Shinzon's bootsteps echoed brightly as he crossed the deck of the main starboard hangar. He moved quickly between the rows of *Zemba*-class dropships, which were arranged in three forward-facing rows of five.

His disruptor rifle was slung at his left side, its strap diagonally crossing his chest. Across his back he wore a slightly curved Romulan longsword. Though its ornate pommel and talon-shaped crossguard were fashioned in an ancient Romulan style, the blade was solid, ultra-lightweight duranium with a monofilament edge. Sheathed on his right hip was a matching shortsword, and on his left hip was a long, double-bladed dagger he had taken off the first Jem'Hadar he had killed, on Tibura Secundus two months earlier.

He felt like he was the only person in the hangar. All his troops were already either aboard the dropships, in the port hangar powering up the fifty *Scorpion*-class attack fliers, or on the bridge of the *Draco.*

Shinzon stepped toward the lead dropship, which was the only one whose aft hatch was still open. Stenciled on the side of the long, battle-scarred ship was the name *Zdonek,* which he recalled was a breed of feline predator found in some jungles on Romulus. He strode up its gangway and slapped the shoulder of AnteCenturion E'Mek, who sealed the hatch behind him.

The main compartment of the battered, jury-rigged dropship, large as it was, had grown ripe with the stench of the Remans' bloodstained, filth-encrusted armor. There was no internal illumination except for some console displays near the forward hatch to the cockpit. Regardless, Shinzon was able to account for all thirty-five members of his command platoon by nothing more than their grunted salutations. He made sure each soldier had obeyed his order to come equipped with at least one long-bladed weapon. Satisfied that they had, he stepped toward the cockpit. The cluster of armored bodies parted before him.

In the cockpit, Vkruk was at the controls. Two other flight crew sat behind him. Shinzon settled into the co-pilot's seat and opened a secure comm channel to the other ships in the attack group. "All wings, this is Shinzon," he said. "We go as soon as the *Draco* drops to sublight. Fighters, concentrate on your targets. Dropships, use evasive pattern *k'nek tal.* All platoons, regroup as soon as we're on the ground. Platoon leaders, begin final weapons check." A flashing light on the *Zdonek*'s console indicated that the warbird was about to drop out of warp. Shinzon nodded to Vkruk, who powered up the dropship's engines. "All ships, stand by to launch."

The hangar door opened, revealing the streaked blur of stars stretched by the effects of faster-than-light travel. Suddenly the stars retracted back into familiar, static points. Dominating the view in front of the warbird was the fiery-edged sphere of Goloroth. To Shinzon it resembled a perfect, larger-than-life eclipse. The *Draco* had dropped out of warp facing Goloroth's nightside and was so close to the planet that only its middle latitudes were visible within the wide, horizontal frame of the hangar entrance.

He keyed the comm. "All wings, deploy."

Vkruk piloted the *Zdonek* out of the hangar. There was a slight crackle of energy across the cockpit windshield as they penetrated the obscuring envelope of the *Draco*'s cloaking device. Off their port bow, both squadrons of *Scorpion*-class fighters raced ahead of them, streaking so quickly toward the planet that the lights of their impulse engines left dark, pulsing blurs slashed across Shinzon's vision.

The *Zdonek*'s tactical display showed the rest of the dropships following close behind. They had launched together in a tight cluster. Within seconds they cleared the *Draco*'s cloaking field and quickly widened their formation. Less than three seconds later the first blasts from the Jem'Hadar's surface-mounted plasma cannon soared up from the planet and vaporized two dropships on the *Zdonek*'s starboard side.

"All wings, increase speed," Shinzon said. "Dive!" Plunging directly toward the planet surface would present the Jem'Hadar gunners with the smallest possible targets, but Shinzon knew that the Dominion's targeting AIs were far more sophisticated than anything the Alpha Quadrant powers had so far devised. At best, steepening the dive might save one or two ships that would otherwise be lost. But he would need every soldier he could get after they landed.

Four dropships accelerated ahead of the *Zdonek* and assumed a covering formation in front of it. No sooner had they maneuvered into position when one suffered a direct hit. The explosion consumed it in a blinding flash and peppered the *Zdonek*'s doubled forward shields with fiery debris. The other three vessels ahead of the *Zdonek* immediately closed into a triangular cover formation.

A nerve-rattling boom shook the *Zdonek* as it pierced the upper atmosphere. Shinzon activated the dimming filters to reduce the glare of the thermal effects caused by the ship's rapid descent. All around the *Zdonek,* each remaining dropship was preceded by a fiery nimbus, as if a squadron of falling stars were raining down on the Jem'Hadar.

The rumble of a distant explosion signaled the loss of another dropship. Shinzon checked his tactical display. He had left the *Draco* only thirty seconds ago, and already he had lost eight dropships and nearly half his fighter escorts.

Outside the cockpit, dim shapes on the surface of Goloroth began to grow more distinct. The *Zdonek* and the other dropships plummeted at supersonic speed directly toward the main Jem'Hadar encampment, which Shinzon was pleased to see was illuminated by fires and explosions wrought by his *Scorpion*-class fighters, which drew most of the enemy fire away from the dropships.

Then the view changed into a sickening blur.

Even with inertial dampeners, Shinzon could feel the gut-twisting G-force caused by Vkruk's rapid shift from power dive to level flight. Shinzon's jaw clenched and his eyes squeezed shut as he was pressed into his seat with merciless, crushing force. When the pressure eased, he opened his eyes to see the jagged, barren landscape of Goloroth blurring past on both sides of the dropship. The battle-scarred craft bobbed along at a dangerously low altitude as it dodged plasma cannon fire coming from the Jem'Hadar base behind it.

"Hang on," Vkruk said, "we'll be out of range in just a few

more—" Blinding light and searing heat accompanied the deafening blast that rocked the *Zdonek*. The dropship pitched forward and began to roll erratically. "Damage report!" Shinzon said. The two flight crewmembers behind him struggled to extract any useful information from their scrambled consoles.

"Direct hit, sir!" one said, shouting over the din of the damaged ship's death spiral. "Port engine gone. Shields have failed."

Shinzon looked to Vkruk, who fought a losing battle against the sparking helm controls. "Can you hold her together?"

Vkruk nodded. "I can make the landing zone."

Shinzon turned and shouted back through the open door to his troops, who were calm and unfazed despite the smoke that filled the troop compartment.

"E'Mek," Shinzon said. "Brace for crash landing." The antecenturion nodded and saluted in reply.

Shinzon turned his attention back toward the landscape ahead of the *Zdonek* as E'Mek barked orders at the troops. The dropship jerked as it sheared off the top of a spire-shaped rock formation and continued its shuddering, unbalanced descent toward the landing zone, which was now only fifty kilometers away.

"Thirty seconds to the LZ," Vkruk said. The dropship's one remaining engine whined in protest, and its fractured hull rattled violently. The wounded ship's persistent clangor was drowned out for a moment by a painful metallic screech, as a chunk of its exterior hull plating was torn away by the shearing force of the winds that buffeted the craft.

Shinzon checked the straps on his seat's crash harness.

"Ten seconds," Vkruk said.

Up ahead, Shinzon could discern the shapes of seven other dropships that had already touched down at the landing zone. Then a secondary explosion, less powerful than the first but still jarring, rocked his ship. The anguished howling of the port engine ceased, and the ship's nose dipped toward the harsh, rocky, and rapidly approaching planet surface.

"All power to navigational thrusters," Vkruk said. The flight crew behind him raced to comply. The low roar of the dropship's guidance thrusters grew to a shriek as the landing zone drew near. As the *Zdonek* passed over the other dropships its thrusters failed. The nose drifted to starboard, then the ship began an unstoppable roll onto its port side. Half a second later the *Zdonek* struck the ground with a sound like thunder caught in a bottle. One thudding impact after another rattled the ship as it careened over the boulder-strewn plain.

Shinzon was transfixed by the tumbling kaleidoscope of darkness and churning dirt visible through the cockpit windshield, which quickly spider-webbed with deep cracks. His body flailed against his seat's safety-harness straps as up and down reversed themselves over and over again. The brutal rolling motion knocked the wind out of his lungs, and every new breath he took was poisoned with the smoke that belched from his console and from every widening crevice in the ship's hull.

The rolling slowed, then stopped for a brief moment. Just when Shinzon thought it might be safe to release the lock on his safety harness, the ship began to roll again—back the way it had come. Several disorienting seconds later the rolling slowed again, and the ship rocked to a stop lying on its port side.

Shinzon exited the wreck of the dropship and coughed. He took a breath of the hot, dusty air and reveled in the darkness of the moonless night. Looking back, he marveled at the scar in the ground that had been cut by the *Zdonek*'s crash landing.

The smoldering gouge glowed like the embers of an old grudge. It was interrupted by patches of pristine ground where the ship had bounced off of one obstacle or another. The cuts in the dirt were strewn with small bits of debris torn from the *Zdonek*'s hull. Slashing across its path were several other burning trails, each of which terminated at the twisted, flaming wreck of a *Scorpion*-class fighter.

Shinzon stepped down the gangway and turned around to look at the shallow, craggy slope that had brought his ship to a halt. By fortunate coincidence, the incline that had stopped the *Zdonek* was less than a kilometer from the landing zone—and it was also the assembly point for the final charge toward the entrance to the hidden Tal Shiar laboratory, which was in the bottom of the crater on the other side of the rise.

Vkruk and the rest of the command platoon followed Shinzon out of the *Zdonek*. The troops from the other dropships were quickly approaching, moving across the plain at a double-quick march as they followed the *Zdonek*'s crash scar. Shinzon made a rough head count and was dismayed to find that, including his own command platoon, just fewer than two hundred fifty of his soldiers had reached the surface of Goloroth alive.

He waited for his troops to gather around him. The Jem'Hadar were probably already deploying their forces into the crater to defend the lab's entrance. There was no time now for rallying speeches. He began walking up the gradual slope and motioned for his troops to follow him. Giving his orders over his shoulder, he and his regiment climbed toward the lip of the crater, seventy-five meters ahead.

"As soon as we go over the top, expect the enemy to open fire. Scout their positions, then take cover." He motioned with his rifle. "The Jem'Hadar will be using their chameleon camouflage, so don't bother aiming—you won't be able to see them. Just lay down as much suppressing fire as you can."

He crouched as he neared the top of the slope. His troops did likewise and spread out along the slope on either side of him, dividing into five-person squads for the attack.

"Remember the plan," Shinzon said, stressing each word. "Once I give the order to charge, we'll only have four minutes. No prisoners, no retreat. No matter what happens—*go forward.*" With grim determination, every one of his troops nodded their understanding.

"Charge rifles," Shinzon said as he activated his disruptor rifle. It hummed to life with a high-pitched tone that was echoed a split-second later by more than two hundred others just like it. "Stand ready."

Vkruk gave a fraternal squeeze to Shinzon's shoulder. "Victory and freedom," he said, loud enough only for Shinzon to hear. Shinzon nodded, hefted his rifle and faced forward.

"Advance!" he bellowed, and led his troops over the edge and down the steep interior slope. The bottom of the crater was lit by the blazing wreck of a *Scorpion*-class attack flier.

He and his men were greeted by a barrage of blaster fire from the concealed Jem'Hadar troops that were scattered across the bottom and sides of the crater.

Shinzon fired back at any flash of light in front of him and sprinted awkwardly toward a large rock formation. Diving forward, he narrowly escaped a blast that had been targeted at his head. He slammed hard against the back of the long, smooth-topped rock barrier and looked back.

In the strobing glow of Jem'Hadar blaster pulses flying over his head and flaring against the sandy crater wall, he counted roughly thirty of his men dead. Their bodies slid and rolled down the steep slope. Their more fortunate comrades took cover behind boulders and other rock formations, then quickly stripped the dead of their weapons.

He activated his comm. "Shinzon to *Draco*."

"Go ahead, sir," said R'Vek, who he had left in command of the warbird.

"Begin your attack in five seconds," Shinzon said.

"Acknowledged. Draco out."

"Down!" Shinzon said, gesturing toward the ground with his open palm. "Close your eyes!"

If his plan worked, all that would remain would be a brutal charge against a force twice the size of his own. If it failed, he would be dead before he felt the sting of regret. He pressed his face to the ground and shielded his head with his arms.

R'Vek had been staring at the computer-generated crosshairs on the main viewscreen since the moment Shinzon had departed the *Draco*. The young Reman was honored that Shinzon had chosen him for this task. It spoke of Shinzon's faith in him as a soldier.

All systems were at full power and standing by when the centurion's voice crackled over the static-filled comm.

"Shinzon to Draco.*"*

R'Vek pressed the switch on the arm of his chair that opened the reply frequency. "Go ahead, sir," he said.

"Begin your attack in five seconds," Shinzon said.

This was it. The order had been given.

"Acknowledged. *Draco* out," he said and closed the channel. "Helm, engage on my mark." *For Remus,* R'Vek told himself.

"Three . . ." *Victory . . .*

"Two . . ." *And . . .*

"One . . ." *Freedom!*

"Mark!"

The helmsman pressed the warp drive master control. For the main Jem'Hadar battalion on the surface, and for R'Vek and the Reman skeleton crew of the *Draco*, the Battle of Goloroth ended three thousandths of a second later.

The night sky above the crater flared white from the supernova-like flash beyond the horizon. The ground quaked for several seconds, then a blistering thunderstorm of fire and sand swept across the plain and roared over the top of the crater. Red-hot ash and sand rained down in torrents on Reman and Jem'Hadar alike. Shinzon winced as it coated his back and singed the hairs on the nape of his neck.

As the maelstrom raged, Shinzon checked his disruptor rifle. It was inert, its power cell neutralized. His plan had worked: The warp-speed suicide attack of the *Draco* had caused a subspace disruption wave powerful enough to disable everything from energy weapons to communications to shields.

Shinzon knew the Tal Shiar lab's shielded backup generators would reinitialize in just over four minutes. Until then, the other half of the Jem'Hadar regiment—who, predictably, had been held in reserve by their overcautious Vorta handler—would remain trapped inside the lab, whose doors would not open without power.

But more important, the Jem'Hadar remaining on the battlefield could no longer pick off Shinzon's men at a distance. Now they would have to fight on the Remans' terms.

Shinzon stood and drew his longsword. "Grenades!" he said, and pointed his blade toward the last observed enemy positions. The Remans stood and plucked chemical-fuse grenades from their belts, then launched the fist-sized orbs on shallow trajectories toward the enemy.

Seconds later, the crater echoed with the sharp reports of one explosion after another. Jem'Hadar bodies were revealed in the flash of each explosion, their chameleon camouflage deserting them in death as they were hurled through the air. As the last explosions' echoes faded, Shinzon heard the low growl of cloaked Jem'Hadar troops moving closer.

He leaped atop the rock that he had used for cover and turned to face his men. He raised his longsword over his head. "Victory!" He drew his shortsword. "Freedom!" He turned to face the oncoming front of Jem'Hadar, and mustered his voice into a thunderous bellow: *"Charge!"*

The Remans' war cries reverberated in the crater as they surged forward, swords drawn, toward their unseen opponents. Shinzon leaped forward and sprinted ahead, leading the attack. The burning husk of the downed attack flier and scattered fires from the Remans' detonated grenades were the only illumination on the battlefield; small patches of greenish flame lighted Shinzon's path as he tensed to strike.

Chameleon camouflage—the Jem'Hadar's chief advantage in hand-to-hand combat—was useless against the Remans. Unlike any other battle force the Jem'Hadar had faced in the Alpha Quadrant, Remans did not need to see their foes in order to fight them. Remans were creatures of darkness who had learned to rely on all their senses in battle: They could hear the invisible Jem'Hadar's footfalls on the gravelly sand; smell the bitter Dominion mind-control drug known as ketracel-white; and feel the tremors in the air and earth as they closed to melee distance.

Shinzon felt his weight pound against the ground with each running step. Gravity and bloodlust pulled him with equal power toward the bottom of the crater. He bounded off his leading foot and spun, letting momentum carry him forward. His longsword flashed around him in a tight arc. It caught the dancing, jade glimmer of firelight as it cut through the scaly throat of a Jem'Hadar soldier. A hot spray of blood that stank of ketracel-white spattered Shinzon's face and tunic. He finished his cut, turned full circle with the momentum of his attack, and lunged forward with his shortsword into the midst of the Jem'Hadar.

The first rank of Jem'Hadar were cut down before they even realized they had been engaged.

The night rang with a symphony of clashing metal and a chorus of guttural death cries.

Shinzon parried a Jem'Hadar's *kar'takin* with a downward swing of his long blade and stabbed forward and up through the Dominion soldier's throat with his shortsword.

He twisted his weapon ninety degrees and cut free of the taut, clinging flesh, cutting the ketracel-white supply tube of another Jem'Hadar, who was rushing past on his left side.

Shinzon pushed his dead opponent backward onto another Jem'Hadar. He used the body as a ramp as he sprinted up its torso and somersaulted forward. He landed hard, with his feet square on the ground and his shortsword plunged into the chest of a Jem'Hadar soldier. The stunned Jem'Hadar grunted and collapsed to his knees under the force of the attack.

Shinzon yanked his blade free, parried another trio of blows coming at him from different directions, and pushed forward. For every lethal stroke he deflected, two or three grazing cuts stung his hands, arms, or back. He ducked under a broadly swung attack and parried another with such force that his foe's weapon shattered. He winced as a flying splinter of steel bit into his cheek.

Shinzon barely saw the edge of the blade as it slashed downward with perfect, terrifying grace toward his skull. He crouched to delay its impact for a fraction of a second and crossed his swords to block the death stroke.

The impact alone sent shooting pains through his arms. A steel-booted foot slammed into his solar plexus with blinding speed and stunning force. The kick lifted him off the ground. He no longer heard the hue and cry of the battle. He felt for a brief moment like he was floating in a warm, comfortingly dense salt sea. Then he hit the cold, rocky ground and felt a jagged stone tear a gash in the back of his shaved head.

He barely rolled clear of the metal boot that stomped down toward his face. He pushed himself onto his knees and was poised to spring back to his feet when he glimpsed the maniacal snarl of the Jem'Hadar First, who kicked him in the chest. Shinzon stifled a shout of pain as he felt several of his lower ribs break. He barely parried another broad swing of the Jem'Hadar's sword, but was unable to dodge the First's lightning-quick left hook. The brutal punch hit Shinzon solidly in the temple.

Shinzon allowed the force of the punch to spin him counterclockwise as he swung his longsword low and parallel to the ground. His blade bit through armor and flesh, severing the Jem'Hadar First's right leg above the knee. The First teetered on his left leg then fell to his right as Shinzon finished his turn with a lunging stab of his shortsword, which speared through the First's breastplate and into his chest.

The First gurgled a mouthful of blood. He focused his shocked and furious glare at Shinzon, who sprang back to his feet, yanked his shortsword blade free, and struck again with both blades, all in one spinning blur.

As the First's severed head hit the ground, Shinzon pressed ahead like a tornado of limbs and steel.

Shinzon sensed the momentum of the battle as it raged around him. A sudden push forward was met by a counterattack that forced the Remans backward. The Jem'Hadar were at a slight disadvantage in the darkness, but they still outnumbered the Remans two to one.

Momentum was everything now. If the Remans stalled in their advance, they would die.

"Go forward!" he commanded, his blades in constant motion. As he rushed ahead, he realized that a wave of Jem'Hadar was closing in on him from every direction. Now that the enemy had realized he was the commander, he'd become their prime target.

He braced himself for the crush of bodies. Then two squads of Reman warriors tackled the charging Jem'Hadar in a flurry of blades and growls. Shinzon twisted his body to avoid the thrust of a Jem'Hadar dagger. A knife thrown from behind him flew past his ear and lodged in a Jem'Hadar's throat.

More Remans pushed in front of him. Some threw themselves onto enemy *kar'takins*, sacrificing themselves to clear the path ahead of him and Vkruk. The sacrificial warriors tumbled to the blood-soaked ground, entangled with their foes, stabbing and slashing with impassioned roars until death took them.

Shinzon broke through the rear rank of Jem'Hadar and sprinted forward. He heard Vkruk and a handful of other Remans following close behind him. He stopped where he expected to find the concealed access hatch to the thalaron core.

"Find the hatch," he ordered. Three of his soldiers sheathed their swords, pulled entrenching tools from their packs, and began digging to find the edge of the sealed emergency bulkhead.

Shinzon turned to face back the way they had come. A squad of six Jem'Hadar had fallen back to pursue them. They attacked in unison. Shinzon and Vkruk stood back-to-back and held their ground.

Shinzon's muscles burned with the effort of defending himself against three Jem'Hadar at once. A fortunate thrust of his longsword blade felled one of his attackers. Then a Jem'Hadar dagger pierced Shinzon's left thigh and struck bone. He staggered as he pulled the blade from his leg. Sharp, crippling waves of pain shot up his spine.

The two Jem'Hadar facing him rushed forward and lifted their *kar'takin*s to strike. Both were skewered from behind by Reman swords, which emerged from their chests, slicked with blood that gleamed like liquid ebony. The Remans behind them pushed the dead Jem'Hadar off their blades. The bodies hit the bloodied ground with a wet and heavy sound.

Behind Shinzon, the three Remans had revealed the edges of the thalaron core hatch and were lining it with explosive charges. The two Remans who had just saved his life moved past him and added their own charges to the demolition effort.

The charges' indicator lights all blinked once in unison. The five Remans sprinted away from the hatch. "Fire in the hole!" one shouted. Vkruk grabbed Shinzon and pulled him away from the hatch. The explosives detonated. A column of fire roared skyward and illuminated the crater with its golden-orange glare. Searing heat accompanied the shockwave, which hurled them away from the blast and flattened Jem'Hadar and Remans alike.

Seconds later the flames expired. A pillar of smoke drifted like a solid object across the battlefield, obscuring everything more than an arm's reach away. The ten-centimeter-thick duranium hatch, which had been blasted skyward, struck the ground with a dull thump only meters from the now-exposed thalaron core control chamber.

Shinzon was the first one back on his feet. Every step with his left leg sent new tides of excruciating pain coursing through him. He transformed his agony into battle-rage as he half-ran, half-limped toward the control chamber. "Secure the perimeter!" he said to Vkruk.

The Remans and the Jem'Hadar all pushed in toward the exposed control chamber entrance. Shinzon reached it first. Vkruk and the Reman soldiers who had blasted it open arrived only a few steps behind him and surrounded the entrance portal.

Beyond them, the wall of swinging blades and falling bodies closed in like a tidal wave. He looked Vkruk in the eye. "Two minutes," he said. "Hold the line." Vkruk nodded once and turned to face the oncoming Jem'Hadar.

Shinzon climbed down the ladder into the control chamber as the clamor of the battle resumed above him.

Vkruk made an upward thrust with both his swords and lifted a Jem'Hadar off the ground. The Dominion soldier's blood ran down Vkruk's blades and trickled in warm rivulets over his gnarled hands. The air was rank with the bitter stench of ketracel-white and chemical explosives.

Vkruk tossed aside his dead foe. From the edge of his vision he saw another Jem'Hadar lunge at him. The enemy's knife slipped under his parrying stroke and plunged into the elder Reman's ribs. The serrated blade burned him as it pierced his skin. *Caustic poison,* Vkruk surmised grimly.

With a furious growl he pushed one of his two swords into his attacker's throat. The dying Jem'Hadar stumbled awkwardly forward and twisted his weapon.

Vkruk howled as the saw-toothed edge tore at his ribs. With a cry of rage he grasped the knife by its blade and wrested it from the dead Jem'Hadar's hand. He pulled it free of his own ribs and, with a flick of his wrist, caught it by its grip and used it to parry another adversary's slashing cut.

Vkruk saw the tide of the battle turning in the Remans' favor. The enemy's advantage in numbers had been overcome; the Remans were clearly more skilled and more at home fighting in the darkness.

However, if Shinzon's plan failed to eliminate the second wave of Jem'Hadar currently trapped inside the laboratory, that would soon change. Fewer than a hundred Reman soldiers were still in the fight, while more than two hundred Jem'Hadar waited inside the lab, eager to join the fray.

A wounded Jem'Hadar fell to the ground beside Vkruk. The Reman elder lifted his foot. *Our fate is with you, Shinzon,* he thought. He stomped with his heel and was rewarded by the wet crack of the Jem'Hadar's neck breaking beneath his spiked boot. *Don't fail us.*

Shinzon wiped the sweat and blood from his hands with a rough smear across his chest. He worked from memory as he disconnected several insulating elements from the thalaron core and channeled its output into the lab's primary power grid.

The lab was still offline, as was the thalaron core. But he knew that the subspace disruption caused by the *Draco*'s suicide attack would dissipate in a matter of moments. If he didn't finish his sabotage of the thalaron core in time, he and his troops would be annihilated.

Many of the core's secondary components were dangerously hot, even after being offline for more than three minutes. The underground crawlspace around the core was pitch-dark, and Shinzon identified each element by touch, comparing the shape against his memory of the core's schematic diagram. The controls of the primary manifold burned Shinzon's fingertips as he reshaped them to a new and deadly purpose.

Above him he heard the grunts and rattling gasps of the dead falling from the battle. Then the metallic cacophony was muffled by Vkruk's telepathic voice inside his mind.

Our fate is with you, Shinzon, Vkruk said telepathically. *Don't fail us.*

The mind message did not trouble Shinzon; it was not the first time that Vkruk had spoken to him this way. Shinzon made his final adjustment to the thalaron core and began inching his way backward to the ladder.

Fear not, father, he replied, reaching out with his mind to the man who had raised him. *Victory is ours.*

As he climbed the ladder, the core hummed back to life.

Inside the sealed and power-deprived laboratory, Rayik stood with his back to his second company of Jem'Hadar troops. He was a fixture of calm in opposition to their seething mass of anxious bloodlust. The serene Vorta could sense that Mogano'gar, the company's First, was brimming with resentment at having been held in reserve.

That is why I am in command, Rayik thought. *That many Jem'Hadar crowded together on the battlefield would only have made a better target for the Remans' grenades.*

Rayik felt a slight vibration through the floor as the facility's generators recovered from what he could only guess had been a subspace shockwave. The door would be open in a few moments when power returned. The emergency lights weakly flickered back to half-strength. He nodded to Mogano'gar.

"I am dead!" Mogano'gar bellowed to his troops. "As of this moment, we are all dead. We go into battle to reclaim our lives."

So single-minded, Rayik mused smugly. *So expendable.*

"This we do gladly because we are Jem'Hadar. Victory is life."

"Victory is life!" The Jem'Hadar soldiers cheered. Rayik sighed quietly. He turned to issue the attack order.

Rayik stared mutely at the swarm of glowing motes that cascaded out of every free power node.

The corridor was filled with the tiny luminescent specks, which swirled down the corridor and flowed through the walls like a river with no boundaries. The shimmering particles passed without sensation through Rayik and the Jem'Hadar. Then, just as quickly as the phenomenon had appeared, it faded away.

A sensation of being incinerated from within filled Rayik's quickly desiccating body. He stared at Mogano'gar. He felt his face start to crumble before he saw it reflected in Mogano'gar's cold, angry eyes. The Vorta's reflection vanished as the Jem'Hadar collapsed into powder at his feet.

The Founders are wise in all things, Rayik reflected, before disintegrating into a cloud of fine, crystalline dust.

Shinzon tied a tourniquet above the wound in his thigh while six of his men, working under Vkruk's supervision, carefully opened the double doors to the Tal Shiar laboratory.

The battle had been over for a few minutes, but Shinzon's body still quaked from adrenaline overload. As always, he had been impressed by the tenacity of the Jem'Hadar soldiers. Even after their defeat had become all but inevitable, they had refused to surrender. He had personally slain the last of them, a veteran who had demanded to face him in single combat.

Now, the forty-one other Remans who had survived the battle were policing the dead. They collected supplies and trophies from bodies that had been dismembered by blades, scorched by still-burning chemical fires, or shredded by grenades.

Shinzon twisted the tourniquet until it bit into his skin. His leg began to grow numb.

He swept his dirt-encrusted hands over his sweaty shaved pate. His burned, blistering fingertips lingered over the jagged gash on the back of his head. At his feet, a Jem'Hadar and a Reman lay side by side in death. Both their faces looked gruesome to Shinzon, who suddenly felt very much like a man alone on a field of monsters.

The Tal Shiar lab's double doors opened with a metallic groan followed by a violent, sibilant hiss.

"Shinzon," Vkruk said. "It's time."

Shinzon nodded and limped stiffly to Vkruk's side. Hefting his now-working disruptor rifle, he led his brethren down the sloped corridor into the lab.

As Shinzon had expected, they met no resistance inside the laboratory.

As the Remans had scanned each corridor and room, they had found no life signs. Not even bacteria had survived the thalaron radiation Shinzon had unleashed; the weapon had annihilated all organic material in the lab at the subatomic level.

Shinzon monitored his troops' progress from the lab's antiseptically clean command center. Twenty of his soldiers were quickly but carefully taking apart the lab's computer memory banks and loading them into two of the dropships, all of which had been moved to the lab's main entrance in the crater. The remaining Reman troops were removing the now-deactivated thalaron core from its underground bunker and loading it into a third dropship.

As Shinzon watched the steady activity on the control center monitors, however, his thoughts were consumed by the information he had just obtained from the Tal Shiar computer. He had always wondered where he had come from; how he had ended up being schooled by the Romulan scientists Tran and Svala; and why the Romulans had enslaved him in the mines of Remus.

He had asked the computer a simple question: "Who am I?"

The answer had torn his identity apart. He was a copy. A fabrication. A living lie. *I'm a clone.*

He had hoped the computer might know *something* about him. He wasn't ready to accept that it knew *everything* about him.

"Shinzon, I've found something," Vkruk said over the comm. *"I think you should see this."* He had sent Vkruk to make a final sweep of the lab's lower levels before they triggered its self-destruct system.

"Where are you?" Shinzon said.

"Sublevel six, compartment five."

"On my way."

Shinzon touched the smooth, metallic-hued skin of the android's face. It stood in its storage pod, eyes closed, its body clad in a drab, gray utilitarian overall.

Shinzon skimmed through the documentation that Vkruk had found with it. The information on the holographic tablet was incomplete, but Shinzon recognized certain names in it from his own recently discovered biography.

"Activate it," Shinzon said, nodding upward at the android.

Vkruk hesitated. "Are you sure that's—"

"Do it." Vkruk reached behind the android's back and flipped a switch. Its eyes fluttered open. It looked back and forth between Shinzon and Vkruk.

"You are human," the android said to Shinzon. It looked at Vkruk. "I do not know what you are," it said simply.

"What is your name?" Shinzon said.

It looked at him blankly. "I am B-4."

"Do you remember how you came to be here?" Shinzon said.

"I used to be in a lab," B-4 said. It looked around the lab, its head jerking in staccato, birdlike movements. "It was not as nice as this lab. I was taken away by people with gray skin. They put me in a box and turned off my power."

The android pointed at a metal examination table. "I woke up here. There were people with pointy ears and angry voices. They yelled at me."

Shinzon studied the android's childlike manner. He suspected the machine was likely not capable of lying. That was a programming defect he would have to correct. "What did the people with pointy ears say to you?" Shinzon asked.

"They told me I was too stupid to be of any use," B-4 said. "They said they would let me know if they needed me for spare parts. Then they put me back in my pod. Now I am here."

"How long you have been here?" Shinzon said.

"Nineteen years, five months, three days, nine hours, eleven minutes, and twenty-two seconds."

Shinzon looked again at the android's documentation. Like Shinzon himself, it was a duplicate of a high-profile Starfleet officer. Also like himself, it had been consigned to oblivion nineteen years ago when the Tal Shiar abandoned an overly ambitious plan that relied on doppelgängers to infiltrate an enemy's military hierarchy.

Shinzon had been engineered from flesh and blood to take the place of a captain named Jean-Luc Picard. This stolen android had been marked to replace an android officer named Data—who, ironically, now served as Picard's second officer aboard the *U.S.S. Enterprise*. It became clear to Shinzon that long ago he and B-4 had been part of the same, aborted Tal Shiar scheme. While he had been exiled to die in the mines of Remus, this android had been abandoned to a mechanical coma and forgotten.

"Can you walk?" Shinzon said to B-4. The android stepped forward. It looked down at its feet, then back at Shinzon.

"Yes."

"Follow us," Shinzon said. "We will bring you to our ship. We will set you free . . ." Shinzon clasped B-4's shoulder. "Brother." Shinzon nodded to Vkruk, who gestured to B-4 to follow. The android exited behind the hulking Reman, and Shinzon walked out behind them. He activated his comm. "Shinzon to Xiomek. Are you finished loading the transports?"

The Reman antecenturion's voice crackled over the comm. *"Affirmative, sir."* Shinzon followed Vkruk and B-4 into the turbolift.

"We're on our way out," Shinzon said. "Set the self-destruct timer for ten minutes, then get to the transports."

Shinzon gasped for breath. He was down on his hands and knees. His fingers clawed at the muddy ground as searing pain tore through his insides. It felt as if it were twisting him in knots until he was about to rip apart.

The viselike sensation abated, and he inhaled greedily. Even though the toxic smoke from the wrecked attack flier burned his sinuses and throat, he was grateful that it had concealed his moment of weakness from his troops.

He lifted one knee, planted his foot, and paused to let his dizziness pass. The smoke thinned, and he saw the dropships less than twenty meters away. Behind them the sky swiftly grayed with the approach of the Goloroth dawn. The day that would follow behind it, darkly overcast as it was certain to be, would be too painfully bright for his Reman troops to bear.

Shinzon wished he could stay to watch it, just this once. Though he considered the darkness-bound Remans his kin, part of him was still tempted to step out of the shadows. His irrepressible fascination with the fine line that separated light and darkness had been what inspired Vkruk to name him Shinzon, the Reman word for *twilight*.

He stood and limped forward toward the dropships. The ground rumbled angrily beneath his feet as the Tal Shiar lab imploded. He stopped short of the gangway to the dropship on which Vkruk awaited his return. He waited until all his surviving men fixed their attention on him. The air was growing warmer, and he felt a fresh sheen of sweat dampening his skin and mingling with the blood-caked mud that flecked his face.

"Our comrades did not fall in vain, my brothers," he said loudly. "But they did not die for Romulus. Nor for the Tal Shiar. Our victory was for Remus—" he lifted his sword and held it horizontally above his head "—and for *freedom!*"

The roar that answered him was long, feral, and deafening. Rather than taper off, it segued into a deep, overpowering chant accompanied by the heavy stomping of the Remans' booted feet: "Shin-*ZON!* Shin-*ZON!* Shin-*ZON!* Shin-*ZON!* Shin-*ZON!* . . ."

Shinzon limped into his dropship. The fanatical chorus continued without pause as the gangway closed behind him. Battered, broken, and bloody, he settled into the cockpit beside Vkruk. As the dropship ascended, the newly self-proclaimed liberator of Remus set a course for a rendezvous with a Romulan senator who had a promise to keep.

Eleven Hours Out

Dave Galanter

War correspondence: This story takes place immediately prior to the *Star Trek: Deep Space Nine* episode "The Changing Face of Evil."

Dave Galanter

Dave Galanter has authored various *Star Trek* projects, among these the *Voyager* novel *Battle Lines*, the *Next Generation* duology *Maximum Warp*, and the *S.C.E.* eBooks *Ambush* and *Bitter Medicine.* His not-so-secret Fortress of Solitude is in Michigan, from which he pretends to have a hand in managing the message board Web sites he co-owns: ComicBoards.com and TVShowBoards.com. He also edits and is the main contributor to his own Web site, SnarkBait.com. Dave spends his non–day-job time there, with family and friends, or burying himself in other writing projects which at some point might actually see the light of day if he ever gets off his duff. He enjoys feedback on his writing, positive or negative, and would appreciate seeing any comments you have on his work. Feel free to email him at dave@comicboards.com.

In the distance there was war, yet Earth sat in an uneasy bliss. No battle touched her shores, no fire singed her sky. But as the bright sun shone on San Francisco Bay, sparkling brighter than any starscape, Captain Jean-Luc Picard could not fully embrace its beauty. Death fogged over all. War always found its way home, if not in deed then in the souls of tired soldiers.

"You're morose," Deanna Troi told him. "I could feel it from the corridor."

Picard turned to look toward the lounge doorway. He thought to mention how lovely Troi looked in her formal gown, then reconsidered, only to change his mind again. "Didn't you tell me you were going to wear your dress uniform instead?"

"That was before I found a dress shop nearby."

As he gestured for her to sit in one of the large, overstuffed chairs, her smile made him smile, if only just a bit, before he lost the expression in more somber thoughts.

"You're going to give me empathic whiplash," she told him as they both sat. "Are you worried about the *Enterprise?*"

The captain tugged at his tunic collar and wondered if he still had time to get into his dress uniform. Suddenly he felt underdressed with Deanna in such formal wear. "Worried? No. Storms delay ships all the time. And we're far enough away from . . ."

"The war."

"Yes." Picard paused. He didn't feel so far away from the battle. "I don't really feel like I'm home," he admitted.

"Maybe you should have visited Labarre?" Deanna suggested, hands elegantly cupped together on her lap. "There was time. You could take the time, after the ceremony and before *Enterprise* returns."

Picard shook his head. "*Enterprise* will be back by 1900 hours."

"You're the captain. You can make time."

He pulled in a long breath. "There's a war on."

"You could still—"

He cut her off with a motion of his hand. "Deanna, there is little there for me now."

Deanna Troi didn't give up quite so easily. She would press this until she knew her captain would take no more. Being an empath, she was quite good at knowing when that was. "What about your sister-in-law? Friends? Other family?"

"I've neither had, nor had time for, extended family. Robert and I didn't even have much use for one another until recently. Without him there seems to be no family left."

She paused, pushed a strand of dark hair behind her ear, and then continued. "I thought we were here to see your niece graduate the Academy."

"Amarante is my sister-in-law's niece," he said with a slight sigh. "I've only met her twice. Marie is trying to give me some sort of family."

"And you're taking it," she said with a short nod. "That's good."

Picard half shrugged and pulled his tunic down in front. "I'm humoring her. She's trying to rebuild her life after Robert and René died in the fire and I want to help by being family to her, but . . ." He looked away a moment, not wanting to think about the fire and the events after and his inability to make it to the funeral. "And the girl and I have talked since she's been in the Academy. She's asked advice. She's smart. We were scheduled to be here, and she asked if I could attend."

"Will Marie be here?" Deanna asked.

"No, no." He brushed something off his trouser leg and leaned forward to take the cup of tea he'd left on the coffee table when he entered the room. "She's not even that close to the girl. But I think she thought since Amarante was going to the Academy, and my background . . ."

"It's good for you, you know. To have family other than us."

The captain allowed himself a thin smile. "Marie says the same."

"Maybe you should take *our* advice."

"I'm here, aren't I?"

"Are you?" There it was, that counselor-having-a-session expression. "That gaze out the window was a thousand light-years away."

"How long had you been watching me?"

"I'm an empath. No watching necessary."

Picard scoffed. "Damned invasion of privacy is what that is."

"Don't broadcast your misery so, and I won't pick it up."

"I'm not miserable." He took another sip of tea, but it was unsatifyingly cold.

"Brooding, then," she pressed.

"I'd like to officially challenge my counselor's interpretation," he said in mock annoyance.

"We're not logging a session, Captain." Deanna leaned forward across the glass coffee table and touched his hand. "We've all lost people. In war, in tragedy, in life."

"You're not telling me anything I don't know, Deanna. I just . . ." It had never been easy for Jean-Luc Picard to put his deepest feelings into words, but if there was anyone with whom he was comfortable doing so, it was his ship's counselor. She'd helped him through some difficult times—ordeals no one should have to live through. He trusted her and her advice, perhaps more than anyone he knew. "You know Robert and I hadn't talked for some years," he said finally, "And then we did, of course, from time to time. Now . . . we can't. I'm not sure even what I'd say if we could. But I wish we had another chance."

She nodded lightly. "You miss him."

"Yes," he said in something only slightly louder than a whisper. "And I didn't think I would." Abruptly, he stood, and his voice was as crisp as always. "I'll be fine."

Deanna slowly rose as well. "I hope so. And remember," she said with a warm smile. "I'll know when."

"I'll need to scan an ID." Jeremy Plenda barely looked at the man in front of him. There was no need. No one beamed anywhere on Earth or off without an encoded ID card that would scan the traveler to verify they were whom they claimed to be. Unless it was some Starfleet yahoo who didn't need normal clearance.

Plenda didn't care for his job, but he did it well, if by the numbers. There was a routine he'd fallen into, a physical memory of how to act during his day and what to do with his hands as he keyed in destinations to other transporter hubs and made detailed and boring logs.

"This'll be just a second." Plenda took the man's card and turned to place it in the datareader. "Please read the screen to your left. If you agree to the terms and conditions of using the QuikPort Transporter Service, Inc. please place your thumb on the pad provided and allow the scanner to pull DNA for our rec—"

Suddenly feeling a burning sensation on his neck, Plenda turned and saw the man grabbing his arm and lowering him into the console chair.

"Wha—" His own voice was thick. He'd been drugged. *Why? In this little podunk backwater city? A ship is easy to hire, why do this? It's not even that expensive to go anywhere on the planet.*

The lights seemed to dim, though Plenda imagined they had not. He could still see, though, and now took as best note he could of the man who'd done this. He was tall and thin, gangly even, and moved quickly to lock the doors and then put up an away message that said Plenda was taking a break.

Plenda tried to croak out a word, but he found himself paralyzed, unable to move, barely able to breathe. He wasn't panicking, though. And that surprised him most of all. What he was doing was *watching*, hoping that when all this was over he'd be able to tell the police all that happened and everything he could about the man who assaulted him.

The man took a large case from in front of the counter. Plenda hadn't noticed it especially, but it wasn't unusual for someone to take luggage with them when they traveled.

As the tall man input coordinates into the console, Plenda tried to see where they might lead. The police would be here soon and he'd want to give them a good statement and a good description. Didn't he just tell himself that? The world was beginning to slow down. If he could move his head . . . just a bit . . .

With a mental grunt and a push that manifested little actual outward movement, Plenda only managed to spin his entire chair on its swivel, but that was good enough. What he saw made even less sense than the entire predicament. It was to a coordinate no one should ever use—into the middle of space in an area no ships were allowed. If a ship *was* there, it would have to be Starfleet's and if this guy was Starfleet, he wouldn't need a land transporter. What was this all about?

Rather than setting the timing controls, the mysterious man wrenched an access panel from the main power hub. With cables he pulled from that case of his, he connected ports on the side of his luggage directly into the transporter's main power grid.

Lolling his head as best he could to see what happened next, Plenda realized what the man had done when his eyes caught a glimpse of the charging graphs. His attacker had added so much power to the transmission system that he could probably beam himself to Mars. Well, that wasn't possible, but whyever he needed the extra power, about two seconds after dematerialization it was going to blow the controls, the buffers, and probably the building itself. If he could have moved more than his diaphragm and his eyeballs, Plenda might have panicked by now, but all he really wanted to know was why was he going to die here, in his dead-end job on a day he'd considered calling in sick for no particular reason? What was it all about?

Stepping onto the number one transport pad, the man pushed a button on a remote in his hand and the dais came to life with a power-stoked hum Plenda had never heard before. Energy washed down over the man as he slowly dematerialized, as if the transmission was struggling to get through the Earth's crust itself.

Finally, sparks flashed when the buffers overloaded with current, and somehow Plenda thought he heard his younger sister laugh. For a moment he wondered if this all might have been some strange joke. Then, in a flare of pain, the universe around him turned white hot and engulfed him in a violent wave. After that came darkness, silence, and he was gone.

The air was fresh, if a bit singed with fire and tainted with smoke, but that was to be expected—he'd had to beam up not just himself, but the atmosphere around him. Once here, if he'd studied the stolen schematics correctly—and he had—it would be easy enough to turn on minimal life support.

Za'dag got to work quickly. He needed no chronometer to know that he had only minutes before his air would become too polluted for life, and minutes more before his associates were within range of the very deadly weapon he was soon to control.

He pulled open the access panel to his left, cursing both his height and the low ceiling of the cramped orbital platform. A tight smile thinly pulled itself across his face, however, when he saw that his schematics were, in fact, accurate. A few switches moved, a few isoliniar chips removed, and life support was on. And before anyone could be notified of the change in conditions, he removed the communications chip, then snapped it in two.

To Za'dag, the coming strike was going to be a thing of beauty, a lesson taught to an arrogant planet and an overbearing Federation. Perhaps this would only bloody the Terrans' noses, but that was enough for now. And if he had to give his life for such a thing . . . well, that would be a glorious end.

After a few more chips were removed and then rearranged, control of the defensive platform was now his. If only, Za'dag thought, it would be possible to turn the power of the satellite back on to the planet. Sadly, it was not. He would have to settle for destroying any approaching Federation starship.

"Admiral? We've lost contact with DP-7." Lieutenant Hackworth had never seen Starfleet Command lose touch with one of the planetary defense platforms.

Nor had Rear Admiral Ling, and he marched quickly toward HQ's main status consoles. "Malfunction?" he asked.

"I'm not sure, sir." Hackworth's nimble hands did a fast dance across her ops station. "Backup systems aren't responding."

"Can you scan it?" Ling turned to his assistant. "Commander, come see this."

"I have it on sensors, sir," Hackworth reported. "It's intact and reads as having functional power output."

Admiral Ling's assistant joined him at the status console. "Sir?"

"DP-7 isn't responding to subspace contact. Is there maintenance on that platform today?"

The young Vulcan shook his head slightly. "No, sir. You or Admiral Mendez would have had to approve it. Admiral Mendez did not."

Ling nodded. "Put a tech detail on it. Have it checked out," he told Hackworth.

"Aye, sir," she said, her brow furrowed with dismay. "Thing is, I should have gotten an alarm on this. I didn't. I mean, we should get a *big* alarm when we lose contact with one of the platforms."

Huffing out a breath, Ling nodded his agreement. "True. Get

me Starbase 1. Let's have them send out an emergency crew right now." Ling twisted toward his assistant. "And let's inform Admiral Gunnell. *Discreetly,* please. He's tired of the leaks to the press."

"With news on the hour, this is United Press Interstellar's Afya Jamilia from the UPI NewsCenter in San Francisco. Top stories today include reports from the front lines by unnamed sources close to the Federation Council that suggest shipping routes necessary to resupply Chin'toka are being disrupted by Dominion forces. Two Cardassian warships were reportedly destroyed when the U.S.S. Starstalker *defended three cargo carriers bringing Chin'toka much-needed resources and defenses. At the Starfleet Command press briefing this morning, Admiral Brian Gunnell refused to comment on any ongoing mission, so we can only assume that the* Starstalker *and the ships she escorts have not yet arrived in the Chin'toka system. We are also hearing some unconfirmed reports that the Cardassians aren't happy with support they're receiving from their Dominion allies. Former Starfleet Commander Lawson Royse, a veteran of the Federation's first war with Cardassia, will be the guest on tonight's* Federation at War *broadcast to discuss the possible validity of those rumors. Join us on most of these affiliated networks."*

"We have three Tellarite freighters on the screen, ma'am. Vector is incoming."

"Let me see a detail scan." Commander Kim Bouse leaned in toward her display console as the graphic detailing the incoming cargo ship filled the screen. "Any Tellarite ship knows better than to violate starbase approach perimeters without clearance." Squinting in some surprise, Bouse shook her head in disbelief. "This is all wrong. I know the captain of the *F'sweiv.* He wouldn't be this far off—"

Choom!

Her console exploding in sparks, cracked bulkheads spewing debris and crackling power conduits, Commander Bouse found herself thrown to the floor as she lost her balance.

Three more explosions pounded into Starbase 1, each burst quaking every bulkhead around her.

"My God," she croaked out, smoke quickly stinging her lungs. "What the hell—"

"Emergency lights," someone ordered and she thought it was her second in command. Temporary lighting flickered on.

"Contact Command!" Bouse struggled to get to her feet. "We're under attack!"

"I can't get a signal out," called her communications officer. "Channels are jammed!"

"Main power is out!"

"Aux circuits are not responding."

"We're losing lighting again—" Another explosion rattled the deckplates beneath her and she nearly fell again. Her knees ached and all the voices began to meld into a cacophony without meaning.

"Never mind lights," she barked. "We need to get a signal out—"

"Comm is on battery, Commander, but all channels are jammed."

"Try non-subspace. We don't have to talk to Tellar, for godssakes! We *have to* talk to Command."

"Admiral, I think we're getting a message from Starbase 1, but not as an answer to my hail," Hackworth said.

"You *think?*" Ling's thin brows rose in surprise. "It's about forty thousand kilometers above us, Lieutenant."

Hackworth shook her head, and as Ling leaned over her console he glanced at her briefly and noticed her worried expression. "This is on a nonstandard channel, sir. I can't make out more than their code—"

Choom!

Ling looked up as the ceiling bore down on top of him. He instinctively bent to cover one of his crew.

She smelled nice, he thought fleetingly, then dust filled his lungs and heat enveloped him until nothing remained.

Usually Jim Stoakes had to be working this time of day, but not today. He'd taken the day off, as he did every wedding anniversary, no matter what projects where on his plate at the office. At first he would take his wife Beth to walk along the Golden Gate Bridge, but now they added their only daughter to the tradition, and the three of them would celebrate their family on the bridge, stopping to eat along the way at one of the many cart vendors who fed the passersby and tourists.

"Ice cream, ice cream," his daughter squealed with glee. "Pleeeease?"

"Like she doesn't get it every time?" Jim asked his wife. "You'd think there was a question." He held up three fingers to the ice cream vendor and mouthed the word "chocolate."

The older man with the apron pulled ice cream bars from his cooler one at a time, handing the first one to the delighted little girl, probably because to make her wait might cause her head to explode right there and then.

Jim took his daughter's hand, and the three of them continued up the bridge. It was a bright day, warm, and the ice cream was already beginning to melt. "Better hurry," his wife told him, "or it will be running down onto your sleeve."

"You're talking to me about eating fast? I usually can't get you to finish half your meal in the time it takes me to finish my plate."

The girl giggled. "Mama eats bird food."

Jim noticed his wife's quizzical look. "Where did you hear that, honey?"

"Gramma. She says you eat like a bird."

A slight smirk pulled Jim's lips tight. "My mother loves you very much."

Beth sneered, more teasing than serious. "She'll love me more when I'm just like her."

"Thanks, dear," Jim said, laughing as he moved to give her a very chocolaty kiss. "That's a notion that will have me in therapy for a few years."

His wife returned the kiss, saying it was sweeter than usual.

"Happy anniversary," she whispered.

"You, too."

They had a silent moment, then their daughter asked, "Daddy, why is this bridge so big?"

"Well, honey, before it was a museum, people used to drive automobiles across it all the time. It needed to be large enough to handle all the traffic for the city. Now anyone with a land vehicle uses the tunnel." He leaned down, finishing the last of his ice cream and mockingly trying to take a bite of hers. "So we can walk it, and enjoy the sun, and eat ice cream and pretzels and fill your tummy with all these bad things!"

She giggled, and Beth laughed, and then the bridge shook more than it should have and his face contorted from grin to abject horror as an explosion pushed out from the center of the bridge.

Cables snapped and swung wildly and the bridge cracked and crumbled just meters from his daughter. Jim Stoakes grabbed her with one hand, his wife with another, and began a dead run for the shoreline. Whatever was happening—an unheard of uncontrolled earthquake—or . . . whatever, he couldn't imagine. Hundreds of people began running in panic. He heard cries, yells, one of them might have been his daughter as he scooped her into his arms, her small stride unable to keep up with his and his wife's. "Don't let go," he yelled to his family. "Stay with me!"

When the plasma bolt hit them straight on, his last thought was for them.

"Congratulations, Ensign," Deanna said. "Were you nervous?"

Amarante couldn't keep from grinning, and Picard also found himself smiling, more because that may very well be a question to which Deanna already had an answer.

"I wasn't as nervous as I thought I would be. So much work went into this—more than I imagined."

"And more is to come," Picard said, but as serious as he was trying to be, he couldn't help being infected by Amarante's enthusiasm. Most of their communications had been either audio or text, but that was their preferences, and Picard was amused that she was just as fervent in person as she was in her letters.

"Do you have orders yet?" Deanna asked her.

"No." Amarante pulled her brown hair out of the more regulation bun she'd worn and shook her head both to free her hair and indicate her response. "But I'm hoping for starship duty. I've studied tactical, engineering, and navigation."

"She's very eager." Deanna beamed a bright grin.

"I see that," Picard replied dryly.

While Amarante hadn't come right out and asked her uncle to pull any strings for her, and likely would never have been so impolite as to do so, she was making her wishes well known. Only youth thought such thinly veiled overtures were subtle.

He *could* get her posted to a starship. Not only would it be easy, but considering her record at the Academy it would be appropriate. But should he? If anything, he was more inclined to get her a safe posting. That wasn't fair to her, and he hadn't yet taken any such action, but it was on his mind. Youth likes risk, and in his youth Picard craved it probably more than even Ensign Amarante Lebel. But could he take an action that would send her off to war? That sad dilemma was why Neela Darren eventually had to leave the *Enterprise*. Deciding life and death was difficult enough without adding a familial relationship into the equation.

"Would you join us for a late lunch, Commander?" Amarante asked, then looked up to Picard to make sure that was his wish as well.

He nodded his approval.

"Oh, please, call me Deanna."

"Deanna, then. We were going to—"

Picard stopped listening to his niece. A distant rumble drew his attention away from the conversation. It sounded like thunder, but the temporary VIP quarters Starfleet had given Picard were supposed to be soundproofed to most outside noise. And, he thought, there was no forecast for thunderstorms. He furrowed his brow and turned toward the computer terminal. That was when the rumbling turned into a howl as the ceiling cracked and the floor shook, and the walls crumbled around them.

"Enterprise to Starfleet Command, come in. This is *Enterprise."* Lieutenant Daniels looked up to Commander William Riker and shook his head despondently. "I can't get through, sir."

Riker leaned forward in the command chair. "Data? Interference from the storm?"

"Scanning." Lieutenant Commander Data leaned over his ops console. "I do not believe the storm is to blame. I am picking up steady navigational beacons from both Vulcan and Andor. Subspace communications from the Sol system seem—" he turned, looked back to Riker, his android brows raised in intrigue "—jammed at the source, sir. No clear channel on any Starfleet frequency."

Not something anyone wanted to hear at a time of war. Riker twisted back around to Daniels. "Try nonfleet frequencies, Lieutenant. Scan the commercial bands, too."

"Aye, sir." Reconfiguring his station for a frequency set not usually scanned, Daniels had to wait a moment for a full scan to complete. "Getting something now. Multiphasic transmissions, sir. Not jammed but so active it's almost a garble."

"Data? Can you make any sense of it?"

"I shall attempt to." Data's fingers moved quickly over the face of the ops console. "The strongest broadcast without waver is from commercial news agencies, sir."

Riker nodded toward the main viewer. "Put one on the screen."

Before them, the starscape warbled out of view, replaced by the charred and melted remains of Starfleet's home.

"—the scene from San Francisco today. Uncounted dead and injured at the Golden Gate Bridge park and museum, but area hospitals are overwhelmed. As well, many of the the buildings that house Starfleet Command have been completely obliterated. Communications with other Starfleet offices have been jammed, and we are unable to determine survivors at this time. The Federation News Service is reporting that recently elected Mayor T'Grell, San Francisco's first Vulcan mayor, has urged calm, and requested that both the state of California and the Federal government designate the city a disaster area. That request has been granted and national, state, and planetary agencies are coordinating with the city. Repeating our top story once again, Starbase 1 has lost all power, trapping one line of Earth defense within its confines. We have reports that the orbital defense platform protecting North America has been disabled as well, leaving this hemisphere utterly without protection from the attacks. This is Wendy Spampinato, reporting from San Francisco, Earth. Back to you, Afya."* She paused awkwardly, then felt for an unseen earpiece. *"Afya? We've lost the connection to the NewsCenter. Jeff? Jeff? I can't read my producer either. It's possible . . ."* The reporter was now choking back tears. *"I think the NewsCenter has been attacked. I'm sorry, I'm going to transfer to Los Angeles."* As the transmission broke down, the reporter could be heard fading away. *"My husband, I need to find my husband!"*

Silence enveloped the bridge until Riker stood. "Red alert," he ordered. "Mr. Daniels, continue to monitor that band for more information. Data, tactical report. Nearest Federation starships?"

Riker joined Data at the ops console.

"*Columbia* is docked within Starbase 1 itself, undergoing refit, sir." The main viewscreen shifted graphics from Starbase 1 to a starchart of their sector. "We and the *Lexington* are the closest starships to the Sol system. *Lexington* is escorting TF-12 to Starbase Midway and is within communications range despite the storm."

"What about the *Indianapolis*?"

"Also within range, sir, though at least five hours away."

Riker pivoted to the ensign at conn. "What's our ETA to Earth at maximum warp?"

Ensign Kell Perim already had that figured as a normal part of her watch procedure. "Eleven hours, sir, if we continue to go around the storm."

Shaking his head, Riker said grimly, "I don't think we have that time to waste." He pointed to Perim's console. "Adjust course to take us straight through."

As soon as he heard that order, Chief Engineer Geordi La Forge pushed off toward the port turbolift. "I'll be in engineering, sir. I can't promise maximum through an ion storm."

"Just batten down, Geordi, and give us the best you can." Riker returned to the command chair, his shoulders suddenly tense and his jaw tight. "Ensign?" Riker lowered himself uneasily into the center seat.

"Course plotted and on the screen, sir."

"Engage. Best possible speed to Earth."

Jean-Luc Picard had seen more battles than he cared to remember, yet he remembered them all. None had been waged on Earth. The dust and debris he now shook from his shoulder was not from a starship bulkhead, but from his quarters at Starfleet Command. Instinctively he reached out for those he knew to be near him when the attack had come. He pulled Deanna from the ground, helping her to her feet, and found he didn't have to help Amarante who was sweeping a thick strand of brown hair behind her ear and out of her eyes.

"An earthquake?" Amarante asked.

"None were scheduled for today, and they wouldn't have let off this much stress in any case." Picard coughed, steadied Deanna who in return tried to bolster him as well when he choked on the thick air. "We're under attack," he said, his throat feeling rough around the words. "Are you both all right?"

"Fine, sir." Deanna nodded and straightened her dress as best she could.

"Unc—Captain," Amarante corrected herself, realizing the situation was now an on-duty Starfleet event. "I'm fine, sir."

The captain jabbed at his combadge. "Picard to Command." Nothing. Communications were possibly down. "I'm going to test your communicator," he told Amarante. "Picard to Lebel."

His niece frowned. "It's not working."

He tapped the combadge again. "Picard to Starbase 1."

Again, only static crackled back.

"Damn," he whispered angrily. "Ensign, I want you to see if you can find some of your classmates. They might still be in the reception room with members of their families. See to the civilians, and then gather your class. They may be needed. Counselor, with me, please."

Amarante nodded determinedly, though he could see she was somewhat shaken.

Gutwrenched not with terror but with dismay and disdain, Picard and Deanna helped one another toward the doorway with Amarante taking the lead. All of them stepped awkwardly over broken furniture, ceiling supports that had dropped, and debris from the floor above. Picard nearly tripped trying to grasp at a tricorder he'd found near the door. Regaining his balance, he dusted the device off and thrust it in his pocket.

"We need to try to get to HQ ops. If we can," he told Deanna as Amarante headed slowly but surely down the corridor in another direction. "I think it's safe to say that operations would have been the target . . ."

"The Dominion, this far into Federation space?" From the sound of incredulity in her voice, Deanna obviously found it hard to believe.

"Not a pleasant prospect," Picard said, stepping over an exposed lighting panel that had fallen from the ceiling.

A loud rumble quaked the walls around them and dust fell as ceiling cracks spider-webbed above. "They're continuing to attack. Hitting the city." He huffed out his breath, the thick air getting to him. "How many people have died?" he rasped. "Not just in here, but outside. People who thought themselves safe."

They reached a dead end where the rubble from above was so high there was no getting around it without breaking through what was left of the ceiling above.

The captain turned back to Deanna and gripped one of her arms. "We have to assume planetary defenses are neutralized and the scale of this attack is larger than just San Francisco. That means we need to be ready to coordinate a defense if Starbase 1 and other fleet offices cannot." She nodded her understanding. "There's a transporter room two levels down. I'm going see if I can make my way there. Meet up with Amarante and I'll join you later. Care to any survivors and to the civilians."

"Aye, sir." She nodded, turning away as he released his grip.

"Find a sidearm, if you can, Commander," he called after her. "And be careful." There was no guarantee that this was just an aerial attack. Ground troops could already be swarming the HQ complex.

She turned to look at him a brief moment, and quietly said, "You too."

"I'd call them morons if they'd not been so successful." Watching the newsfeeds on the viewscreen, Captain Richard Husband watched with anguish as news cameras showed the starbase dock in which he and his ship were locked. He'd never seen Starbase 1 without power before. It was eerily dark when only lit by the sun. The picture was a surreal one.

Husband still wasn't sure exactly what enemy had made the sneak attack. Whoever they were, they'd effectively jammed Starfleet communications, but had left lower frequency commercial channels untouched. Not the first time that mistake had been made in the history of warfare, but maybe that loophole had never appeared in this enemy's experience.

The news, if it was right, spoke only of the attack on the starbase and San Francisco. If true, it was likely meant to have more a psychological impact, to terrorize the population, hoping that would weaken the Federation's resolve to defend itself. *They don't know us very well,* the captain thought.

"Lieutenant Chawla, keep monitoring commercial communications, and let me know when you can piggyback one of those transmissions in a secure way."

"Aye, sir. I should have the algorithm worked out by the time we have main power."

Main power wasn't *supposed* to be restored for another four days, but without current from Starbase 1's spacedock it was important to make a change in that schedule. The trouble was, there was only one full shift of crew on board the *Columbia.* Clark and the rest were on leave or day passes. That made it hard to work on more than a few damaged systems at a time.

Husband had to keep himself from bothering Commander Anderson and the rest of his engineering staff. Mike was having enough problems with all the captain had given him to do without needing to answer "Are we there yet?" every five minutes.

Lifting himself anxiously from the command chair, Husband made his way across the dim bridge toward the rear engineering station. To conserve energy it was shut down, but he tapped in a command to tie it in to the whole system so he could check on battery power.

"Twenty-two percent left on batteries," Husband said more to himself than anyone else, then pivoted toward the science station. "Mr. Ramon, any luck?"

Ilan Ramon shook his dark head of curly hair. "There are a million ways to break through those doors with force, but not if you want to do it without destroying that entire section and perhaps everyone in spacedock, us along with them."

"What about cutting our way out? Fine-tuned phaser beams at certain points—"

Ramon cut his captain off—something he normally would not do. "It would take more time than we likely have, and we won't have the phaser power until the mains are back online anyway, sir."

As if by omen, an increasing hum and brighter lights suggested for a moment that main power was back. But then, an instant later, everything returned to battery power. Before Husband or Ramon could do more than exchange a disappointed glance, however, power returned. They both waited—the entire bridge crew waited—looking at one another, and their now bright consoles, making sure this time the power would be maintained.

Almost startling them all, the comm crackled to life. It was Anderson. *"Sir—"*

"You don't even have to say it," Husband told him, then turned to Ramon. "Let's get to work."

"Sir?" Chawla pulled his attention toward her then motioned to the view screen. "I think you should see this."

"Get started," Husband ordered Ramon, then looked toward the main viewer.

A now familiar news broadcast filled the screen.

"—now confirmed that Starfleet has scrambled low orbit fighters to combat three unknown vessels that most surely outgun anything but a starship. Forces spread thin because of multiple war fronts, only the U.S.S. Columbia was in Earth orbit at the time of the attack, and she is reportedly locked behind the powerless spacedoors of Starbase 1's refit docks. Starfleet headquarters in the bay area is little more than a mound of rubble. Obviously orders are coming from somewhere, but that information is being kept classified, likely to avoid that base from being attacked. As I speak, we've lost contact with our offices in San Francisco and have verified that the Golden Gate Bridge and Starfleet are not the only targets in this slow, methodical attack. Both civilian populations as well as centers of infrastructure are being bombarded by plasma weapons from this unseen and unknown enemy. Casualty counts are . . . there's no way to know at this early date. The National Guard has been mobilized to shore up any possible defenses and bring all available mobile medical units to this city. FEMA has already beamed onto the scene, as has the Interstellar Red Cross/IDIC Kula'na, the joint Terran/Vulcan civilian support organization. Vulcan defense ships have been dispatched as well,

*but will not cross into the Sol system for at least another hour. Until
then, Earth sits defenseless."*

"Keep monitoring, but get it off the main screen," Husband ordered, then spun back toward Ramon. "We need to get out of
here now."

The transporter room Picard hoped to find was there, but without
power. There was a battery backup system, but circuits had been
crushed by falling debris and the captain could not fix them alone.
He made his way back to where he knew Deanna, Amarante, and
the other Academy graduates and their families would be. Along
the way he checked every door he could open for survivors, and
every communications console for power, but neither quest bore
fruit.

It was once he was reunited with Deanna and his niece that the
real work began.

Controlling and consoling the mass of graduate relatives,
Deanna was already in full counselor mode before Picard even
pulled together Amarante and her classmates and the few other
Starfleet personnel that had found their way to the lounge. Some
of those Deanna said she'd met on her way from Picard's VIP
quarters. No wonder he encountered no one on his way back. For
that reason and because most staff would either be on shift in ops
or in offices off base.

"I don't know your names," Picard said, meeting each new ensign's eyes with his own, "and I'm not sure I have time to learn
them. But those of you here, having seen to the safety of your
loved ones and the injured without panic, are already holding
yourselves well as Starfleet officers. I need you all to stay that
course." He paused in dramatic effect that only starship captains
and the finest actors possessed. "Many are likely dead. Those of us
who remain . . . need to *be* Starfleet Command."

The captain had seen more than one eager ensign in his career,
and he saw the same determination in every face that looked back

at him now. And as well a touch of fear. That was normal, and natural, and they would have to set it aside.

"Very well," Picard said. "Who here majored in communications?"

Two hands raised and one other of the young officers said, "I
did."

"You three, then. Take two others, not in your field, and get to
the surface. There's an emergency stairway two doors down that is
clear. Once outside, find *ground* transportation, as aerial may be
compromised. We don't know if this is to be a full-scale invasion
or not, but I want you out of the air. Get to the nearest intact
communications hub, and I don't care if that's governmental or
commercial. We need to know if communications are jammed lo-
cally, globally, and to what extent. If you're able to get a signal out
of the city, you're to set us up with a link to the nearest Starfleet
office."

"And if they're *also* under attack, sir?" one of them asked.

It was a good question. "If they've attacked Mexico City as
well, then try Detroit, or Houston. Then New York, Toronto, Santi-
ago, Tokyo, London, and keep expanding outward. Cover the globe
if needed. There's a reason we have offices and operations spread
over the planet. Find sidearms or phaser rifles before you go, then
head out."

"Aye." The three of them stood and quickly marched out of the
room, exchanging quick glances, Picard noticed, with those who
must have been relatives.

"Amarante," Picard called for his niece and then corrected himself to call her, "Ensign Lebel."

"Sir?" Her eyes were wide, expectant, not so much excited as
they were impatient for something to do.

He handed her the tricorder he'd taken from his quarters.
"Connections from this to main Starfleet libraries are jammed.
Modify the connections, searching for links to less secure networks. There's not enough power in this to transmit very far, but
we should be able to receive outside nets."

She nodded and almost grabbed at the tricorder. "Yes, sir."

The captain turned back to the rest of them as Amarante moved off to work. "Now, who wants to be an engineer?" A few of them nodded. "You'll get your chance. You." He pointed to one of them. "Find a working computer that has local storage. Get me detailed plans of the HQ complex. You'll know what to look for. Meet us back in the transporter room two levels below."

The one at whom Picard pointed moved off. "On it, sir."

They were holding up well. They were young, and they graduated from Starfleet Academy in a time of war. They thought they knew what to expect. They were wrong, because war wasn't something that was so easily related in a class—it had to be, sadly, experienced. Their real training began now.

"The rest of you new engineers will join me in the transporter room. All others, comb as much of the building as you can for survivors. Bring them here, and then Counselor Troi will bring you all to the transporter room as well. Understood?"

Most of them nodded, and a few said, "Aye, sir." The most eager ones added an extra "Aye."

Picard hoped that enthusiastic attitude would serve them all well. "Make it so."

Enterprise was storm-tossed, thrust from side to side as the ion storm wreaked havoc with its warp field. Support struts creaked and structural integrity field generators sizzled with overloads as the deckplates seemed to shimmy beneath Riker's feet.

"We're losing number two shield, sir." Daniels's voice was stressed, but Riker himself wasn't as calm as a sleeping puppy.

Riker had left a comm connection open to engineering. "Geordi, number two shield?"

"Generators are weakening, Commander. Ionic disruption in the storms is messing up our systems, and more power is needed to maintain a stable warp field."

"We can't lose the shields, Mr. La Forge."

"I'm aware of that, sir."

And Riker knew that, and regretted stating something so self-evident. "Do your best, Geordi."

Data turned slightly, catching Riker's gaze. "Should we lose the shields, deflector systems will be overwhelmed and we will be torn apart, sir."

Riker sighed deeply. "Data, I would sincerely appreciate if you'd turn off your obvious chip."

Because Data now actually had a working emotion chip he rarely turned off anymore, Data managed a somewhat wry smile. "Sorry, sir."

"How much longer, Ilan?" Captain Husband was awash in tension.

"I'd say we're about half done, sir," Ramon said, adjusting the phaser controls.

"Any way to speed it up?"

"This is as fast as it gets."

Columbia was a coiled snake, spitting slow phaser fire in a controlled beam when she wanted to be slinging photon torpedoes at a brazen enemy.

"You know what would help?" Ramon offered suddenly.

His captain hovered over him with intent. "Tell me."

"A tractor beam," Ramon said, wagging a finger at the doors on the main viewer. "To pull from the other side."

"I don't understand," Husband admitted. "Why can't we just push on this side?"

"Our phasers would disrupt the tractor. If someone could pull as we're cutting away the inner door supports, the doors would be flung right off."

Nodding, the captain moved toward the tactical station. "We need some co-ordination. Chawla?"

"Sir?"

"Get on the K band."

★   ★   ★

"Where is that coming from?" Amarante asked of the explosions in the distance.

"The city," one of the other Academy graduates said. "They're attacking the city."

"This makes no sense," someone else muttered.

"How did they get past all our defenses?"

"A few ways, I'd guess," Amarante offered, and Picard listened with some interest to her theories. "First, notice that they're using conventional and rather weak plasma weapons. More high energy phasers or photon torpedoes would have been impossible to hide from scans at checkpoints. And I'll assume they somehow made it past, or disabled, or destroyed, planetary defenses."

Exchanging a long glance with Deanna as they all worked on the transporter circuits, Picard was fascinated by how spot-on Amarante was in her analysis.

"Also," she continued, "a slow, continuous attack makes people feel as if it may never end. I don't think this is an attack on anything more than our will to continue the war."

"It won't work."

"Indeed it won't," Picard agreed with whichever ensign spoke.

"She's remarkable," Deanna whispered to him as they closed the access panel they'd been working under.

"She is. But—" Another explosion, closer, rattled the walls as well as a few of the youngsters within them. Even Amarante seemed a bit spooked. "There's much left to do and we shall see if she's up to it," Picard added.

"Do you have an equal level of skepticism in the other graduates?"

"Of course."

Deanna accepted that. "All right."

"I tried to get to ops on my way to meet you and the others," Picard told her in a more hushed tone.

"How far did you get?"

"Quite far," he said, holding out his hand for a scanner from the toolbox. "The ops level is destroyed."

"Admiral Ling?" She handed him one item, then readied another.

The captain shook his head. "I doubt anyone survived. The tricorder I gave to Amarante . . . I'd used it to scan for life signs. There were none."

Deanna paused a moment, holding in what in a less experienced officer might have been a gasp. "Then why are we working on the transporter? I assumed you wanted to beam survivors out of ops or . . ."

"I don't remember the exact year," Picard began quietly, "but it was after a similar attack on the Earth. It may even have been before the founding of the Federation. A bunker was built deep below here, protected from attack, protected from earthquake, protected from all access but transporter and one elevator. Now, I don't know where that lift shaft is, which is why I'm hoping we can get schematics of the building. But if we can't, this is our way down there."

"And what's down there?"

"Duplicate systems from ops."

"Modern? This has been maintained?"

"It's supposed to be. It certainly was when I graduated from the Academy." Interlocking one conduit to another, Picard finished the second connection he need to. He also didn't remind Deanna that his Academy graduation was almost five decades ago. "Before being transferred to Starbase Earhart I did some duty here at Command and was given a tour. That's the last time I saw it, but it should be good enough. From there we'll be able to coordinate with others, and get them information about the attack."

"Won't communications still be jammed?"

"From the bunkers below, all outgoing communications are physical land lines protected by the Earth's crust itself."

Amarante approached and handed Picard his tricorder. "Captain, I can access both the globalnet and if I could get more power to this, I think I could link into Marsnet as well."

"This will do," Picard said, taking the device.

"May I ask, sir, what you're looking for?" Amarante was never afraid to ask a question.

"Nonstandard communications. If Starfleet frequencies are being jammed, there's an alternative." After making a few adjustments to the scanning range, Picard handed the tricorder back to her. "Monitor all sub-bands on every commercial channel."

"Ah, of course. Starfleet will piggyback communications on the commercial nets."

"If they can," Picard said. "We won't be able to communicate back with that, but—"

Another ensign, a Bolian, stepped over from the main transporter console. "Sir, I think we've got it now."

"Battery power to the transporter?" the captain asked.

"Yes, sir."

Picard nodded his approval and felt his face flush with the fancy that came with taking more aggressive action. "Excellent, Ensign. I don't trust this structure. Bring all survivors here for transport."

"Arrival at outer Sol system in thirty-four seconds, sir," Data reported.

Riker gripped the arms of the command chair, more for something physical to do than because of nervous tension. "Maintain warp speed until the moon, then slow to one half impulse power."

"Until the moon, sir?" Perim asked.

"We're not wasting time with an impulse approach from Jupiter, Ensign."

"Aye, sir."

"Twenty seconds now," Data said.

"Tactical, stand by on all weapons."

Daniels was practically riveted to his console. "Standing by."

Picard nearly bounded off the transporter dais while still materializing, and as soon as his feet touched the floor, lights automatically snapped on. He crooked his hand over his shoulder at Amarante. "See to the safety of all personnel. There should be a medical center for anyone injured."

"I've been trained as a medic, sir," one of her classmates said.

The captain nodded. "You're my chief medical officer, then. Go."

"Aye, sir!"

"Counselor, with me, please."

As they strode into main complex, the air was suddenly light with freshly created oxygen.

"Computer, this is Captain Jean-Luc Picard, commanding the *U.S.S. Enterprise.* I am assuming command of Starfleet Command Headquarters, authorization Picard-Gamma-two-seven-three, Sigma-nine-nine."

"Picard, Captain Jean-Luc. Identity recognized, authority granted."

"Computer, transfer Starfleet HQ Command to Bunker SF-Zero-One."

"Transferred." Console after console around a large control center semicircle lit up and chirped to life.

Soon after Deanna and Picard slid into two of the more central chairs, Amarante entered. "Sir, I'm picking something up on the K band."

"Let me see." Picard looked down at the tricorder, reading the frequency from it, then pivoted toward the communications console. "Weak, but there." He punched in the frequency and tried to boost reception as best he could. Once he saw the ID coded into the transmission, he turned to Deanna. "We're not alone."

"Sir, I've got Starfleet Command. Audio only."

Captain Husband expectantly jumped down to his command chair. "Put it on the speaker."

"—read you, Columbia. *Come in."*

"This is Husband on the *Columbia.* Go ahead, Command."

"This is Picard, on coded channel 46-A, Captain."

Husband nodded. "Acknowledged, Captain. I read you on that channel."

"Good to hear your voice, Rick. We'd thought the worst, down here. What is your status?"

"We're without main power, and even if we could restore that, the spacedoors are closed and would need to be pulled open from the outside. I'm sure we couldn't cut through them."

"We have no one to spare to help, Captain. There are three ships up there, attacking the city. That's our main concern."

Smiling, Husband let himself relax just a bit and he leaned back in the command chair. "Wish we could help, Jean-Luc. I guess we'll have to wait this one out. I could use a five-minute nap anyway."

"Acknowledged, Captain. We'll be in touch. Picard out."

"He's going to take a nap?" Amarante was indignant and incredulous. "Is he insane?"

"Ensign," Deanna admonished. "You're speaking of a starship captain!"

Picard didn't have time to explain and not work at the same time, so he merely reminded his niece of that which she should already know. "Regulation 46-A, Ensign. If you've not remembered that one I recommend you look it up."

"I—" She pulled in a deep sigh. "I'm sorry. Of course. I just was listening so closely—"

The captain smiled. "So closely that you didn't hear everything that was said. That's why you're an ensign, and not a captain."

"Yes, sir." He didn't mean to, but by her expression one might have thought Picard had stepped on her kitten.

She'd have to get over it fast. "Now, we have less than five minutes to help pull the doors off Starbase 1."

"Hold off. Full stop. Keep us behind the moon." Riker spun a small monitor toward the captain's chair and studied the code for himself. "You're sure that's from the captain?"

Daniels half shrugged. "As sure as I can be, sir."

Riker looked up toward ops. "Data?"

The android nodded, his brown hair looking more orange under the bright red-alert lighting. "It is not coded, but he does mention—"

"I see that," Riker said. "Clever. You know what's strange? Those three ships should have noticed our entry into the system, but they're maintaining their attack on the city and ignoring us."

"Maybe they missed it?" Daniels asked.

Riker shook his head. "Or maybe there's a reason they're not worried about us."

"I can't get to planetary sensors," Deanna called from one of the stations. It was the second one she'd moved to as she quickly set up more and more ensigns to monitor certain consoles for the captain.

What had been distant rumbles above them now grew louder.

"They're attacking above us," Picard mumbled. "Trying to get through to the bunker. I'd say they figured out where we are."

"Can they get through?" Amarante asked.

"Eventually, but as soon as we beamed down here, shielding clicked on. They can't transport down here, and they can raze a crater above us but—"

Another explosion, closer, and the lights and console power browned out for only a split second.

"Or, perhaps they're more tenacious than I thought." Picard stood. "We have a contingency if they get through the shields. For now, however, we need to get sensors up."

"I don't see how, sir," one of the ensigns, the taller one who looked to be a bit Vulcan, said. "They are jamming all sensor frequencies."

"You were monitoring news reports," Picard said to his niece, as he thumbed his chin thoughtfully. "Did they have visual channels from satellites?"

She nodded slowly, seeming to search her memory. "I think so."

"Let's bring that up."

Beginning to work like an actual team, Amarante and her class-mates functioned as a more cohesive unit than just twenty minutes before, when all this had begun. "I've got a picture of Starbase 1, Captain."

"One minute until the *Enterprise* makes her move," Picard said, checking the monitor and then a chronometer. "And as a little dis-traction . . ." He called up a console that would use the K band and opened a channel to the moon. "Lunar Base 3, this is Picard, are you ready?"

"Ready when you are, sir."

"Look sharp, and wait for *Enterprise.*"

"Now!"

The *Enterprise* shot out from behind the moon, pushing quickly toward Starbase 1.

"The three enemy vessels are in low orbit, continuing to attack the city." Data's hands were a flurry over the ops console. His fin-gers were practically a blur as Starbase 1 grew large on the main viewscreen.

"Several runabouts have been launched from the moon and—" Daniels's voice choked. "Sir! DP-7 is firing on the runabouts."

High in his chest Riker felt a heavy lump. There was little he could do to help them now. "Follow the plan, Data. Maintain course, Ensign."

"Tractor beam ready," Data said.

"Engage."

Kalpana Chawla's hands were doing their own dance across her console. "Short range sensors show *Enterprise* on the other side of the space doors, sir."

"Ramon?" Husband leaned forward, willing his ship forward with him.

"We're ready," Ramon called.

"Go!"

With a crackle of electric flame and a wrench they could neither hear nor feel, the large space doors of Starbase 1 fell forward and swung away.

Husband was ready for *Columbia* to move. "McCool?"

"Course set."

"All ahead full," the captain ordered. Unable to sit, he was at Willie McCool's back, gripping onto the headrest of the pilot's chair. "Come about once we're clear."

"Captain," Chawla called, "the runabouts are drifting, powerless."

"Survivors?" Husband asked, his upper body twisted toward tactical.

Chawla shook her head in dismay, her lips pressed into a thin line. "Minimal life signs."

The captain tapped his combadge. "Transporter room, stand by to beam casualties directly to sickbay. Bridge to Dr. Brown. Stand by with emergency medical teams."

"Standing by."

Before Husband could bark another order, high-powered phasers, stronger than any starship could have mustered, pounded into *Columbia's* underbelly from the DP-7 platform.

The captain nearly lost his footing as he jabbed at his combadge again. "Mike, we need more power for the shields."

Anderson replied after too long a pause. *"We weren't fully repaired, sir. We got some major coolant leaks here and not enough staff. Relays to the shield generators are overheating."*

"Mike, work with me, buddy."

Sighing, as all chief engineers were wont to do with their captains, Mike Anderson said, *"We'll do our best, sir."*

"Columbia is venting plasma, sir."

"Advise them to back off." Frustrated by what he saw on the

tactical display, Riker shoved the side monitor away from his view. "We need to do the same, lock on torpedoes when out of range of fire from the platform."

When they were far enough back, and *Enterprise* fired her white-hot quantum torpedoes, they never made it to target. Intercepting fire from the defense platform detonated the munitions well before Earth orbit.

"We have to go in," Riker said, his voice firm and taut. "We'll distract the platform while *Columbia* attacks the three ships."

"Sir," Data said, too busy to turn away from his console. "The platform can handle contact with several ships—"

"What did I say about that obvious chip, Data?"

"I do not actually *have* such a chip, sir."

I know, Data, Riker thought, and that this time he didn't get the joke could mean Data had turned off his emotion chip, perhaps to give himself a better edge. They'd need it.

"Evasive pattern zeta-three-three," Riker ordered. "Engage."

"Thanks, Fahim. An unexpected turn of events, as the Federation Starship Enterprise *surprisingly returned to the system, hours ahead of schedule. Our lunar office brings you these images, a UPI exclusive, from the battle playing out above Earth orbit. Here you see several small Federation craft destroyed by the North American defense platform as* Enterprise *seems to hover near Starbase 1. Then, quickly, the* U.S.S. Columbia *joins the* Enterprise *in what we believe was meant to be an attack on the three vessels firing on San Francisco. But our own defensive platform has somehow been turned against us, its massive firepower trying to pull our starships from the sky."*

"Search all frequencies for one with activity," Picard ordered. "Someone is controlling that platform remotely."

"Nothing, sir. However . . ." Amarante paused. She wanted to be sure, obviously, but Picard didn't have time to wait for insecurity.

"Ensign, report!"

Startled a bit, she did. "It's possible the platform is the source of all the frequency jamming."

Picard pondered that a moment, then pointed to one of the ensigns monitoring ops itself. "Transfer all power to the transporter room."

"All *available* power?" the young man asked.

"Negative. *All* power. Now."

The captain turned toward the emergency transporter, calling for Deanna first, than deciding to leave her in charge. "Commander, you have the conn. Ensign Lebel, with me."

Once in the transporter room, Amarante admitted what she wouldn't have among her classmates. "I don't understand."

"Someone is on that platform," Picard told her as he furiously programmed coordinates into the transporter controls.

"I thought it was constructed with materials resistant to beaming."

"It is. Which is why I'll need all power."

Taken aback, Amarante first whispered, "No," and then spoke more clearly. "We're putting it all through the transporter? It will blow the buffers and kill you."

"You're going to bypass the buffers entirely," he told her, stepping up to the transporter dias as he set his hand phaser and checked its charge.

"And what happens if I can't get you through to the platform? Without the buffers you'd be gone."

Standing on the transporter pad, Picard pursed his lips a moment, pushed out a quick breath, then spoke in his best firm yet caring tone. "Amarante, there are hazards to being a Starfleet officer, I shouldn't need to tell you that. We take them, when necessary, because to not do so risks more. There are times—often in this career—when inaction is worse than action, no matter the danger."

She looked down at the console, then back up at him. "We have full power available. Buffers are offline."

"Energize."

She hesitated. "Uncle—"

"Give my best to your aunt," Picard said, and brought his phaser up to an aiming position. "Now energize."

Before Picard had even fully dematerialized he was beginning to thumb the trigger on his phaser if need be. "Don't move."

Obviously startled, the thin man in the tight console smiled a whispy smile and checked his watch. "I actually expected someone at least five minutes ago."

"Step away from the console," Picard ordered.

"Oh, I'll do better than that. I'll—"

Before the tall man could move more than a centimeter, the captain fired his phaser, set to heavy stun, and the alien collapsed into a gangly heap.

What looked to be a small palm-disruptor fell from the man's hand, and Picard quickly snapped it up and pocketed it.

"I don't really have time for a chat," the captain said dryly as he spied all the modifications that had been made to give the intruder control over the platform. "I don't have time to undo all this neatly, either." Firing again, the internal panel flashed into a storm of electrical flame. Then power was gone from the entire platform and only the light of sizzling circuits lit the alcove in which Picard stood.

But, at least, the frequency jamming should be gone.

He tapped at his combadge. "Picard to *Enterprise.*"

"Enterprise, Riker here."

"I've secured DP-7. Go, Will."

Grinning at his captain's ingenuity once again, Riker pointed toward Perim. "All ahead full, two-one-zero mark five."

"All ahead full."

"Mr. Daniels, lock on and fire!"

Twisting one way, then another, *Enterprise* swooped down, an angry eagle spitting raw power from its maw. Hot bars of phaser fire blasted through the nearest enemy vessel and the ship's hull seemed to melt and congeal again, then disappeared to reveal a different configuration underneath. No one thought they were actually Tellarite freighters, but this certainly proved it.

Columbia dove into the fight, attacking both of the other enemy ships, white torpedo bulbs pounding into each vessel, disrupting the holographic projectors that cloaked their true design as well.

"Breen ships, sir," Daniels said.

Riker nodded grimly. "Maintain fire."

The Breen warships turned away too slowly, and their armaments were for destroying a city, not doing battle against two starships. As *Enterprise* pummeled the first ship with quantum torpedoes and phaser flame, *Columbia* added a few shots as it remaneuvered for another go at the last two.

The first vessel caved in on itself, then thrust forward in a massive explosion that bulldozed out, pushing away her two sister ships as they drifted, listlessly disabled.

Beamed right to his bridge from the now useless defense platform, Captain Jean-Luc Picard nodded to Riker and slowly, somberly lowered himself into his command chair.

Space calmed as both *Enterprise* and *Columbia* fell into quiet orbit. Below, Riker thought sadly, there were wounds to tend, and honored dead to bury.

"In a statement broadcast via subspace but not personally delivered today, the Breen ambassador to the Federation Council declared that official diplomatic associations with all Federation members would be restricted and that the Breen were formally entering into an alliance with the Dominion. There was no comment on the Breen attack on the Earth yesterday, but unofficial channels suggest the Breen government is not denying responsibility. Federation President Min Zife this morning, at an impromptu press conference in Paris, said the Breen statement was a very loud, aggressive threat to the Federation and interstellar peace. The Coun-

cil's office said President Zife would be joining the United Earth Prime Minister and the President of the United States in touring the battle-ravaged city of San Francisco. Final casualty counts are still not determined, but early and unofficial sensor reports put injuries in the millions, and deaths in the hundreds of thousands. We'll have more on this, and the disturbing reports of increased Breen activity near Chin'toka, later in this hour."

"Captain?" Deanna Troi touched his arm and Picard slowly turned his gaze away from the San Francisco sky. The fires were out, more quickly than he thought they'd be. For some reason he had hoped the day would be overcast, or at least hazy. The sun was too bright for an occasion as unpleasant as a funeral.

"Counselor." He acknowledged her with a nod, glanced briefly back at Amarante and the other officers gathered at the ceremony, then turned back away.

Deanna came up along side him and also watched the sky.

"This is a very old cemetery," Picard said softly. "The first where any Starfleet officer or noncom was buried after the Federation was founded."

She nodded. "Admiral Ling was a friend?"

"He was," Picard said. "Not that being one matters so much. There's enough death in this city today to mourn without knowing each name or touching each life."

"If not for you, there would have been more dead to mourn." He took little comfort in her words and said nothing. "It's true," she told him finally.

"Never should numbers matter less than when talking about death, and yet never do numbers matter more."

"Who said that?" she asked.

"I just did. That's why it's hardly profound." He followed a seagull as it floated almost aimlessly toward the bay, its large white wings flashing against the sapphire sky.

Deanna smiled and gave his elbow a squeeze. "You're very hard on yourself."

Amarante came up beside them, and Deanna greeted her warmly, then left the two of them alone.

Picard turned to her, and was surprised when Amarante hugged him with such strength that he nearly lost his breath. "Well—" He returned the hug as best he could. Not practiced in such embraces, he felt a bit awkward.

She released him and took a half step back. "I'd always felt as if I knew you from our correspondence, but . . ." She looked up at him, her hazel eyes very bright and a bit moist. "I respect you a great deal, and . . . love you very much."

Looking up only a moment, Picard noticed Deanna was standing by a far tree, trying unsuccessfully not to watch him and Amarante. If she wasn't within earshot, she was certainly within the range of his emotions.

"I have been very impressed with your courage and strength," he told his niece, and then realized he'd sounded more like a professor complimenting an Academy student than an uncle showing the true affection he'd come to feel for his niece. But it was also true that he *was* impressed with how she'd handled the situation into which she'd been thrust. It was why he'd decided to see she got her starship assignment. "Amarante . . ." he leaned down, almost telling her he loved her as well, but he pulled back at the last moment. "I can talk to the captain of the *Lexington* if you'd like," he said finally. "See if she needs an able ensign, and—"

"Oh," Amarante interrupted, bringing a hand to her lips in surprise. "Didn't I tell you? I asked for duty here."

"Here?"

"Starfleet Command needs to be rebuilt," she said. "And after seeing how much needs to be done here and at the starbase," she leaned forward and whispered, "not to mention the defense platform you destroyed . . ."

Impulsively, Jean-Luc Picard embraced his niece again, this time of his own volition. "I do believe you're dismissed, Ensign. Don't make me have this insubordination put on your record."

She giggled and gave him another tight squeeze.

"I love you too," he whispered finally, so low he wasn't sure even she heard him.

Stepping away again, Amarante wiped a small tear from one eye and nodded a salute at her uncle. "I'd like to still keep in touch, sir."

"You're under orders to do so, Ensign."

"Aye aye, sir," she said, and added, "Thank you, Captain-Uncle," as she moved toward the transport that would take her back to the temporary buildings being used for Starfleet Command.

As Picard walked toward Deanna to join her at the transport point, he knew she had overheard more than he'd have liked. She greeted him with a very bright grin. "Softie," she murmured.

"Belay that," he grumbled, then tapped his combadge. "Picard to *Enterprise*. Two to beam up."

As they dematerialized and San Francisco disappeared before them, Picard was almost sure he heard Deanna's voice. "Aye aye, Captain-Uncle."

Safe Harbors

Howard Weinstein

War correspondence: This story takes place just prior to "The Changing Face of Evil."

Howard Weinstein

It's been thirty years since Howard Weinstein sold his first story at age nineteen ("The Pirates of Orion," an episode of the animated *Star Trek* series in 1974). Since then, his varied credits include six *Star Trek* novels and sixty *Trek* comics. Howard's last *Star Trek* comic work was *Enter the Wolves*, a WildStorm special issue coscripted with Ann Crispin, from Ann's story about the lifelong conflict between Spock and Sarek. His most recent book is *Puppy Kisses Are Good for the Soul and Other Important Lessons You and Your Dog Can Teach Each Other*, the nonfiction account of his fifteen-year relationship with his wonderful Welsh Corgi, Mail Order Annie. It's filled with funny and heartwarming tales of life with Annie, and the lessons she had to teach about dogs, humans, life, and love. A lifelong baseball fan, Howard had the pleasure of writing a biography of his childhood hero, Yankees star Mickey Mantle. Howard's other main occupation these days is Day-One Dog Training. He calls himself a "doggie social worker" and enjoys using Annie's valuable lessons to help dogs and humans have the best possible life together.

McCoy . . . personal log . . . Stardate 52603.2.

Everything that happened was so real. But it wasn't.

But it *was*.

It began with the loudest crash of thunder I've ever heard. When it hit, I practically fell out of bed. The clock said 2:49. A heartbeat later, I knew it wasn't thunder at all, when a chain of bone-rattling booms rolled across San Francisco.

Way back in medical school, I learned the hard way that emergencies don't wait. Over a century later, it's still second nature for me to wake up in a flash. So when those explosions shook the rafters, I threw back the covers, and rushed to the window.

"Blinds—open!" I called out. The opaque layer embedded in the glass took a few seconds to clear completely, but I could already see the hellish glare of flames leaping from Starfleet Headquarters across the promenade from my apartment tower. Dear God almighty.

I flinched as a squadron of alien fighters screamed through the dark smoke billowing from the ruins, cannons blasting as they swept across the skyline . . .

Somehow, next thing I knew, I was down there, right on the promenade. That was such a beautiful space, with the reflecting pool and trees shading the paths. That very afternoon, that perfect afternoon, I'd had my lunch there, and that sun felt so good and warm. Now, in the middle of the night, I was there again, dodging debris, choking on ash, racing across in the flicker of fires burning all around. Other people rushed away from the Starfleet building, trying to escape. And there I was, plunging toward it, like I was being pulled by a magnet.

And then I was inside. Twisted metal, railings and girders and beams, and shattered glass everywhere, crunching under my feet with every step. And the fires! I've never felt anything so hot. I heard the screams of the dying as I stepped over the dead. At first, it was just a few voices, then ten, then a hundred or a thousand . . . I couldn't even tell. And there wasn't any time to care. In all that noise and heat, I homed in on two voices I'll always hear inside my head, as long as I live. Finding them was all that mattered. God knows how I knew where they were.

But then I saw their blistered, bloody faces, caught in the maze of buckled steel and tangled wires. I had to shout over the sounds of the people and the building, all dying. "Jim! Spock! Hang on!" I tried to fight my way through the flames to reach them. There was no way they could reach me. They were trapped, their bodies broken and pinned by all that rubble.

Then I felt the ground shiver, like an old subway was running right underneath me. The shiver became a rumble, and then a roar. And I looked up, and the whole building was coming down, collapsing on us. The noise drowned out everything else, except Jim shouting out my name, and then Spock moaning. And I didn't know whether to run or to pray. I tried to turn, but my foot got caught and I fell. And I screamed, because I didn't know what else to do. . . .

"McCoy . . . *McCoy!*" It was a different voice yelling my name, louder than the scream in my own head. I felt hands, strong hands, shaking me. Lifting me. I opened my eyes and I was looking into *Scotty's* face. *Where the hell did he come from?* He looked so worried. But the heat from the fires was gone. In fact, my clothes were drenched in cold sweat and I was getting damned chilly.

"What—? Scotty?! Where are we?"

"You're on the *Hudson.*" There was something about that brogue that made me start feeling better, safer. Maybe it's knowing that Scotty can fix pretty much anything. After all these years, I know this: if I had to be stuck in a leaky rowboat in the middle of the ocean, there's nobody I'd rather be stuck *with* than Scotty.

I looked around, trying to get myself oriented. I wasn't on Earth—or on fire, thank God. I was in a cramped room. A ship's cabin? When I tried to talk, my voice was shaking, kind of like the rest of me. It's fair to say I wasn't exactly firing on all thrusters. "On the . . . the what? The *Hudson?*"

"Aye. She's a runabout," Scotty said. "You were takin' a nap and y'must've had some nasty nightmare. Y'fell right outta your bunk."

My legs felt all rubbery. Scotty helped me sit back on the bed. "Where are Spock . . . and Jim?"

He looked at me like I was crazy. "Spock? Still on bloody Romulus. And Jim's been gone for eighty years."

Nothing made any sense. I had this dim memory of hearing about an accident, on the *Enterprise*-B, a long time ago. Jim—lost? But my brain couldn't let go of what I was sure I'd just seen. "Eighty years? But . . . they were just here . . . or, I was there."

"Where?"

"San Francisco. Starfleet Headquarters. We were under attack! Earth . . . Earth was under attack . . . by the Dominion. But . . ." I stared at Scotty's face. The wrinkles around his eyes, the silver hair. "When did you get so old?"

Then those eyes of his crinkled and he chuckled. "You think *I'm* old? Have you looked at yourself lately?"

I was still pretty wobbly, so he gripped my elbow and helped me over to a little alcove with a sink and a mirror. And I leaned forward and saw a white-haired creature with sags, bags and jowls staring back. I looked older than the mountains, with twice as much dust. "Good God, I must be a hundred and fifty."

"Close, but not quite," Scotty said. "Are y'sure you're all right?"

I took a deep breath and straightened up, trying to summon up a little dignity. "All right? At my age, I'm lucky to be breathing."

By the time we made our way back to the little mess table and food replicators in the aft cabin, I'd pretty much recovered my senses. Still wasn't too happy about being so goddamned old—but old is better than dead. Scotty got us two mugs of coffee and we sat down. I tried to tell him how real that nightmare felt. "The explosions . . . heat like a blast furnace . . . the stench. Like the whole city was burning. And Jim and Spock . . . and I couldn't get to them." I closed my eyes, hoping the image would disappear, but I pretty much knew it was seared into my brain forever. "Maybe I'll just stay awake from now on."

"After drinkin' coffee this strong, y'might have no choice in the matter."

"Scotty, what if the Dominion really does attack Earth?"

"What—just because y'had a dream? All of a sudden, you're psychic?" Scotty took a donut from a plate on the table. "There's no place in the galaxy as well defended as Earth. Starfleet's seen to that."

"Have they? I guess. But we've never been up against anything like this Dominion. What kind of monsters would unleash something like that nasty virus—it killed dozens of Vulcans, and almost took that damned Bajoran space station before we found a cure. And that's just the tip of the iceberg."

"Aye, but we're still here, aren't we?"

"For now." Then, out of the blue, I remembered something I told Spock once, on some godforsaken planet. Omega IV, I think. Christ, these days I can't remember by dinnertime what I had for breakfast. But *that* I could remember. "Remember Omega IV, when Jim was about to fight that crazy captain? What was it—Tracey, that was his name, mad as a hatter. A fight to the death. And I told Spock that evil usually triumphs, unless good is *very, very careful.* What if Starfleet's not careful enough?"

"When we get back, you can tell 'em that."

"I'd give anything to go back to the good old days," I said, "when all we had to worry about were Klingons and Romulans."

"Aye. They may've been devils, but at least they were somethin' like us. But these shapeshifters, and genetically engineered Jem'Hadar—" Before Scotty could complete his thought, an alarm sounded.

"Engineering alert," the computer said, in that damned calm voice.

Scotty swore under his breath and got up fast. I guess engineers also learn that emergencies can't wait. "I was hopin' she'd hold together before—"

"Before what? What is it?" I hobbled to my feet and followed him to the midship engineering compartment.

"There was a variance in the plasma injector sequence. When it misfires, it can destabilize the whole warp field. For the last two hours, while you've been havin' nightmares, I've been tryin' to keep these engines runnin' long enough to get us home."

As usual, I didn't know exactly what he was talking about, but I caught enough of it to give me a good case of the jitters. "Are you telling me Starfleet sent us gallivanting across the galaxy, inspecting field hospitals and repair bases, in a bucket of bolts?"

Scotty blew out a long, tired sigh. "Let's just say this old girl's way overdue for an overhaul."

"How overdue, *Captain* Scott?!"

"There's a shortage of ships, *Admiral* McCoy. You know that."

I did know—I just didn't want to think about what that meant about our ship. He opened an access panel and frowned as he checked diagnostic grids and graphs on the little computer screen next to the glowing ship's guts inside there. "Well? How bad is it?" I asked.

"The variance started out around two percent off normal performance."

My eyebrows went up with relief. "Two percent? That doesn't seem like much."

"Aye, not if she held at that," Scotty said as his fingers tapped the keypad. The computer screen kept displaying new data, too fast for me to make any sense out of it. "Any variance over ten percent and we'll have to drop out o' warp."

"So what's it at now?"

"Computer, status report."

"Injector misfire variance now at nine-point-nine-three-five percent, and increasing at a variable rate."

"That tears it. Computer, initiate warp-drive shutdown."

"You mean we'll have to go to impulse power? We could *row* home faster than that!"

With another sigh, he replaced the access panel, and we went back to the cockpit. "We'll not be goin' home. Not just yet."

Just what I wanted to hear. "Then where the hell *are* we going?"

"To find the nearest repair station."

The search turned out to be brief, and didn't turn up many choices. At top sublight speed, the only repair facility within two days of where we were limping along turned out to be run by the Bakrii, a reclusive species who'd had the gall to turn down four invitations to join the Federation. Now, Starfleet background reports tend to be pretty bland documents, but whoever approved this particular dossier let a little bite slip in there. Despite the fact that they'd benefited mightily from the peace, security, and free trade afforded them by Federation military power, the Bakrii government had made it damned clear that they preferred to remain neutral during the war against the Dominion.

Knowing that, neither of us figured on a warm welcome when Scotty eased the *Hudson* down at the Bakrii shipyard on a northern continent. But their reception was even chillier than we expected.

While Scotty shut down and secured ship's systems, I took a good look out the window. From what I could see, the Bakrii spaceport looked almost as long past its prime as I did. Scotty had set the *Hudson* down at the open end of a massive horseshoe-shaped complex, with ten huge hangars, each big enough to accommodate four or five ships the size of the runabout. But most of the hangars were empty, with crews at work in only three of them. One other ship was being lowered beneath ground level on an elevator platform, presumably to subterranean facilities. The main horseshoe structure was patched and shabby, with more than a few broken and boarded windows. The weather looked as bleak as the outpost itself, cold and windy, with an iron-gray overcast shrouding a dim sun. I opened a storage compartment, pulled out a pair of jackets and tossed one to Scotty. "Remind me to defrost in Hawaii when we get back."

"Let's hope the Bakrii'll help us get there sooner rather than later."

Just then, I looked outside again and saw a dozen armed guards trotting double-time out of a bunker not far from the landing pad, and surrounding the runabout. "Not exactly a brass band out there. Guns pointing at us before we so much as say howdy is generally not a good sign."

Scotty popped the hatch. As we climbed out, a biting wind hit us right in the face. And the way the circle of guards leveled their rifles at our chests wasn't terribly comforting either. I've never seen a Bakrii before, but they all had characteristic rough wrinkles and folds around their facial features, kind of like elephant skin, and I wondered if it made all their expressions look grave. Then one older Bakrii man in a uniform cut through their line and came toward us, and I didn't doubt for a second the expression on *his* face—about as friendly as your average batch of fire ants.

He strode over as fast as he could, as if he didn't want us taking even a step away from the runabout. "Starfleet ships," he barked, "are not welcome here."

Scotty narrowed his eyes. "Captain Montgomery Scott, sir. This is Admiral Leonard McCoy. We don't plan on settin' up housekeepin'. Just here for emergency repairs. You are listed as a repair station, are you not, Mister—?"

"Vuko. Supervisor. Yes, we are a repair station, but—"

"Then give us a hand, Mr. Vuko," Scotty said, "and we'll be outta your way before y'know it."

Vuko pursed his lips, and the folds above his brow nearly obscured his amber eyes. "Your presence is a delicate matter, Captain Scott. Dominion ships have been sighted in the sector. We don't want or need any trouble."

That made me hopping mad. "Trouble? Starfleet's kept the peace for decades, allowing you Bakrii to go about your business. You'd think you'd actually have some idea who the enemy is!"

"We have no enemies, Admiral. That's the point of neutrality. In that spirit, we will extend the use of our port to you." He turned toward a deferential younger Bakrii woman who'd slipped up behind him so quietly I hadn't even noticed. "Deputy Supervisor Mezta here will assist you in getting your ship repaired and away with all possible haste. You should be leaving in no more than three hours." With a sort of subtle precision, like they were doing an old dance step, the Bakrii woman moved aside just enough for Vuko to scuttle past her before we could argue with him.

I glanced at this Mezta's face, trying to get a feel for how much she agreed with her boss. Unfortunately, she was either very good at hiding how she felt or had nothing to hide. She looked like one of those people who didn't doubt for a second the job she was told to do. All business. Too bad for us.

"Captain Scott," she said, "we will have your ship moved to Bay Five. Then I will review all your relevant data, and assign a repair crew to work with you. As you can see, we're not that busy just now. I hope we'll be able to help you get your repairs done before you have to depart."

The picture of efficiency, Mezta didn't even wait for Scotty's answer. She went right to delivering her orders through her wrist communicator. Almost immediately, a crane lowered its boom from the roof of the building, stopping directly above the *Hudson*.

A tractor beam locked on, lifted the runabout and moved it into Bay Five, lowered the ship to the floor, released it and retracted.

Always the gentleman, Scotty waved Mezta toward the *Hudson*'s open hatch first. We followed her in. While they went directly to the engineering compartment, I went to the cockpit. They hardly needed me back there, and I wanted to see if I could contact Starfleet Command. So I sat in the pilot's seat, and activated the comm system. "Runabout *Hudson* to Starfleet Command." After a few seconds of staring at the Starfleet symbol on the screen, I tried again. Still nothing. I tried a few other frequencies. And then I started to get worried. Was the comm system even working?

"*Affirmative,*" the computer said. "*Subspace signal has been transmitted.*"

"Did it get where it was going?"

"*Insufficient data for response.*"

"All right, then. Is Starfleet Command's comnet operational?"

"*Insufficient data for response.*"

"Then give me some damn good reasons why I'm not getting through to them—if it's not too much trouble."

"*Potential causes include subspace interference, outdated encryption codes, active jamming, malfunctioning receivers—*"

Well, I sure as hell didn't like the sound of any of those. And the computer didn't know enough to narrow down the list of possible problems. I wondered if I should interrupt Scotty's repair work to tell him. There could be a perfectly innocent explanation—*or* the universe as we knew it could've ended. I started thinking of all the disasters that could've struck without us having a clue.

At that point, I didn't know how much of what I was thinking was that nightmare talking, or even that blasted industrial-strength coffee. Even if I told Scotty, there was nothing to be done other than getting the *Hudson* shipshape and resuming our voyage home. On the other hand, I've never been terribly fond of cruising toward the unknown. I'd just about decided Scotty should know, when a sudden crackle from the comm speaker nearly made me jump clear out of my skin.

The image on the viewscreen stuttered and froze and rolled with interference. Through all the static, I could barely make out the grim face of a pretty young woman in a Starfleet uniform. She had short, dark hair and dark eyes, and there was a sober urgency in her voice. "U.S.S. Saladin *to any Starfleet vessel in the vicinity,*" she said. *"Repeat—this is the Federation Starship* Saladin. *Any Starfleet or allied vessel receiving this message, please respond."*

I fumbled with the companel for a second, then spoke up. *"Saladin,* this is the *Hudson."*

"Hudson? *Thank God you're all right!*" I took her relief as a sign that they'd been out looking for us. At least somebody cared enough to notice we weren't where we were supposed to be. She identified herself as Commander Julia Rivera, first officer.

"Dr. Leonard McCoy, at your service, ma'am."

"Admiral McCoy?!" When she heard my name, Rivera's eyes bugged out. I'd seen that look often enough to know that she'd just realized she was talking to the oldest active human in Starfleet. I just wasn't in the mood for another "living legend" moment.

Then I stopped being annoyed long enough for it to dawn on me: if Rivera's ship had been searching for us, she'd have known the only two people on the *Hudson* were Scotty and me, and she wouldn't have been surprised to find me on the other end of the conversation. "You weren't out looking for us, were you?"

"No, sir. Should we have been?"

"Well, we're overdue arriving back at Earth. So I just thought . . ." My voice trailed off, met only by a long, awkward silence from Rivera. "Then, if you weren't looking for us—"

"You don't know, do you, sir?"

Oh, I didn't like the sound of that. "Know what, Commander?"

"Sir, we've lost contact with Starfleet Command."

"Well, that makes two of us. Is there something else you're not tellin' me?"

Another long silence from Rivera chilled my blood. Then she swallowed and spoke up. *"Earth's been attacked . . . by the Breen. They've allied themselves with the Dominion."*

The words hit me like a punch in the solar plexus. "Good God! Were you there?"

"No, sir. We were part of a combined Starfleet-Klingon patrol. We engaged a Jem'Hadar task force. We took losses but we walked away. They didn't."

I tried to sound upbeat. "Well, that's good news. Is your captain there?"

"Captain Shinoda . . ." Rivera's voice caught. *"She's dead, sir. We took some casualties. I'm in temporary command. We did manage to capture prisoners—one Jem'Hadar soldier who died, and one Vorta, who's pretty badly wounded. Our doctor was also killed, so we sure could use your help keeping this prisoner alive for Starfleet to interrogate."*

Then it was my turn to swallow hard. "If there's any Starfleet left."

"Doctor, we've located you on Bakrii. We'll be landing there in a few minutes."

As soon as she signed off, I got up as fast as these creaky bones would move. *Now* it was time to tell Scotty. Then we rushed outside the ship, just in time to see the *Saladin* landing in the center of the repair complex. She was one of those newfangled *Defiant*-class ships, with NCC-74350 marked on her battle-scorched hull. Compared to the starships I was used to, big ships like the *Enterprise*s, *Saladin* was small. But she was still a whole lot bigger than our runabout. As *Saladin* touched down in the heart of the complex, Vuko and his guards rushed up, looking even less happy than when we'd arrived.

We came up behind Vuko as the starship's hatch opened. Rivera climbed down and introduced herself. Her uniform was streaked with soot, and she had a bloodstained rip where she'd suffered a shoulder wound.

Seeing her for the first time without comm static obscuring her face, I was stunned by how young she looked. Couldn't be more than twenty-five. But that's how wars go. As the more seasoned troops are killed, the ones who come next just get younger and younger. If they survive, they advance through the ranks long before their time. And they get to live with the psychic scars of war far longer than anyone should have to. Rivera was just one of the latest generation unlucky enough to be part of an old story, replayed century after bloody century.

Speaking of replays, Vuko gave Rivera the same hostile reception as he'd given us—and then some. Having one Starfleet vessel here during perilous times was bad enough. Having a second—and one that was a lot more heavily armed and just escaped from mortal combat—was even worse.

"What if the Dominion ships you fought come looking for you?"

"They won't," Rivera said softly. "We destroyed all five. They never had time to send any maydays. Nobody's hunting us."

On their own, out of context, Rivera's words could've sounded boastful. But there wasn't any bravado in her voice. I looked at her eyes, and all I saw was numb acceptance of the reality of her situation.

Then Mezta spoke up, and what she said surprised me. "They're here, Vuko. We have the crews available. We can get them both repaired."

That didn't sit too well with Vuko. "Do it," he huffed. "But the time limit stands."

Scotty and Mezta huddled with Rivera and her blue-skinned Bolian engineer. That Mezta wasn't one for wasting time. She decided right then and there what needed to be done, assigned teams to each ship, and they got right to work. The *Saladin* got squeezed into the work bay next to the *Hudson,* which meant Scotty could keep an eagle eye on both ships as the Bakrii swarmed around them. But it didn't take long for him to be as impressed as hell by their tools, skills and professionalism. Maybe it was because he trusted Mezta, but he decided to let the Bakrii work without his needing to watch every diagnostic scan and turn of a bolt. He asked where she'd found so many good engineers.

"It's in the Bakrii blood, you might say," she told us, letting her pride show through for the first time. "Our planet's climate is harsh and resources aren't abundant, so we've had to develop a culture based on efficiency and inventiveness."

"Aye, nothin' like a cold wind and the wolf at your door to inspire a clever mind."

"I'd never phrased it so poetically, but that's the sum of things here."

Rivera's combadge chirped. It was one of her officers from the bridge. *"Commander, you'd better get up here."*

All of us, even Mezta, followed Rivera to the *Saladin*'s cramped bridge. Her first officer was staring at a viewscreen showing a ragged Federation Newsnet signal that kept cutting in and out. But it was clear enough for us to hear a reporter's hushed voice attempting to describe the indescribable—images from all over Earth of fire, smoke, rubble, and death . . . collapsed buildings and bridges, craters where cities used to be, and the powerless hulk that was all that was left of Starbase 1. Then a wave of static washed the signal out for good. Even Mezta was shocked by what we'd just seen. No one knew what to say.

Somehow, I found my voice first, though it was more like a croak. "Not as well defended as we thought."

"The Dominion did that to your planet?" said Mezta. "Why?"

"Because they're bastards," I said. But there wasn't much point in standing around, so I turned to Rivera. "Commander, let me see this Vorta you captured."

Rivera led us down a deck to their cramped sickbay, where the Vorta was lying unconscious on a diagnostic bed, a portable life-support unit over his thorax. She handed me a medical tricorder, already loaded with what little we knew about Vorta physiology from the Starfleet database.

I picked up a scanner and passed it over the Vorta's body, starting at his feet and moving north. And I thought *Vulcans* had peculiar ears. Nature sure does come up with some ornate handiwork. I'd bet cash money that Vortas can hear a whisper at a hundred paces.

"How is he?" Scotty asked.

"There's internal bleeding. If we're going to save this son of a bitch, I'm going to have roll up my sleeves and do some surgery. Commander, have you got any crew with medical training?"

"Just me, sir," Rivera said. "I qualified as a field medic. Never had any actual experience, until yesterday. But I can assist."

Mezta looked confused. "Why are you trying to save him? He wanted to destroy your world. Commander, your captain was killed by this Vorta's ships."

I *wanted* to tell her that I planned to gut him and mount his head on a pike. Instead, I said, "If he'd died in combat, when it's us or them, we'd be cheering. But I'm a doctor, and a life is a life. Even if I'd rather slit his throat, it's my job to keep him breathing."

"Would he do that for you?"

"Only to torture us for military information," Rivera volunteered.

Mezta nodded slowly. "Ahh. So your Starfleet will want to do the same."

"He'll be *interrogated*, long and hard," I said. "But much as we might be tempted, we don't torture prisoners."

"Your people have never done anything like that?"

"Oh, on the contrary," I said, "we've had a history full of barbarism and cruelty like you wouldn't believe. We keep trying to evolve, though, even though sometimes it's not easy to be better than you want to be. But when it's hardest, that's when you have to try the most."

A deep frown furrowed Mezta's creased brow. "But he would torture you . . . and then probably kill you. Your lives would mean nothing to him." She was damned right about that. "But you're still going to try to save his life."

"Aye," Scotty said. "Somethin' your people might want to consider."

"Commander," I said to Rivera, "you ready to see what's inside this weasel?"

"Yes, sir."

Scotty and Mezta left us to go do their own kind of surgery, and we got ready to work on our patient. "I'm a mite rusty," I said to Rivera as she organized the instruments, "and these hands aren't quite as steady as they were, oh, say, seventy-five or eighty years back. Can you handle an exoscalpel?"

"Good enough to carve a turkey, sir," she said, surprising me with her quip.

"Good enough for him, then."

"Did you really mean what you told Mezta? Do you really believe a life is a life?"

"Sometimes I do," I said. "And sometimes . . . I wish I didn't." I've never felt that way more than I did on that particular day. And for the umpteenth time in my life, I thanked my lucky stars that long before me, people far smarter than me decided doctors had enough to worry about just patching up their patients, without also worrying about delivering justice. That'd be up to somebody else.

By the time we were finished stitching him up, the Vorta was out of danger. Rivera had gone to clean up, and I was alone with our patient when he woke up. I wasn't going to say a word to him, but something Mezta had wondered about was stuck in my head: *Why did the Dominion attack us?* I wanted an answer. So I asked.

"The Founders cherish order in all things," the Vorta said, rather calmly considering his circumstances. "Disorder equals danger. You who reject the Dominion are the antithesis of order."

His purring voice made my blood run cold. "That may be. But we've never done a thing to threaten the Dominion."

"Your quadrant has a long history of selfish and violent disunion, punctuated by a perverse propensity for occasional interspecies unity. The periods of conflict do not concern us, since fighting among yourselves makes you weak. But when you unify, you expand your reach. If you are not stopped, it is inevitable that you will try to extend your grotesque devotion to anarchy into our quadrant."

"Where the hell did you people get that idea?"

"Experience and persecution have taught the Founders a hard lesson: That which you control cannot hurt you. Thus, your very existence is a threat which cannot be tolerated. This war is a clash of civilizations, which we intend to win."

Not a lot of room for compromise there. The same could be said of our situation with the Bakrii. Despite top-notch work by their repair crews, there was more damage than they could fix within Vuko's time limit. After Rivera and I got done with the Vorta, I went with Mezta and Scotty to the supervisor's office to plead for more time. To her credit—and our surprise—Mezta really tried to change his mind.

"Are the Starfleet ships in condition to depart?" Vuko asked.

"Yes," Mezta said, "but repairs won't be complete, and neither ship will be safe enough to assure their return to Earth."

"That's not our problem."

"The hell it isn't!" Mezta growled. "When we come to work here, we swear an oath that no ship will leave until the job is done to the best of our ability. Are you dismissing that oath? Because if you are, that's a disgrace to every ethic we believe in."

"You and your crews have fulfilled your oath. That the agreed-upon time limit prevents you from completing the work does nothing to negate that."

The more we listened, the madder we got. I wanted to give Vuko a piece of my mind, but Scotty *shushed* me with a hard look. I guess he knew I had a way of popping off and making a bad situation worse. So we both held our tongues, figuring Mezta had the best chance to sway her boss. But the more she argued, the more mule-headed he got.

"Vuko, if any of these Starfleet people are injured or killed because their ships were substandard, your time limit will never hold up before a review board."

"No review board will ever hear this case. I'm following government guidelines regarding combatant vessels."

"No, you're interpreting government guidelines. And the review board will question your judgment!"

"Speaking of judgment, Mezta, remember that your promotion came about because of what happened to your predecessor when he challenged my authority. Give that some thought."

Well, that took the wind right out of Mezta's sails. And Scotty must have figured a lost cause couldn't get any more lost, so he just blew up at Vuko. Mad as a wet hen in a tote sack. I'd have done the same, but he beat me to it. "Of all the pinheaded, addlebrained, blockheaded asses I've ever met, you take the cake! With a little bit o' bad luck, which you richly deserve, maybe you'll get a chance to see just how much freedom you'll have under the Dominion. Give *that* some thought." Then he turned and we marched out of the office.

As we walked back toward the ships, I started to say, "Not that I disagreed with what you said, *Captain* Scott—"

Scotty waved his hands. "Don't start, *Admiral* McCoy. I'm an engineer, not a diplomat."

"That's my line. And as I believe you've noted once or twice in the past, now the haggis is in the fire for sure," I said, doing my best impression of an angry Scotsman.

That's when we heard the whine of a small, buglike ship coming in for a landing. It swooped over us and settled down in the center of the repair complex. Scotty recognized it as a Ferengi trader.

We waited for the Bakrii unwelcome wagon to show up. But no Vuko, no armed troops, just a service van pulling up to work on the engine pods. So when the hatch opened and the Ferengi pilot hopped down, we went over to find out why. His name was Migg, and he explained that he had a standing service contract with the Bakrii. Since Ferenginar was officially a noncombatant, he expected the contract to be honored. "What's your destination, humans? I'm sure I have something to sell that you can use on your journey."

When he heard we were headed for Earth, his beady eyes widened and the color actually drained from his cheeks. "Oh, there's no Earth to go back to," he said, shaking his knobby head.

"What do you know about it?" I said, not wanting to believe him. After all, the word of a Ferengi isn't usually worth much.

"I was in Earth sector. Rule of Acquisition Number Thirty-Four: War is good for business."

"Wasn't that kind o' risky?" Scotty said.

"Rule Number Sixty-two: The riskier the road, the greater the profit. But I digress. When that Breen attack fleet came screaming in, it was the worst fighting I've ever seen. The most one-sided, too. Not that I'm a betting man, since the house always wins. But if I had been—and before I saw what I saw—I'd have put my latinum on you, Starfleet. But your defenses might as well have been paper."

"You obviously didn't stick around," I said.

He looked up at me from beneath that bulging brow-ridge of his. "I'm greedy; I'm not an idiot. Carnage isn't my favorite sport."

Scotty turned pugnacious, getting right in that Ferengi's face. "So you don't have any idea what finally happened."

"Well, no, not really. But I know what I saw, and that wasn't pretty for your side, Starfleet. If I were you, I wouldn't want to be seen in that uniform when the Dominion gets here. And I'd be choosing another destination. Get on with your lives. But if you're still determined to find out all the gory details of what happened on that Earth of yours, I'll be happy to send you a message when I get back there."

I stared at him. "You're going back?! After what you just told us?"

Migg stared right back at me, like I had two heads. "Fighting doesn't last forever. And that's when Rule Number One-Sixty-Two takes over: Even in the worst of times, someone turns a profit. Now if you'll excuse me, I have to bargain down the price of my service here."

We watched the Ferengi scuttle off to find Vuko, and Scotty and I looked at each other. What if he was actually telling the truth? What if there was no Earth to go back to? We returned to the hangars in time to see the Bakrii crews packing up their gear. Both ships had been moved outdoors in preparation for departure. Mezta came over to us, her head hanging a bit. "We got as much done as possible. I'm sorry we couldn't do more."

"You did what you could," Scotty said. What happened wasn't her fault.

She walked with us toward the runabout. As we came around the stern of the *Saladin,* we saw Rivera giving a pep talk to her twenty surviving crew members. That was the first time we'd seen them all together. Humans, a Bolian and an Andorian, both with their blue skin, and officers from three other nonhuman species. That was what Mezta noticed the most. "We meet a lot of off-worlders," she said softly, "but not many live here. And we don't see a lot of interspecies crews like this. Is that unusual for Starfleet?"

"Matter of fact," I said, "that's what Starfleet and the Federation are all about. Living together, working together. Fighting together, when we have to."

"Hmmm," was all she said. Then Scotty and I exchanged sad little nods with her, and she walked away. Rivera came over to us as her crew boarded their ship.

"My God," I said to her. "They're just a bunch of kids."

Scotty shrugged. "That could be because at our age, everyone looks like kids."

Rivera managed a tired half-smile. "Even at my age, they look like kids. But they're a good crew. They've been through hell and they're still standing. So, now we go home and see what's what."

"Aye," said Scotty. "We'll stick together, and we'll make it."

It may not be Starfleet protocol, but I gave Rivera a hug, and by the way she hugged back, I knew she appreciated it. Scotty squeezed her hand. And then we each boarded our ships, not knowing what we'd find once we got back into space. And maybe it would've been better not to know. Unfortunately, while Scotty fired up the *Hudson's* main systems, I plotted our course for Earth and ran a long-range sensor scan. Scotty could tell just by the look on my face: there was a Breen patrol out there, and they were heading this way. We both knew there was a very good chance that our little two-ship convoy wouldn't get very far.

We called Rivera, but she'd already seen the same thing on her sensors. "How smart is it to fly straight into a hornet's nest?" I wondered.

"Well, the Bakrii've made it clear we're not welcome here," Scotty said.

"Sir, even if we were," Rivera said, *"if those Breen ships find us here, we're dead."*

"We're just as dead if we run into them in open space," I said.

"The no-win scenario," Rivera muttered. *"How I hated that test."*

"Maybe we need to follow the example of an old friend of ours, who didn't believe in no-win scenarios," I said. "We need to change the conditions of the test."

Scotty grimaced. "And how're we goin' to do that, *Admiral* McCoy?"

"I haven't figured that out yet, *Captain* Scott. Maybe there's someplace we can hide. Or some detour where they won't be able to track us. Some nebula, or asteroid. How the hell do I know?" I snapped. "I'm a doctor, not a navigator."

And then we took off, flying up through the low-hanging clouds. At Scotty's suggestion, once we'd cleared the atmosphere, we started a geosynchronous orbit around the planet, just to make sure all the repaired systems were actually functioning. We were in better shape than the *Saladin,* mostly because we hadn't had any battle damage. Scotty was pretty sure our warp drive wouldn't go haywire again. But the *Saladin* had one computer core down, warp drive at only sixty-percent capacity, and half her weapons offline. The phrase "spit and chewing gum" came to mind.

Just as I was wondering what the hell we might do if we ran into that Breen patrol, the computer announced that we were being hailed. To our surprise, it was Mezta.

"Captain Scott, you probably already know this," she said, *"but our long-range scanners show a Breen squadron approaching our space."*

"Aye. We've been debatin' some alternatives—and we're open to suggestions."

"Return to Bakrii," Mezta said. The fact that Scotty and I immediately exchanged confused glances made it obvious we'd heard the same thing, and neither of us understood what the hell was going on.

Scotty's eyes narrowed. "You're not tellin' us Vuko changed his mind."

Mezta hesitated before answering, as if she was sitting on something she'd just as soon not share. *"Um, never mind about Vuko."*

"With all due respect," I said, "we're no safer if they find us on Bakrii than if we ran smack into them out in space."

"That's the point, Admiral. The only way you'll be safe is if they can't find you."

"Lassie," said Scotty, "you've lost me. First, Vuko won't let us stay. Second, how can they miss us if our two ships're sittin' out there in the open at your spaceport, like a coupla clowns with our drawers down around our ankles?"

"We can hide your ships."

Scotty started to smile. "Aye, now you're talkin'. And whatever you said to make Vuko change his mind—"

Mezta cut him off. *"Vuko is my problem. If this is going to work, you'd better get back here immediately."*

We called Rivera, turned around in a hurry, and made a beeline back to the repair complex. We'd no sooner landed than both ships were hauled, side by side, into two empty hangars. Mezta told us to stay aboard, and with both crews still inside, the elevator platforms under the ships started dropping underground. We passed three unoccupied work levels, and kept dropping. The shaft took us down past another thirty meters of solid rock, and we finally jolted to a stop on the floor of a cavern.

By the dim light from utility lamps mounted along the rocky walls, we saw big metal doors rolling on tracks twenty meters above us, closing across the shaft, and sealing us into the cavern. There were catwalks, a turbolift tube, and narrow metal stairs spiraling up what looked like an emergency access shaft. Both elevators had lowered into the same cavern, which was so long that we couldn't see either end out there in the darkness.

"Welcome to the wine cellar," Mezta said over the comm speaker. *"When we built this complex, we had the foresight to include subterranean chambers within rock formations with natural sensor-deflecting properties. Just to be on the safe side, keep your power output to a minimum. The cavern is ventilated, but it's not very hospitable, so you'll probably be more comfortable waiting in your ships. Other than me, only three of my most trusted senior staff know you're down there. Any questions?"*

"Just one," Scotty said. "How did you convince Vuko—"

Mezta cut Scotty off in mid-sentence. I guess that was her way of avoiding the topic. *"This will be my last communication until we're certain it's safe for you to return to the surface. I'll contact you as soon as possible."*

And that was that. We checked in with Rivera on the *Saladin,* and we wondered some more about Vuko. Entombed a hundred meters below ground, what the hell else was there to do? But that particular topic petered out pretty fast, since we had nothing but speculation to work with. Scotty muttered about wishing he'd brought along some Scotch, then decided make good use of the time by helping Rivera's crew with more repairs. He asked if I wanted to go with him. Not that I could have done much to help.

I think he mostly felt bad about leaving me by myself. And maybe I should've gone. But I didn't.

That left me alone with my thoughts, maybe not the best company for somebody my age, entombed a hundred meters underground . . . or did I already mention that? I tried to occupy myself with medical journals, but I couldn't seem to concentrate. Then I struggled with a crossword puzzle for a bit, and I'm sure the computer was laughing at me somewhere deep in its isolinear brain. But what I kept doing, despite my lame attempts otherwise, was thinking about Earth. What would we find when we got back . . . *if* we got back? How many cities were smoking ruins? How many people died?

Was that damned Ferengi right? Was there even any Earth to go back to? In all my years in space, I'd seen a score of worlds reduced to cinders, some by nature, some by the stupidity of their own inhabitants, and some by enemies bent on destruction. Were we going to end up refugees, with no world left to call home? What if the Breen ships incinerated the Bakrii, too? What if there was nobody left to let us out of this cavern? Believe me, as old as I am, and as much death as I've seen, I'm pretty damned sure there's no great way to die. But getting blown to bits in space had to be better than being buried alive.

Like I said, being alone with my own thoughts wasn't the best company.

The company improved when Rivera came knocking on the hatch, asking if I'd mind a visitor. But that child sure did look tired. She sunk into the pilot's seat next to me, and I noticed the dark circles under her eyes. I asked if she'd had any sleep since her ship tangled with the Dominion.

"I'm okay, sir," she said with a shrug.

"Poppycock," I snapped. "And that's not what I asked, young lady."

Rivera shook her head. "Every time I close my eyes, my brain won't shut down. Might be better if I had an on-off switch, like that android on the *Enterprise.*"

"You could take something."

She shook her head again, more emphatically. "No medication. I'm the one they look up to, now. I have to keep it together, stay sharp."

"You can't be sharp if you're exhausted, now can you?"

"I can sleep later, sir."

I started to get the feeling that she came over as much for herself as for me. That poor girl needed to talk, and she had no one to listen but me. I was glad to be of service. "When you try to sleep, what do you see?" I asked gently. I didn't know if she was ready to open up just yet.

She took a deep breath. "Captain Shinoda's face. She's the only captain I've served under." She caught herself. *"Was* the only captain I've served under. Tell me about Captain Kirk. He's been one of my heroes since I was seven. I read everything I could find about him. What was he like?"

"Driven. Compassionate. Single-minded. Open-minded. Stubborn as a mule—always had to be right, but still the first to admit when he was wrong." I was glad to see an innocent sparkle in Rivera's eye as I talked about Jim. "The best starship captain who ever lived. Maybe the worst admiral. And about the most courageous man I ever knew."

"So he was never afraid?"

"Where'd you get an idea like that, child?"

"But you said—"

"Nobody can be courageous if he doesn't know what it means to be afraid. I may be just an old country doctor, but I can tell you this—*everybody's* afraid of something, unless he's a damned fool."

"Maybe it's because I'm so tired, but I don't understand."

"Not being afraid when there's a good reason for it, well, that's plain stupid. Courage is when you're scared out of your wits, and you *still* do what you have to do. What you've done since your captain got killed—*that's* courage." I could tell that the notion of anyone thinking of her as courageous didn't sit well with Rivera. But after all these years, and serving with the crewmates I've known, I know courage when I see it.

"Well, it doesn't feel like courage," she said, tilting the seat back and resting her heels on the console. "It just feels . . . empty."

Then I told her about my first combat casualty. "I was as green as grass. We were scouting a planet and ran into some Klingons, back when we hated each other. There was an explosion. Knocked me off my feet. When I came to, I saw my lieutenant, just lying crumpled in the dirt like a rag doll somebody threw off a roof. There was blood everywhere. And when I tried to wipe it off his face, blood was all that was there. I tried to give him an emergency tracheotomy, so he could breathe. There was this sound from his chest, like nothing I ever heard before. And then he was gone."

Rivera stared at me, without a blink of those pretty, long lashes. Her voice came out a whisper. "What did you do?"

"I puked my guts out. That's over a century ago, but I'll never forget it."

"They don't tell us it'll be like this. War, I mean."

"No, they don't."

"I joined Starfleet to explore. I never thought about . . . this."

I reached out and took her smooth hand in my old wrinkled claw. "You'll do some exploring. I have no doubt about that. And you'll never forget the thrill of seeing a new world for the first time, or discovering some stellar phenomenon no one's ever seen before, or making a successful first contact with some new species. And you'll know you're the latest link in a chain that goes back to Magellan and Neil Armstrong and Jonathan Archer . . . and Jim Kirk."

"And what about this? I suppose I'll never forget this either."

"No, no, you won't, my dear. It's part of who you are, but it's not all. Not by a long shot."

And then, finally, she dozed off, just like a baby. I hoped she'd be seeing new worlds in her sleep, and not the faces of the dead.

Scotty came back after an hour or so, and Rivera woke up and went back to her ship. We were all wondering what was going on up on the surface. We got our answer about thirty minutes later, when we saw Mezta's face on the comm screen.

"The Breen ships are gone," she told us with a smile. *"We're bringing you up, and if you're not in a hurry, we'd like to complete those repairs."*

Well, that was a big enough surprise all by itself. But when the elevator platforms got us back to the surface, I couldn't believe what was waiting for us—at least twenty Bakrii, standing around long tables where they'd set up all kinds of food and drink, all for us. They had fresh pastries, fruits and vegetables, steaming stews and soups. And at least half the people there to greet us looked like teenagers. Mezta was waiting for us as Scotty and I climbed out of our runabout.

Rivera came down the *Saladin*'s ladder first, her mouth just gaping open in shock. Her crew seemed like they weren't sure if they should follow, but she waved them out impatiently: "Come on, come on!"

Mezta could see we were all a little flummoxed, so she gestured us toward the tables and the friendly faces of the people who couldn't wait to feed us. There was a shy little Bakrii girl, the size of an eight-year-old human, sort of hiding behind her mother. She was holding a bouquet of flowers, and her mother gently pushed her toward Rivera. She held the flowers out, and Rivera took them and knelt down and gave the girl a hug. Well, that little girl scurried back to her mother, but she was beaming a mile-wide smile.

"This is the welcome you deserved," Mezta said to us. "I'm sorry we weren't able to give it to you the first time."

"Beggin' your pardon, lassie," Scotty said, "but how did you change Vuko's mind?"

"Well," Mezta said, "the truth is, I didn't."

I shook my head. "Now I'm really confused. If he didn't change his mind—"

"I changed mine," she said.

"And Vuko let you do all this for us?" said Scotty.

"Uhh, not exactly. Let's just say Vuko is . . . hmmm . . . tied up at the moment."

My eyebrows went up fast. "Literally?"

Mezta nodded, and Scotty and I couldn't help laughing. As she guided us over to all that delicious-smelling food, she explained. "When he refused to extend your stay, I got so angry that I started talking to others on our staff. And it became clear that nobody shared his opinion. When he wouldn't see reason, we . . . ummm . . . narrowed his choices. He's under house arrest."

"Mutiny isn't usually a smart career move," I pointed out.

"I'll worry about that later. Vuko may not care who rules the quadrant, but I think most Bakrii do. As a new friend told me recently, it's sometimes difficult to be better than you want to be. This seemed like one of those times when it was worth the effort, and the risk."

While we and the *Saladin* crew enjoyed the Bakrii's genuine hospitality, Mezta's crackerjack repair teams went back to work on our ships. It did my heart good to see Rivera's young crew actually smiling and laughing. Some of the Bakrii children were asking the *Saladin* crew about their homeworlds, and their families, and the excitement of being in Starfleet. And some of the older Bakrii women hovered around like mother hens, making sure everyone had enough to eat. It was just a short respite for those kids from the *Saladin,* but beggars can't be choosers.

Then I saw Rivera, off in a corner near her ship, with a baby-faced ensign who looked barely a day over eighteen. Old as I am, my hearing's still sharp and I could hear him crying, just overwhelmed by everything he'd been through in the last few days, and by the fuss the Bakrii were making over us, thanks to Mezta. I thought about going over and lending a hand, but Rivera was doing just fine by herself. She spoke to that ensign like a big sister, just as calm as you please. She told him what he needed to hear, and maybe what she needed to say, too. She smiled. She wrapped her arm around his shoulders. And she sent him off to have a good time, while there was time. I knew right then and there that she was going to make a great starship captain, and I planned to tell that to Starfleet first chance I got.

And then I saw her slip behind her ship's landing pad, saw her shoulders slump, saw tears sliding down her cheeks. I wanted to go and do for her what she'd done for that ensign, but before I knew it, she'd wiped those tears away, squared her shoulders and marched over to join her crew with a smile on her face.

Well, soon enough, Mezta came over to tell us that her repair teams were done. Both our ships were ready to go and face whatever might be waiting for us out there. We thanked her, and all the other Bakrii who'd ended up making us feel as welcome as family. Rivera's crew, weighed down with boxes of food for the trip, boarded the *Saladin*. Scotty gave Mezta a hug and climbed into our runabout. Then I linked my arm in hers, so she couldn't get away without answering what I had to ask. I needed to know what made this apparently ordinary woman do this extraordinary thing.

"It had to be more than what *we* said or did," I said. "It had to be something inside *you*."

Mezta took a deep breath. "Before I was born, we Bakrii spent fifty years living under an alien dictatorship. We lost a lot of young people fighting for the resistance. Their blood bought the freedom we have today—including the freedom to choose our allies. When I met Commander Rivera's crew, and saw how young they are, I thought about how I'd want our young soldiers treated if they were in your situation. That made it easier to do the right thing."

I clasped Mezta's hands in mine. "Well, we're sure glad you did."

We said our goodbyes, and then our little convoy took off, looking for a safe route home. Were we worried about running into the Breen or the Jem'Hadar? You bet we were. But no matter what the dangers, we knew where we were needed. And like my new friend Mezta said, that made it easier to do the right thing.

All the way back, we kept trying in vain to contact Starfleet. We kept hoping we'd run into some other allied ships that might've escaped the attacks on Earth. But it felt like we were the last two ships in the universe. Space never seemed so empty. The closer to home we got, the more we expected the worst.

Finally, five hours out, the Starfleet channel crackled to life. We got the news that Earth was battered, but safe . . . for the moment. And all hands on two lonely little ships cheered like it was New Year's Eve. When Starfleet asked Rivera if her crew was prepared for a new assignment, I was afraid she'd feel obligated to say they were ready, willing and able. Instead, she said they needed a day or two of R & R first, and *then* they'd be ready to march into hell. Just then, the way she looked out for her crew, she reminded me of Jim. Starfleet approved her request, told her to report to Mars Base first and then to Starbase 4. As the *Saladin* peeled off from our tiny formation, I said a silent prayer for her and those kids under her command. And Scotty and I continued on toward home.

As we made our final approach to mother Earth, I was glad we'd seen those news images, so at least we knew what to expect. Even so, my stomach got all queasy and sick when we first saw the wrecked spacedocks, the blast-craters pocking the planet, and the smoke plumes rising from her beautiful cities.

"Scotty," I suddenly said, "take us in over New York."

"Why?"

"Just do it, okay? Why does everything have to be a big debate? All I ask is a simple little course change, and you start a big argument. Every time—"

Scotty rolled his eyes. "All I said was, 'why.' "

"Does it matter why? Good God almighty!"

"Well, you're the admiral and I'm *just* a wee captain, so New York it is."

I just didn't feel like telling him, 'cause it seemed so silly. But there was something I had to see. It was night on the American east coast as we broke through the bottom of a cloud cover, crossing on a diagonal over the rocky coast of Maine, then passing over New England, and I could feel Scotty cut our speed. I know he did it for me, cranky old son of a gun that I was. Whatever it was I wanted to see, that was all right with him. When we caught sight of New York City, first thing we saw was all the damage, just like the rest of the planet.

Then we rounded the south tip of Manhattan, and I saw what I was afraid I *wouldn't* see. There she was, standing on her island in the harbor, her back straight, torch held high and burning bright.

Scotty glanced at me, smiled, and flew a lazy circle around her. When they first built her, five hundred years ago, she became a symbol of hope for the hopeless, no matter where they came from. Back then, there weren't a lot of free places on Earth. America stood for something better, and, like the poem says, generations of "huddled masses yearning to breathe free" were drawn by that light in the harbor.

The history books tell us how it was touch and go there in the twenty-first century, when cultures clashed and terror seemed to be hiding in every shadow. For a while, it looked like the good guys might lose the very things that made them good. If ever there was a time when good needed to be very, very careful, that was it.

Somehow, we survived all that. And, eventually, the people of Earth came together. When every land became the land of the free, it looked like that lady in the harbor might've outlived her purpose. Instead, she became a symbol for the whole planet. Then, when the Vulcans came down out of the sky to let us know we weren't alone in the universe, and Earth eventually became the capital of the Federation, that torch needed to burn even brighter. The ideas she stood for needed to reach a whole galaxy.

That's the world I was born into. And I'll never forget the first time my parents took me to New York. We made the same pilgrimage to the statue that millions of families have made for hundreds of years. Of course, we've lived with so many technological wonders for so long now, you might think a simple, mute copper statue on a little green island would seem a quaint relic so ancient that it couldn't possibly convey anything important centuries after they put her up on that pedestal.

But that statue's done a miraculous thing—she's evolved. She started out as the "Mother of Exiles," welcoming her world's "wretched refuse" to a place where they could build a good, new life they'd only dreamed of before. And when there were no more "homeless, tempest-tossed" to bring *in,* she started beaming her message *out.*

So, the truth is, the longer she stands, the more she means. And the longer *I* stand, the more I *under*stand that some ideas never go out of style.

"After all these years, and all these wars," I said to Scotty, "I was afraid that this time . . ."

"Aye."

Then we flew west for San Francisco, both of us looking straight ahead. After a while, Scotty said, "Don't tell me you're gettin' sentimental in your old age."

"I most certainly am *not.*" Then I added: "And even if I was, do you have a problem with that, *Captain* Scott?"

"Not at all, *Admiral* McCoy."

That's one of the nice things about having old friends. After a century or so, you pretty much understand each other, without having to say a whole hell of a lot.

Field Expediency

Dayton Ward & Kevin Dilmore

War correspondence: In 2000, Pocket began publishing *Star Trek: S.C.E.*, a monthly series of eBooks focusing on the adventures of the Starfleet Corps of Engineers on the *U.S.S. da Vinci*. Though the eBooks primarily deal with the period after the Dominion War, the *da Vinci* did serve in that conflict. "Field Expediency" tells the story of one such mission.

Dayton Ward & Kevin Dilmore

Dayton Ward has been a *Star Trek* fan since conception (his, not the show's). After serving for eleven years in the U.S. Marine Corps, he discovered the private sector and the piles of cash to be made there as a software engineer. His start in professional writing came from placing stories in each of the first three *Star Trek: Strange New Worlds* anthologies. He is the author of the *Star Trek* novel *In the Name of Honor*, the science fiction novel *The Last World War*, and the short story "Loose Ends" in *Star Trek: New Frontier: No Limits*, as well as having cowritten several *Star Trek: S.C.E.* adventures and two *Star Trek: The Next Generation* novels with Kevin Dilmore. Though he currently lives in Kansas City with his wife Michi, he is a Florida native and still maintains a torrid long-distance romance with his beloved Tampa Bay Buccaneers. You can contact Dayton and learn more about his writing at (www.daytonward.com).

After fifteen years as a newspaper reporter and editor, Kevin Dilmore turned his full attention to his freelance writing career in 2003. Since 1997, he has been a contributing writer to *Star Trek Communicator*, writing news stories and personality profiles for the bimonthly publication of the Official *Star Trek* Fan Club. With Dayton Ward, he has written seven installments of the continuing eBook series *Star Trek: S.C.E.* as well as the *Star Trek: The Next Generation* novels *A Time to Sow* and *A Time to Harvest*. On his own, he wrote the story "The Road to Edos" for *Star Trek: New Frontier: No Limits*, and also conducted interviews with some of *Star Trek*'s most popular authors in the *Star Trek* Signature Editions series of trade paperbacks. A graduate of the University of Kansas, Kevin lives in Prairie Village, Kansas, with his wife Michelle and their three daughters.

Kieran Duffy was sweating like a pig.

More than once, he had to stop what he was doing and wipe perspiration from his face. Even with his damp uniform tunic sticking to his back and chest, the chilled air inside the wreckage of the Breen scout ship did not cool him.

Clock's ticking, Duff. Hurry up.

He would have loved a chance to study the vessel's onboard systems in more detail. It was a natural inclination for any technical specialist, whether or not they served with the Starfleet Corps of Engineers as Duffy currently did. Unfortunately, time was a luxury he did not possess. He would instead have to content himself with retrieving the one piece of equipment they had come for in the first place and getting away from this uninhabited world of Lamenda Prime, hopefully before alerting anyone in the area to their presence.

"Hold on a second," said Fabian Stevens. Duffy turned to where his shipmate and friend crouched next to him, a frustrated expression on his face. Both men hunkered down at the rear of the ship's cramped passenger area, aided only by the feeble illumination of their worklights as they worked to extricate one of the vessel's control consoles.

"Another sneak circuit," Stevens said, holding up his tricorder for emphasis. The device's status indicators glowed in the near darkness as he used it to point inside the console's open panel. "See

the small cylinder there? A battery-operated, miniaturized trans-
mitter." Indicating the small laser-cutting tool in his other hand, he
added, "Cut the connection between it and the panel, it sends a
signal back to the explosive cartridge we thought we'd bypassed
half an hour ago."

Duffy sighed in exasperation. After nearly an hour scanning the
workstation with their tricorders and moving with agonizing
slowness to sever the numerous connections linking the console to
various onboard systems, both men were well past the first tinges
of frustration.

Damned thing's fighting us every step of the way.

Supposedly, "the thing" was a prototype for a new form of encryption technology conceived by the Breen, at least if the briefing given to Duffy and the other members of the *U.S.S. da Vinci*'s
S.C.E. team was accurate. The engineer knew enough about the
success Starfleet had enjoyed breaking enemy communications
codes to realize the implications of this new development.

According to Commander Hrevet, the Starfleet Intelligence
agent assigned to oversee the recovery operation, the deployment
of such technology among Breen ships as well as those of the
Jem'Hadar and the Cardassians would deal a massive setback to the
Federation and its allies. Breaking the new codes would require
time—weeks if not months. Therefore, acquiring information on
the new mechanism was a top priority, even if getting it was proving to be a colossal headache.

"Direct shielded interfaces to the ship's computer and the communications system," Duffy said, "along with a separate central
processor and data storage." It was an easy guess that this part of
the device stored and executed the encoding and decoding sub-
routines, both from within protected computer memory. "And on
top of it all, four different methods of self-destruct." Shaking his
head, he added, "They weren't kidding around when they built
this thing."

Studying his tricorder once more, Stevens paused to wipe

sweat-matted locks of black hair from his eyes. "At this rate, it'll take us at least another hour to get this thing removed along with all of its accompanying hardware, and that's if we don't find any more booby traps."

"Are you saying you can't do it?" a stern voice asked from behind them. Turning, Duffy had to look around for a moment before he saw the speaker, Commander Hrevet, standing just inside the scout ship's open hatchway and cradling a Type-III phaser rifle in her arms. Like the rest of the away team, the Bolian was dressed in the black uniform variant worn by Starfleet ground forces. Only the red departmental stripe across her chest and the tinge of her powder blue skin prevented her from blending into the shadows of the vessel's interior.

"That's not what he said," Duffy replied, irritation lacing every word. "What he said was that it would take time."

Hrevet, regarding him with narrowed eyes and a mouth held tightly shut in a thin line, seemed unimpressed with Duffy's clarification. Instead, she turned away from the engineers, muttering something he could not hear as she stepped outside the ship to where she had placed the body of the ship's lone occupant. Duffy watched as the Bolian knelt and gazed down at the human's lifeless form for several seconds before slowly shaking her head.

"How well did you know him?" Duffy asked.

The man, identified by Hrevet as Commander Tobias Donovan, was dead when the away team arrived and forced the scout ship's hatch open. Duffy knew nothing about the man save for the information Hrevet had passed on during the premission briefing. Also an Intelligence operative, Donovan had infiltrated a Breen installation in the Kavarian system with the original mission of kidnapping the scientist responsible for developing the new encryption device.

"Well enough to expect that he'd try something like this," Hrevet replied.

According to encoded communications he had sent, Donovan's

mission had failed and forced him to improvise, a desperate action resulting in the killing of the Breen scientist and the destruction of his computer records. That accomplished, the agent escaped with the scout ship, already outfitted with the encryption prototype.

Reaching down, Hrevet adjusted the fold on the emergency blanket in which she had wrapped Donovan's body, preparing her fallen comrade for transport back to the *da Vinci* and, ultimately, to Earth for final interment. "He should have known they'd plan for somebody stealing the damned thing."

"I don't think he could have anticipated the lengths the Breen would take to protect this thing," Stevens said from where he continued to work on the control panel. "They've really thrown the whole smash at this."

Duffy nodded in agreement. While the cause of the ship's crash was unknown before arriving here, a tricorder scan of its dormant data banks had quickly solved the mystery. "In addition to the security protocols built into the hardware and software, the onboard computer has a few extra features, including a special command sequence programmed into the navigational subprocessor."

"As soon as he set a course out of Breen space, the computer initiated a security override," Stevens added. "Its instructions were to divert to the nearest Breen base." The computer logs told the rest of the story, with Donovan trying everything in his power to regain control of the craft, up to and including the ejection of the warp core. He had then taken a phaser to the computer's central processor, though its destruction had given him only partial control of the ship. While it was enough to effect a controlled crash landing here, it had not been enough to ensure the agent's survival.

"Given what we've found here," Duffy said, "I don't know anyone who could have gotten away with this."

Hrevet waved the consolation away. "What's important now is retrieving the equipment and any data he was able to gather and getting it back to Starfleet." Looking up at Duffy and Stevens once more, she asked, "What's our status?"

"I wish he'd left us some instructions on getting this thing out," Stevens replied. Holding up his tricorder, he added, "The onboard computer doesn't contain any information on it." He cast a tired look at Duffy. "Have I thanked you for dragging me down here yet? This'll teach me to keep my mouth shut at briefings."

Chuckling humorlessly, Duffy shook his head. This entire operation was an improvisation in progress, put into motion the moment the *da Vinci* had received its new orders. As part of their latest in a string of courier-type missions undertaken since the beginning of the Dominion War, the ship was already carrying Hrevet and her team to Starbase 585.

The agents' original assignment was scrapped, however, in favor of the more pressing need to recover the encryption prototype and, if possible, the operative who had liberated it from Breen hands. When the scout ship proved to be in no condition to fly back to Federation space and too large for the *da Vinci*'s transporters to beam into a cargo bay, only one option remained: Remove the equipment from the vessel. Without the necessary technical expertise to remove the equipment on their own, the field operatives required the talents of the *da Vinci*'s cadre of engineering specialists. The ship's captain, David Gold, and its S.C.E. detachment commander, Salek, had wasted no time placing the responsibility for the mission's success squarely on the shoulders of the team's most experienced engineer: Duffy.

"It's nice to be loved," Stevens had blurted out at the premission briefing, but Duffy smiled at the memory of the grin melting from his friend's face as he realized that his mouth had indeed gotten him into trouble. Again.

Not that Duffy would have excluded him from the mission. Since coming to the *da Vinci* following his tour aboard the *Defiant* and Deep Space 9, Fabian Stevens had proven to be a talented engineer who could think fast on his feet, especially when a situation deteriorated from bad to worse. He was a valuable addition to any away team, and Duffy had quickly come to rely on the man's skills.

Unfortunately, both men's talents, technical or otherwise, were proving insufficient for their current task.

"Da Vinci *to away team.*"

Commander Salek's terse, controlled voice erupted from Duffy's combadge, nearly making him jump out of his skin. Cursing to himself, he reached up to tap the badge. "Duffy here."

"*A Breen vessel has just dropped out of warp. Our sensors detected the activation of their transporters just as they entered orbit, and we register seven Breen life-forms on the planet surface, closing on your position.*"

"We've got trouble," Duffy told his companions even as he heard the sounds of running footsteps coming from outside the ship. The away team turned toward the hatch in time to see Hrevet's fellow field agent, Lieutenant Commander Rondon, appear in the opening. A Zaldan, Rondon had an imposing, muscular figure. Duffy had a hard time believing he could be frightened of anything, but there was no mistaking the anxious expression on the agent's face.

"Life signs, heading this way," Rondon said as he climbed through the hatch and took up a defensive position, his phaser rifle looking more like a toy than a weapon in his massive webbed hands. "My tricorder registered seven, but there could be more."

Scrambling away from the open access panel, Duffy and Stevens reached for their own phaser rifles, and Duffy tried to ignore the knot of unease forming in his stomach as he checked his weapon's power setting. Other than his Academy training courses, Duffy had little experience with the rifle. For that matter, he had never been subjected to anything resembling a ground combat action.

You're about to get a crash course, pal.

Moving for a better vantage point toward the front of the ship, Duffy peered through the shattered remnants of what had once been the cockpit's canopy in search of the new arrivals but saw nothing. The vessel had come to rest in a small valley cutting through a line of rolling hills, with a wall of rock lay less than ten meters from the ship's port side, rising straight up nearly fifty meters before angling away. At least no one could approach them from that direction.

"*Lt. Commander Duffy,*" Salek's voice said through Duffy's combadge, "*are you all right?*"

Duffy started to reply when he heard the distinctive sound of disruptor fire, and the ship's hull shuddered from the impact of multiple energy blasts. Rondon wasted no time launching a response, the report of his phaser almost deafening in the confines of the vessel's cockpit.

On the bridge of the *U.S.S. da Vinci*, Captain David Gold leaned forward in the center seat, his brow furrowing in concern. The unmistakable whine of weapons fire filtered through the ship's intercom system.

"Stand by for beam out, Duffy," he said. Addressing the ship's comm system, he began, "Gold to Feliciano. Beam them out of—"

"*Captain, you can't do that,*" a new voice shouted over the speakers, one he recognized as belonging to Commander Hrevet. "*Our mission's not over.*"

"I'm sorry, Commander, but the Breen don't seem sympathetic to our concerns." Before he could say anything more, he was interrupted as Lieutenant McAllan called out from the tactical station.

"Captain, they've charged weapons and they're coming about!"

"Battle stations," the captain said.

Red alert klaxons wailed as the Breen ship fired on the *da Vinci*.

"Report!" he called out over the alarms.

McAllan replied, "I got the shields up in time to prevent any damage, sir. They're holding at ninety-three percent."

Looking to Commander Salek, Gold said, "Get the away team up, now."

"No time, sir." The Vulcan first officer shook his head. "They are coming around again."

At the helm, Songmin Wong shouted, "Incoming!"

Gold cursed to himself as a second salvo struck his ship. He knew he had to get the *da Vinci* moving if he was to have any chance of confronting the enemy vessel on anything approaching equal terms.

To the comm system, he said, "Commander Hrevet, the Breen have closed the issue for the moment. We're under fire and have to take evasive action."

"Do what you have to do, Captain," Hrevet replied, *"but I need more time down here."*

Gold stiffened at the Bolian's tone, his jaw tightening as he rose from his chair. He knew that leadership structure aboard a ship assigned to S.C.E. duty often blurred into gray areas, with the captain's role sometimes relegated to that of a ferry driver while the engineering specialists carried out orders given directly from Starfleet Command. While the occasional interpretation of his authority did not normally bother him, the knowledge that two of his people were in danger lent an edge to his voice.

"I understand the importance of your mission, Commander, but I stop caring about what you need when my people's safety is concerned. You'd do well to keep that in mind."

Sounds of phaser fire erupted from the speakers again and Gold turned to Salek. "What's their status down there?"

"Scans show that their position is defensible against seven ground troops," the Vulcan replied. "That could change if the Breen are able to send down reinforcements." Indicating the main viewer with a slight nod of his head and the image of the Breen vessel dominating it, he added, "And we do have concerns of our own."

Gold nodded. No less important than his engineers on the surface were the forty-odd personnel aboard the *da Vinci*. "Break orbit, evasive maneuvers," he ordered. Though he was worried about his people on the ground, he had no choice but to communicate his confidence in both the engineers and the Intelligence operatives who had taken them into harm's way.

"Commander Hrevet," he said, "We're going to try and buy you some time, but I will yank you out of there if it comes to that. My people are merely on loan, and if you want a ride home, you'll bring them back to me in one piece."

"Understood," the Bolian replied, and Gold heard the first hint of humor in her voice. *"Starbase 585 is a bit of a walk from here."*

Unwilling to sever the connection without reassuring his engineers in some fashion, Gold added, "And Duffy? You and Stevens behave yourselves down there. Here's your chance to make the S.C.E. look good to Starfleet Intelligence."

"Oh sure, Captain," Duffy answered, somewhat out of breath. *"Put that burden on me."* Gold allowed himself a slight smile at that. Though some ship commanders might not tolerate such flippancy in their junior officers, the *da Vinci* captain had learned to accept Duffy's levity as easily as he had come to rely on his technical expertise.

More for himself than anyone else, he said in a low voice, "You'll be fine, Duffy."

If the second officer replied, Gold never heard it as static erupted from the bridge speakers.

"Jammed from somewhere on the surface, Captain," Salek reported. "The Breen ship is closing on us again."

Gold's response was instant. "Bring us about, Wong. Stand by phasers."

As the *da Vinci* bridge crew snapped to their captain's orders, Salek stepped down into the bridge's command well. "Sir, tactical scans show that the Breen vessel's weapons are superior to ours. It may be advisable to retreat and attempt to draw them away from the planet."

"You said the away team could hold its own for the time being," Gold said. "If we leave, the Breen could simply let us go while they send down reinforcements. I'm not giving them that choice." Eying his first officer, he added, "Besides, they're liable to concentrate more on us if we start dishing it out for a change."

The change in Salek's expression was subtle, but Gold recognized thoughtful approval on the Vulcan's face when he saw it. "Unconventional, yet logical, Captain."

Nodding, Gold addressed the rest of the bridge crew. "All right, people, our team needs more time to work, and I'm tired of being shot at. Let's see what we can do about both."

Static burst from Duffy's combadge, drowning out Gold's voice.

"Captain?" he prompted, tapping the device again before looking up to Hrevet. "They must be jamming us."

Stevens held up his tricorder. "That's not all. I can't get a solid reading on anything. We won't be able to track their movements."

"We won't have to," Hrevet said quietly as she moved closer to the front of the cockpit, bringing her phaser rifle up.

Had she seen something? Duffy jerked his head to look beyond the shattered canopy, his eyes struggling to see whatever had caught the agent's attention. Something moved to his left, or did it? Nothing more than a patch of black darker than the surrounding shadows, for an instant he thought his eyes might be tricking him.

They weren't.

"There!"

Orange light flared in the near darkness before Duffy could react, the whine of Hrevet's weapon assaulting his ears as the energy beam struck the approaching Breen. Less than fifteen meters away, the soldier staggered before falling unconscious to the ground.

Studying the stunned alien for a few seconds, Duffy realized now why he had almost missed seeing it. Its earth-toned insulation suit and the dull finish of its helmet, which immersed the wearer in a refrigerated environment similar to that of the Breen homeworld, also functioned as effective camouflage. Aided by the darkness and the drab landscape surrounding the scout ship, the Breen were all but invisible.

"They're getting bold," Hrevet offered, not turning her attention away from the rocky terrain flanking the ship's starboard side.

Crouching near the main hatch, Rondon said, "Keep your eyes open. They might be getting ready to charge."

Until now, the Breen had made effective use of cover and concealment as they moved closer to the ship. It was obvious from their tactics that they were trying to avoid unduly damaging the craft, most likely to facilitate their own retrieval of the encryption prototype. Hrevet had sought to use that to the away team's advantage by concentrating heavy fire on the most likely avenues of approach to the vessel. So far, the improvised strategy had succeeded in keeping the Breen at bay, but if the probing actions of the soldier Hrevet had stunned were any indication, their aggressors were adjusting to the defensive scheme.

Or, perhaps they were simply running out of time and patience.

"What now?" Stevens asked, his voice barely a whisper. He positioned himself as Rondon directed on the opposite side of the hatch from the Zaldan, allowing the two of them to overlap their fields of fire and cover each other's blind spots. His anxiety was impossible to miss, and matched Duffy's own. Out of their element here, and with the *da Vinci* unable to retrieve them, the engineers were dependent on the field agents to guide them through the chaos now enveloping this mission.

"If we stay here we're as good as dead," Hrevet said. "Our only chance is to make them move before they're ready."

Confusion creased Duffy's brow. "How do we do that?"

The Bolian's answer came as she adjusted the power setting on her phaser rifle. "With a little landscaping."

Rising from her crouch, Hrevet aimed through the cockpit's ruined canopy. Phaser energy erupted again, only this time the effects were much more powerful. One large boulder perhaps thirty meters from the ship exploded, launching countless fragments of stone shrapnel in all directions. Hrevet fired again, destroying a second rock before moving the rifle in a straight line to her right, chewing up more and more chunks of the hillside.

Her actions had an immediate effect as Breen soldiers scampered back from positions of concealment ahead of the destructive swathe. They fired as they ran, but many of their shots went wild. A few struck the side of the ship and Duffy felt it shudder again from the force of the impacts. Trying to ignore it, he concentrated instead on tracking the movements of their aggressors with his phaser rifle. Doing so was difficult amid all the dust and debris thrown about by Hrevet's unorthodox actions.

"They're pulling back," Rondon called above the din as the agent and Stevens fired their weapons. Peering through the open cockpit, Duffy saw several Breen scrambling among the rocks. One attacker was carrying a companion slung over his shoulder, his movements slowed by his additional burden. It would have been easy to shoot the struggling soldier in the back, but Duffy saw no point to that.

There were rules, after all, even in war.

"Look out!" Hrevet shouted as a disruptor bolt struck the ship just below the windshield. The Bolian dropped to the deck in search of cover as a second volley burst inside the cockpit above Duffy's head. Sparks and debris rained down on him and he threw his arms up to protect himself, tiny points of fire biting into his exposed skin. Stars danced in his vision, each a telling reminder of just how close the shot had come to hitting him square in the face.

The echo from the blast faded and Duffy became aware of someone inside the ship screaming in agony. Rolling onto his side, he turned and saw Stevens writhing on the deck, his hands clamped around his thigh. Blood, a lot of it, streamed between his fingers and soaked the leg of his uniform. Already it began to pool on the deck beneath him.

"Fabian!" he yelled. Scrambling across the deck plating, he ignored the sounds of weapons fire all around him as he went to the aid of his friend. Without thinking he covered Stevens's hands with his own and pressed against the wound. "What happened?"

Stevens hissed through his teeth. "Shrapnel."

"His femoral artery's been cut," a deep voice said from behind him as a huge hand settled on his shoulder. Duffy turned to see Rondon leaning over him, his expression one of stone. Only then did the engineer realize that the shooting had ceased.

"They've retreated," Hrevet explained. "For now, anyway." She tapped her communicator. "Away team to *da Vinci*. Requesting emergency transport directly to sickbay." When no response came, she repeated the call but achieved the same result.

"They're still jamming us," Duffy said. "Dammit!"

Another burst of phaser energy rattled the ship's interior, startling him yet again as the beam crossed in front of him and struck Stevens. The wounded engineer collapsed instantly and Duffy instinctively jumped back. He whirled to see Rondon aiming his hand phaser at Stevens, who now appeared to be unconscious, or dead.

"What the hell are you doing?"

Standing next to Rondon, Hrevet held up a hand as Duffy moved back toward his friend. "He's just stunned. It will make what Rondon's going to do easier."

Eyes wide with anger and confusion, Duffy watched in open-mouthed shock as the Zaldan intelligence operative adjusted the setting on his phaser.

"If we do not stop the bleeding, he will die," Rondon said. "This will be more effective than a tourniquet." He turned back to Stevens and tore the material of the engineer's jumpsuit, exposing the still bleeding gash in his thigh. A moment of probing with his hand produced a jagged piece of metal, which Rondon extricated from the wounded leg. Then, holding the phaser like a fat, bulky pen between his large webbed fingers while he pulled the edges of the wound together with his free hand, the agent pressed the weapon's firing stud.

A thin line of orange energy lanced from the phaser. As it made contact with the edge of the wound, a dreadful sizzling sound filled the cabin. Duffy covered his mouth and nose with his hand to block the stench of burning flesh as he watched the phaser beam cauterize the injured tissue.

"Disgusting, but I can't argue with it," he said, his stomach threatening to heave its contents all over the inside of the ship. "Straight out of the *Starfleet Survival Guide.*"

Not looking up from his task, the Zaldan replied, "They taught us the technique in our field medical training, but this is the first time I've tried it, or even seen it for that matter." His work complete, he reset his phaser to its original power level before returning the weapon to its holster. "That will do until we can get him back to your ship, but he has lost a considerable quantity of blood."

"Nice work," Duffy said, impressed with the agent's quick thinking and decisive action that was, like everything else on this mission, a product born from the desperate necessity of the moment.

Rondon waved the sentiment away. "Of course it was. He still lives, does he not?"

Duffy bit down on the impulse to respond to the callous words when he remembered to whom he was talking. As a people, Zaldans detested most forms of social courtesy, viewing such overtures as a ploy to hide real feelings and motivations. Were it not for their tendency toward dramatic emotional displays, they could almost be Vulcan in their regard for total honesty, no matter how harsh or unwelcome the truth might be.

Having apparently forgotten the exchange already, Rondon reached for his phaser rifle and checked its setting. "It will be light soon. If I were the Breen leader, I would launch another attack before sunrise. We cannot stay here."

From where she was keeping watch near the hatch, Hrevet looked to Duffy. "How long will it take you to extract the device?"

Shaking his head, Duffy said, "At least another hour, maybe more, and that's without our friends shooting at us."

"Too long," Rondon said. "The Breen are almost certainly stranded here, at least so long as the *da Vinci* is able to keep their ship from getting close enough to send down reinforcements. They outnumber us, and I suspect that they won't hesitate to destroy us and the ship if we're here when they come back. The easy course would be to eliminate the prototype ourselves, find a defensible position and await the *da Vinci*'s return."

Hrevet shook her head. "I'm not ready to do that just yet, so our only other choice is to do a better job of protecting the ship and the device until we can get it removed."

"Easier said than done," Duffy replied. "For all we know, half the systems aboard this ship are tied into that thing. We could spend a week examining the equipment in here and still not figure it all out."

The Bolian's expression was at first one of disapproval, but it disappeared a moment later. "I'm no engineer, but I'm smart enough to listen to one. We'll find you the time you need."

"Wow." Despite everything that had happened, Duffy still managed a small grin at that. "Any chance you could talk to our security chief when we get back?"

Spinning . . . no, rocking . . . I'm rocking . . . why am I rocking . . . make it stop. . . .

The first thing Fabian Stevens saw as he forced his eyes open were clumps of grass and loose dirt streaming past, up and away from him. Blood rushed in his ears and pounded at his temples. Every breath he tried to draw was forced out of his lungs as something unyielding pushed into his stomach with no discernible rhythm.

"Unh . . . what's happening?" Stevens said, his words slurred as he struggled to talk between the punches to his gut.

"Quiet," a voice replied. "We're almost there."

Rondon? What the hell are you doing?

Opening his eyes wider, Stevens made out a pair of boots below him. He shook his head a bit and got more of a bearing on his predicament, realizing that Rondon was carrying him slung over his shoulder. Judging by the Zaldan's movements as he navigated up the uneven terrain, he was in a big hurry.

"Hold on." Stevens forced the words out as nausea washed over him. "I think I'm going to be si . . ."

Unable to stop himself, he vomited down Rondon's back.

Wiping spittle from his lips, Stevens mumbled, "Sorry," but the agent's only reaction was to keep climbing the rocky slope.

The engineer's stomach was still heaving moments later when Rondon pulled him from his shoulder to deposit him uneasily on the ground behind a rocky berm. The abrupt movement elicited a jolt of pain from his injured leg and he groaned in response.

"Lie still," Rondon ordered as he moved toward the berm, and Stevens watched as the agent shifted a few rocks aside and up-rooted a pair of scrawny shrubs with his bare hands. Tossing the pitiful vegetation away, Rondon peered over the berm through the opening he had created and nodded in approval before turning back to the engineer. "How are you feeling?"

Sitting up so he could inspect his injuries, Stevens noted how his torn trouser leg had been pulled back together and secured with a length of Starfleet-issue optical cabling, doubtless from his or Duffy's toolkit. "Like a runabout landed on me." Looking up, he added, "Sorry again about the, uh . . ."

"Forget it," Rondon replied. "I've encountered worse."

Stevens found himself believing that, but his stomach prayed that the Zaldan would refrain from offering specific examples. "What are we doing up here?"

"Taking the high ground," Rondon said as he dropped his rucksack to the ground and passing Stevens his engineer's tool kit. "Our job is to cover Hrevet and Duffy while they attempt to re-trieve the device."

Feeling the cobwebs clearing from his mind, Stevens watched as the agent began to root through his rucksack when an odd odor drifted to his nostrils. "What is that? Did something burn?"

"That smell," Rondon replied, not even bothering to look up, "is you."

Stevens stared down at his leg, his hands moving to pull aside the material of his torn trousers and inspect his wound, but a new protest from his still-quivering stomach stopped him. Instead, he tried not to think about his injuries as he reached for his satchel. Fishing inside the bag, he pulled out his tricorder along with a worklight and his kit of engineering tools. Important to him when carrying out his normal duties, his equipment seemed all but useless now.

Looking over at Rondon's stockpile, Stevens saw that in addition to his phaser rifle, the Zaldan had also set out a trio of hand phasers along with two tricorders, one of which looked to have been heavily damaged.

"Four phasers?" he asked.

"One of them is yours," Rondon replied. "Two of them have low charges. They will not last long if we encounter prolonged resistance."

Motioning for his companion to hand him the weapons, Stevens said, "Let me see what I can do." As Rondon watched, Stevens detached each phaser's power cell and connected them with a strand of monofilament line from his toolkit.

"Very resourceful," Rondon said, nodding appreciatively.

"This is a bit riskier than it looks, so don't try it at home," Stevens said and smiled. "I can even use this to drain the power from our combadges, if it would help."

Rondon declined the offer as he pulled a new item from his bag, a polished metal ring with three curved blades around its outer edge. Noting his rapt audience, the burly Zaldan actually offered a slight smirk. *"Kligat,"* he said, "for when the phasers run dry."

A nervous lump formed in his throat as Stevens considered Rondon's words. "I've never seen anything like it."

"It is the weapon of choice among the people of Capella IV, with a rich and storied history." He held up the kligat to inspect its blades. "I won this from a royal guardsman there a few years ago."

"Won it how?"

Rondon smiled. "I won it honorably."

Figuring his companion was not going to offer anything more on the subject, Stevens opted instead to study their surroundings. "So now we wait?"

"For now," Rondon replied, moving back along the berm to the observation post he had created. Reaching again into his rucksack, he extracted a pair of what Stevens recognized as Starfleet emergency ration bars. "Are you hungry?"

His stomach lurching at the very thought, Stevens shook his head. "Hardly."

"Too bad," Rondon said, tossing a bar his way. "You need energy. I'm done carrying you."

Stevens grimaced as he retrieved the bar and unwrapped it. Biting into it, he silently thanked Starfleet nutritionists for the flavorlessness of the field-issue bars that met the minimum meal requirements for most of the Federation's member races.

"The Breen will find us, you know," he said between mouthfuls.

"Almost certainly," Rondon replied. "We have nothing to shield us from their scanners."

Pausing to think a moment, Stevens said, "Yeah, but we don't have to be completely surprised, right?" He indicated the pair of tricorders near Rondon's leg. "Pass those over."

Studying the first of the tricorders, Stevens frowned at its damaged condition. "What the hell happened to this one?"

"That was Commander Donovan's," Rondon said, as if that were sufficient explanation.

Stevens decided that it was as he inspected the broken unit again. It took only seconds to confirm that the tricorder was inoperative, though there was a chance its memory core could still be salvaged. Tucking it into his satchel, the engineer then opened his toolkit and selected a pair of sonic emitters.

Setting to work, Stevens began to integrate the emitters with Rondon's tricorder, repurposing them from their more exacting and intended handheld uses to something more appropriate for their current situation. The process took several minutes, after which he tied the hastily improvised device together with a few more loose monofilaments, using his teeth to pull the knots tight.

"Here we go," he said, admiring his handiwork. "One motion sensor." Seeing Rondon's puzzled expression, he added, "All I did was boost the sonic emissions and set the tricorder to detect any movement. It's highly directional and probably not any good past a hundred meters or so, but if you point this toward the way you expect the Breen to be coming, we should get a decent heads-up."

Rondon reached over and grasped Stevens's contraption. Eyeing it before setting it on the berm, he said, "I'm starting to see the benefits of having an engineer along for covert operations. Have you ever given thought to joining the Intelligence branch?"

Stevens could not resist the playful chuckle as he set to work on his own tricorder. "I'm an engineer. I'm too smart for Intelligence."

Movement behind him made Duffy jump, and he lurched around to see Hrevet sighting down the barrel of her phaser rifle at something outside the ship.

"What?" he whispered.

After a moment, the Bolian lowered her weapon, convinced that all was still quiet. "Nothing," was all she said before returning to her silent role as sentry. How many times had something caused her to react in such a fashion since all this had started? Duffy had lost count, but her behavior was beginning to fray his nerves.

Of course, it was possible that the strain of the team's current situation was wearing on the agent, as well. She was better at hiding its effects than he was, of that Duffy was certain, but even an experienced field operative had to be susceptible to the stresses of combat, right?

Without their tricorders to help them scan for the presence of Breen soldiers, Duffy and Hrevet had kept watch for Rondon as he carried Stevens up the steep hillside to an area of what looked to be flat ground. The agents had decided that the ridge would make an ideal position from which to defend the vessel while Duffy and Hrevet tried again to retrieve the encryption equipment.

It seemed to take forever for Rondon to transport his wounded charge up the hill, with Duffy's pulse racing each time an odd noise echoed among the hills or a shadow seemed out of place amid the rocky terrain. Now back inside the ship, he at least could focus on his work.

"Commander?" he asked as he continued to work, "this isn't the first time you've had an assignment like this, is it?"

"No," Hrevet replied, "but it's been a long time since I've been involved in anything this intense. I guess I'm out of practice more than I want to admit." She shifted in an attempt to get more comfortable. "When I was an ensign and new to Intelligence, my team went on several missions into Cardassian space. This was before we signed the treaty, of course, so tensions tended to run high. Once in a while, one of those missions went bad and we ended up fighting our way out."

She nodded toward the hatch, beyond which still lay the shrouded body of Commander Donovan. "I probably would have died on one of those trips if not for Tobias. He was a lieutenant when I joined his team and had already had a few run-ins with Cardassians. He taught me things you don't learn in school, things that keep you alive when the plan goes wrong." She sighed, directing her gaze back through the open hatch. "I guess there are still some things to learn, though." Duffy said nothing, intending to allow her whatever time she might want to spend in silence, but after a few moments, Hrevet turned back to him.

"What about you? You've never had a mission like this before, have you?"

The engineer chuckled. "What gave it away?" It was a weak attempt at humor as he returned to the partially disassembled control console. "There's never been much call for this sort of thing until now, at least not for our crew. I mean, we've had a few scrapes since the war started, but nothing like this. I can only imagine what the ground forces are going through, dealing with situations like this every day."

Nodding, Hrevet replied. "In war, it's important to remember that we're all soldiers first, and specialists second. Many of us could find ourselves fighting on the front lines, whether in space or on some planet with strategic value, simply because there is no one else to send."

A lump formed in Duffy's throat in response to the vision evoked by the agent's words. The Dominion War had raged for nearly two years now, and was fast becoming the most costly conflict in Federation history with regard to lives and resources. Even the losses suffered on both sides of the Earth-Romulan War, fought before the Federation's founding, paled in comparison to the widespread carnage inflicted in recent months.

Trying to push the disturbing thoughts away, Duffy looked down to see that his hands were shaking. Clasping them together, he willed them to stop as he exhaled in a frustrated burst. "I could say I wasn't scared right now, but I'd be lying."

Hrevet nodded, the hint of a smile on her face. "I would not believe you, anyway. Still, there's no shame in being scared. It takes courage to admit one's fear in the first place."

"Then I must be the bravest man on this planet," Duffy countered.

"And resourceful, judging by the progress you've made." Hrevet indicated the various components and other equipment lying on the deck in a semicircle at Duffy's feet.

His hands under his control once more, Duffy surveyed the scene around him. "This is one of the most complex pieces of communications technology I've ever seen." The mess before him was the result of nearly an hour's work, and he had been forced to perform much of the console's disassembly without most of his diagnostic instruments, thanks to whatever jamming method the Breen were employing. While his tricorder's basic functions such as data storage and retrieval were unaffected, it was of little use in helping him identify and remove all of the hardware associated with the encryption prototype. The going was even slower than he had anticipated. He needed more time, which he was sure the Breen would not give him.

And where the hell is the da Vinci*?*

The away team had not heard from the ship since losing communications with them earlier. Was Captain Gold still facing off with the Breen ship? Had reinforcements arrived, forcing the *da Vinci* to retreat in the face of superior numbers? Could she have been destroyed?

No, Duffy scolded himself as he shut down that line of thinking. He knew that his captain was an experienced and innovative tactician, though it was a facet of his personality that Duffy had witnessed on only a few occasions. Still, he was convinced that David Gold was far more than a chaperone for a shipload of engineers. If there was a way to handle the Breen, the *da Vinci*'s captain would find it.

Something outside the ship caught Duffy's eye. "Look," he said, rising from where he was working and pointing toward the cockpit canopy. Out among the rocks, light flickered in a regular pattern.

Faced with the jamming effect employed by the Breen, the away team had devised other methods of communicating with one another. Duffy had suggested they use their worklights along with a quickly conceived set of simple signals. Repeated flashing, for example, meant that the Breen had been spotted and were moving in their direction.

"They're coming," Hrevet said, recognizing the prearranged signal.

A disruptor bolt slammed into the hull an instant later.

"Cover!" she barked as she positioned herself next to the open hatch. She was returning fire even as Duffy skulked back toward the cockpit, searching for signs of the approaching enemy. He saw nothing at first, but then Hrevet fired again and the flash of the phaser beam illuminated a shadowy figure darting between the rocks. Breen.

"How many do you think there are?" he asked.

Hrevet fired again before replying. "I'm not sure. Three, perhaps four."

Where are the others? Duffy wondered even as he caught sight of another fleeting figure. He fired his phaser rifle, hitting a boulder behind the Breen soldier as the alien dashed for concealment among another grouping of rocks.

The sounds of more weapons drifted down from the hills to his left, and Duffy looked up to see the flashes of phaser and disruptor fire up on the ridge. Stevens and Rondon were under attack too!

Though he was no tactician, even Duffy could see what was happening. The Breen, able to use their own scanning devices to pinpoint the away team's locations, had split their forces and launched a simultaneous offensive. Forced to defend themselves from the new threat, Rondon and Stevens would be unable to provide covering fire in support of their teammates, and the Breen still had a large enough force to overrun Duffy and Hrevet.

If they got close enough.

Movement to his right. Duffy swung his phaser around and fired, but he was too late as the Breen jumped into a depression and out of sight. The soldier was less than forty meters from the ship now. Where were his buddies?

"Duffy," Hrevet called out, "I need to know now. Can you re-move that thing or not?"

Though his engineer's pride scoffed at the idea that there was a task he could not accomplish, Duffy sighed in resignation. Even if he could get all of the necessary components identified and removed before the Breen overtook their position, there was no way he and Hrevet could move and protect it until the *da Vinci* returned for them.

That left only one option if they hoped to keep the device out of enemy hands.

Hrevet seemed to recognize the look in Duffy's eyes. "That's the way it has to be, then. You know what to do."

Duffy nodded. "But how?" he asked, more to himself than to the Bolian as his eyes scanned the interior of the scout vessel. With the warp core gone and with no torpedoes or other weapons systems of which to take advantage, his choices were limited.

Other than the obvious one, of course.

"Get ready to bug out," Duffy said as he opened the access panel on the side of his phaser rifle and began to tinker.

Looking over her shoulder, Hrevet saw what he was doing. "Setting it to overload may not be enough to destroy the entire ship. There might still be something the Breen can recover."

Duffy could not help a mischievous grin. "Trust me."

Stevens fired his phaser and caught the Breen in full charge, the soldier's body enveloped by the weapon's energy as he slumped to the ground. The alien was so close that dirt and bits of rock kicked up by his impact hit Stevens, peppering his uniform and stinging his exposed skin.

"One down, two to go," he said as he searched for another target. Their only warning had come from the tricorders Stevens had rigged to act as motion sensors, mere seconds after the two officers had seen weapons fire down on the rocky terrain surrounding the scout ship. Despite whatever the Breen had done to interfere with their equipment, the engineer's efforts had been enough to alert them to the trio of Breen trying to sneak up on them.

It had not been hard to figure out their opponent's new strategy, dividing their numbers and launching synchronized attacks on the separated away team. Rondon had counted four sources of disruptor fire down below, aiming toward the scout craft, which meant the remaining three soldiers were working their way in this direction. The ridge where Stevens and Rondon had positioned themselves precluded assaults from all directions save two, and the Breen had wasted no time in exploiting those to the best of their ability.

Something moved to Stevens's right. Rondon saw it, too, because he reacted by sweeping his weapon in that direction and firing. The shot went wide left, and though Stevens did not understand the curse the Zaldan muttered in his native language, he could guess its meaning.

"They are as elusive as Denebian slime devils," Rondon snapped, frustration lacing his words.

"But not as cuddly," Stevens replied, just before a disruptor bolt struck the base of the boulder he was using for cover. He recoiled as stone shrapnel exploded in all directions, the heat from the blast singeing the skin on his hands and face. The sudden movement directed a fresh jolt of pain through his injured leg and he bit his lip to keep from crying out, wondering as he did so why he had bothered. After all, the Breen knew exactly where he and Rondon were.

His ears were still ringing when a second volley tore into the dirt to his left, between where he and Rondon were lying. Mixed in with the soil and rock this time were pieces of composite metal and plastic shrapnel, all that remained of a tricorder and one of their worklights as they too were caught by the blast and disintegrated.

"Look out!" Rondon warned as yet another barrage was unleashed on their position. The agent rolled to avoid a disruptor bolt that narrowly missed him, striking his phaser rifle instead. Sparks and black smoke erupted from the weapon and Rondon tossed it aside as he pushed himself to one knee. In one smooth motion he drew his hand phaser and fired with a confidence gained through years of practice and hard-won experience. To

Stevens's astonishment the Zaldan's aim was true, catching another Breen in his helmet.

No sooner had the soldier fallen than Stevens detected more
movement to his left. He turned in time to see a third Breen, rising
up from his place of concealment behind a small rise and aiming
his disruptor at him.

Oh shit. . . .

His own weapon hand came up almost without his conscious
thought and his phaser fired. The shot lacked Rondon's accuracy
and instead hit the dirt embankment, throwing soil and rock into
the air and causing the Breen to step back out of reflex. That was
all Stevens needed to check his aim and fire again, this time striking the alien in the chest.

"Nicely done," Rondon said as he pulled himself to his feet and
ran to the edge of the ridge that formed their original defensive
position. "Come on, we have to see how Hrevet and your friend
are faring."

If I know Duffy, he's probably holding off the Breen with some of his
bad jokes, Stevens thought as he pulled himself to his feet, gritting
his teeth as pain lanced once more through his injured leg. He
tried to walk, but had to steady himself against a boulder for a moment before stumbling forward to stand alongside his companion.

For the first time, Stevens realized that the darkness was fading.
Looking up he could see the first glow of sunrise peeking over the
horizon. The shadows were beginning to retreat and their surroundings were taking on the first hints of substance and color.
Mineral deposits in the soil reflected the feeble predawn light, and
Stevens could make out the jagged features of the bland, almost
barren landscape.

He also saw Breen, four of them, moving with deliberate purpose toward the downed scout ship, their movements partially
camouflaged by the rocky terrain. Stevens thought he could make
out one person moving inside the ship's cockpit, but it was hard to
be sure at this distance.

Then he saw Hrevet and Duffy lunge from the open hatch and head toward the rear of the vessel, firing phasers as they ran. They disappeared behind the craft, heading for a small ravine and the meager cover it offered.

"Oh damn," he whispered, understanding the reason behind his companions' evacuation. "They're going to blow up the ship."

"Keep moving!"

Duffy felt Hrevet's hand in his back as the Bolian pushed him farther down the rocky slope and into the ravine several dozen meters behind the crashed ship. The engineer fumbled with his tricorder, trying to study its miniaturized display as he ran.

He had programmed the unit to link with his modified phaser rifle and order it to trigger its overload sequence. All that remained was for him to send the final command, but already he was detecting trouble with his hastily concocted plan. Even this small distance from the ship, the link he had established with his phaser rifle was fading. It was a testament to the Breen jamming equipment that it could disrupt even this simple, low-level function of the tricorder.

"Wait," he called over his shoulder. "I'm losing the signal the farther we go."

"Then blow it," Hrevet said, firing her phaser back the way they had come as a Breen emerged from behind a large outcropping. Her shot missed and the soldier answered with a volley of his own as he ducked back around the rocks.

"This close?" Duffy exclaimed. "We'll be caught in the blast, or worse, buried under an avalanche."

While the phaser rifle's overload yield was sufficient to destroy a Starfleet runabout, the Breen scout ship's larger size and robust construction made Duffy doubt the weapon's effectiveness. With no room for error, the engineer had decided to attach the rifle to the ship's main drive plasma reservoir. The phaser's detonation would act as the catalyst for igniting the craft's remaining plasma, their combined force more than enough to incinerate the ship and anything inside it.

"We're dead anyway," Hrevet said as she exchanged fire with the Breen, "but we can't take the chance of them recovering that equipment." When Duffy hesitated an additional few seconds, she turned back to him, her expression angry and determined. "Do it now!"

With a silent plea to any deity or omnipotent superbeing who might be watching the final act of this insane play, Duffy closed his eyes as his thumb pressed the tricorder's transmit key.

Then his eyes jerked open as Hrevet grabbed him by the arm and dragged him farther into the ravine. "I didn't say I was going to stand here and wait for it," she snapped.

The normal overload sequence would take thirty seconds, with an extra couple added on for the transmit delay. Duffy tried to count as he ran but gave up any hope of keeping track of the time as more disruptor fire burst around them.

Luckily for him, Hrevet was picking up the slack.

"Down!" she yelled, pushing Duffy behind a large boulder and firing one last time back up the ravine before dropping next to the engineer.

Three seconds later, dawn erupted.

At least, it seemed to. The explosion resulting from the combination of the phaser rifle's overload and the ignition of the plasma was more than enough to simulate daylight for a few fleeting seconds. Duffy felt the ground tremble beneath them as the blast swept over them, the shockwave enough to make his teeth rattle. Debris showered the landscape, slamming into the hillside and anything between them and the center of the detonation.

Anything, and anyone.

Unmistakable cries of agony filtered to Duffy's ears from somewhere behind them as the explosion faded. Out in the open at the time of detonation, the soldier had doubtless been unable to reach cover before being caught in the debris storm. Mercifully, the sounds died out after only a few seconds, leaving an eerie silence in their wake.

"I wonder where the others are?" Duffy whispered a moment later.

Hrevet rose to a crouch and studied their immediate surroundings, searching for threats. "It's possible that one or two of them went for the ship instead of following us." If that was the case, Duffy realized, those soldiers would be dead, vaporized along with the rest of the vessel's interior. How many did that leave?

At least one.

Duffy saw movement among the rocks the instant before the disruptor blast ripped into the soil at his feet. He scrambled back behind the boulder, his hand reaching for his phaser but instead closing around the empty holster at his waist.

Uh oh.

Getting to her feet, Hrevet was bringing up her phaser rifle when the next energy bolt slammed into her shoulder. She cried out in pain as the force of the strike hurled her to the hard unforgiving ground.

"Hrevet!"

Moving to help her, Duffy was already conscious of the sounds of someone running down the slope toward them. His heart racing, he reached for Hrevet's phaser rifle but stopped at the sound of a high-pitched, digitally synthesized voice from behind him.

Duffy couldn't understand the words, but he comprehended the tone well enough.

Holding his hands away from his body, he then heard another squawked instruction, and slowly turned around to see a disheveled Breen standing before him. Gray soil covered much of the soldier's tan uniform and armor, and dark, wet splotches stained several rips in the fabric of his clothing. Vapor escaped from cracks in his helmet, a sure sign that his suit's environmental systems had been damaged in the explosion.

"Look," he said, "it's over. The ship's gone, along with everything onboard." Duffy hated the words as they left his mouth, his first verbal admission that he had failed in his mission here. "Killing us won't accomplish anything."

The Breen's breathing was labored, and several seconds passed before he responded. This time, Duffy didn't have a clue what he was saying, but he doubted the Breen was agreeing with Duffy's assessment of the situation.

Duffy judged the distance separating them to be only a few meters, but with the disruptor trained on him it may as well have been a light-year. Fatigue and pain was evident in the Breen's voice, even filtered through his helmet, though Duffy doubted the alien's injuries would prevent his thwarting any attempt to overpower him.

An odd whistling sound echoed among the rocks. He thought at first that it might be some kind of bird or other animal, but it seemed oddly artificial as it drew closer.

Then something crossed Duffy's line of sight from the left, a blurred whirling object slicing through the air to bury itself in the Breen's shoulder. His disruptor barrel jerked into the air and pushed the soldier off-balance, and Duffy ducked as the weapon discharged and an energy bolt screamed past his head.

Seeing the Breen still reeling from whatever it was that had hit him, Duffy lunged for him.

His opponent recovered first, bringing his weapon around to aim at Duffy.

A phaser whined and orange energy streaked past the engineer, hitting the soldier and sending him collapsing to the ground. Duffy stood frozen in place, his mouth open in muted shock. Then he heard running footsteps and turned to see an enormous figure lumbering down the slope toward them.

"Rondon!"

The agent knelt beside Hrevet, leaning over her to inspect her injury. After a moment, he patted her on her uninjured shoulder with one massive hand. "You will be fine." Rising to his feet, he regarded Duffy. "Are you unharmed?"

"I am now. Nice timing." Duffy pointed to the odd weapon still sticking out of the wounded Breen's shoulder. "Nice aim, too. What is that thing, anyway?"

Moving to retrieve the odd blade, Rondon smiled. "A long story. Suffice it to say that it comes in handy on occasion."

Duffy picked up the Breen's disruptor rifle before turning to look back up the slope, his eyes tracing the plumes of smoke rising from the decimated remains of the scout ship. "Well," he said to no one in particular, "I can't wait to write the report for this one."

Two of the Breen had been killed when they entered the ship prior to its destruction, while a third had fallen victim to flying debris from the explosion. Rondon and Duffy treated the injuries of the remaining soldiers as best they could, after which the away team could do nothing but wait for the *da Vinci* to return. The ship arrived nearly forty minutes later, and it was a simple task for the ship's tactical officer, Lieutenant David McAllan, to locate and destroy the jamming apparatus the Breen had used on the surface to interfere with the away team's equipment.

"Sorry for the delay," the relieved voice of Captain Gold said through Duffy's combadge. *"The Breen tried to make it interesting for us by calling in reinforcements. We played hide and seek around the moons of Lamenda IV, but with Wong's piloting skills and McAllan's sure aim, we finally got them to turn tail. They'll be back with reinforcements soon, though, so I'd like to get out of here. Get ready for transport."*

Asking the captain to stand by for a moment, Duffy severed the connection as he walked to the small clearing among the rocks where the rest of the away team and their Breen prisoners were situated. Hrevet and Stevens sat nearby, trying to remain still in light of their respective injuries, and Duffy moved to kneel beside his friend.

"I can't wait for Dr. Tydoan to get a look at you," he said, imagining the response the *da Vinci*'s irritable chief medical officer would have upon examining Stevens's injury and the crude technique that had saved his life. "He'll fix it, all right, but he's liable to kill us both afterward."

Stevens chuckled as he tried to get comfortable with his back propped against a rock. "Well, assuming he doesn't, I'm putting in for shore leave. I think we've earned a vacation after this."

"I know just the place. It's this bar on Syrinx III. You'll love it."

"Syrinx III?" Stevens echoed. "The resort planet with all the ancient temples? I heard that place can be rowdy. You're not trying to get me into more trouble, are you?"

"Perish the thought," Duffy said, leaving Stevens to ponder the possibilities as he rose and moved to where Rondon stood covering the remaining Breen soldiers with his phaser.

"They're ready to beam us up," he offered to the Zaldan before directing his attention to the leader of the Breen group. "My captain reports that more of your ships are on the way. We plan to leave you here to wait for them. Our mission was to retrieve the prototype, or destroy it. While I'm not happy we won't be taking the thing home with us, at least you won't be, either."

From behind him, another voice said, "Don't be such a pessimist."

It was Stevens, holding up . . . something . . . for everyone else to see. To Duffy it looked like a padd, but it had obviously been disassembled and reconstructed with parts from other equipment. All of it was banded together with a length of optical cabling.

"Donovan's tricorder was beat up pretty bad," Stevens said, "but its memory core was still intact. Ordinarily I'd have connected my own tricorder to it and retrieved the data that way, but it was destroyed during the fighting."

"And since padds don't have a direct data transfer capability," Duffy said, "you created your own interface?"

Stevens nodded. "It's not perfect, but it was enough to let me get a look at what Donovan stored. From the looks of things, he copied all of the schematics for the prototype. The software to run it isn't here, but there's enough information to at least have a go at reverse-engineering the thing." Glancing at the Breen, he said,

"They'll probably build another one. But when they do, we'll be ready for them."

Next to him, Hrevet said, "It was a lot of work to accomplish that. Why did you simply not wait until we returned to your ship, when the task would have been easier?"

Stevens pointed to where the covered body of Commander Tobias Donovan had been relocated, awaiting transport to the *da Vinci*. "I wanted to make sure his efforts weren't wasted." Indicating the Breen, he added, "And I wanted them to know it, too."

While the Breen offered nothing in the way of response, Rondon smiled at the engineer in genuine approval. "It takes a great deal to impress me, human, and here you've done so yet again. Excellent work."

Duffy saw the expression mirrored on Hrevet's face, and offered an appreciative nod of his own. Improvisation and imagination had been the order of the day from the moment they beamed down, though they had proven insufficient to accomplish their primary goal. Still, he had prevented the Breen from recovering the vital technology, and Stevens's own talents had provided some measure of success to their mission while at the same time reassuring Hrevet and Rondon that their friend's sacrifice had been a worthy one.

It was a small victory, Duffy realized, perhaps even irrelevant in the larger scheme of the Dominion War.

But it's enough, he decided, *at least for today.*

A Song Well Sung

Robert Greenberger

War correspondence: The *Star Trek: The Next Generation* novel *Diplomatic Implausibility* introduced the *I.K.S. Gorkon* and its crew, among them Captain Klag, a character first seen serving aboard the *I.K.S. Pagh* in the *TNG* episode "A Matter of Honor." The adventures of the *Gorkon* continue to be chronicled in the *Star Trek: I.K.S. Gorkon* series. "A Song Well Sung" tells the tale of one of Commander Klag's battles during the war while still serving on the *Pagh.*

Robert Greenberger

Currently a senior editor at DC Comics, Robert Greenberger has worked most of his adult life there. In addition, he finds time to write fiction (most notably, but not exclusively, *Star Trek)* and young-adult nonfiction on a wide range of subjects (from Pakistan to Godzilla). His latest works have been released in the summer of 2004: *A Time to Love* and *A Time to Hate*, both part of the nine-book set-up for the events seen in *Star Trek Nemesis*. He makes his home in Connecticut with his wife Deb and kids Kate and Robbie. While never having served his country, he remains proud of those who have.

The first thing Klag noticed was the smell.

Burning circuits fused with smoldering flesh. It was unpleasant, but he had smelled far worse. Klag blinked several times, trying to get the smoke to stop stinging and blurring his vision. When that failed, he concentrated his efforts, trying to sort out the sounds that assaulted his ears. The hissing sounded like the fire-suppression equipment, and the warning bleeps indicated the sensors were still online. The *Pagh* might have been old, but it was sturdy. It was that toughness that no doubt saved the lives of the crew, although the number of honored dead would be high.

As the seconds passed, a key sound was missing. No one was on the communications system, nor was there any sound of breathing on the bridge. He wasn't deaf—he had proven that already—but something was amiss. That in itself was enough for Klag to gather his strength and try to move.

It only then became apparent that he was pinned down under something bulky. Odd, he didn't seem to feel the discomfort, but then again, he always prided himself on his ability to withstand pain. Right now, he assumed his senses were overloaded and he was in shock from the crash landing on Marcan V. His last memory was of the engineering *bekk,* a beardless youth, reporting the stabilizers had failed and the landing was to be rough. Then they were tossed about the dim bridge like sacks of wheat as the *K'Vort*-class ship first met the atmospheric pocket surrounding

Marcan V and, seemingly seconds later, impacted with the ground.

Finally, the haze began to clear away and Klag saw the outline of the captain's chair between himself and the floor. Its armrest was uncomfortably jabbing his abdomen, something he felt through the leather armor he wore. The corpulent form of Captain Kargan was fortunately not in the chair, but that raised another question he did not dare ask as yet. No, the first thing he had to do was regain freedom of movement.

He tested the wrecked chair and found that it was wedged between other twisted portions of command stations. Try as he might, Klag could not even get his right fingers to wiggle, let alone grip the chair. He gingerly moved to his knees, debris cutting through leather, bracing his left shoulder against the cushioned seat. With his left leg braced against one of the few intact support struts, Klag pushed against the chair, trying to force it forward. While the metal groaned at the effort, it only moved slightly. Klag let out a curse and coughed as the smoky air filled his lungs.

He paused a moment to note there were no responses to his curse. Could it be that the rest of the bridge crew was dead? With renewed effort, he pushed at the chair and noted it moved just a bit more. Changing tactics, he pulled at the chair and it moved more freely, and he continued to exert force, willing the twisted metal and leather to be gone. And like a cork released from a keg of bloodwine, the chair popped out of its crumbled housing, causing Klag to lose his balance and tumble face down to the damp deck.

While he had momentarily thought he had actually opened bloodwine, his eyes focused on the cause of the wetness: the blood of the pilot, whose sightless eyes and his own were only centimeters apart. The wound nearly severed the head from the woman's neck and her heart had long since stopped pumping the blood through useless veins.

Taking a deep breath, Klag got to his knees and then to his feet.

Standing at last, he began to survey the destroyed bridge but finally stopped to examine an odd sensation in his right shoulder. Glancing down, Klag saw in horror that the shoulder stopped and no arm extended from it. He looked further down and saw his appendage lying on the deck, blood pooled at the ripped end and the fingers curled into a fist with nothing to strike at.

For a moment Klag, first officer of the *I.K.S. Pagh,* took stock of what the future held for him. There were many decorated warriors still active in the Klingon fleet missing an eye like General Martok, or a hand such as *Dahar* Master Lethik. But an arm? Could he still serve with honor? The one thing he knew was that he would not, could not, return home to sit beside his father M'Raq and await death without honor.

He needed to return to productive duty and now. Blood continued to drip from his wound so that needed attending to first. There was no sense in waiting to see if anyone else was still alive to come to his aid. All his training prepared him for survival on this waste of a world. His eyes darted about the bridge and he took in the bashed bodies and damaged equipment. Clearly, the *Pagh* would never again take to the stars, and for that he was sorry. It was a worthy ship, even if its captain was a weak fool.

Finally, he spotted the helm still sparking, a small fire crackled from exposed circuitry. With careful steps, he made his way over the mixed bits of metal and soldier, stopping before the active station. With his remaining good hand, he waved it over the station, sensing its heat. This would have to do, he decided. He kneeled, taking several deep breaths, and then leaned his damaged shoulder into the hot metal.

There was more pain than he had ever before endured. Involuntarily, his teeth clamped shut with a clack, a scream constricted in his throat. His eyes wanted to shut, but he willed them to remain open, watching as the high heat did its job. He focused on the drying blood.

Again he was assaulted by the smell of charred flesh, but this time it was his own as he cauterized the wound. The sizzle stopped the blood flow and sealed the damaged nerves, tendons and veins from the infectious air. But with each popping and hissing sound, Klag felt as if doors on his career and his path to *Sto-Vo-Kor* were being slammed in his face. He endured the pain, now no worse really than the painstiks during the Age of Ascension, but this time the agony extended to his soul.

After a minute, Klag withdrew from the station and regained his feet. He saw with his eyes what he knew in heart was to be true. Captain Kargan, the weak-willed, close-minded animal, was on his large belly, his neck at an unnatural angle. Kargan was from the powerful House of K'Tal and had used his position to stay in command and keep Klag from rising up the ranks. How he wanted to challenge the older man, but Klag knew that even if he won such a challenge, his own life would be forfeit at the hands of House K'Tal's agents. Klag's own House would also suffer, and it had endured enough with the way his father M'Raq lay in bed on the Homeworld waiting for death. So Klag remained under Kargan's heel—until now.

Others from the crew were scattered around the bridge, all dead, and try as he might, no one responded to a single call over the partially working communications network.

It was possible he was the sole survivor on Marcan V. His blood, what was left of it, burned for the fate dealt his shipmates. Most deserved better than this, he knew, and to die, deprived of a chance to end life in battle, served to make him angry. First, at Kargan for foolishly leading them for so long and second, at the Dominion for fighting in an honorless manner.

Reinforcements were on the way, Klag knew, so it was only a matter of time before he was rescued. But there was still business to conduct. After all, if he managed to survive the crash, so too might the despised Jem'Hadar. One of their ships also survived the battle in the Marcan system, and it was on a trajectory to crash on the fifth planet as well. With working sensors, he quickly determined that they had indeed landed, not far from his position.

Trying to refine the reading, he reached to his right, but there was no hand to touch the control. He withheld the curse this time, recognizing it was time to train himself to function. Crossing with his left hand, he triggered the control. The sensors clearly showed eight life signs moving in the *Pagh*'s direction—seven Jem'Hadar, one Vorta. Good, they were coming to him, it would save him from hunting them down.

Klag knew he would be tested in the coming struggle. His shoulder ached, there were cuts and bruises all over his body, his uniform in less than perfect condition, and of course, he had lost a considerable amount of blood. There was to be no time to rest, certainly no time to heal—the enemy was coming.

And he smiled, baring teeth.

His *mek'leth* remained strapped to his right leg, and he took some trouble to transfer it to his other leg. Then he stuffed a disruptor into his belt holster. So fortified, he was ready to go out and meet them.

But before leaving his dead ship, he had one final duty to perform. He stood on the bridge, surrounded by the bodies of his shipmates. His eyes were bright and Klag took several short breaths before one, long deep inhalation of smoke and blood-tinged air. From the bottom of his wounded soul, Klag summoned a fearsome war cry, alerting the sentries at the River of Blood that a ship full of warriors was about to enter *Sto-Vo-Kor*. Even that *petaQ* Kargan.

It also served notice to the Jem'Hadar that victory was not theirs to have.

Now it was time to go and mete out revenge.

Without stopping to grab water or rations, Klag worked his way from the battered bridge to the corridor that connected the bulbous head to the remainder of the vessel. There he found a rupture in the hull with bright sunlight filling the empty space. There were no bodies, nor was there any smoke. Klag sensed the planet's heat from outside but was prepared to endure any environment Marcan V had to offer. He worked his way through the jagged tear in the vessel's body and emerged, blinking against the sun, onto the planet.

The Marcan system was resource rich, one of the first systems conquered during the Klingon's early days of expansion as an empire. It was raised into a productive system through sheer force of Klingon will. It was therefore highly coveted by the enemy. The *Pagh* was part of a fleet assigned to protect the sector and almost immediately they encountered resistance. Jem'Hadar attack ships and Breen forces had been patrolling the sector first, and immediately responded to the Klingon fleet of twelve ships. Klag paused a moment, letting his eyes adjust to the sun, feeling refreshed from the warmth.

While the Jem'Hadar were renowned as warriors in hand-to-hand combat, their smaller ships could not withstand the coordinated efforts of the determined Klingons. Klag reflected with pleasure that here, they were clearly superior. While their deflector screens were more advanced compared to Klingon technology, the combined might of torpedoes and disruptor cannons picked off one ship after another.

Marcan V was an arid world, hotter than Qo'noS, with a slightly heavier gravity. Like Klingons, the Jem'Hadar probably also trained in heavier environments. Given the breadth of the Klingon Empire, all soldiers regularly trained in varying atmospheres and gravities, but the Dominion was also of great breadth, and though they had no honor, the rulers of the Dominion were no fools. Still, at least the oppressive heat did not put Klag at a disadvantage. Cold would have been an issue, but Klingons thrived in heat.

Klag stumbled over rocks and lost his balance, reaching out with an arm that no longer existed. The fall filled his mouth with dirt and once more he cursed out loud. He had to force himself to concentrate and compensate for his body's new proportions.

As he made his way toward the dark column of smoke that could only be the downed Jem'Hadar ship, his mind filled with images of the glorious battle in the black skies above this system. Even Kargan acquitted himself well, for a change, as the *Pagh* took out two Jem'Hadar ships with just one well-aimed torpedo. It was the stuff of song, Klag concluded. No tune, though, presented itself. In fact, he noted, he was having uncharacteristic difficulty in concentrating.

Within an hour, the numbers on both sides had been whittled down to just one *K'Vort*-class cruiser and one Jem'Hadar ship. They danced and chased and fired upon one another until the cursed Jem'Hadar dove toward Marcan V. Kargan, of course, followed, disruptors beating out a tattoo with repeated blasts. The engineer called out that the stabilizers were off-line, and suddenly Klag was in the desert, trudging toward the enemy to complete his duty to the Empire. Possibly his final duty.

The surface was tan and dusty, the ground dried out by an unforgiving sun. Marcan V was exploited for its mineral properties, he knew, but had no population to speak of. Therefore, no hope of help. That was fine by him. Klag barely noticed the light breeze that blew across him as he marched, his eyes carefully sweeping the horizon in search of the eight victims coming his way. The sun was past its zenith so he knew there were but hours before darkness, when the advantage would be entirely theirs. Trained eyes sought protective cover or ambush spots, but the few hills were squat and opportunity was scarce. There'd be no element of surprise for him, while the Jem'Hadar had those damned personal cloaks that allowed them to fight dishonorably.

While Klag marched and scanned, his mind drifted, from running battle scenarios to thinking about his drinking mates or the last woman to share his bunk. Every so often, the Klingon recognized he was not as sharp as he should be and forced himself to focus on a singular point ahead of him, detailing it to himself, making certain his mind remained alert. He strained his nostrils and ears for any telltale sign of the enemy but he was met only with the faint scents of the local plant life.

It took him a torturous hour or more to cross the distance between the two wrecked ships. On the way he continued to drift in and out of focus, his mind returning to Qo'noS and his father. M'Raq was captured by Romulans and later escaped without divulging a single Klingon secret. The cruel Romulans refused M'Raq's request to die an honorable death. Instead, he returned home, his secrets intact but his spirit broken. All he wanted to do now was sit and await death from old age. It was not a proper way for a warrior to die, and Klag had chosen not to speak with him rather than sully his own reputation. Klag's heart grieved for what his father had been and what he allowed himself to become. M'Raq's wife, his mother, tended to the disgraced warrior, running their House and doing whatever was possible to remind her mate of the glorious past. Dorrek, his younger brother, felt differently and took Klag's silence as a betrayal of their father. Klag had not spoken with him, either. His brother, though, had fought bravely in the war, which gave Klag some small measure of pride. Last he heard Dorrek had received another field promotion so both did their fair share to restore pride to their House.

His ruined shoulder began to throb with pain. Klag ignored it, gritting his teeth, using the pain to stay aware of his surroundings, pushing images of M'Raq and Dorrek to a far corner of his fevered mind. The burning of his brain and his blood would prepare him for battle.

Soon after, the enemy ship was finally in sight and this heartened Klag, who blinked back sweat while studying it. The vessel also seemed unworthy to test the vacuum of space, which quickened Klag's heart. Still, he watched, and listened. And smelled. The slight breeze carried what his eyes could not see—Jem'Hadar were nearby. Their stink was of living in close quarters with those pathetic Vorta. Perhaps just over the rise of a nearby hill, scant meters ahead. Klag's left hand grabbed the disruptor and fired several shots while he simultaneously dove to the plains. His shots struck nothing but air, although it worked, forcing the nearby Jem'Hadar to fire back, giving away their position, for they could not fire weapons while shrouded. So predictable. It took Klag two shots to target his first soldier, a shot more than it should have. Klag was ashamed at his weakness. He watched with delight as the soldier's entire right side was blackened from the impact.

One down. Six more Jem'Hadar and their keeper were still loose. But even one dead alien improved the odds. Klag was ready for a fight but was also no fool—he was outgunned, he was wounded, and time was against him. There'd be no chance for stealth or careful planning; he would need to strike ferociously, making each shot or stab or even punch count.

The sounds of fire worked both for and against him. True, it did deliver him his first kill of the afternoon, but it also revealed his position. Exposed to the sun, his ravaged body was no doubt visible. Perhaps, he considered, this would make them overconfident and he could use that against them.

They were out of eyesight, cloaked cowardly soldiers. Klag decided to head straight toward the point where the dead Jem'Hadar was. It was directly before the ship and made sense to him as a starting point. The others had probably scattered, looking for their best opportunity to strike. The Vorta would be in the ship where it was safe.

Bits and pieces of the alien ship wreckage littered the ground between Klag and the remains. No body parts, which disappointed him, but also no footsteps in the sandy spaces between conduits, hull plating, and other debris. They scattered before this point. He cautiously approached the dead vessel, stopping frequently to sniff the air and listen. A shift in the dirt behind him and to the right, perhaps a foot slipping on a stone. He tensed his body and a small smile crept over his lips.

They were not fools, Klag knew, but neither was he. With a steel-tipped boot, the Klingon carefully balanced a piece of hull plating on his right foot. Then, he kicked it to the right, letting it rattle amidst other pieces of wreckage. As it landed, he darted left, zigzagging toward larger pieces that would provide better cover. Klag paused underneath a large, dull gray piece of hull, controlling his breathing and listening. No more footsteps as the dislodged piece of shrapnel stopped scratching against the ground. The breeze, Klag finally noted, was dying down from almost nothing to nothing. His ears and eyes would have to become sharper.

Remaining still and breathing shallowly helped. Minutes passed in utter silence and then there was the unmistakable sound of a footfall. The cloaked enemy was to his right, maybe five meters away. He was clearly picking his way through the debris to get closer. Klag merely gritted his teeth in preparation and slowly removed his disruptor. His thumb changed the setting, going from a narrow-focused beam to a wider one. Perhaps less effective, he knew, but more likely to strike first.

Another faint sound from the same direction allowed the Klingon to narrow his aim. For a moment, his mind shifted from Marcan V to Qo'noS, and his first kill. It happened while still drilling for duty as a warrior. There was . . . odd, he couldn't recall the man's name. They had just finished training on the firing range, getting used to a new model disruptor, each boasting of their accuracy. There were the normal shouts and head butting, but this one man—no, youth—was insulting, not boastful. He took exception to Klag's House, intimating Klag's mother must have bedded with someone on the High Council to earn him a spot in the Defense Force. While the others laughed, Klag seethed. A single backhand swipe from his now-missing arm sent the nameless one stumbling into a cluster of laughing colleagues. The fight was on, with Klag's blood rushing in his ears, drowning out the laughter. The backhand was followed with a heavy booted kick to the side, forcing the trainee to sprawl. Without waiting, Klag hefted the other one up and smashed him headfirst into a support column. He smelled blood, which only encouraged him. The other one waved his arms, trying to force Klag off him or reach for a weapon, he never knew which. Instead, Klag held on tighter, kicking once again into his ribs and laughed when he heard one crack. This contest was clearly one-sided, and his opponent was totally unworthy of the effort. It was brief and the man fell and was left to bleed to death as Klag and the others walked back to the barracks. None screamed on the dead one's behalf. The moment of the kill was glorious for the youth, especially since it was committed with bare hands. That enhanced his reputation with his instructors and ensured him a peaceful night's sleep.

Klag blinked several times, casting aside the mental image of the dim hall where the fight with the forgotten *petaQ* occurred, replacing the vision with the desert reality. He paused to note how far the sun had dropped, estimating as best as he could how much longer before dusk arrived. Then he took aim, squeezing the trigger. A burst of light and the high-pitched whine of release gave away his position but also found its target. There was a muffled exhalation of air and then the sound of a body collapsing to the ground. Klag fired a second time and this time the body barely shifted on the ground. A second Jem'Hadar had fallen to a superior combatant.

Quickly, Klag scuttled from his hiding place, toward the body and then past it. He needed a new place to position himself, knowing the others would come. Five were still a formidable number, but he chuckled at the notion that five was less than six.

Eyes rapidly scanned for other large pieces of the Dominion ship to use and he chose one that was barely going to cover his body but brought him closer to the wreck. Should dusk find any Jem'Hadar alive, he needed to bring the battle into the ship where even emergency lighting would prove useful.

How he wanted water to slake his thirst, but he had neglected to bring anything with him save his weapons. Even his wits threatened to depart as the pain in his shoulder continued unabated. Were his comrades still alive, he knew, Klag would have been left back on the ship, seen as useless in combating the Jem'Hadar. He would prove them wrong; prove that even one-armed, a Klingon warrior could vanquish this enemy.

Klag needed to work with the pain, use it to help keep his mind focused on his surroundings. Rather than let his mind drift, he used each sense one at a time to get a feel for where more cloaked Jem'Hadar might be hiding. There was nothing to hear, nothing to smell . . . he would have to wait until something became obvious. Similarly, he knew that to stay hidden left his sight as useless to him as his taste. He did note with increasing alarm the sun's descent, revising his estimate for dusk.

A shot from behind forced Klag to flatten himself in the dirt. How did anyone get behind him, the warrior wondered as he crawled away from his hiding spot. The taste of dirt was getting bothersome, only serving to remind him how thirsty he had become. His body was tense, anticipating another discharge, but when nothing came in the seconds that followed, Klag once more strained his tired senses. The disruptor was comfortable in his left hand, but it had no target. He could only guess where the soldier was now, certainly not in the same place as before. Wildly shooting would be a waste of energy and that, he knew, needed conserving. Instead, he slowly moved first to his knees and then to a crouch, scanning the horizon.

There! In the loose dirt dislodged by the ship's crash, there were footprints. Spaced unevenly and intended to throw off being tracked, but there was the clue Klag needed. They were deep from their greater weight, but not so deep as to indicate they were moving in single file. It was just one Jem'Hadar, Klag concluded, and he felt emboldened by the even odds. The trail implied the soldier had been moving in a circular pattern, surrounding Klag, seeking the best shot to either kill him or drive him into the open. Since the shot failed to accomplish either goal, Klag laughed to himself about how fearsome these genetic abominations were deemed.

The Jem'Hadar lived to fight, as did the Klingon people, but they did nothing but train and fight. None were assigned to build weapons or starships. As a result, they could overwhelm their opponents with sheer numbers, directed by those other genetic miscreants, the Vorta. Together, the Klingon Empire and the United Federation of Planets, and even the honorless *petaQ* of the Romulan Empire, had the people and matériel to defend their quadrant, but the battles were too often lopsided. The Federation fought bravely, Klag knew, but they were too resistant to finish off the enemy, preferring to reclaim star systems or stations and declare victory. He shook his head at their notions of mercy and their own rules of engagement. To the Klingons, their code was simple: *Hoch 'ebmey tIjon.* Capture all opportunities.

Klag continued to scan the footprints, moving slowly under cover of debris, following the soldier's path. It seemed to be circling again, in the same area as the first shot. He was going to try again now that Klag had moved. Shadows caused by the lowering sun made spotting every footstep difficult, but not impossible. Instead, Klag steadied himself and then began to anticipate the soldier's likely position. After all, for the shot to be true, a clear line of sight would have to extend in both directions. He let his eye and hand drift a bit to the left and then, acting on a mix of experience and instinct, he lowered the disruptor half a meter and squeezed the trigger.

The sound seemed deafening in the silence, but the weapon's aim was true. The Jem'Hadar's shroud shimmered and died as the soldier, who was indeed crouching for a better shot, fell backward. If five soldiers were formidable, then four was almost too easy.

As he was mentally congratulating himself, Klag felt a blow to the back of his head and he tumbled forward, off balance once again. Reptilian hands were almost immediately at his throat, and the wounded Klingon was instantly fighting for breath. His Jem'Hadar assailant made no sound, not even labored breathing, as opposed to Klag, who was now grunting and gasping with every shortened breath.

Klag tucked his knees to his chest and kicked out. The effort worked, the hands left his throat, and the Jem'Hadar fell backwards. In that moment, his disruptor, still in his clenched hand, fired repeatedly. However, the Jem'Hadar dodged the blasts, and Klag let out a hoarse curse.

He turned slowly and as he did, a stone came hurtling from a short distance away and knocked the disruptor from his hand. His assailant was once more upon him, punching at his neck and near his eyes. Both men fell backwards, with Klag's back hitting the dirt first. His shoulder stung anew but he ignored the pain. Klag did not try to strike back, but instead withstood the blows and reached for his *mek'leth*. One punch landed next to the left eye and he winced. Then a foot to his stomach forced him back. The pain that once nestled itself in his shoulder now trooped across his body. A warrior did not complain about physical discomfort, he told himself, and besides, there was no one to share that complaint with. He let himself chuckle aloud, which probably confused the Jem'Hadar. He never heard them laugh, suspected they were not bred with a sense of humor, and for a moment he considered that a sad thing.

The alien aimed a weapon at Klag. The Klingon's lips turned into a sneer. He quickly hurled himself forward, the direction least expected, somersaulting—more of a roll actually—toward the soldier and slicing at his legs with the sharp blade. The metal found the fleshy part of a calf and the Jem'Hadar staggered backward.

Klag swept his arm upward and nicked against the torso, quickly changing direction so the blade made a horizontal incision against his abdomen. The Jem'Hadar clasped his hands together and brought them with crushing force against his stump. The pain caused spots to form before his eyes and extended throughout the Klingon's entire body. It took every iota of will he still possessed to not let go of the *mek'leth*. If anything, he held on to it tighter, focusing everything he had left on his grip. His knuckles whitened.

The Jem'Hadar was going for another blow when Klag allowed himself to sink to one knee, letting the swing miss. Instead, the *mek'leth* followed his body's momentum and at the right moment, it sank into the Jem'Hadar's neck, severing the thin tube carrying the ketracel-white nutrient. The head was now mostly severed, and the body began to flail about, allowing Klag the luxury of several deep breaths, which helped him clear his mind and control the pain. One more swing of the curved blade and the head rolled off the body and sank nose first into the dirt, which greedily absorbed the dark fluids that drained.

Four dead, three alive. And the damned Vorta, who was probably armed to the teeth.

Klag felt himself exposed, having been found by a sharpshooter and a brawler. He needed to move but found himself disoriented from exhaustion, pain, and a still-hot sun.

That sun was a hand's breadth away from the horizon, so the shadows were now elongated. He suspected with the cloudless sky that the heat would radiate away quickly and the night would be cool. And natural predators might come out, drawn by the blood scent. Klag needed to be done with his job before then so he could secure his ship and await rescue. They would come. They had to respond to Kargan's last signal. No warrior should be abandoned when all were required to repel the Dominion.

Klag desperately needed a drink, but there was nothing available except within the hulk mere meters before him. Within lay a opponent. Honorless, true, but one who could just as easily kill him as a Jem'Hadar soldier. And the three that were still roaming were no doubt approaching his position. There was nowhere new or especially useful to hide, so his best bet was to keep moving. He hoped he would find more tracks but after the scuffle just completed, the dirt and sand around him were a mess and useless to his eyes.

That is, if all three were still outside and none were within, protecting the Vorta. After all, reports indicated they were sycophants and cowardly. So, how many would be inside and how many still on the prowl out here? His mind had trouble focusing on the math. The pain radiating from the aggravated stump was finally fading a bit, but he felt sore all over. His left eye was beginning to swell from the sucker punch but so far his vision was clear.

Did Jem'Hadar feel fear? Klag did not know, but he would show these laboratory-grown monstrosities that they faced an honorable foe—and their last foe as well.

"Jem'Hadar, hear me," Klag shouted. "I am Klag, son of M'Raq! I have killed four of your soldiers. And I am coming!" He didn't recognize his own voice, which startled him.

He began walking with purpose, his disruptor once more comfortably in his grip. Klag set out in a westerly direction, toward the setting sun, his pace steady. He would walk a few more meters and then make a turn as if he detected motion.

After three more meters, Klag paused at the sound of footsteps approaching. A soldier was making no secret of his approach, desperate as he was to protect his fellow combatant. At the sound, Klag twisted about, took aim, and fired. Three pulses shot out and there was the sound of contact, a skidding in the dirt and the fall of a lifeless body. A fast death and perhaps too quick. One cannot, however, complain about a clean kill.

At that moment, the sun finally had fallen below the horizon and night was beginning. With little choice, Klag moved toward the ruined starship, a source of light, heat, and, more importantly, water. His chances of success and survival were now greater inside the vessel.

Klag couldn't remember the name of the planet. Or the last time he had eaten. Or how long he had been killing Jem'Hadar. He lost count of the Jem'Hadar he had killed. Klag did know, though, that he was now entering the hulk of their craft.

The Jem'Hadar ship was smaller than the *Pagh,* which proved to work to his advantage since at best it could carry just a dozen or so, plus flight crew and troops. It was half as large across the beam, which meant there were fewer places for them to hide amidst the debris and dead bodies. Emergency lighting was still functioning as Klag crept down one corridor. He had to slosh through pools of coolant and over the dead. When he awoke earlier, Klag thought the stench of the Klingon dead could not be topped, but here, the smells of alien death were worse. It was the first time he ever regretted his people's superior sense of smell. The warrior wanted to control his breathing, keep what little remained in his stomach intact, and still move. He heard the sizzle of burning circuits, the steady drip from deep within the hull, and the groan of deck plating that wanted to collapse.

What he did not hear was any sound of life.

The Vorta was certainly within this metal carcass, and probably the remaining Jem'Hadar. Or were there two left? Klag took stock and recognized that despite his warrior's physique, he didn't have much time left before dehydration, blood loss, and physical exhaustion would make him vulnerable. He decided to pause; actually finding a bench still attached to the wall and let his body slump down. The Klingon practiced breathing exercises that he had barely remembered from his training—these were designed to allow a warrior to regain control of his body during battle. He was also dimly aware how comfortable it was to sit and how much he wanted to remain there. Klag's mind reacted in alarm and he struggled back to his feet.

Aktuh and Melota faced similar travails, Klag recalled. He was not a follower of opera, but everyone raised in the Empire knew their story. As he began to move forward once more, Klag imagined his own exploits immortalized in song. They would sing of this battle on ships throughout the fleet. Or maybe it would be turned into an opera to rival *Aktuh and Melota* and he would sit in a prized seat next to Chancellor Gowron.

No, wait. They didn't write operas about living warriors. He would have to die to have his story told. But no one was here to witness the battle and if he were to fall before reinforcements arrived, who knew how they would interpret the scene? Klag knew this was a story worthy of a song—at the very least. He began to assemble the events since the engagement above this world . . . what was its name again?

Marcel? Martok? Marisol? No, Marcan! He was standing on Marcan V, a lone Klingon soldier against a horde of Jem'Hadar. Did seven make a horde? They were more than a squad, less than a division. . . .

He blinked five times and took four deep breaths and felt more focused.

What he focused on, though, were two Jem'Hadar soldiers, aiming rifles at him. They arrived silently, he realized, or his wits were duller than he admitted.

His mind snapped into focus and in the next second, his training took over. Klag could not move left or right in the narrow corridor. The ceiling was dented and ruptured in spots, but offered no solution. He dared not turn his back on the soldiers so going forward was his only option.

Or was it?

Dangling from a torn juncture box were some form of cables, with one of them still sparking. The Jem'Hadar were standing in such a way as to block the corridor but also left them standing with their boots touching something wet. The liquid would conduct, but was there enough to do the job?

Only one way to find out.

As the Jem'Hadar gestured for the Klingon to drop his disruptor, Klag did just that. The moment his hand was free, he bent for the exposed cables, continuing in a fluid motion, as the wire touched the thick liquid. Upon contact, the sparking cable ignited nothing short of a fire that rapidly spread toward the soldiers, who were already backpedaling. The fire outpaced them and engulfed their boots and licked at their pants. One soldier continued to fire at Klag, who had bent low, retreating down the corridor, away from the conflagration.

One shot grazed his hip, sending him sprawling. Klag's teeth snapped shut as he rolled onto his back. He took stock, noting the pain was sharpest in his left shoulder and right hip, with various other points of head and body vying for attention. Two more shots passed over his head but created flying shrapnel from a destroyed door. Pieces banged off his back but several scratched his cheek. The blood felt hot as it ran into his beard. He drew strength from the fresh wounds.

Looking at the soldiers, he was amused to see them writhe in agony from the flames and their inability to snuff out the fire. No emergency equipment was visible, nor were there blankets or coverings to smother either torched body. They were done for; it would just be a matter of time.

Ignoring the pain once more, Klag tried to count the Jem'Hadar dead by his hand today. He thought there were six, maybe seven, possibly even eight. That would suffice as he hunted down the Vorta, who, while probably well armed, was not bred for fighting. It was almost going to be too easy.

The Vorta was probably trying to contact his people for help. That meant the bridge, which he needed to find. And quickly as he noted that focusing in the flickering light was getting difficult. He already had trouble concentrating, so he needed something clear.

Not bothering with stealth, Klag moved through the ship, deck by deck, room by room. No sign of the bridge, or the Vorta. In fact, it seemed this ship took more damage than the *Pagh*, a small thing but another example to Klag of the Klingons' eventual superiority in the war. He revised his thinking that if there were no computers running, then the Vorta was likely working to restore them, which meant he might be at the computer core. Given its value to all starships, the core tended to be housed in the thickest portion of the design, and the second most shielded section right after the warp core. Klag saw nothing that resembled the main computer, so he continued moving. Given his size and breadth, the corridors felt stifling and the air close and cloying.

The fatigue that had been creeping up on him was nagging at his mind as stray images appeared. They were a jumble starting with his father sitting at home, polishing a sword . . . Dorrek and Klag building targets out of mud when they were children . . . a fellow trainee ripping off her leathers after losing a wrestling match . . . Will Riker flipping Klag to the deck of the *Pagh* . . . a fight when Klag came to the rescue of his friends when they had shore leave on Barratas . . . a flying creature that nearly killed him on a planetary survey. . . .

So many experiences but none to match the one he was now enduring. He wanted to continue adding stanzas and wondered who could add a tune. He liked tunes with a steady beat and a rousing chorus so the deck plates themselves would ring.

Stop it, he told himself. Find the Vorta, the song would finish itself.

He descended lower into the ship, fighting to stay focused and find the computer core and the Vorta. If he could dispatch six, no seven, Jem'Hadar, a lowly clone should pose little problem. But he remained elusive, which angered Klag. He stalked the decks with a purpose to his step but found himself frequently forcing himself to focus, first his hearing, then his eyesight. His prey wouldn't dare go outside, exposed to the elements. After all, he had no protection.

The lower he went the more Klag began to doubt his conclusion. Of course, he had yet to find the computer core, so it was hard to say if that was so. There was one branch that seemed to narrow, and Klag wedged himself along the walls, curious. The lighting was even dimmer, as if this were a little-used section and he wondered what was housed here.

Clank.

His eyes widened at the sound of metal against metal, although

muffled by the door before him. There were no signs telling anyone what was beyond the doorway and he guessed that was a security measure, one he approved of. The sound repeated itself and
Klag debated between his *mek'leth* and his disruptor. He decided to
honor his ancestors and went for the blade. It felt good in his
hands, much like the days he spent hunting *targ* at home. Even
then, there was competition with Dorrek, but it was good competition and they battled like brothers should.

He shook his head, clearing his mind one final time and focusing on the sound. The Klingon crept along the corridor, cursing its
tight confines since it would hamper a retreat or even twisting to
fight.

The door was ajar, pried off tracks not damaged from the crash.
The Vorta purposely sought this out, so it had to be important.
Klag stood before the doorway, narrowing his focus over every
edge, looking for traps. He doubted there was time for any, but he
refused to take an unnecessary risk and die a fool's death.

Satisfied there was nothing hindering his entrance, Klag regripped the *mek'leth* and stepped into the room, expecting his
minimal noise to be masked by the banging. The Vorta was in profile to him, absorbed in trying to repair something through brute
force. Of course, he was weak and his idea of brute force was
laughable to a Klingon. What surprised him was that this was one
of the phased polaron beam control rooms, not the central computer. He seemed more interested in having ready defenses than a
functioning means of communications. For this, Klag mentally
gave him credit.

"Ah, my opponent arrives to exact some finality to this exchange," the Vorta said in its annoying singsong way. "I salute your
courage."

"Your soldiers are dead," Klag gruffly responded. He towered
over the Vorta and was pleased to note the room gave him space to
maneuver. The Vorta seemed to stop working, and the pistol was
out of reach. What was it humans said, shooting ducks in a barrel?

"They fought bravely but lost to a no doubt superior combatant," the clone said with a smile. He even nodded his head in Klag's direction. This was going to be too simple and the warrior wanted a challenge. "You must kill me now, before I have the opportunity to kill you."

Klag laughed out loud at the notion of the Vorta managing to kill a Klingon, especially in these circumstances. His opponent frowned like a hurt child and then his features returned to their neutral, placid expression. Klag began to step closer, ready to use the *mek'leth* to end this charade.

The Vorta raised his hands and looked ready to surrender. Klag smiled and a part of him wanted this over so he could heal and a part of him wanted a challenge.

He must have lost focus or blinked, for suddenly Klag was losing his balance. He fell heavily to the deck, losing his breath with the impact. As he struggled to rise, his boots felt a tug. The damned creature had taken the time to rig a trap. And Klag, curse him, missed it and was now ensnared in some form of wire.

As he attempted to turn over and use his *mek'leth* to cut himself free, a heavy weight knocked him back to the deck. It was the damned Vorta; he jumped and landed heavily on his back once more. As the enemy leapt into the air to land a third time, Klag managed to roll onto his side and the landing figure only straddled him, missing altogether.

The Vorta reached into a pocket and withdrew a handheld device that glowed green in the dim light. A thumb depressed a trigger and a pointed object emerged. Klag didn't know what it was, nor did he care. What mattered was that anything pointy in close proximity was a threat, especially in his weakened condition. He rolled hard to his right and knocked his opponent off balance, but not enough to make him fall.

Again, his reflexes were slow, and Klag was struck by the Vorta's weapon. It was being gripped and regripped as if the Vorta had never held it before. Then Klag saw that it was actually a tool that

tapered to one end, imitating a knife. He truly was an inexperi-
enced fighter, but even those could be dangerous when fighting
for their lives.

The tool was waved back and forth, trying to keep Klag at
bay. Instead, he was timing the Vorta, noting that he moved in a
predictable fashion. Three-second arcs, the Klingon counted as
he backed up. His enemy's expression was still neutral which ir-
ritated Klag no end. Klag twisted to move in time with the arc
and thrust with his *mek'leth,* coming close to the defenseless
Vorta.

The blade bit deep, organs being sliced into pieces and blood
rushing out the widening wound. Klag knew this was a killing
blow and would have nothing further to worry about. The Vorta
looked at the wound, then at Klag. He muttered, "Oh . . ." and collapsed to the deck.

Klag made certain he would move no more and then left the
room. The wounded Klingon made his way back toward the
rip in the hull where he would wait for his comrades-in-arms.
As he approached the new exit, he saw the stars in the night
sky. They twinkled and it was bright with a biting chill in the
air. It made Klag think of the time he and B'Ursana snuck away
from home to go lie under the stars, two naked youths with
their futures yet to be written. The air was just as crisp, the sky
filled with possibilities. As Klag slumped obliviously to the
deck, he swore he felt B'Ursana's teeth bite his neck, just like
the first time. . . .

When Klag next opened his eyes, his first thought was that *Sto-Vo-
Kor* looked too bright.

As his vision cleared, he saw several Klingons clustered by a
monitor. One saw Klag was awake and announced himself as
Ganok, captain of the rescue fleet. His first officer, Melik, had
given Klag up for dead until he groaned when warriors hefted
him from the Dominion ship.

"The Jem'Hadar scattered out here," Ganok said, gesturing toward the all-too-familiar plains.

"My kills," Klag simply stated.

Ganok nodded in satisfaction.

"There are more inside I claim," Klag continued. "Including their Vorta handler."

"Yes, we found him. You killed six. . . ."

"Seven," a clear-headed Klag said with authority.

"Seven Jem'Hadar and a Vorta with just one arm?"

"Yes."

Ganok reared back and laughed, then clapped a hand on Klag's good shoulder. Clearly, this was an entirely different kind of captain than Kargan. Klag liked him immediately.

"I am Klag, son of M'Raq, first officer of the *Pagh*."

"Ganok, son of Ganthet, captain of the *Ro'Kronos*," his host said. "Your ship is no more."

"But it died in service to the Empire," Klag said with solemnity.

"You are the sole survivor of Marcan V, an excellent soldier," the captain admitted.

"What of the fleet?"

"My fleet has been dispatched to replace the one destroyed here. But no Dominion ships are here to challenge us. Marcan is once again ours, and soon the entire Allicar Sector will be free."

"So what do we do now?" Klag couldn't imagine being retired after his exploits here. He dreaded the notion of sitting beside his father, both warriors reduced to jokes.

"My orders are to leave engineers to study this ship. There is much to learn here."

Klag looked at Ganok, studying the captain. He was maybe a decade older than himself and he wore scars of battle on one cheek. The full beard was knotted at chest level and the hair was pulled back and sporting a matching knot in the rear. He carried himself well, comfortable with command.

"And there is much my crew could learn from the Hero of

Marcan V. Join us in the mess hall—if you have nowhere better to be."

Klag sat up, his head swimming from fatigue and hasty medical repair. Maybe it was not a good day to die, but instead, a good day to continue his battle.

Idly, Klag began to imagine a new ship, a new crew, and new songs to be sung.

Stone Cold Truths

Peter David

War correspondence: In 1997, Pocket Books premiered *Star Trek: New Frontier.* Developed by Peter David and John J. Ordover and written by the former, *New Frontier* was the first novel series that didn't directly tie into one of the existing TV shows. Taking place on the *U.S.S. Excalibur* under the command of Captain Mackenzie Calhoun, *New Frontier* also features *Star Trek: The Next Generation* guest stars Elizabeth Shelby, Robin Lefler, and Dr. Selar, as well as several original characters. The series has gone on to include over a dozen novels, a short story anthology, and even a comic book. That comic book, *Double Time,* was a time-travel adventure, which ended with the *Excalibur* accidentally leaping eighteen months into their future, from a time prior to the *Star Trek: Deep Space Nine* episode "In the Pale Moonlight" to a time just prior to that show's final episode, "What You Leave Behind." This story takes place between *Double Time* and the novel *Star Trek: The Next Generation: Double Helix* Book 5: *Double or Nothing.*

Peter David

Peter David is the *New York Times* best-selling author of numerous *Star Trek* novels, including the incredibly popular *New Frontier* series, the next book of which is the forthcoming hardcover *After the Fall*. In addition, he has also written dozens of other books, including his acclaimed original novel *Sir Apropos of Nothing* and its sequels, *The Woad to Wuin* and *Tong Lashing*. David is also well known for his comic book work, particularly his award-winning run on *The Incredible Hulk*. He recently authored the novelizations of both *Spider-Man* motion pictures, as well as that of the *Hulk* film. He lives in New York.

Zak Kebron was feeling his age.

It wasn't simply that the Brikar's body was more attuned to the shifting seasons on the like-named planet of Brikar, and that those changes inflicted heretofore unknown pain into his joints.

No, it was that he was seeing himself.

As it so happened this particular day, with the sun high in the sky and the temperature a relatively balmy one hundred and twenty degrees in the shade, Zak heard himself before he saw himself. He heard a thudding, a thumping, the ground shaking as something large approached. The Kebron home was largely devoid of furniture, as were most Brikar homes, since they were minimalist beings and saw little need for such frivolities. Nevertheless, what few bits of decoration were there trembled under the sustained impact, and Zak shook his head.

Actually, Kebron didn't exactly shake his head. More accurately, his entire massive torso swayed a bit from side to side, since Kebron wasn't possessed of a neck. His head was joined squarely to his shoulders, and the entirety of his humanoid body was covered with skin so thick and impenetrable that it was often perceived to be akin to rock. They'd had to develop new sizes of Starfleet uniforms just to accommodate him when he had joined up. At home on Brikar, as was the case with the rest of his race, he simply went unclothed. But Starfleet tended to be a bit more provincial.

He came as close to a smile as his physiognomy allowed him.

Starfleet. That had been so long ago . . . so very, very long ago. He hadn't thought about it in years, and when he did, it was almost as if he was dispassionately watching someone else's life unfold in his mind. It had so little to do with the being he was now.

The source of the trembling drew closer and closer, and then the door to the three-room domicile burst open and Cal was standing there. Cal, looking so much as Zak had looked at that age. It was almost like staring into a mirror that opened up a portal back through time . . . which, now that Zak thought about it, he had on one occasion. This circumstance, though, wasn't fraught with time paradox possibilities.

In essence, he was Kebron in miniature, except his outer husk was the typical gray of young Brikar. Although very young for a Brikar, not even an adolescent, he was already as large as a typical Terran adult and could easily break one of those poor, delicate creatures in half.

He had been stomping particularly hard in his approach, indicating that he was upset about something. He said nothing, though, just glowered at Zak, which indicated that somehow he felt whatever was bothering him was Zak's fault. Zak, of course, had done nothing. That didn't bother young Cal, who was perfectly content to blame Zak for whatever troubles befell him simply because Zak Kebron was responsible for his being born.

"Rough day at school?" asked Zak.

More glowering, although the intensity level seemed to have been notched up a bit.

"You're my homework," he said.

This announcement took Zak a bit by surprise. "Am I."

"Mentor Kelner said we are to begin studying the glories of war."

"The . . . glories of war." Zak considered that. "That was the Mentor's exact phrasing. The glories of war."

"He said that wars are great endeavors, in which the truth of the enemy always comes out."

"Did he, now."

"You keep doing that," Cal said. "Saying things that sound like questions, except there is no actual question in your voice."

"Have I been doing that."

Yet more glowering. It was comforting to Zak that, if he had the need to get Cal to glower, he knew how to go about it: Say anything aloud and that would provoke it. "I do not understand," he said, "how your Mentor's views on war translates into my being your homework."

"He assigned me," said Cal, sounding as if Zak were the greatest moron ever to walk the planet since he had not figured this out already, "to ask you about your experiences during the Opinion War a hundred and fifty years ago."

Zak stared at him for a moment, his mind flying back a century and a half to try and recall what the hell it was that Cal was referring to. Tentatively, he said, "You mean the Dominion War?"

"I think so."

"You think so. You should try to be sure, Cal, since the Dominion War *happened* and the Opinion War . . . well, that's ongoing, I suppose, on every planet everywhere."

"Who *cares?*" Apparently he thought that by adding even greater emphasis to the question, it would have more weight.

"Not I," said Zak Kebron mildly. "I have retired from caring. So . . . I am to describe to you my involvement in the Dominion War."

"That's right. In as much detail as you can recall."

"For your Mentor who celebrates the glories of war and the great purity of its moral truths."

"Yes."

"Let me consider it for a bit."

Cal stared at him. "Consider it?"

"Precisely what to say and how to say it. Much happened. Plus, it was quite a long time ago. My memory may not be everything it once was."

"Father . . ."

"Plus," Zak said with quiet emphasis, "a 'please' might not be out of line."

"Is that what this is about?"

Zak said nothing. He simply sat there. Finally he heard a low, growled word trickle from between Cal's lips like water drops from a rusted spigot.

"I didn't quite catch that."

"Please," Cal repeated, a bit louder and far more resentfully.

"Very well," Kebron said at last. "Take extensive notes on this. I am quite sure you will want to write this up."

And then he began to talk . . .

I stood on the bridge of the *Excalibur* in my customary spot at the tactical station. Ahead of us was the Starship *Corinth,* hurtling through space as quickly as its warp engines would propel it. Behind us, hanging in space and effecting repairs—but not quickly enough to be of any use—was a Romulan warbird. The reason it was crippled was because of us, and we were desperate to try and undo the damage we had done.

Understand that the return of the *Excalibur* could not have been at a more poorly timed moment. We had been time traveling, you see . . . leaping through time by hurling ourselves around a sun at top speed. Our return from the past had not gone exactly as we would have liked, unfortunately, since we'd overshot our original time of departure by eighteen months. The result was that for eighteen months of relative, "real" time . . . the *Excalibur* had ceased to exist. Starfleet had lost track of us, and the general belief was that we had been destroyed.

The problem was, we didn't dare attempt to go backward and then forward yet again. First, the continued strain of time jumping might well have torn the vessel apart. And second, since a "reality" had been created in which the *Excalibur* was MIA for a year and a half . . . we didn't dare to "unwrite" that reality. There was no way of calculating the ripple effect such a move might have had. Frankly, considering we had just had a singularly unpleasant and unfortunate encounter with the realities of changing reality on the planet Haresh, none of us—particularly Captain Mackenzie Calhoun—had the stomach for embarking upon such a venture yet again.

Nor was Captain Calhoun's first officer, Commander Shelby, especially happy with him. More often than not, she would try to confine their disagreements to behind the closed doors of his ready room. But she was feeling somewhat frazzled at that point, and I cannot say I entirely blamed her.

"With all respect, Captain, this is a hell of a fix you've gotten us into," she told him.

"I appreciate the respect, Commander," replied Calhoun with that trademark sarcasm of his. In retrospect, it's hard to believe that some months later they would wind up getting married. Or perhaps it's not all that difficult to believe, at that. "Mr. Kebron . . . kindly inform Starfleet of our return."

I went ahead and did so without even acknowledging that he had spoken. I think I grunted slightly. That was about the most I did to let someone know their request had been heard. I was not remotely the erudite father you've come to know and . . . well, know.

Then, while preparing to send out word of our return, I noticed something coming through on the tactical warning systems. Before I could say anything, however, Robin Lefler—I think she was an ensign at that time—spoke up. Lefler was at the ops station, and very little, if anything, escaped her notice. "Captain," she said abruptly, "we've picked up a starship heading toward us, bearing 227 mark 3, moving at warp five."

"It appears we have company," said Calhoun, but he sounded suspicious. When I first met Mackenzie Calhoun—and for a good portion of the time thereafter—I was wary of him. But slowly I learned to trust him, at least as much as I trusted anyone. And one of the things I knew of a certainty was that his instincts were unimpeachable. If something felt off to him, the reason for it was that it was off.

"Confirming approach, Captain," said Lieutenant Soleta. Soleta was the Vulcan science officer. At least, we thought she was a Vulcan at the time, although we learned differently later. "Energy signature identifies her as the *Corinth,* a *Cheyenne*-class starship."

"That's Captain Taggart's boat," said Shelby.

"You know him?" asked Calhoun.

She nodded. "A bit. Very much by-the-book. You'd like him, Captain, if you happened to be completely different from the way you are now." She turned to me and said, "Mr. Kebron, open a hailing frequency—"

"Belay that," Calhoun said. "Maintain radio silence."

Shelby looked at him in surprise. "May I ask why, Captain?"

"You may," he said, pacing the bridge. Without giving her time to inquire, he called out, "Bridge to Engineering."

"Engineering, Burgoyne here."

"Burgoyne," said Calhoun, "shut down power throughout the ship. I want us to look dead."

Well, naturally this caused some confusion among the bridge crew. "I want to see what he does," was the only explanation Calhoun would give us.

Within moments, everything but the auxiliary power and emergency lighting was off. Which isn't to say that we couldn't crank up at a moment's notice; we could. But Calhoun clearly felt that something was amiss. He had some sort of awareness for danger that bordered on the supernatural, and he'd learned that to ignore such concerns was to court disaster. So he never ignored them.

The *Corinth* almost went right past us without slowing, but then dropped out of warp space at the last moment. She circled back around and then hung there, just staring at us.

"What do you expect to happen here, Mac?" asked Shelby.

"If he's by the book," Calhoun told her, "he'll hail us. Attempt to establish contact. Possibly even raise shields . . ."

"Sir!" Lefler suddenly announced. "They're bringing shields on line—"

"See?" Shelby said. "Totally by the b—"

"And they're running weapons hot. Targeting our primary and secondary engines."

Shelby's head snapped around. "What?!" she practically barked.

"Shields up!" called out Calhoun. He didn't sound at all perturbed.

I brought the shields up . . . and suddenly our entire viewscreen was filled with another image altogether. The starship was blocked from view by none other than a Romulan warbird, shimmering into existence barely a thousand klicks to our starboard. In terms of distance in space, that was practically right in our laps. The warbird was between us and the *Corinth*.

Shelby sounded almost relieved. "The *Corinth* wasn't aiming at us! She was targeting the warbird!"

"How?" demanded Calhoun. "How did they penetrate the cloaking device?"

"We've been out of touch for eighteen months, Captain," Soleta pointed out. "New developments in technology could easily have—"

"The warbird and the *Corinth* are exchanging fire, Captain!" Lefler suddenly said.

She was absolutely right. The Romulan warbird was firing upon the *Corinth* with as much ferocity as the starship was shooting at the Romulan ship.

With only seconds to make a decision as to whose side to take, Calhoun took the only reasonable course. He ordered us to fire upon the Romulan vessel.

This we immediately did. Our forward phasers ripped into her and the warbird staggered under the dual barrage of ourselves and the *Corinth*.

Just as suddenly, however, Calhoun ordered me to open a channel and, once I did, said, *"Excalibur* to *Corinth.* We've got a handle on the Romulan. Back off and let us take charge."

Under ordinary circumstances, the *Corinth* would have done exactly that. Once again, though, somehow Calhoun anticipated the result. At the very least, he wasn't surprised by it.

As the critically wounded Romulan warbird dropped down and away from us, the *Corinth* angled around and opened fire on us.

The shields absorbed the brunt of the attack, but the *Excalibur* still trembled under the assault. Systems went out throughout the ship. "All auxiliary power to shields! Mr. Kebron," called Calhoun over the pounding, "kindly inform the *Corinth* that we don't appreciate their attitude."

We returned fire, hitting the ship's port nacelles and striking a glancing blow off their engineering hull. But that was about all the damage we were able to inflict, because the *Corinth* was smaller and more maneuverable than the *Excalibur.* It peeled out of there immediately, leaving us floating nearby the newly crippled Romulan vessel.

That was when the Romulan commander appeared on our screen, and he was extremely angry, to put it mildly. What he told us sounded insane, as if the entire galaxy had been reordered in our absence.

The Romulans were now our allies, thanks to the revelation of a Dominion-backed assassination of a prominent Romulan senator. As for the *Corinth* . . . she'd been captured by the Cardassians.

The *Corinth* had been stolen out of drydock by Cardassian spies and was being piloted, at high speed, out of Federation space and toward Dominion space. If she was able to make it there, it would provide the Dominion with a world of information about Starfleet vessels that we didn't want them to have.

As the Earth saying goes, we had been thrown into the deep end of the pool. Out of touch all those months, and suddenly we were in the middle of a key moment in a war that had only just started when we left.

But did that slow us down? It most certainly did not.

Making best possible speed, we took off without hesitation after the *Corinth*.

There was a good deal of tension on the bridge, not much conversation. Calhoun watched the stars hurtle past, a look of fixed concentration on his face. Every so often, Burgoyne would send updates from engineering as to how repairs were coming along. Even the normally chatty Shelby was silent, although I noticed that one or two times as she passed Calhoun, she allowed a hand to rest briefly on one of his shoulders. It was as if she drew comfort from it.

There was no strategy or elegance in what we were doing at that point. It was a pure race. We were able to follow the *Corinth;* it was purely a matter of being able to overtake it. Our navigator, Mark McHenry, was doing everything he could to try and plot an intercept course, but there really wasn't any way to do it when the ship you're chasing is making a beeline.

We were also faced with the harsh reality that, if we didn't get them soon enough, we'd wind up in Dominion space along with the *Corinth,* and they'd have two prizes instead of one.

"Are we going to make it, Mac?" Shelby asked.

"We always do," he said. He didn't lack for confidence.

"Sir!" It was Lefler. "*Corinth.* dead ahead. Fifty thousand klicks and closing. At current rate, we will be able to overtake her in four minutes."

"Ready tractor beams."

"Tractor beams remain out of commission," I had to tell him.

"Very well," he said. "Bring the port photon cannons on line. Prepare the grappling hooks and lines. Mr. Kebron," he said briskly, getting to his feet, "prepare a boarding party of about twenty men."

"Will you be leading us, Captain?" I asked.

"Of course," he said.

Shelby took him briefly in her arms, held him tight. "Good luck," she said breathlessly.

"I make my own luck," he assured her.

Just as Lefler has foreseen, within minutes we were alongside the speeding *Corinth*. We, the boarding party, were poised atop the saucer section, our space suits protecting us from the ravages of space. You see, firing upon the *Corinth* would have done us no good because the ship's shields were up. However, individual men could easily pass between them, and that was our plan. Our boots magnetized, each of us was holding a grappling gun, and we waited for the captain's order.

"*Open fire!*" the captain called through the comlink in his helmet.

The port phaser cannons snapped out of the engineering section and targeted the *Corinth*. Within seconds they were firing, hammering the sides of the fleeing starship, trying not to destroy it, but to slow it down. In this regard, the cannons succeeded. The *Corinth* began to slow, and it was at that point that Captain Calhoun called out, "*Fire grappling guns!*"

We took aim and fired. The hooks sailed across the vacuum of space and, with perfect precision, sank into the hull of the *Corinth*.

"*Go!*" shouted the Captain, and we swung across the void, firing our phasers as we went. Several of our men were blown off into space as the *Corinth* tried to pick us off with their phasers, but the rest of us managed to land on the side of the runaway starship.

"*Get us inside, Zak!*" Calhoun ordered. It was not a problem. We had landed right near an access port. I gripped the side of the port door, pulled with all my strength, and the entire port came away in my hand. It left a gaping hole in the side of the vessel through which we were able to enter.

We stampeded through the corridors. The Cardassians came at us, trying to pick us off one by one, but they had no success. We were too thorough, blasting at anyone coming near us. The Cardassians were blasted backwards and, with the sort of efficiency that only a crack team can command, we made our way up to the bridge.

None of us knew, of course, that the Cardassian commander was a shapeshifter . . . one of the members of a race called the Founders.

"You are most resourceful to have gotten this far," he told us. "But you will go no further."

His skin began to ooze and twist, and suddenly he was the size of . . . well, of me.

"Get back, Captain!" I shouted, putting myself between the Founder and my commanding officer. The Founder charged, slammed into me, and I staggered inside my space suit.

"Kebron!" Calhoun cried out, "don't sacrifice yourself for me!"

"Just doing my job, sir," I assured him. The fortunate thing was that the Founder couldn't do much damage unless he was willing to harden his body. Every time he did, I pounded on him, harder and harder. We struggled, grappling, and I shoved him up repeatedly against the wall, until he cried out in pain and then shattered into a thousand pieces.

And so ended the attempt hijacking of the *Corinth*. It was our only major involvement in the Dominion War . . . but if we hadn't been there, who knows how much the new information from the stolen ship would have prolonged it . . . or even changed its outcome. I even received a Federation Medal of Valor for my actions during the incident.

It was a proud time for us all.

Zak Kebron was not entirely surprised when Cal's Mentor demanded to see him. He made an appointment at his leisure to visit with the Mentor at the school. When he arrived, not only was the Mentor waiting for him, but so was Cal. If Zak thought Cal had given him dirty looks before, they were nothing compared to what was being fired his way now.

As was customary, the Mentor addressed Zak by house name, since he was the seniormost of his family. "Kebron," he said tersely, seated behind his desk with his massive fingers resting lightly on the surface. "Cal turned in his report today on your time in the Dominion War."

"I see."

There was a pregnant pause. "Is there anything you wish to say?" the Mentor asked him.

Zak thought about that. "Nice weather."

The Mentor leaned forward. *"Grappling hooks?* Side mounted *phaser cannons?"*

"Do they present a problem?"

"Somewhat. The means by which you describe boarding the *Corinth* is, in fact, classically associated with Earth pirates, circa the seventeenth century. The pirates would soften up the sailing vessel they intended to plunder by opening fire with their cannons—usually projecting out the side of the ships—and then would swing across onto their victim and board via grappling hooks."

"Imagine that."

"You lied." It was Cal who had spoken.

"Yes," said Kebron.

"What possible reason," the Mentor demanded, "could you have to lie to you son?"

"To counter the lies you told him," shot back Kebron. "About the glories of war. The wonders of it." He shifted his gaze from the Mentor to Cal. "There is no glory in war, Cal. There are great individual accomplishments. But these occur in spite of war, not because of it. They come from the individual spirit refusing to be beaten down."

"You could make your point without lies," Cal said.

"No. Because that's what war is. Lies. All wars are based upon lies. All wars are fostered by lies. The specifics of the lies may change. 'The war will be quick.' 'The war is blessed by God.' 'We will kill as few people as possible.' 'We will only commit a handful of troops.' 'The war will be over soon.' 'You can trust me.' 'Wars end.' So many lies, on and on and on—"

"Kebron," Mentor began.

Zak didn't let him speak. "You wish to know the truth? The truth is that our one brush with the Dominion War involved responding to a distress signal from a Romulan warbird and arriving too late. The Romulan ship was gone. The *Corinth*—which, indeed, had been stolen by the Cardassians—was also gone. Although 'gone' may be too broad a word. Wreckage hung everywhere. We moved through it, and it was like a graveyard in space. Romulan bodies, pieces of them, arms, legs, heads, mixing with similar death and dismemberment from the Cardassians. We didn't even fully understand what had happened until we spoke to Starfleet.

"Heads in EVA helmets bounced off our viewscreen. You haven't experienced the glories of war, Mentor, until heads have bounced off your viewscreen."

"It was for a good cause," the Mentor said tightly, "and it flies in the face of what you said. There were no lies in the Dominion War . . . and it did end."

"Really."

"Yes. Really."

Zak turned back to Cal. "The Mentor has apparently forgotten the Sisko lie."

"The . . . what?" asked Cal, looking interested in spite of himself.

"That hardly can be taken into consideration," Mentor told him. "Since it was hardly pivotal, and—"

"Remember when I spoke earlier of the assassination of a Romulan senator by the Dominion? That was a lie, concocted by a Starfleet space station commander, to guarantee the Romulans would ally with the Federation. The Romulans didn't find out about it until many years later. That led to the Third Great Earth-

Romulan War. And more wars after that. Always more and more wars. Considering it's something that every race becomes involved in so reluctantly, you'd think it would be more popular than it is."

"Sometimes," the Mentor said, "there is no other way."

"And that's the most popular lie of all."

"I do not need to be lectured by you, Kebron," said the Mentor. "You've done enough damage to this child for one day. Grappling hooks, of all things."

Zak Kebron stood and gestured for Cal to follow him. Cal did so, and then the Mentor called after him, "Claiming you were awarded a medal . . . another lie, I suppose?"

"No, it's true. I was awarded a medal. Just not for that."

"For what, then?"

"For killing my best friend," Kebron told him. "But it was connected to a war . . . and that justifies everything that one does. Does it not, Mentor?"

"I think," the Mentor said stiffly, "you may want to consider alternate means of education for your son in the future, since we clearly do not see eye to eye on these matters."

Zak Kebron walked out of the office, and Cal fell into step next to him. "You made me look stupid," Cal said.

"Yes."

"But you made the Mentor look more stupid."

"I did."

"Why?"

Stopping and turning to face his son, Zak said, "Because I was in a war for shaping your views . . . and he needed to be a casualty of that war."

Cal stared at him for a very long time. "You're very strange," he decided.

Zak Kebron chuckled low in his throat. "You, my son, do not know from strange. Let me tell you about what happened with Mark McHenry."

"Does it involve lies?"

"It's bizarre enough not to require any."

"Is there a war?"

"Actually . . . yes."

"Great," said Cal. "Let's hear it. I love stories about war, true or not."

Zak Kebron sighed. "Splendid."

Requital

Michael A. Martin & Andy Mangels

War correspondence: The bulk of this story takes place at the end of the war, during the final *Star Trek: Deep Space Nine* episode, "What You Leave Behind."

Michael A. Martin & Andy Mangels

Michael A. Martin's solo short fiction has appeared in *The Magazine of Fantasy & Science Fiction*. He has also coauthored (with Andy Mangels) several *Star Trek* novels, a pair of eBooks in the *Starfleet Corps of Engineers* series, and three novels based on the *Roswell* television series. Martin was the regular cowriter (also with Andy) of Marvel Comics's *Star Trek: Deep Space Nine* series, and has written for Atlas Editions' *Star Trek Universe* subscription card series, *Star Trek Monthly*, *Dreamwatch*, Grolier Books, WildStorm, and Platinum Studios. He lives with his family in Portland, Oregon.

Andy Mangels has coauthored several *Star Trek* novels, two *Starfleet Corps of Engineers* eBooks, and three novels based on TV's *Roswell* (all written with Michael A. Martin). Flying solo, Andy has penned *Animation on DVD: The Ultimate Guide; Star Wars: The Essential Guide To Characters; Beyond Mulder & Scully: The Mysterious Characters of The X-Files;* and *From Scream To Dawson's Creek: The Phenomenal Career of Kevin Williamson*. Mangels has written for numerous licensed properties as well as a plethora of entertainment and lifestyle periodicals. He lives in Portland, Oregon, with his longtime partner, Don Hood, and their dog, Bela. Visit his website at www.andymangels.com.

The approaching Jem'Hadar were relentless. Dozens of them drew inexorably nearer to the defense perimeter. They were massive, scowling gargoyles, their heavy bodies moving quickly on incongruously catlike feet.

Sweat ran down Reese's dust-caked brow and stung his eyes. He ignored the irritation, raised his phaser rifle, and drew a bead on one of the nearest Jem'Hadar soldiers. The captured ketracel-white tubes that dangled from Reese's neck—his trophies of war—clattered like an orchestra's percussion section in the relative silence of the arid Chin'toka wasteland that surrounded him.

Reese's orders were to hold the captured array for Starfleet—and to keep the Jem'Hadar from reclaiming it—at all costs. He and about a hundred and fifty other Starfleet soldiers had spent the past five months doing just that.

Now Reese was one of only forty-three surviving defenders. He was certain that in a few seconds that number would decline even further.

But there was no time to worry about that now. He had a job to do. Letting his training overcome his fatigue and fear, Reese held his breath and fired.

The first Jem'Hadar went down. The men and women who crouched beside Reese in defense of the perimeter, all of them Starfleet soldiers and engineers who were every bit as tired, frightened, and angry as he was, fired as well. The harsh traceries of intermittently crossing phaser beams briefly turned the postsunset gloaming into high noon.

Jem'Hadar were falling, crashing to the hard-packed, dusty earth like so many boulders. But behind them, scaling the mounds of the dead and dying, still more came. Their faces bore testament to their berserker rage; they were every bit as implacable, every bit as contemptuous of death as those who had just preceded them into its jaws.

The phaser fire became more frantic all around Reese as the Jem'Hadar front line drew steadily nearer. Men and women screamed in pain and rage as some of the Jem'Hadar stormed across the perimeter, penetrating the front line.

Breathe. And keep firing, *Reese told himself silently, his heart pounding.*

He heard a distant shriek; it sounded like Kellin, one of the engineers in charge of figuring out—unsuccessfully, so far—how to tap into the Dominion communications array. Reese turned and saw a Jem'Hadar shoot Vargas right between the shoulder blades before he could get off a shot of his own.

Reese mowed down Vargas's killer. Where are the goddamned reinforcements?

He glanced to his right. Captain Sisko was crouched there, fighting hand-to-hand against a pair of snarling Jem'Hadar. The captain's uniform was still improbably pristine, spit-and-polish clean.

That's because he hasn't been stuck in this hellhole for the past five months. *A flicker of anger toward the senior officer flashed across Reese's mind, but it was gone as quickly as it had ignited.*

A Jem'Hadar leapt straight at Reese from across the trench that marked the front line. Reese swung his rifle like a club, landing a stunning blow on the Jem'Hadar's temple. Letting the rifle dangle from its strap, he drew a wicked-looking knife he'd taken off a Jem'Hadar corpse after an earlier battle and sliced his current foe's throat from ear to ear. The monster collapsed into the dust, gurgling, already well on its way to the same place its kind had sent Captain Loomis, Commander Parker, Lieutenant Mc-Greevey, Chief Larkin, and so many other good people—

Reese turned and saw that two more Jem'Hadar soldiers had suddenly cleared the barrier, their rifles and razor-sharp kar'takin *raised high in Sisko's direction. One of them struck the captain, and he went down, ap-*

parently unconscious. As one of the enemy raised a rifle to deliver the death
shot, Reese rushed him. Bobbing and weaving, he buried his blade deeply
in the creature's belly and twisted with all his strength. A phaser blast
struck the Jem'Hadar beside him, blowing an enormous hole in the crea-
ture's torso.

"Die, you bastard," Reese hissed as he withdrew his gore-slathered
knife, then shoved the Jem'Hadar's heavy body away from him.

Time seemed to stop as the creature swayed. Then, in spite of an appar-
ently mortal abdominal wound, the Jem'Hadar steadied itself.

And began to laugh.

"It doesn't matter how many times you kill us in your sleep," it said, its
voice a sepulchral rumble. "It will change nothing."

"That's fine," Reese said. "I'll just keep killing you over and over
again. Until you quit coming."

"But that is exactly my point, Reese. We will not stop. We cannot stop.
Any more than you were able to prevent this."

The Jem'Hadar grinned and held up a human head.

It was Billy, his eyes empty, his bloodless lips forming an ellipse of
horrified surprise. Until now, Reese had thought he'd been vaporized
a year earlier.

Reese screamed his rage and pain. His knife raised, he threw himself
straight at the grinning Jem'Hadar.

"Rough night, Reese?" Nog said, hobbling toward the table and
carrying his breakfast tray with one hand. The little Ferengi leaned
heavily on a metal crutch, his newly installed biosynthetic leg evidently still too weak to support his weight.

"I've had rougher ones," Reese lied, then tore off another hunk
of his too-dry bran muffin. He offered Nog a smile that he hoped
would discourage any more questions. "About five months of
them, when the Jem'Hadar were doing their damnedest to kill me."

Reese had spent many of his mornings with Nog since arriving
at Starbase 235's convalescent hospital, a facility that specialized in
treating wounds that left no external scars.

"I've had a nightmare or two of my own," said Nog, who was staring intently into a plate of wriggling tube grubs.

"Understandable," Reese said, wondering what it would have been like to have lost a limb permanently the way Nog had. "I take it they've got you visiting with a counselor?"

The young Ferengi nodded.

"Does it help?"

"Sure. At least that's what they tell me."

Now Reese saw the same haunted look in Nog's eyes that he'd seen in the mirror every day for the past few weeks. Deep down, he knew that no amount of counseling could fix that.

"How about you, Reese?" Nog asked. "Do the Jem'Hadar still visit you in the dead of night?"

Reese took a large swallow of hot coffee, actually reveling in the pain as it burned its way down.

He recalled the empty, terror-stricken eyes of the only woman he'd ever truly loved—the woman the Jem'Hadar had taken from him. He shivered slightly as the memory of the nightmare-Jem'Hadar's cruel laughter returned unbidden.

"I wouldn't know," he said, pushing his plate aside as he rose from his chair. "I don't have dreams anymore."

That night, Reese's nocturnal wanderings returned him yet again to the dusty Chin'toka flatlands. He was standing on the arid plain near the cavern that housed AR-558, near Captain Sisko and Lieutenant Commander Worf. The Klingon seemed quietly impressed as he surveyed the dozens of Jem'Hadar dead that were strewn about the exterior of the captured Dominion communications bunker.

Reese turned away from the facility, watching as the group of Starfleet officers that had just arrived from the U.S.S. Veracruz began settling in and cleaning up the detritus of the recent battle. After five months of keeping AR-558 out of the hands of the Jem'Hadar, relief had finally arrived. The Veracruz was rotating out the injured and exhausted.

And bringing down more spring lambs for the slaughter, *Reese thought, with their fresh pressed uniforms and their full bellies. How long will it take for them to break? To become like me?*

Reese glanced down at his own disheveled body, which was clad in tattered Starfleet-issue pants and undershirt. He had wondered why the new arrivals had resolutely refused to sustain eye contact with him, until he considered the necklace of ketracel-white tubes that still hung around his neck like evil talismans.

Only then did he notice that he was turning his captured Jem'Hadar knife over and over in his sweaty, grime-caked hands. Dried blood flaked off the blade, sprinkling onto his hands like cinnamon-sugar on toast.

Willing his hands to be still, Reese turned his attention back to the impossibly well-turned-out young reinforcements. "Children," he said.

"Not for long," Sisko replied, sounding older than God.

Reese looked down at the edged weapon in his hand. It had tasted so much blood that he had almost come to see it as hate itself made tangible. And that kind of hatred wasn't something he wanted to carry home with him as a souvenir.

With a supple motion, he threw the blade to the ground. It buried itself almost hilt-deep into the hard earth, like the fang of some malevolent serpent that wanted to inject the planet itself with its lethal venom. He lifted his foot and stomped down, sending the hilt into the dirt further. It was almost invisible now, and the dust would soon cover the weapon. Eventually it would be lost to time.

"Let's go," Reese said, finally feeling free of the buildup of toxic emotions the last five months had forced upon him.

He wouldn't realize how wrong he was about that until after several weeks of nightmares and counseling.

"Thank you for speaking with me, sir," said the young man on the other end of the comlink.

"Not at all, Mr. Reese," Captain Benjamin Sisko said, sitting erect in the padded chair in his office overlooking Deep Space 9's busy ops center. "According to the after-action report from AR-558, I owe you my life. What can I do for you?"

"I've just been certified as fit to return to duty," the younger man said. *"I'd like to get back as close as I can to the front lines."*

Sisko noticed that Reese seemed almost to burn with a barely restrained intensity that he had rarely seen, except in the heat of battle. It made him feel a need for caution.

"I'm not sure I can help you, Mr. Reese," he said.

But Reese seemed determined that Sisko hear him out. *"The rumor going around is that the final assault on Cardassia will be launched from DS9. When the allied forces get under way, sir, I'd like to be there with them."*

Sisko shuddered inwardly, recalling another place he had seen that same angry intensity: in his shaving mirror, for the first three years after the battle at Wolf 359 had taken Jennifer from him and Jake. Sisko could see that Reese wasn't merely making a request of a superior officer; for some reason, Reese *needed* to be present at the final assault on the heart of all Dominion power in the Alpha Quadrant.

Would I *have been any different if we were still at war with the Borg? Or if I hadn't discovered that my destiny is wrapped up with that of Bajor?*

"Welcome to Deep Space 9," Sisko said after a silent moment, hoping he had just granted a tortured soul some small measure of mercy. "Colonel Kira and Lieutenant Dax will see to the paperwork." He paused. "You remember Lieutenant Dax, I'm sure. She's the station's counselor."

At the mention of the word "counselor," Reese appeared to flinch almost imperceptibly. Perhaps he'd had his fill of counselors since his five-month ordeal in the Chin'toka system had ended. That, too, was perfectly understandable, given the young man's obvious eagerness to return to the front lines.

"Yes, sir, I do remember her. Thank you, sir," Reese said just before signing off.

Afterward, Sisko stared into the empty computer screen on his desk, recalling all the death and horror he'd witnessed during the bloody conflict with the Dominion. Faces from this war and others paraded past his mind's eye: Declan Keogh and the crew of the *Odyssey*; Jennifer, Captain Storil, and all the others who had died aboard the *Saratoga* at Wolf 359. He remembered those who had lost their lives aboard the *Okinawa* years earlier, during the Tzen-kethi war.

Those faces no longer plagued his dreams, at least on most nights. But he knew they would remain with him always, no matter how much new horror the Dominion forced upon him as the current war roared toward its inevitable final battle.

Sisko rose and headed for ops, hoping that Reese's new posting would finally help the young man lay to rest whatever demons had hounded him since he'd left AR-558.

Once again, good people were dying all around Reese. But this time, most of them were expiring in silent blossoms of distant light.

He thought he'd experienced the worst imaginable carnage at AR-558. But that was before he'd come aboard the *U.S.S. Defiant*, which seemed to be leading the allied forces straight into the maw of hell itself. If anything, the Jem'Hadar were even more vicious when battling across many klicks of empty space than they were at close quarters.

From his post at one of the bridge's aft tactical stations, Reese saw space become brilliant with interlacing phaser beams. *Defiant* shimmied and rocked as Captain Sisko barked orders and Ensign Nog guided the starship through an unending inferno of random explosions. All around *Defiant*, allied and Dominion vessels alike spouted molecular flames as they vented atmosphere and warp plasma.

Despite the loss of what had to be dozens—or perhaps hundreds—of allied ships, *Defiant*, the two attack wings escorting her, and the assault force elements led by Admiral Ross and General Martok pressed on toward Cardassia Prime.

"Another Jem'Hadar to port," said Nog, seated at the helm.

Near Reese, Worf worked a console with surprisingly nimble fingers. "Transferring auxiliary power to the port shields."

"Dax," said Sisko, "we need some support from our attack fighters." Sparks erupted from an aft science station, and the bridge shook from another hit. Reese's teeth rattled as he assisted Worf in routing additional power to the shields.

"Breen ship off the starboard aft," Nog reported.

"Sir, most of our fighters are either destroyed or under attack themselves," Lieutenant Dax reported calmly from her console.

Sisko barked another order to the Ferengi helmsman. "Ensign, get us out of here." *Defiant* rocked again, hard.

"I'm trying, sir."

Reese's tactical console revealed an ominous tableau: several Jem'Hadar and Breen warships were rapidly closing on *Defiant*. The Breen vessel approached to within a few klicks, its weirdly organic-looking weapons tubes glowing with a menacing green light.

See you soon, Billy, Reese thought, silently marveling at how fatalistic AR-558 had made him.

Then a golden brilliance flooded the bridge for a split second as the main viewer displayed yet another colossal explosion.

It took Reese a moment to realize precisely what had happened, and just how unlikely that event was.

The Breen ship nearest to *Defiant* had been utterly vaporized.

Odo stared at his console, a stunned expression on the security chief's half-formed, masklike face as he addressed the captain. "Sir, the Cardassians—they're attacking the other Dominion ships."

"They've switched sides," Dax said, looking as surprised as the shapeshifter.

"Yes!" Nog shouted in triumph. Reese grinned.

Sisko's features remained impassive. "The timing couldn't be better. Come about and head for the center of their lines. This is our chance to punch through."

"Aye, sir," Nog said, busy at the helm.

Working with Worf, Reese quickly took stock of the status of the ship's armaments. After all, the battle was still anything but over, even with the Cardassian fleet apparently now fighting on behalf of the allies.

"Sir, phaser banks are fully charged," the Klingon reported. "But we are down to forty-five quantum torpedoes."

"That'll have to do," the captain said, pacing the bridge. He turned to face Dax. "How are you holding up, old man?" The nickname jarred Reese every time he heard Sisko use it when addressing the counselor; it was difficult getting used to the fact that the youthful-looking officer actually carried many lifetimes worth of experience within her.

"All things considered, I'd rather be on Risa," she said.

"Well, that makes two of us." Sisko moved toward Odo, who was still staring intently at his station's monitor.

"Have you seen these reports, Captain?" Odo said, his voice tinged with disbelief. "The Dominion has begun destroying Cardassian cities. Millions of people are dying."

And the orders to do that were no doubt cut by somebody very much like you, Constable, Reese thought, sparing a sidewise glance at the sandy-colored shapeshifter.

Nog spoke up, breaking the spell of stunned silence that had momentarily engulfed the bridge. "Captain, we're approaching the Dominion defense perimeter."

"Well, let's see what they have waiting for us," Sisko said. "On screen."

Cardassia, Reese thought incredulously as the limb of the planet sketched a dull brown crescent across the main viewer an instant later. *We've actually made it all the way to the middle of the Dominion's biggest Alpha Quadrant beachhead.* Dots of orange light opened like flowers across the night side as cities burned.

Reese tried not to think about that as the sun crested the planet's terminator, revealing hundreds of weapons platforms, Breen vessels, and Jem'Hadar attack ships in orbit. This ferocious array reminded Reese that everyone aboard *Defiant* could still die at any moment, and probably would. Nevertheless, he took some grim satisfaction at having sent countless Jem'Hadar to hell ahead of him.

"Now we know," Sisko said quietly, his eyes riveted to the all but impassable barrier that lay in *Defiant's* path.

Rest easy, Billy, Reese thought, casting a wary glance across the bridge at Odo. *We can still rid the universe of some of the architects of all this misery. Before they finally manage to kill us.*

Sisko could hardly believe that the fighting was finally over. But too much blood had been spilled on both sides to allow him to exult in the allies' victory the way General Martok had. And far too much work still lay ahead for Sisko to consider the war truly over.

Taking Cardassia had cost *Defiant*—and the rest of the massed allied fleet—dearly, both in terms of casualties and damage to the ship. *And we got off easy,* Sisko thought as he made his way into transporter bay one.

"Beam them up, Mr. Reese," he said, nodding to the young veteran who had taken over for the transporter chief, killed hours earlier by a Breen fusillade.

"Aye, sir." Reese said, pausing to verify the transporter lock before entering the energize command. Several humanoid forms immediately began to shimmer into existence on the transporter stage.

An exhausted-looking Kira Nerys, still dressed in the Starfleet uniform she'd worn while assisting the late Legate Damar's uprising against the newly fallen Dominion regime—her temporary Starfleet commission a necessary concession to Cardassian prejudice—stood beside a meter-high cargo container. On the other side of the container stood Odo, his expression as unreadable as ever.

As Kira and Odo stepped down from the platform, Sisko's eyes were drawn to the pair of figures who stood behind them. The first of these to step down from the dais was a young but hard-looking Cardassian soldier. The next was a female changeling, whose half-formed facial features bore an incongruously beneficent expression.

Looking into the Founder's sharp, intelligent eyes, Sisko felt his body tense involuntarily. Despite her having ordered her forces to surrender, Sisko remained wary. This creature was, after all, the very embodiment of Dominion aggression.

During the war's twilight hours, she had ordered the deaths of upwards of a billion Cardassian civilians.

Sisko stood silently as Kira reached his side and Odo and the Cardassian soldier escorted the female changeling toward him. Her movements were supple and graceful, almost boneless. The skin of her face was smooth and lacked any visible pores, all vestiges of the wasting illness with which Section 31 had afflicted her people now gone, thanks to Odo's intervention.

"Captain," the female changeling said, nodding respectfully as she came to a halt a meter from where Sisko stood. "For my crimes, I am ready to accept whatever judgment your leaders see fit to pass upon me. Odo has assured me that I can expect fairness from you and your people."

Sisko thought of everyone who was dead because of her. Just for a moment, he wondered if Odo might not be a foolish optimist.

"We'll do our best."

She closed her eyes and nodded once again. "My fate is in your hands."

Sisko found it difficult to accept her words at face value. But for the moment he had no viable alternative. "Thank you," was all he could think of to say.

Turning, Sisko trained his gaze on the Cardassian who stood beside the Founder. He, too, was eyeing her warily, though his weapon remained holstered.

"This is Glinn Ekoor, Captain," Kira said, anticipating Sisko's question. "He was part of Damar's uprising. Saved us all from summary execution by the Jem'Hadar, in fact. If not for his help, we might not have made it into the Dominion Command Center in time to persuade our—" she cast a flinty look at the changeling. "—guest to cooperate with us."

"Of course," Sisko said, nodding politely to the young Cardassian. The soldier couldn't have been much older than twenty-five or so, though he had the eyes of a much older man. That didn't surprise Sisko a bit, given what Ekoor's homeworld had just endured.

"Welcome aboard the *Defiant,* Glinn Ekoor," Sisko said. "Colonel Kira told me that Mr. Garak had asked you to accompany us back to DS9. We'll be happy to accommodate you."

"You are most gracious, Captain," Ekoor said with a smoothness that belied his years. As was the case with Nog, this glinn had evidently been strengthened and tempered by the crucible of battle.

Sisko spread his hands. "I'm not certain how quickly we can bring you back to Cardassia Prime, though."

The glinn nodded soberly. "I understand completely. However, Garak has asked me to take all the time I need safeguarding the items I've brought." He gestured toward the crate that sat on the transporter platform. "At least until the allied authorities take possession of them. And I expect to assist the Cardassian diplomatic delegates who are to attend the signing of the official Dominion surrender papers. Afterward, I can find my own transportation home, if necessary. I may even book passage with one of the relief convoys that I'm sure will soon pass through the Bajor sector on its way to Cardassia."

Sisko knew that with the fires of the war's last battle still burning, no completely accurate assessment of Cardassia Prime's casualties and infrastructure damage was yet available. But he also had no doubt that DS9, both because of its strategic location and the generosity of the Bajoran people, would indeed coordinate some much-needed Cardassian relief efforts.

"Of course," Sisko said. Raising an inquisitive eyebrow, he took a couple of steps toward the crate on the transporter stage. "What's in it?"

"Certain matériel used by the Dominion and its . . . clients. It is now a token of Cardassia's appreciation for the allies' assistance in ending the Dominion's rule over Cardassia," Ekoor said, drawing an angular Cardassian padd from his belt. He handed the padd to Sisko. "Here is a complete manifest."

Sisko took the padd and quickly scanned its table of contents. Among the items listed were handheld Dominion long-range site-to-site transporter controls, disruptor weapons, and a pair of still-functional Breen refrigeration suits. Sisko supposed that the suits must have been taken by Cardassian rebels during the war's final chaotic hours, or perhaps even by members of Damar's own resistance cell.

Starfleet Intelligence will be very *interested in taking this stuff apart,* he thought.

Handing the padd to Kira, he said, "Colonel . . ." He stopped when his gaze fell upon the collar of her Starfleet uniform, which bore a trio of gold pips. "Or should I address you as 'Commander'?"

She smiled, then looked down at her current uniform as though seeing it for the first time. "I suppose 'Commander' will have to do until I get a chance to change back into Bajoran Militia gear."

Sisko returned her grin. "Well, Commander. Please see to stowing our cargo." He turned to Odo. "Constable."

"Yes, Captain?"

"I want to be on the bridge when we break orbit. Would you mind escorting our . . . guest to some appropriate accommodations?"

Odo looked uncomfortable, as though unsure whether he should be steering the other changeling toward crew quarters or the brig. "Not at all, sir. But . . ." He trailed off.

The female Founder sighed and shook her head, obviously

sensing Odo's quandary. "Put your mind at ease, Odo. Your highest security area will do quite nicely."

Now that *Defiant* was crossing nearly three parsecs of quiet space on her way back to Deep Space 9, the bridge was able to function with a mere skeleton crew. There was no need for extra tactical personnel in the absence of raging space battles.

Well aware that the last battle had left other sections of the ship shorthanded, Reese approached Colonel Kira and volunteered to help guard the shapeshifter. If the Bajoran officer had glimpsed the fire that still burned in his soul, she betrayed no sign of it.

A few minutes later, Reese stood outside the brig. Through the shimmering blue force field, he studied the creature that sat on the cell's narrow cot, its eyes closed in apparent meditation. When he'd run the console in the transporter bay, Reese had kept his eyes downcast, not wanting anyone to sense the blinding hatred that had seized him the moment he'd laid eyes on the Founder.

The Founder. The vile thing to whom the Vorta and the Jem'Hadar ultimately answered. The inhuman monster whose pliant hands were spattered with so much innocent blood. The fiend who had filled his dreams with visions of Billy's death-slackened face and sightless eyes. The beast that had sent Loomis, Parker, McGreevey, Larkin, Kellin, Vargas, and so many others beyond the veil of mortality, simply to gain power and territory.

She's the one who's responsible for all of it, Reese thought, wishing his eyes were charged phaser banks while still struggling to keep his expression as blank and unreadable as that of the shapeshifter.

He stood there, letting his need for vengeance burn like the sweet agony of an anticipated sexual tryst. He continued studying her, standing as unmoving as the changeling until the Cardassian glinn came to relieve him four hours later.

As he brushed past Ekoor, Reese was careful not to meet his eyes, lest the cauldron of rage within him overflow.

That evening, Reese ate alone in a corner of the small mess hall. He had no particular desire to talk to anyone, though nearly a dozen other officers were present, dining, drinking, and conversing with the celebratory conviviality that came only with the triumphant resolution of a war.

But *Defiant*'s small mess hall had only four large tables. On an occasion such as this, it simply wasn't possible to be as alone as one might wish, even with the crew's numbers diminished.

Reese wondered how long Ekoor had been standing in front of his table before he'd noticed the Cardassian's presence.

"Have a seat," Reese said, though he wished fervently that the glinn would go someplace else, anyplace else, instead.

"Thank you," Ekoor said as he took a seat across the table from Reese, who returned his attention to his replicated Reuben sandwich, French onion soup, and Telluridian synthale.

A few moments later, Reese noticed that Ekoor wasn't eating or drinking anything. He set his sandwich down.

"Can I do something for you?"

The Cardassian leaned forward and spoke in a low tone, obviously not wishing to be overheard by anyone seated at any of the other three bustling tables. "I've watched you at the brig, Mr. Reese. I've seen you studying the changeling."

Reese felt his hackles rise. New allies or not, surveillance by Cardassians was always cause for alarm. "Just staying alert. In case you haven't noticed, Captain Sisko can't spare a lot of warm bodies for the security detail."

"I know. That's why I volunteered. Or at least that was my pretext for volunteering."

Reese slowly pushed his lunch tray aside. "What are you trying to say?" he asked very quietly, not wishing to attract anyone's attention. Ekoor was clearly up to something.

"Only that I've taken the liberty of reading your service record, Mr. Reese. And that I've never seen such malice in the eyes of a non-Cardassian as I've seen in yours. With the possible exception of the Jem'Hadar themselves."

Reese stood, but continued to keep his voice down. "I don't need to sit here and listen to this."

Ekoor remained seated as he glanced around the room. Reese noted that everyone else seemed too caught up in their own private conversations to pay any heed to his tense exchange with the Cardassian.

"I need your help in doing precisely what I'm certain that you, too, want done," Ekoor said, almost whispering. "I want to discuss it with you tonight. In private." He leaned forward and looked up at Reese. "Once the Founder leaves Terok Nor for the war crimes tribunal, there won't be a lot of opportunities to do what we both know has to be done."

Ekoor's cobalt eyes blazed with a supernova intensity that he recognized at once. Reese understood the glinn's meaning all too clearly. In a fit of pique, the Founder had devastated the Cardassian's homeworld, nearly committing genocide in the process. Ekoor was revealing his abiding hatred, just as Reese must have inadvertently displayed his own during the changing of the guards outside the shapeshifter's security cell.

He must be pretty desperate to get some Starfleet help to carry out his plan, Reese thought. *Or else he wouldn't have risked having this conversation with me.*

"Sorry to disappoint you, Cardassian," Reese said, *sotto voce.* As full of rage as he was, he still hoped he'd left his very worst impulses back on the Chin'toka battlefield, where he'd discarded his Jem'Hadar knife. "I'm better than that."

"Ah. Of course." Ekoor favored him with the creepy, wide-mouthed expression that seemed to pass for a smile among Cardassians, his eyes taking on a pop-eyed innocence.

Reese turned and left the mess hall without saying another word.

I can't believe I'm actually considering going along with this, Reese thought, perspiration pooling beneath his collar in the Cardassian's too-warm quarters. But the earnest young glinn had presented him with an irresistible opportunity. Reese found it strange to think that they might have treated each other as shoot-on-sight enemies as recently as yesterday. But their exchange earlier in the mess hall had refused to leave his mind until he had found himself pacing in the corridor outside Ekoor's guest quarters.

"The allies will no doubt have the Founder sign the official surrender documents aboard Terok Nor," Ekoor said, perched on the edge of his narrow bunk.

Reese remained standing, his arms folded across his chest. His earlier distrust of Ekoor flared up again. "We like to call it Deep Space 9 these days."

Ekoor blinked. "As you say. Regardless, the allies will then take the Founder away to stand trial for war crimes."

"Assuming we can reach an agreement with the Klingons and the Romulans over who has jurisdiction," Reese said with a dry chuckle. After all, the Dominion had inflicted horrendous casualties upon the forces of those two empires as well.

"My people may also have some thoughts on the matter," Ekoor said, almost growling. "A lengthy Federation trial will disgrace the memory of hundreds of millions of brutally slain Cardassians."

And of Billy, Reese thought. He shrugged, crushed by the futility of it all. "Of course, once the allied authorities get her off the station, she'll be beyond your reach." *Beyond our reach,* Reese added silently.

"I'll see to it that we're both present when she signs the surrender papers. Once that's finished, we can make our move."

As much as he wanted to see the Founder suffer for her crimes, Reese found Ekoor's plan entirely too simplistic. "How do you propose getting past Odo? From everything I've seen, he won't exactly sleepwalk through his security preparations. And then we'll have to get away afterward."

Ekoor chuckled and reached for a padd that lay on the edge of his bunk. He lifted it so that Reese could see the graphics on its display surface. One was a handheld Dominion transporter unit; the other was an image of an all-concealing Breen helmet.

"Leave those details to me," he said, smiling a shark's smile. That smile gave Reese a chill of revulsion.

And a rush of anticipation.

Sisko watched in silence as the Founder accepted the document that the Vorta sitting at her right placed before her on the wardroom table. With quiet dignity, she took the stylus in her left hand and placed her mark at the bottom of the page.

"The war between the Dominion and the Federation Alliance is now over," she said as she rose and handed the surrender treaty to Vice Admiral William J. Ross.

Standing ramrod straight in his dark duty uniform, Ross addressed the room, which was filled with witnesses representing the victors: Starfleet, the Klingon Empire, and the Romulan Star Empire. Also present were the vanquished, including several Cardassians and a pair of cold-suited Breen officers—unarmed, of course, per Odo's careful security screening prior to the ceremony—who stood silently at parade rest near the bulkhead behind the Founder's chair, which was flanked by her Jem'Hadar bodyguards.

"Four hundred years ago," Ross said in solemn tones, "a victorious general spoke the following words at the end of another costly war: 'Today the guns are silent. A great tragedy has ended. We have known the bitterness of defeat and the exultation of triumph, and from both we have learned there can be no going back. We must move forward, to preserve in peace what we've won in war.' "

The brief speech seemed to linger in the air momentarily. Sisko found Ross's words perfectly appropriate; judging from the expressions on the faces all around him, from Chancellor Martok and the Klingon contingent to Praetor Neral and the Romulan delegation, so did the allies.

Even the hardest warrior has to look forward to a campaign's end, Sisko thought, idly wondering how long the current peace among the Federation, the Klingons, and the Romulans would last now that the common purpose of defeating the Dominion no longer existed.

Sisko's eyes lit on the two Breen soldiers who stood behind the Founder's chair, their battle-scarred metal helmets, face masks, and eerily glowing visors completely obscuring their faces. So far as he knew, nobody except the Breen themselves knew what lurked beneath all that headgear.

The Founder rose from the signing table and approached Odo with graceful, gliding steps. "It's up to you now, Odo."

Odo, a pair of Starfleet security officers, and the Breen bodyguards quietly escorted the Founder from the wardroom. Sisko knew that she was to be returned to one of Odo's holding cells until the time came to bind her over to the allied tribunal for her war crimes trial.

Watching the Breen soldiers depart, Sisko recalled seeing the rubble of part of the Starfleet Headquarters complex, and the twisted wreckage of San Francisco's Golden Gate Bridge. He thought of all the good people who'd died during the Breen sneak attack that had brought down those venerable monuments.

For a moment he wished the Breen guards would give him half a reason to throw them into a cell along with the Founder.

Then, glancing at the small Cardassian delegation, Sisko noted that one gray, ridged face was conspicuously absent. Feeling a sinking sensation in his gut, he considered signaling Odo via combadge right then and there. He decided against it; the "Breen" who accompanied him would overhear, and—if his suspicions turned out to be warranted—might do something desperate.

Instead he approached Colonel Kira, who was standing in one of the far corners of the wardroom, and spoke very quietly to her for a few moments. After giving him a grave acknowledgment, she moved discreetly toward a rear exit as Sisko joined Admiral Ross and Chancellor Martok, who were in the midst of an enthusiastic discussion about Worf.

Sisko accompanied Ross and Martok as they exited the wardroom and entered the adjacent corridor. Sisko was about to mention the precautionary order he had just given to Kira when Worf and Dax approached the group from the opposite direction.

But there's no point in bringing it up until Kira and Odo look into it further, Sisko thought. Besides, something in Martok's aggressively joyful manner—particularly the uncharacteristically expectant way he was looking at Worf—told him that other matters now required his immediate attention.

"Commander Worf," Sisko said, catching his tactical officer's eye. It was clear that Martok was about to drop a bombshell on Worf, and that Ross was anxious to see Worf's reaction.

Worf and Ezri put their own conversation on hold and came to a stop. "Captain," the Klingon said simply.

"Can you spare a moment?" said Sisko.

"Yes, sir."

Fixing his one eye firmly on Worf, Martok said, "We've been discussing your plans for the future."

Though Worf remained as impassive as ever, his eyes widened marginally. "I was not aware I had any plans."

Smiling at Worf, Ross said, "Commander, how would you feel about being named Federation ambassador to Qo'noS?"

Worf evidently found the notion as surprising as Sisko had when Martok and Ross had first broached it to him hours ago. "I am not a diplomat."

"And I am not a politician," Martok growled good-naturedly. "But sometimes fate plays cruel tricks on us, Worf. Come. Qo'noS needs you. And what's more, *I* need you."

"You helped him become chancellor," said Ezri, looking up at Worf. "Can't very well turn your back on him now."

Worf seemed to mull the offer over for a moment before turning to Sisko. "Well, my first loyalty is to you, Captain."

"Thank you, Mr. Worf," Sisko said, feeling genuine warmth for the Klingon, and sadness over what he knew was coming. "I'll probably regret this in the morning, but if it's what you want . . . then by all means."

Worf answered with his usual decisiveness. "It has been a great honor serving with you."

"The honor is mine," Sisko said.

Worf trained his piercing gaze on Martok. "I accept."

Roaring with martial ebullience, Martok clapped Worf on the shoulder. "Excellent! An ambassador who'll go *targ* hunting with me." He laughed again, already resuming his course down the corridor. "Well, perhaps being chancellor won't be so bad after all."

Leaving Worf and Ezri standing alone, Sisko continued down the corridor for another few moments beside Ross and Martok. *So much change,* he thought. *And it's all happening so quickly.* Recalling that Chief O'Brien's departure for a Starfleet Academy teaching post was also imminent, Sisko tried to will himself to expect still more change in the future; after all, any number of such transformations were inevitable now that the war had ended.

Except for the unnecessary and tragic changes that could be prevented by quick action. Once again, he considered the clandestine order he had given to Kira.

He excused himself and strode purposefully toward the security area.

★   ★   ★

Sisko saw that the wormhole aliens had taken the forms of two of his former shipmates from the Saratoga: *Doran, a young woman whose specialty was planetary science, and Hranok, a blue-skinned male Bolian tactical officer. They had both been aboard the* Saratoga *on the day the Borg had come.*

Though he knew he was really somewhere inside the Bajoran wormhole—the Celestial Temple of the Prophets—Sisko seemed to be standing with Doran and Hranok in one of the Saratoga's *burning, debris-strewn corridors. Visible through the haze of smoke was the open door to the quarters Sisko had shared with Jennifer and Jake. The Borg were attacking yet again, as they had done in countless dreams since the Battle of Wolf 359.*

Only this scenario seemed far more vivid than any dream Sisko had ever experienced. Part of him wanted to sprint down the corridor and try again to rescue his wife. But another part of him understood that such an act would be an exercise in futility.

Jennifer will still be dead, *Sisko thought, turning away from his quarters.* I can't go back in there again. I won't.

Sisko noticed the Hranok-alien eyeing him quizzically. "But this is your existence," the alien said, as if challenging him to try to rescue his dead wife.

Sisko nodded. "It's difficult to return here. More difficult than any other memory."

"Why?" asked the Hranok-alien.

"Because . . . because this was the day I lost Jennifer," Sisko said, pausing as waves of exhaustion threatened to overwhelm him. "I don't want to be here."

Reese watched in silence through the helmet's visor, biding his time. The internal refrigeration unit in the too-tight Breen coolsuit was doing little to prevent him from sweating. Reese assumed it must have been damaged by whoever had acquired the suit; a real Breen would no doubt already have expired from heatstroke.

"Raise the force field, Deputy Etana," Odo said after he had emerged from the holding cell into which he had just escorted the unresisting Founder. One of the two deputies present, a female Bajoran with a severe haircut, immediately complied. A male Bajoran deputy and a pair of Starfleet security officers looked on attentively, their hands never wandering very far from their sidearms.

Reese noted that all of them except for Odo were armed with phasers. Standing quietly outside the cell beside Ekoor—who, like Reese, was still disguised as one of the Founder's Breen guards—Reese completely understood the hypervigilance of the security people. The presence of a pair of Breen, even if ostensibly unarmed, had to be making everyone jumpy.

Of course, the female shapeshifter was anything but jumpy. Indeed, she struck Reese as the very essence of calm and serenity. Now safely confined in the cell, she had taken a seat on the edge of the chamber's single narrow bunk. Secure, at least for the moment, behind the cell's unblinking light-blue forcefield, she smiled blandly up at her guards.

Reese felt that his hatred alone just might be sufficient to pierce the energy barrier. He turned to look at Ekoor. Like Reese's, the Cardassian's facial expression was unreadable, thanks to his Breen helmet and mask. But the glinn's body seemed almost to vibrate with tension.

Now is the time, Ekoor's body language seemed to be saying. Not for the first time, Reese found himself wondering whether he had the courage to continue. Or to stop. Perhaps it didn't matter either way. Once again, an image of Billy's dead, vacant eyes came to him unbidden.

The only way out of this is through it, he thought, feeling the reassuring weight of the disruptor that was concealed in the small scan-proof compartment on his thigh. *I have to do this thing.*

Reese heard footfalls behind him and turned toward the sound.

"Back away from the cell, please," said Colonel Kira, her sharp gaze trained first on Ekoor, and then on Reese. Reese saw that her hand hovered near the phaser she wore at her side as she took a single deliberate step toward them. "We'll take charge of the Founder from here."

Damn! She's onto us, Reese thought, feeling the sweat pooling in the small of his back. He remained motionless.

"I said back away," repeated the colonel, who was now drawing her weapon. Reese turned his head and saw that Odo and the armed personnel were now eyeing both Reese and Ekoor with evident suspicion.

Judging from the garbled sounds he could hear through his mask whenever either he or Ekoor spoke, Reese knew that the vocoders that altered their speech—and that completed their disguises as enigmatic Breen soldiers—were still working. And if their scan-shielded disruptor weapons been detected, surely an alarm would have sounded, either here in the security area or back in the wardroom during the armistice signing ceremony.

Reese wondered whether either he or Ekoor had somehow raised the colonel's suspicions with a stray movement or gesture. Or maybe Kira had discovered that Ekoor had taken the coolsuits from the crate he had brought aboard *Defiant.*

He decided it was pointless to speculate and willed himself to relax. *As far as anyone can tell, we're both exactly what we appear to be.*

Ekoor, however, chose that moment to pull his own weapon from a thigh-flap. Rolling onto the floor, he fired at Kira, who was already in motion, as was Odo. Acting on instinct, Reese threw himself to the floor as an alarm klaxon sounded; he knocked over a Bajoran deputy and a Starfleet security guard even as Kira returned Ekoor's fire.

Rolling swiftly onto his side, Reese pulled his own weapon and shot out the keypad that controlled the security forcefield, which abruptly crackled out of existence. Ignoring the firefight that raged around him, he immediately somersaulted into the Founder's cell and came up in a crouch directly behind where she sat, impassively watching the brief battle. If Kira or any of the oth-

ers were to open fire on him now, they'd have to go right through
the shapeshifter to hit him.

Of course, Reese couldn't help wondering whether anyone
other than Odo would have had much of a problem with that.

"Hold your fire!" Odo and Kira shouted, almost in unison. Except for the wail of a security alarm, silence descended over the
small cell block.

When Reese placed the barrel of his disruptor against the
changeling's puttylike temple, she made no move to resist him. She
simply continued sitting. Rather than showing fear, her expression
revealed an attitude of quiet contemplation.

Then Reese heard a deep, familiar voice coming from outside
the cell. "We've got your accomplice. You might as well give up
and drop your weapon."

"I don't want to be here," Sisko said.

*One of the wormhole aliens now wore the form of Jennifer, and was
dressed in the same fetching two-piece bathing suit she had worn on the
day they had met, so many years ago. Still standing in what appeared to be
the* Saratoga's *burning corridor, Sisko was taken aback.*

*"Then why do you exist here?" the Jennifer-alien asked, her face a
study in earnest perplexity.*

Sisko, too, was at a loss. "I don't understand."

*The confusion of the Jennifer-alien seemed only to escalate. "You exist
here."*

Sisko entered the security area at a run. The alarm signaling the
unauthorized discharge of a weapon sounded just as he bounded
across the threshold.

One of the Breen guards, a disruptor in his hand, was caught in
a cross fire laid down by Kira, two Bajoran deputies, and a Starfleet
security guard. The Breen soldier dropped slackly to the deck,
landing near a second Starfleet security officer who had evidently

been knocked off his feet during the melee, his shoulder scorched where he'd been grazed by a Breen disruptor blast.

Inside the holding cell that lay beyond sat the Founder. Her remaining Breen guard held a disruptor pistol to her head.

Sisko arrived at the unconscious Breen soldier's side just in time to see Kira kneel beside him and remove his mask and helmet. The flashing green lights of the visor went dark as she dropped the helmet and face-covering to the deck.

As Sisko had suspected during the armistice signing, the Breen under the headgear was no Breen at all.

The face beneath the visor belonged to Glinn Ekoor.

Of course, Sisko thought, confirming his growing belief that Ekoor must have planned from the beginning to use the Dominion artifacts he had brought from Cardassia to avenge that world's slain millions.

Sisko walked toward the threshold of the holding cell, whose force field, he noted, wasn't working. The keypad beside the cell door was a charred ruin. There was nothing to prevent the person with the disruptor from opening fire either on Sisko or on the others who stood in the security area.

But that also meant that phasers could be fired *into* the cell.

"We've got your accomplice," Sisko said to the figure holding the disruptor. "You might as well give up and drop your weapon."

"Captain," Odo said, holding up a flat, palm-sized device for Sisko's inspection. "Glinn Ekoor was carrying this—his escape route, apparently."

Sisko took the item and turned it over in his hands, studying it carefully. He recognized it as the control padd of a Dominion site-to-site transporter. A few months ago a group of Pah-wraith cultists led by Gul Dukat had used just such a device to abduct Colonel Kira, bringing her across a distance of three light-years to the derelict Cardassian space station Empok Nor.

Lifting the device so that the helmeted man with the disruptor could see it easily, Sisko said, "I suppose if you were carrying one of these as well, you'd already have done your dirty work and beamed yourself out of here." He noted that the Bajoran deputies and Starfleet security personnel alike all had their weapons trained on the second *faux* Breen, whose green visor lights now moved from side to side in a way that suggested to Sisko either fear or rage, or perhaps both.

Whoever this individual really was, he was clearly cornered. *And therefore doubly dangerous,* Sisko told himself as he handed the transporter control back to Odo.

Sisko remembered the phaser that hung at his hip, and momentarily considered drawing it. For a brief interval, his own war-weariness—a cumulative revulsion for the unending pageant of death and horror to which the Dominion and its allies had subjected him over the past two years—threatened to overwhelm him. How easy it would be to simply pull his weapon, fire it, and end the standoff by taking down both gunman and hostage at once. After all, the Founder was a brutal war criminal. Hundreds of millions of deaths could be laid at her feet.

No. This damned war has taken enough lives.

But the anger remained incandescent within Sisko's heart, reminding him of the day, now seven years gone, when he had first come aboard DS9 as its new commander. Back then, the Prophets had yet to reveal how his destiny and that of Bajor intertwined. And this god-forsaken, half-gutted Cardassian ore-processing station was the last place in the galaxy he had wanted to be. He never would have considered raising his son in such a hellhole. In fact, he had quickly—if temporarily—decided to resign his commission before doing such a thing to Jake, who was all that remained of his beloved Jennifer. Her death during the Borg battle at Wolf 359, then less than three years in the past, had still been an open wound in those days.

Sisko had never felt such a primal, atavistic desire to destroy another sentient creature as he had on his first day on the station. He had come aboard the visiting *U.S.S. Enterprise* that day, and found himself standing in the presence of Captain Jean-Luc Picard—the man who had, at the very least, presided over the deaths of Jennifer and so many other good people at Wolf 359.

Locutus of Borg.

"Have we met before?" Picard asked him.

Sisko's response was hard, each word a lethal projectile. "Yes, sir. We met in battle. I was on the Saratoga. *At Wolf 359."*

From beside Sisko, Odo addressed the Founder. "You don't have to sit there and just let him kill you."

She smiled, her expression as serene as ever, her voice tranquil. "Perhaps I do, Odo."

"It isn't right," Odo said. "This isn't the way the things are supposed to be done here."

"There are always exceptions to the they way things are supposed to be done, Odo." Her tone was casual, as though she were discussing the weather on her homeworld. "Like the introduction of the viral disease that has nearly destroyed the Great Link and all of our people."

Odo shook his head. "That wasn't sanctioned by the Federation. You know that. It was the work of rogue elements."

"Indeed. As are the actions of these men." She nodded toward the weapon that stood ready to blow her head apart.

Odo took a step forward.

The "Breen" spoke sharply, obviously issuing a challenge, though all Sisko heard was a series of unintelligible, electronically altered sounds. Odo froze in his tracks. The disruptor remained pointed at the female Founder's head, and she still made no move to protect herself.

"Do not endanger yourself on my behalf, Odo," she said. "You must survive. You must bring the cure for the illness back to our people. And you must assure them of the Federation's peaceful intentions. My own death is inconsequential. And perhaps it is even just."

"I'd prefer to let a formal war crimes tribunal determine what's just," Sisko said.

That thought brought him to a chilling realization: When Odo returned to the Founder homeworld and linked with his people, they would learn everything that had happened here. Odo's species was already predisposed to aggression and paranoia by millennia of conflict with non-shapeshifting "solids."

How would they react to the cold-blooded execution of their supreme military commander?

"Why not take off the mask?" Sisko said to the gunman, hoping that his evolving suspicion about the "Breen's" real identity was wrong. "There's no point in trying to pass yourself off as a Breen soldier any longer. One way or another, this is over."

After a lengthy pause, during which the "Breen" apparently considered the five weapons that were trained on him from outside the cell, the gunman opened the catches on his helmet and mask. Without allowing his disruptor to waver for an instant, he used one hand to doff his head coverings and let them fall to the deck.

An intense feeling of disappointment and anger seized Sisko when he saw the face beneath the mask.

"Don't try to stop me, Captain," Reese said, now sweating profusely into the stifling Breen uniform. He knew that decision time had arrived. And that no matter what he decided, he wasn't going to get out of this alive.

Billy's dead, vacant eyes still haunted him. Spurred him. Inspired him.

"I trusted you, Mr. Reese," Sisko said, glowering dangerously as he stepped toward the threshold of the holding cell.

Reese dug the disruptor's barrel into the Founder's ductile skin. "Don't. Come. Any. Closer." Even in his own ears, his voice sounded brittle, dangerous, an emotional rockslide liable to be triggered by even the gentlest of shocks.

Sisko stopped, his gaze intense and angry, his stance aggressive. Reese wondered if the captain was going to charge him, disruptor or no disruptor.

Then, surprisingly, Sisko's features slackened, taking on a more thoughtful cast. His body relaxed visibly. "I was like you once, Mr. Reese," he said, his voice low, his emotions unguessable.

Reese chuckled, prompting him to wonder if he really was finally beginning to crack. "I doubt that, sir."

"Why?"

"Did you ever spend five months in hell—trying to hold onto a little piece of dirt there—while the Jem'Hadar kept sending everything they had against you?"

"I was there," Sisko said. "At least for the end of it."

Reese's finger tightened on the trigger. He snorted, and said, "And you would have died there if not for me. I saved your life."

"I know that," Sisko said, nodding slowly. "Now I'm trying to return the favor."

"Too late," Reese said. He heard braying, disturbing laughter. His own, he realized belatedly. "It's too late to change my mind about this."

"No, it's not." Sisko turned and pointed toward the insensate body of Ekoor, which lay partially within Reese's line of sight. "We change our minds all the time. Old enemies can become partners, under the right circumstances. Maybe even friends."

"Ekoor and I aren't friends. I just happen to want to see this monster dead as much as he does."

"Because you spent five months in hell," Sisko said. The captain's acerbic tone suddenly reminded Reese of one of his Academy drill instructors, an angry, red-faced man whose favorite disparagement had been *"whiner!"*

The unwelcome memory raised both his hackles and his ire. "With all due respect, sir," Reese snarled, "I'm used to drawing jobs that are a lot less cushy than yours."

"Let me tell you something, Mister," Sisko said, his eyes narrowing, his tone once again as deep and dangerous as an ocean rip tide. "I've seen more hell than you can ever imagine, courtesy of the Borg collective."

Reese's breath caught in his throat. He hadn't heard that Sisko had faced the Borg in battle. But he did know that the chances of surviving an encounter with those Delta Quadrant cyborgs were pretty slim.

"The Borg killed my *wife,* Mr. Reese," Sisko continued implacably. "Along with about eleven thousand other people. The collective destroyed thirty-nine starships that day—and their attack was directed by a fellow Starfleet officer."

Reese closed his eyes. Billy's sightless gaze awaited him in the darkness, as it did more and more frequently these days. His eyes were empty.

"A couple of years later, I came face to face with the same man again," Sisko continued. "He'd recovered from what the Borg had done to him. But I hadn't yet."

Reese blinked as sweat rolled down his forehead and obscured his vision. The memory of Billy's dead stare persisted behind his eyes, as though burned onto his retinas by an exploding houdini mine.

Reese opened his eyes. Sisko had resumed moving forward, crossing the threshold of the holding cell. He was now just two meters away. The captain would be splattered with the Founder's body fluids if Reese fired the disruptor. *When* he fired the disruptor.

"I wanted to kill him, Reese. I actually thought about killing him. And I actually *could* have killed him. It probably wouldn't have been much harder than firing that weapon you're holding right now."

Reese noticed that his gun hand was shaking involuntarily. He found that he was powerless to stop it.

"What did you do?" he said, his voice a hoarse croak. It sounded as though it was coming from someone else, someone standing between him and the Founder.

"I backed away from the precipice. You can, too."

Reese shook his head. *It's too late. Too late for me. For Ekoor. For Vargas, and Kellin, and Loomis, and Parker.*

For Billy.

"This monster's got to die for what she's done," Reese said, somehow maintaining his grip on the quivering disruptor. The Founder still refused to move, or to defend herself. "There's nothing you can say that will stop me."

Sisko came to a stop less than a meter away from the shapeshifter, who was gazing up at him from her bunk, her expression attentive and curious.

"You're right," Sisko said. "Though I *can* tell you that killing this changeling won't bring back whoever you've lost in the war. But you already knew that. Didn't you?"

Billy.

"Whoever you're trying to avenge," Sisko said, "would they want this? Would they want you to leap into the abyss? Or would they want you to live a life they could be proud of? If you throw that life away now, you'll demean the deaths of so many others.

"Is that what you want, Mr. Reese?"

Reese closed his eyes again. As always, Billy awaited him in a foul midden of memory and death. And just as in the past few weeks—a time filled with dreams of ever-escalating horror—his eyes were desolate, bereft of life.

But this time, the darkness within them *accused* him.

Reese felt his quaking hand suddenly go slack. The weapon slid from his nerveless fingers and into Sisko's outstretched hand.

After tossing Reese's disruptor aside, Sisko caught the younger man when he sagged toward the deck. Sisko guided him to a corner, where Reese sat, staring at nothing. Kira and Odo rushed into the cell, followed by the deputies and security guards.

Odo hastened to the Founder's side to make sure she hadn't been harmed. "Solids," she said simply, evidently none the worse for wear. Still seated on the edge of the bunk as though nothing of significance had happened, she looked over at Sisko. "You are so very contradictory. Humans, I mean."

"You'll get no argument from me," Sisko said as Kira summoned medical help for Reese, Ekoor, and the Starfleet security guard who had been grazed by the Cardassian's disruptor. "Fortunately, we're able to overcome our worst impulses."

"At times," the Founder said.

A wry smile came to Sisko's lips. "Usually when it counts the most. Maybe we can't change our shapes, but we can change our hearts." Sisko paused, again wondering what the Great Link would make of her experience here today. Would the changelings find their ingrained suspicions justified? Or would they see Reese's decision not to commit murder as a reason for hope?

"Your people are no different," Sisko continued. "I think you proved that by giving up the fight."

"Let us hope that you're right," the Founder said. "About both our species."

After the deputies had conducted the Founder to an adjacent cell—one with a functioning force field—Sisko, Odo, and Kira stood together in companionable silence in the center of the security area. They watched as Dr. Bashir and a pair of medics arrived and gently placed Ekoor's unconscious form onto an antigrav stretcher. Once that was done, Bashir and one of the medics helped Reese to his feet. Joined by a Starfleet security guard, the group conducted the two broken soldiers out of the security area and toward the infirmary.

"Reese and Ekoor both have got a lot of healing to do," Sisko said quietly. Ezri was going to have her work cut out for her.

Odo nodded. "So do we all. This war is going to leave scars on just about everyone."

With nothing to add to that, Sisko began walking toward the exit. Kira and Odo followed him out onto the Promenade.

"I think you were wrong about one thing, Captain," Kira said.

"And what's that?" Sisko wanted to know.

"You really aren't anything like Reese. Or Ekoor. You aren't capable of fixating on horror the way they did."

Sisko remembered sitting beside Jake inside the escape pod. He had watched through the transparent aluminum window as the *Saratoga* exploded, immolating the corpse of his beloved wife, the mother of his son.

He offered Kira a rueful smile. "Far be it from me to undermine your faith in the Emissary, Colonel."

Standing beside Sisko just outside the dreamlike re-creation of his family quarters aboard the Saratoga, *the Jennifer-alien gently placed a hand upon his shoulder.*

Looking into the rubble-filled room, Sisko saw an image of himself as he had been on that horrible day. Hranok, the Bolian tactical officer, handed the unconscious form of young Jake Sisko to other crew members who were on their way to the ship's escape pods. Hranok soon began grabbing Sisko's struggling earlier self by the shoulders, trying to manhandle him out of the room.

Jennifer lay pinned beneath a tangle of metal debris, just out of the other Sisko's reach. According to a quick tricorder scan Hranok had taken moments earlier, she was already dead.

Hranok was shouting to the other Sisko that it was time to leave. The Saratoga *rumbled and shook, clearly in its death throes. The heavily battle-damaged* Miranda-*class ship was only minutes away from a warp core breach. Sisko stood and watched the Bolian as he lifted his younger self off his feet.*

"Damn it, we just can't leave her here!" the other Sisko said, struggling and crying out incoherently as Hranok half-carried, half-dragged him out of the room.

A realization struck Sisko as he quietly regarded the wormhole alien who stood beside him, wearing the form of the beloved wife whom Locutus had slain.

"I've never left this ship," Sisko said, finally coming to grips with his unmet need to put paid to his grief, lest it devour him.

"You exist here," the Jennifer-alien said.

"I exist here." He watched as the Bolian led his other self down the corridor toward the escape pods.

Sisko advanced into his family's quarters. He could deny it no longer.

He knew he had to leave this place behind. He had to move on, or join Jennifer in death.

But not just this second, *he thought, kneeling beside Jennifer's lifeless body, which still lay pinned beneath a twisted pile of wreckage. He took her hand.*

"I don't know if you can understand," he said to whichever wormhole aliens might be present and listening. "I see her like this every time I close my eyes. In the darkness. In the blink of an eye, I see her. Like this."

The Jennifer-alien stood nearby, regarding him impassively. "None of your past experiences helped prepare you for this consequence."

Overcome with emotion, Sisko slowly shook his head. "And I have never figured out how to live without her."

"So you choose to exist here," the Jennifer-alien said, approaching him more closely. Sisko found it unnerving to hold his dead wife's still-warm hand while conversing with a living alien who so closely resembled her.

"It is not linear," she observed.

"No. It's not linear," he said as hot tears distorted his vision and streamed down his cheeks.

He looked to his right and saw that the Jake-alien was watching him, his youthful face a mask of concern. The simulacrum of his son reminded Sisko forcefully that he needed to live in the present if either he or Jake were to have a future.

Very gently, he released Jennifer's limp hand, rose to his feet, and turned toward that future. There could be no looking back.

Sisko, Kira, and Odo walked on quietly together for a few minutes longer, until Kira and Odo went off on their own. Sisko was happy to let them go so that they could exchange their own private farewells. Perhaps they would be saying good-bye permanently. Once Odo left for the Founder homeworld, who knew when he'd be coming back this way?

Sisko strolled the Promenade by himself, letting the crowd of passersby swirl around him. He felt unaccountably contented as he watched the ceaseless torrent of diverse humanoids, their individual movements and motivations as unpredictable and unknowable as the outcome of a baseball game. In addition to its usual panoply of habitués, the busy arcade also thronged with weary and wounded Starfleet personnel, along with Klingons and Romulans. The sense of shared joy at the war's end was palpable. He knew it couldn't last.

So much is ending now, Sisko thought with an exultation that surprised him. He remembered that he was due within the hour at the holosuite in which Vic Fontaine's Las Vegas program ran perpetually, to toast his senior officers and whatever lay ahead for each of them. He knew that he might not see some of them again—like Worf and Chief O'Brien—for quite a while. *But nothing ends without beginning something else.*

His thoughts turned toward Jake, then to his new wife Kasidy, and the child that was now growing within her. He smiled to himself as he visualized the house they planned to build near the Yolja River in Bajor's Kendra Province, and the life they were going to share there. A private Shangri-La on twelve hecapates of virgin land.

As he walked past the Bajoran shrine, Sisko thought again of how close Reese and Ekoor had come to reigniting a transquadrant war. All in the name of requiting the brutality of that war's aggressors.

There but for the grace of the Prophets go I, Sisko thought as he moved across the thronging Promenade toward Quark's.

The Dominion War Timeline

compiled by Keith R.A. DeCandido

Some entries have bracketed indicators: *DS9*=episode of *Star Trek: Deep Space Nine*. *LOD*=story in *The Lives of Dax* anthology. *PC*=story in *Prophecy and Change* anthology. *TDW*=story in *Tales of the Dominion War* anthology (this volume). *CB*=comic book (published by WildStorm). *SNW#*=story in whichever *Strange New Worlds* anthology indicated by the number #.

Novel/eBook/comic book prefix abbreviations: *TNG*=*Star Trek: The Next Generation*. *DS9*=*Star Trek: Deep Space Nine*. *SCE*=*Star Trek: Starfleet Corps of Engineers*. *NF*=*Star Trek: New Frontier*.

2373
- The Dominion takes control of Deep Space 9, marking the more-or-less official start of hostilities. The station is returned to its original name of Terok Nor. However, before abandoning the station, Starfleet mines the wormhole entrance, preventing Dominion reinforcements from coming in from the Gamma Quadrant. ("Call to Arms" *[DS9]*)
- A Vorta named Sejeel and a garrison of Jem'Hadar set up a communications and supply depot on a pre-warp planet near Federation space called Illarh. Unknown to them, Captain Gilaad Ben Zoma is undercover on Illarh as a scientific observer, and is able to feed intelligence on the Dominion activity to the *Enterprise,* leading to the depot

being eliminated. ("What Dreams May Come" by Michael Jan Friedman *[TDW]*)

2374

• A team from the *Enterprise* prevents the Dominion from constructing an artificial wormhole to the Gamma Quadrant. (*TNG:The Dominion War* Book 1: *Behind Enemy Lines* and Book 3: *Tunnel Through the Stars* by John Vornholt)

• The *U.S.S. Valiant,* a training ship out with a crew of cadets, is trapped behind enemy lines when the war breaks out. Captain Ramirez and the senior staff are killed in battle with the Cardassians at El Gatark, and the trainee crew, led by Cadet Tim Watters, continue to fight the Dominion from behind the lines for eight months. *("Valiant" [DS9])*

• Captain Benjamin Sisko and the *Defiant* continue to fight the war, with Lt. Commander Worf serving under General Martok on the *I.K.S. Rotarran* and serving as liaison between the Klingon Defense Force and Starfleet. The Federation and Klingons suffer major losses at Tyra, losing almost a hundred ships; one of the ships that survives is the *U.S.S. Lexington.* ("A Time to Stand," "Rocks and Shoals," "Sons and Daughters," "Behind the Lines," and "Favor the Bold" *[DS9]; SCE: War Stories* Book 1 by Keith R.A. DeCandido)

• Major Kira Nerys leads a Bajoran resistance movement on Terok Nor that includes Security Chief Odo, Jake Sisko, Quark, Rom, and Leeta, among others. They are able to disrupt activity on the station, use an anonymous newsfeed to sow confusion among the Dominion overseers, and get coded messages to Starfleet, though Rom is ultimately caught and imprisoned following a failed sabotage attempt. ("Rocks and Shoals," "Sons and Daughters," "Behind the Lines," and "Favor the Bold" *[DS9];* "Three Sides to Every Story" by Terri Osborne *[PC]*)

- The *U.S.S. Lexington* and the *U.S.S. T'Kumbra* are part of a task force that manages to hold the Setlik system, though the losses are great. *(SCE: War Stories* Book 1 by Keith R.A. DeCandido)
- A Changeling spy acquires the codes to bring down the minefield blocking the Bajoran wormhole, but her efforts to bring those codes to Terok Nor are sabotaged by the Beta XII-A entity, which feeds off negative emotion, and wishes to prolong the war for its own purposes. ("Night of the Vulture" by Greg Cox *[TDW])*
- A task force led by the *Defiant* retakes Terok Nor, with help from Kira's resistance group, which now includes Gul Skrain Dukat's daughter, Tora Ziyal. Just prior to this, the Cardassians managed to dismantle the minefield, but Sisko convinces the Prophets to stop the invading Dominion reinforcements. The station is rechristened Deep Space 9 and returned to Federation/Bajoran control. Ziyal is killed by Glinn Corat Damar; Weyoun, the Female Changeling, and Damar escape; Dukat is captured. Jake writes Ziyal's eulogy, delivered by Kira at her funeral. ("Sacrifice of Angels" *[DS9];* "Three Sides to Every Story" by Terri Osborne *[PC])*
- Worf and Lt. Commander Jadzia Dax get married on Deep Space 9. ("You are Cordially Invited . . ." *[DS9])*
- Starfleet brings a group of genetically enhanced humans to Deep Space 9 to consult on the war effort. ("Statistical Probabilities" *[DS9])*
- Quark, Rom, and Nog lead a team of Ferengi to rescue Ishka—mother to Quark and Rom and paramour of Grand Nagus Zek—from Dominion capture on Empok Nor. ("The Magnificent Ferengi" *[DS9])*
- Dukat, now consumed by madness, escapes Starfleet imprisonment. ("Waltz" *[DS9])*
- A shrunken runabout helps stave off a boarding party of Jem'Hadar on the *Defiant.* ("One Little Ship" *[DS9])*

- Starfleet Intelligence stops an attempt to assassinate the Klingon ambassador to Farius Prime. ("Honor Among Thieves" *[DS9]*)
- Worf and Dax fail to retrieve an undercover Federation operative within Cardassian Central Command; the operative is killed. ("Change of Heart" *[DS9]*)
- Continuing to operate in Sector 221G—being held in reserve in case the war goes badly for the Federation—the *U.S.S. Excalibur* comes across a planet whose inhabitants have been exterminated by the Redeemers. The crew employs time travel to prevent the tragedy, but overshoot their own time period by eighteen months when they make the return trip. *(NF: Once Burned* by Peter David; *NF: Double Time* by Peter David, Michael Collins, & David Roach [CB])
- The *Enterprise* attempts to get the Gorn to join in the war effort, and find themselves in the midst of a *coup d'état* on the Gorn homeworld. *(TNG: The Gorn Crisis* by Kevin J. Anderson, Rebecca Moesta, & Igor Kordey [CB])
- Section 31 attempts to recruit Dr. Julian Bashir. ("Inquisition" *[DS9]*)
- Betazed falls to the Dominion. ("In the Pale Moonlight" *[DS9]*; "The Ceremony of Innocence Is Drowned" by Keith R.A. DeCandido *[TDW]*)
- Romulan Emperor Shiarkiek is assassinated. While Ambassador Spock secretly investigates the murder, Sisko and Elim Garak manipulate the Romulans into abrogating their nonaggression pact with the Dominion and entering the war, allied with the Federation and the Klingon Empire. ("In the Pale Moonlight" *[DS9]*; "Blood Sacrifice" by Josepha Sherman & Susan Shwartz *[TDW]*)
- Jake and Cadet Nog wind up on the *Valiant*. Nog joins the crew as chief engineer. Most of the ship's complement is killed in an ill-advised attack on a Dominion battleship. Only Jake, Nog, and Cadet Dorian Collins survive. The

former two return to DS9, the latter goes home to Sector 001 to recover. *("Valiant" [DS9]; "Dorian's Diary" by G. Wood [SNW3])*

- Dax and Bashir, along with Romulan Subcommander T'Rul are assigned to work on a scientific "think tank" called Project Blue Sky, an attempt to find new ways to fight the Dominion. ("The Devil You Know" by Heather Jarman *[PC]*)
- Allied forces take the Chin'toka system. ("Tears of the Prophets" *[DS9]*)
- Now an emissary of the Pah-wraiths, Dukat attacks Dax and closes the wormhole. Jadzia dies, but the Dax symbiont is preserved and sent back to Trill on the *U.S.S. Destiny*.Sisko takes a leave of absence and returns to Earth, leaving Kira in charge of the station. ("Tears of the Prophets" *[DS9]*)

2375

- A Vulcan ship is found and brought to Deep Space 9 by the *Enterprise,* with the entire crew infected by a Dominion bioweapon. The combined resources of Bashir, Dr. Beverly Crusher, and the *Enterprise's* Emergency Medical Hologram are required to solve it, with long-distance aid from Dr. Leonard McCoy, unexpected aid from a Romulan intelligence agent posing as one of Bashir's nurses, and a treatment by a twenty-second-century Denobulan physician named Phlox. ("Mirror Eyes" by Heather Jarman & Jeffrey Lang *[TDW]*)
- Due to an emergency on the *U.S.S. Destiny,* the Dax symbiont is implanted in Ensign Ezri Tigan, who becomes the latest Dax. ("Second Star to the Right . . ." by Judith & Garfield Reeves-Stevens *[LOD]*)
- The *U.S.S. da Vinci,* along with the *Appalachia* and the *Sloane,* repair a communications relay and maintain a Federation hold on the Phicus system, and also neutralize a Domin-

ion prototype weapon. *(SCE: War Stories* Book 2 by Keith R.A. DeCandido)

- Odo uncovers an "underground railroad" of Cardassian war refugees spearheaded by Thrax, his predecessor as station security chief. ("Foundlings" by Jeffrey Lang *[PC]*)
- The *Enterprise, Defiant,* and three other ships, with the aid of the Betazoid Resistance, liberate Betazed from Dominion control. *(TNG: The Battle of Betazed* by Charlotte Douglas & Susan Kearney)
- Shinzon and a batallion of Remans are sent on a suicide mission by the Tal Shiar to destroy a base held by the Dominion before either the Dominion or the allied task force being sent to retake the planet find the Tal Shiar's cache. Shinzon manages to survive the mission, and make off with a variety of material that the Tal Shiar think is now destroyed. ("Twilight's Wrath" by David Mack *[TDW]*)
- Colonel Kira prevents the Romulans from establishing an armed base in the Bajoran system. ("Image in the Sand" and "Shadows and Symbols" *[DS9]*)
- The *Rotarran,* crewed by Martok, Worf, Chief Miles O'Brien, Quark, and Bashir, win a victory dedicated to Jadzia. ("Image in the Sand" and "Shadows and Symbols" *[DS9]*)
- Sisko, with the help of Jake Sisko, Joseph Sisko, and Ezri Dax, finds the Orb of the Emissary on Tyree and reopens the wormhole. He then returns to Deep Space 9 and retakes command of the station; Ezri becomes the station's counselor. ("Image in the Sand" and "Shadows and Symbols" *[DS9]*)
- A "defective" Weyoun clone tries to defect to the Federation, and reveals that the Founders are suffering from a disease. ("Treachery, Faith, and the Great River" *[DS9]*)
- *Dahar* Master Kor wins a victory over the Dominion, sacrificing his life in the process. ("Once More Unto the Breach" *[DS9]*)

- Deep Space 9 crew members aid in holding the outpost at AR-558, though Ensign Nog loses a leg in the battle. Nog recovers at Starbase 235, along with Reese, another of the soldiers assigned to AR-558. ("The Siege at AR-558" [DS9]; "Requital" by Michael A. Martin & Andy Mangels [TDW])
- Nog slowly recovers from the trauma of losing his leg. ("It's Only a Paper Moon" [DS9])
- A Vulcan suffering from post-traumatic stress starts a methodical killing spree on Deep Space 9. He is ultimately stopped by Dax. ("Field of Fire" [DS9])
- Bashir is caught up in a Section 31 scheme to get rid of Romulan Senator Cretak, thus placing Koval higher in the Romulan hierarchy. ("Inter Arma Enim Silent Leges" [DS9])
- Worf's ship is ambushed in the Badlands. Dax tracks him down in a runabout and rescues him. They are subsequently captured by the Breen, who turn them over to their new allies, the Dominion. ("Penumbra" and "Till Death Do Us Part" [DS9])
- Sisko buys land on Bajor and marries Captain Kasidy Yates, despite warnings from the Prophets that the marriage is a mistake. ("Penumbra" and "Till Death Do Us Part" [DS9])
- Frustrated by growing Cardassian losses and unconscionable concessions made to the Breen by the Dominion on Cardassia's behalf, Damar helps Worf and Dax escape confinement and return to the Federation. The pair bring intelligence of both the Breen alliance and of Damar's shift in loyalties. ("Penumbra," "Till Death Do Us Part," and "Strange Bedfellows" [DS9])
- The Breen announce their alliance with the Dominion by attacking Earth, destroying much of San Francisco. The *Enterprise* and the *Columbia* are involved in the aftermath of the attack. ("The Changing Face of Evil" [DS9]; "Eleven Hours Out" by Dave Galanter [TDW])

- While returning from an inspection tour, McCoy and Captain Montgomery Scott's runabout breaks down, and they must take refuge at a netural repair station, just as the Breen attack Earth. ("Safe Harbors" by Howard Weinstein [*TDW*])

- The Dominion retakes Chin'toka, with the Breen utilizing an energy-dampening weapon against which the allies have no defense. The *Defiant* is among the ships destroyed. ("The Changing Face of Evil" [*DS9*])

- The Starfleet Corps of Engineers team aboard the *da Vinci* must salvage a vital piece of encryption technology from a crashed Breen scout ship on a moon in the Lamenda system. ("Field Expediency" by Dayton Ward & Kevin Dilmore [*TDW*])

- Damar breaks away from the Dominion government and launches attacks on Dominion targets. Starfleet sends a team led by Kira (given a temporary Starfleet commission and the rank of commander) that includes Odo and Garak, to help Damar organize his resistance group into an effective fighting force. ("The Changing Face of Evil," "When it Rains . . . ," and "Tacking Into the Wind" [*DS9*])

- A Klingon ship accidentally stumbles on a way to resist the Breen weapon. While Starfleet and the Romulans try to reverse-engineer this for their own ships, Chancellor Gowron orders ever-more-aggressive attacks by the Klingon Defense Force, in part to discredit Martok in the face of the latter's growing popularity. Realizing that Gowron's recklessness is sabotaging the war effort, Worf challenges Gowron, defeats him, and installs Martok as the new chancellor. ("When it Rains . . ." and "Tacking Into the Wind" [*DS9*])

- Damar learns that the Dominion has had his family killed. Unbeknownst to him, his son Sakal has survived and lives on the run on Cardassia. ("Tacking Into the Wind" *[DS9]*; "An Errant Breeze" by Gordon Gross *[SNW3]*)

• The Cardassian resistance captures a Jem'Hadar ship outfitted with the Breen energy-dampening weapon, giving the Federation the means to neutralize it by studying the weapon itself. ("Tacking Into the Wind" *[DS9]*)

• A team of cryptographers on Starbase 92 are able to crack the Dominion's latest code, with the help of a Ferengi trader. *(SCE: War Stories* Book 1 by Keith R.A. DeCandido)

• Bashir is able to cure the Founders' disease after extricating information about the disease's nature from a Section 31 operative. ("Extreme Measures" *[DS9]*)

• Now able to defend their ships against the Breen weapon, the allied forces go on the offensive, aided by Damar's resistance. ("Extreme Measures" and "The Dogs of War" *[DS9]*)

• The *U.S.S. Sentinel* is the only surviving ship in a mission to sabotage a Dominion outpost, which paves the way for an offensive in the Orias system. *(SCE: War Stories* Book 1 by Keith R.A. DeCandido)

• Several Klingon ships, including the *I.K.S. Pagh*, fight Jem'Hadar and Breen ships at the Marcan system. The Klingons are victorious—culminating in Commander Klag defeating the surviving Jem'Hadar and Vorta single-handedly on Marcan V. *(TNG: Diplomatic Implausibility* by Keith R.A. DeCandido; "A Song Well Sung" by Robert Greenberger *[TDW]*)

• The *da Vinci* must dispose of an alien ship that has entered the Randall V system, which contains a Federation listening post that must be kept secret from the Dominion. Commander Salek is killed over the course of the mission. *(SCE: Collective Hindsight* Book 1 by Aaron Rosenberg)

- A new *Defiant* is assigned to Deep Space 9. The Cardassian resistance is betrayed and broken, though Damar, Kira, and Garak survive and continue to rally the people on Cardassia Prime itself. ("The Dogs of War" *[DS9]*; "Face Value" by Una McCormack *[PC]*)
- The *Excalibur* returns from their time-traveling mission, having missed their return point by eighteen months. They encounter a Romulan ship, thinking them to be an enemy, and have to deal with the consequences. *(NF: Double Time* by Peter David, Michael Collins, & David Roach [CB]; "Stone Cold Truths" by Peter David *[TDW]*)
- The *Defiant* leads a major offensive into Dominion territory, aided and abetted by a large number of Cardassian ships that turn on their allies. Cardassia Prime is taken, though not before Damar is killed, and the Dominion orders the planet decimated, wiping out a huge chunk of the population, including Sakal. ("What You Leave Behind" *[DS9]*; "Requital" by Michael A. Martin & Andy Mangels *[TDW]*; "An Errant Breeze" by Gordon Gross *[SNW3]*)
- The Dominion surrenders and withdraws from the Alpha Quadrant in exchange for the cure to the disease that is ravaging the Founders and Odo's return to the Great Link. ("What You Leave Behind" *[DS9]*)
- Sisko stops an assassination attempt by Reese and a vengeful Cardassian on the Female Changeling after the surrender ceremony on DS9. ("Requital" by Michael A. Martin & Andy Mangels *[TDW]*)

LaVergne, TN USA
03 November 2009
162842LV00003B/4/P